WEDDED SPIRITS

ALSO BY ALICE DUNCAN

The Daisy Gumm Majesty Mystery Series

Strong Spirits

Fine Spirits

High Spirits

Hungry Spirits

Genteel Spirits

Ancient Spirits

Spirits Revived

Dark Spirits

Spirits Onstage

Unsettled Spirits

Bruised Spirits

Spirits United

Spirits Unearthed

Shaken Spirits

Scarlet Spirits

Exercised Spirits

Wedded Spirits

Domesticated Spirits

Library Spirits

Spirits Adopted

Rosy Spirits

The Mercy Allcutt Mystery Series

WEDDED SPIRITS

A DAISY GUMM MAJESTY MYSTERY
BOOK 17

ALICE DUNCAN

May 2022
Hardcover ISBN: 978-1-64457-236-8
Paperback ISBN: 978-1-64457-235-1

ePublishing Works!
644 Shrewsbury Commons Ave
Ste 249
Shrewsbury PA 17361
United States of America
www.epublishingworks.com
Phone: 866-846-5123

AN INVITATION TO READERS

Enjoy 1920s hospitality right from Aunt Vi's Kitchen. Don't miss the recipe for Aunt Vi's Raisin Pie at the end of the story.

Wedded Spirits is dedicated to the memory of Nina Paules who, along with her husband Brian, created and ran ePublishingWorks!. ePW has done more for me and my writing career than any publisher I've ever been with (and I've been with most of them). ePW is carrying on, but everyone associated with the house will always miss Nina.

ACKNOWLEDGMENTS

Thanks to Diana Jackson, Margaret Cronk, Sue Krekeler, and Georganne James for going over this manuscript and attempting to find all the typos. I read it approximately 7,000 times, too, but I generally see what's supposed to be there rather than what is. Among us, I hope we cleaned it up well enough.

And thanks also to Nancy Arellano for sending me the clipping from the May 28, 1888 *New York Times* regarding the city's ban on hiring Italian workers to pave East Washington Street.

ONE

In the little back bedroom where the bridal party gathered, I knelt at Regina Petrie's feet and made sure the hem of her beautiful wedding gown—which I'd created my own personal self—didn't dip in the wrong places. "There," I said with what I believe to be not undeserved pride. "You're beautiful, Regina."

"Yes, you are," said another Miss Petrie, this one being Regina's aunt. This Miss Petrie's Christian name was Susan, and she was filling in for Regina Petrie's mother, who had, sadly, passed away in 1922.

When I got to my feet, rather spryly since I'd been taking an exercise class at my church for several weeks, I smiled at Susan Petrie. She gazed at her niece, hands clasped to her bosom, and sighed deeply. I'd made her almost-mother-of-the-bride's dress, too, by golly.

The eleventh day of July, 1925, had arrived in spite of itself; and Regina Petrie, my favorite librarian, would in a few minutes be married to a nice fellow named Mr. Robert Browning (not the poet). There had been many days—even weeks—during 1925 when I hadn't believed this day would come. Well... I don't mean that precisely. I knew the day would arrive; I just didn't think I'd live to see it. It had been a rough year, and it was only a little more than half over.

"I'll never be able to thank you enough, Daisy," said Regina in her soft, sweet voice. "Not only did you introduce Robert and me, but you made gowns for my entire wedding party."

"Happy to help," I told her. It was but the truth. I loved to sew, and I thought Regina and Robert made a terrific couple.

She'd asked me to be her matron of honor, so I'd made myself a dress for the occasion, too. The only jarring aspect of Regina's wedding ensemble—I was probably the only one who didn't adore the trend—was the beaded hat covering her pretty light brown hair from which a short veil depended. When I married my Sam, I aimed to wear a bandeau. The new fashion in wedding hats left me cold.

A tap came at the door, and we all turned to see who had tapped.

"May I come in?"

"Is that you, Dwight?" asked Susan Petrie.

"Yes. Are you ready? Pastor Calvin asked me to ask you. Everybody's here, he thinks."

Regina looked at her bridesmaids and me. "Ready, everyone?"

We all nodded our assent.

Susan Petrie said, "We're ready, Dwight."

"Good. You come out first Susan, and I'll take you to your seat."

For the record, Dwight Fitzgerald was another of Regina's relatives. Maybe a cousin. Because Regina's father had also passed away, Mr. Fitzgerald had been asked to give the bride away, and he'd agreed. Most of Regina's family had come from Tulsa, Oklahoma, but Mr. Fitzgerald and his family lived in Oxnard, California. I considered this a good thing, as most members of the Oklahoma side of Regina's family tree were rotten limbs. Because they embarrassed her, Regina pretended they weren't related to her. That's only a tiny reason she'd be glad to become Mrs. Browning this day. The other—big—reason, of course, was that she and Robert adored each other.

Anyhow, the door to Robert's parents' back bedroom opened,

and Mr. Fitzgerald gently took Susan Petrie's arm, led her across the hall, down the stairs and out of the house to her seat. The wedding was being held in the Brownings' spectacular garden in back of their lovely home in Pasadena, where most of the rest of us lived, too.

The wedding breakfast had been quite good, considering it hadn't been prepared by my aunt, Viola Gumm, who was acknowledged to be the very best cook in all of California if not the entire United States. Vi would prepare my own wedding breakfast when Sam and I tied the knot. That's providing we both lived to see the day. Our venue had yet to be decided because every single one of my clients wanted us to have the ceremony at his or her home.

Elopement was sounding better and better to me, although I wanted my father to give me away to Sam. Not that it matters, but the custom of "giving away" a daughter (or any other female relative) to another man also irks me. Not quite as much as wedding hats, but almost. I figured *I* was the only one who should decide with whom I'd spend the rest of my life. Sometimes I feel out of place in the world.

But all that is neither here nor there. The music began downstairs, played on the big grand piano in the back parlor by the organist of the Pasadena Presbyterian Church. This was the cue for the rest of us who comprised the wedding party to walk downstairs and stand in a line.

When Mrs. Calvin, the minister's wife, gave a nod, Robert's two adolescent cousins, Phyllis and Janet, made their way one at a time to where the Reverend Mr. Calvin, Robert Browning, and his best man stood. The men had to squint in the sunlight, but they both smiled too, so their squints didn't detract from the beauty of the scene. The Brownings had bought—or maybe rented—a pretty gazebo for the occasion. After Phyllis and Janet, it was my turn to join the wedding knot as soon as Mrs. Calvin gave me the signal. My family attended the First Methodist-Episcopal Church, but nobody minded the mingling of the churches. Heck, my fiancé, Sam Rotondo, was Italian and a former Roman Catholic.

Mrs. Calvin nodded at me and, with a glance back at Regina

and her uncle, I started on my own way to the gazebo. Robert made quite a handsome groom, for a chemist. That's not to say chemists on the whole are ugly or anything. In truth, he was the only chemist I knew. At least I think he was.

I smiled broadly, happy about the weather, which had cooperated and was pleasant. Sometimes the weather during June and July could be a little overcast and chilly in the beautiful city of Pasadena, California, but not that day. While Regina had chosen a hat covering her whole head, her bridesmaids and I wore straw hats, which were probably cooler than her head covering. Because our gowns were blue—Regina's was white—blue flowers adorned the brims of our hats. Regina's bouquet contained pretty blue hyacinths, hydrangeas and baby's breath.

I'd recently learned hydrangeas were toxic if eaten. I'd told Sam that and he'd said, "I doubt anybody will eat her bouquet." I'd laughed.

Silly me.

The ceremony didn't take long, and everyone seemed happy when the couple cut their cake and mingled with the guests for fifteen minutes or so. Then Regina tossed her bouquet—straight to me, bless her—and then she and I took a trip upstairs so I could help her change into her traveling clothes. Her beautiful wedding gown had a lot of hooks and snaps for us to deal with. Not to mention the many beads I'd sewn in a gorgeous pattern onto the front and hem of the skirt. I'm sure no one wanted any of them to snag on anything. I sure didn't, anyway. It had taken me *hours* to decorate that wedding dress and its accompanying hat. Even though I didn't care for the hat, I'd beaded it to perfection, by golly.

I put the bouquet I'd just caught next to my handbag on a dressing table and said, "I'll stand on the bed. If you back up to the footboard, you can hold up your arms so I can lift the gown over your head without wrinkling it."

"Sounds good to me."

So, after removing my shoes, I climbed onto the bed, and Regina dutifully backed up against the footboard. I unhooked and unsnapped like a mistress of the art, which I pretty much was. "How does it feel to be Mrs. Robert Browning?" I asked as I lifted.

"I'm not sure. It hasn't sunk in yet."

We both giggled.

"My aunt is going to save this beautiful dress, Daisy." Regina held her arms straight up in the air, and I carefully lifted the gown. "She hopes Robert and I will have a little girl who can wear it at *her* wedding." I'd made the dress out of a silk-satin fabric that wrinkled easily, so I laid it flat on the bed.

After I'd made sure all was well with the gown, I said, "That's so sweet." I meant my words as regarded the sentiment behind Regina's aunt's hopes. I doubted any young woman in twenty or so years would want to wear *this* gown again, unless she had it altered a good deal first. Fashion trends changed. I didn't tell Regina my thoughts on the matter.

She and Robert were going to take a train to Los Angeles and, from there, a steamer to Hawaii where they'd honeymoon. Hawaii sounded exotic to me. Sam and I aimed to go to New York City via train and then travel to Auburn, Massachusetts. That's because we had relatives in the two cities. The only problem I envisioned when we honeymooned involved Sam's family. They didn't approve of me because I am neither Italian nor Roman Catholic. Fiddlesticks.

Anyway, after Regina changed clothes, she and I went downstairs again and mingled with the guests for another half-hour or so before we all headed out to the front yard. From there Regina and Robert drove off in Robert's nice new Lincoln Model L sedan. Two giggly young women named Madge and DeeDee (Robert's relations, I think) followed the couple in Madge's Model-T to the Santa Fe Station. From there, either DeeDee or Madge would drive Robert's Lincoln back to the Browning residence to await the happy couple's return.

I'd traveled by ship once. Never been so sick in my life, although I think my illness had more to do with my own emotional circumstances than actual seasickness.

Standing next to Sam, who had an arm around me, although he

couldn't get too close because of my hat brim, I sighed deeply. "What a lovely wedding."

"Yeah. It was nice," Sam agreed. "Ours will be better."

"I hope so, although I'm afraid I'm going to offend a whole host of my clients by not having the wedding at one of their houses."

"You can only use one venue," Sam said reasonably. "If we get married at your parents' home or your own church, nobody can complain without stretching the point past breaking it."

"You're probably right."

"You know I am." Sam had a lovely, deep voice when he wasn't hollering at crooks or me for one reason or another. Since he was a detective for the Pasadena Police Department, and because I—through no fault of my own—seemed to stumble over corpses quite often, I didn't hear his lovely deep voice as often as I'd like.

After heaving another big sigh as the two automobiles turned a corner and vanished from our sight, I said, "Guess I'd better go back in and get my things." The idea of taking Regina's wedding bouquet home made me happy, although I wasn't sure what I'd do with it once I got it there. Can one press an entire wedding bouquet between the pages of a book? Guess I'd find out. "I suppose you have to work this afternoon, right?"

Sam heaved a sigh of his own. "Yes. Afraid so."

"Do you want to stop and get a sandwich at home first?" The home to which I referred was the attractive little bungalow owned by my parents, Joe and Peggy Gumm. Well… the truth is, I'd mostly paid for the house because I made more money than anyone else in my family, but I figured it belonged to all of us.

Sam and I had another, larger, bungalow across the street from my parents' house. As for Sam's house, he'd bought it—paying in cash, for crumb's sake—at the first of the year. Bless his heart, he didn't have to survive on the salary he earned as a police detective. That's because his family had owned jewelry stores in New York City since the mid-1800s, and he had some pretty big bucks. I'd been knocked all of a heap when I'd learned about his mazuma—not literally, but almost, because of the circumstances abiding at the time—but I didn't mind. And no, I'm not being sarcastic. Not very, anyway. I'd loved Sam even before I knew he had money, and his having money hadn't made a difference.

It was nice to know we had a cushion upon which to fall back if everything else in our lives suddenly slid askew. Mind you, I was only twenty-five years old at the time of Regina's wedding but my life, through no fault of my own, had been anything but smooth sailing.

Sam chuckled. "After that huge breakfast and that chunk of cake, I think I'll be full until dinnertime."

"Yeah. Me, too. I'll just trot upstairs, grab my handbag, Regina's gown, and the bouquet, and you can drive me home."

"Good idea."

So Sam and I went back into the house with the other guests who'd gone outside to see Robert and Regina off on their journey to wedded bliss. Miss Susan Petrie stood at the foot of the staircase chatting with Mr. Fitzgerald, and they both appeared satisfied and happy.

Susan Petrie and Mr. Fitzgerald turned and smiled at Sam's and my approach to the staircase. "Oh, Daisy, wasn't Regina a beautiful bride?" cooed Miss Petrie.

"She was, indeed," I agreed.

"It was so kind of you to sew up all the gowns for the wedding party. I love mine!" She looked down upon her dress, which was quite a marvel if I do say so myself. Made of a cream-colored silk-taffeta fabric with a pale blue lace overdress, it was, quite frankly, superb.

"Regina knows how much I love to sew, so it was no bother. Anyway, I still owe her for years and years of keeping my family supplied with wonderful books to read."

"I still think you were terribly kind to make *everyone's* dresses."

I smiled at Susan Petrie, repeated, "I love to sew," and jogged up the stairs. When I reached the little back bedroom where the bridal party had gathered before the nuptials, I opened the door, took a step inside and stopped.

A man lay on the floor. Since Prohibition had become the law of the land and the Brownings were law-abiding people, I knew no alcohol had been served at the wedding breakfast or the reception. Therefore, unless this fellow had carried a flask with him, I was pretty sure he hadn't passed out from over-indulgence in spirituous liquors.

Then details began registering in my brain. His feet, which flopped slightly outwards, were aimed at me, and his head was hidden from my view by the bed's footboard. I hesitated for a moment, but then figured I pretty much *had* to get into the room if I wanted to fetch my handbag and bouquet and Regina's gown—and I did. Therefore, I took in a deep breath and hoped the fellow wasn't playing some stupid joke. Or hadn't had a fit or a seizure or anything else of the kind.

As soon as I saw the young man's face, I realized he wasn't joking and probably hadn't had a fit or seizure, unless it had been brought about by ingesting poison. His face was a grayish-purple color, and his mouth overflowed with hydrangea and baby's breath petals. Little bell-like hyacinth flowers cascaded down his chin.

"Oh, no."

Sam. I had to get Sam.

So, without touching anything—I wished I hadn't touched the doorknob, but I hadn't anticipated anyone actually eating Regina's bridal bouquet—I stepped into the hallway. With my back pressed to the door, I called, "Sam!"

No answer.

My heart sped up. Oh, Lord. I needed Sam. Now.

"*Sam!*"

The merry chitchat I'd heard at the foot of the staircase stopped abruptly.

Into the silence, I heard Sam's voice. "What is it?" He sounded the least little bit cranky.

"Please come here."

"You need my help or something?"

"Yes. No. Yes. I need you. Now." I detected the note of panic in my voice and wasn't surprised when I heard Sam's big feet clumping up the staircase runner.

He arrived before me a few seconds later, frowning. "What's wrong?"

"There's a dead man in there." I jerked my head to indicate the room behind the door against which I leaned.

"What?" He squinted at me. "Is this some sort of—"

"*No!*" I didn't mean to bellow. In a calmer voice, I said, "There's a dead man—well, a young man—in there. I'm… pretty sure he's dead."

"Step aside," said Sam resignedly.

So I did.

TWO

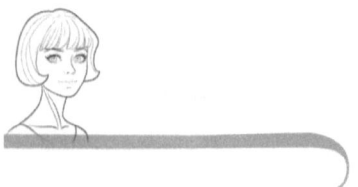

Tiptoeing behind Sam, I entered the room, too. Then I plastered my back against the door and watched Sam examine the body. I didn't want to look at it again.

"You say you found him like this?" Sam.

"Yes." Me.

"What's he doing with these flowers in his mouth?"

"Dying?"

"Did he eat them? Did somebody shove them down his throat?"

"How should *I* know? He was like that when I found him." I told myself not to snap at my fiancé. He was a good man only doing his job. "Sorry."

"Not a problem. I'm sure you were upset."

"I still am. Those flowers in his mouth are poisonous. I can't imagine why he'd want to eat a bridal bouquet."

With a soft grunt, Sam got to his feet and stood there, staring down at the body, his fists on his hips. Then he heaved a gigantic sigh and said, "I'd better call the station. I wish you'd stop finding dead people."

"So do I. And I was just wondering how to preserve those flowers as I walked upstairs to fetch them and my handbag. Now I don't want them any longer." I felt tears well in my eyes and ruthlessly suppressed them.

"Yeah. Well, nobody's going to remove anything from this room until we get a doctor or the medical examiner to certify to this fellow's condition. I'll need a couple of uniforms for crowd control and a couple more to take statements from people, too."

"Oh, Sam! This was supposed to be such a happy occasion. I hate to ruin it for everyone."

"Unless you're the one who bopped this bird, you aren't the one who ruined it." He squinted down at the body some more, frowning. "Who is this mug, anyhow?"

"I don't know. As far as I know, I've never seen him before, although if he attended the wedding, his face probably wasn't that color, and he surely would have been upright, so I honestly can't say." I shuddered.

"Right. Well, do you know where the telephone is?" Turning, he scowled at me, although I don't think I was the one with whom he was annoyed. "And somebody's going to have to begin telling people not to leave. Dammit, we need another person."

"Why? I can stay here while you tell people not to leave."

"And the ghost you conjure will call the station?"

"Oh."

"Yeah."

A slight diversion here. Perhaps you wondered, when I wrote about my clients, why I had any. Clients, I mean. It's also possible you believed that when Sam asked me about conjuring a ghost, he simply plucked that particular ethereal image out of nowhere. You'd be incorrect if you surmised those things.

You see, I made my living—and most of my family's—by working as a spiritualist-medium for wealthy people in Pasadena, California, most of them women. The rich ladies for whom I worked wanted me to conduct séances and chat with dead loved ones, or use my Ouija board to answer their questions, or read tarot cards to advise them how to get along in the world. Occasionally I'd even use a crystal ball. In other words, I, at the ripe old age of twenty-five, was giving spurious advice to women twice or thrice my age. What's more, most of those ladies had resources enough to buy sixty-seven or more sweet little bungalows like the ones my family and Sam lived in.

I mean, honestly, you don't think I *believed* the hogwash I spewed, do you?

It's not my fault. Ever since the fateful Christmas of my tenth year, when my Aunt Vi brought home an old Ouija board given to her by Mrs. Algernon Pinkerton (who was then Mrs. Eustace Kincaid), I'd been monkeying with the spiritualist business. Also, because the male members of my family were, through no fault of their own, unable to work, I'd been the primary breadwinner for the family for at least eight years by the time of the Browning wedding.

Back to the scene of the crime. "Well, crumb," I said. "Maybe Mr. Fitzgerald can come up here and watch the door while I call the coppers and you tell everyone not to leave the scene?"

"Is he the fellow from Oxnard?"

"Yes."

"All right. Bring him here—alone—and then telephone the station. As soon as Mr. Fitzgerald knows what's what, I can start taking statements."

"Yes, sir." I saluted my intended and scurried out of the room with its ghastly contents.

Once I found him, Mr. Fitzgerald was easy to persuade. Miss Petrie wanted to go with him, but I asked her to show me where the telephone was, so she altered her plan. She did look at me rather oddly, probably because she didn't live in the house and wondered why I thought she knew where the telephone was. I reckoned she'd understand my reasoning—well, Sam's reasoning—soon enough.

As luck would have it, the telephone was located in a small alcove off the kitchen, so there weren't too many people around. Also as luck would have it, Susan Petrie stayed with me as I called. The police station had a direct number, so I dialed it. Sycamore seven-three-zero-zero-zero.

"Pasadena Police Department, Officer Windham speaking."

"Yes," I said, wishing Susan Petrie would go away. She didn't. So I just blurted it out: "I'm Mrs. Majesty, and I'm reporting on behalf of Detective Sam Rotondo. There's been a murder in this house, and he wants uniformed policemen to come to his aid in taking statements and so forth. He also needs a doctor or the medical examiner." I gave the policeman the address of the Browning residence while Susan Petrie gasped and covered her mouth with both hands. I reached out to grab her shoulder, just in case she got faint or wanted to run around telling people whom I'd just telephoned and why.

"Detective Rotondo, you say?" Officer Windham said, sounding as if he thought I might be spoofing him.

"Yes. Detective Sam Rotondo. I'm his fiancée, and he needs people here *now*."

"Yes, ma'am." He rattled the address back to me.

"Correct," I said, my hand still gripping Miss Petrie's shoulder and wrinkling the lovely fabric with which I'd made her frock.

"Right away, Miss Majesty."

I didn't bother to correct him, but hung the receiver on the candlestick with a sigh. Then I turned to Miss Petrie, who appeared horrified, a reaction I understood.

"Daisy!" she said. "What on earth?"

Because she'd spoken loudly, I put a finger to my lips. "Shhh. Come with me, and I'll tell you about it."

Sam manifested himself at my side, making me jump about a foot and a half. For a big man, he could walk incredibly softly when he wanted to. "Everything under way?" he asked.

"Yes. I spoke to an Officer Windham, and gave him all the information I have. Had. You know."

"Yeah." He smiled ruefully at Miss Petrie. "So sorry about this, ma'am. And on this day, of all days." Sam could be sweet and kind when the occasion called for it.

"But what happened?" she asked, squeaking slightly.

"Daisy had better tell you about it. I have to get to work," he said. Turning to me, he said, "Go on upstairs and keep people away from that room. Mr. Fitzgerald might need help."

Gee, Mr. Fitzgerald had looked like a big, strong man to me. I figured Sam just wanted me out of the way. That was all right with me.

"Let's go upstairs, Miss Petrie—"

"Call me Susan, for heaven's sake," said she, her voice stronger than it had been.

"Thank you, Susan. Let's go upstairs, and I'll tell you about it."

So we went upstairs, and I told her about it.

"The bouquet was in his mouth?" she asked incredulously.

"Yes. I can't imagine how it happened. I mean, a young man wouldn't deliberately attempt to eat a bridal bouquet would he?" Remembering some young men of my acquaintance, I amended my statement. "Unless, of course, some idiot bet him he wouldn't do it, so he did it to win the bet. But half of those flowers were poisonous."

"Oh, dear. Who is the poor fellow?"

"I don't know. I can't recall seeing him before, although…" I decided not to tell her about his blue-gray face. Rather, I said, "I couldn't really tell what he looked like with his mouth full of flowers and with him flat on his back."

We'd reached the top of the staircase and saw Mr. Fitzgerald standing at attention in front of the death room. Ew. What an awful thing to call it, even though the name fitted. Poor room.

"Dwight," said Susan as she got to her brother-in-law and took his arm. "Do you know who it is?"

"I'm not sure, but I think it's one of the Turner twins."

Turner. Turner? Nope. Didn't ring any bells.

"Who are the Turner twins?" asked Susan so I didn't have to.

"I'm not altogether sure. I only met them today. I think they're friends of Madge and DeeDee, Robert's cousins."

"Oh, dear. What happened? Do you know?"

"No. Detective Rotondo said Mrs. Majesty walked into the room and found the body. I'm standing guard so he can organize things downstairs." Mr. Fitzgerald looked at me as if for confirmation, and I nodded.

"Perhaps a doctor will be able to determine how the young man died. And maybe why," I said without confidence.

"He's not a pretty sight," said Mr. Fitzgerald with a small shudder.

"That's for sure," I agreed.

"Oh, dear. What a dreadful thing to happen," said Susan.

Neither of us disagreed.

The three of us turned at the sound of stomping feet. Mr. Browning, Robert's father, looked mightily put out as he approached us.

"What's this nonsense about a dead man in that room?" he demanded.

"I'm afraid it's true," said Mr. Fitzgerald.

"Open that door and let me see for myself," said Mr. Browning. "This has to be some kind of vulgar joke."

"Detective Rotondo asked me to keep people out of the room," said Mr. Fitzgerald without a lot of vigor.

"Damnation, this is my house! I want to see for myself. I'm sure it's some idiotic trick those silly girls have perpetrated."

"If it was a trick," I said, using my soothing spiritualist's voice, "It was a truly tasteless one." I shot a glance at Mr. Fitzgerald before saying to Mr. Browning, "I know Sam doesn't want anyone going in there, but if you don't touch anything, I guess it would be all right. As you said, it's your house."

"Indeed it is, young woman," Mr. Browning said haughtily.

"Well…" Mr. Fitzgerald appeared uncertain.

Disdaining uncertainty, Mr. Browning nudged the other man aside and grabbed the doorknob. I almost protested, but then realized finding a perpetrator's fingerprints on the doorknob was already a lost cause.

"I'll go in with you," I said firmly. "Go ahead and look, but be sure not to touch anything. Maybe you'll know who it is." It? I amended my statement. "Who he is, I mean." Is? "Who he was, I mean."

Pausing at the door and frowning down at me, Mr. Browning said, "You shouldn't look at such things, Mrs. Majesty."

"I'm the one who found him," I said, even more firmly. "I've already seen him, and I haven't swooned yet."

Mr. Fitzpatrick cleared his throat and said, "Mrs. Majesty is correct, Mr. Browning."

With a huff, Mr. Browning said, "Very well," and opened the door. He took one big stride inside the room, and then, after seeing the dead fellow's feet splayed outward, shortened his steps and went almost the rest of the way to the corpse. He stopped a few feet away and lifted a hand to his mouth. Then he turned abruptly and nearly ran me down getting to the door.

Guess my nerves were steelier than his. Sometimes men annoyed the heck out of me.

Flinging the door to the room open, Mr. Browning ran chest-first into Dr. Benjamin, our wonderful family doctor.

"Doctor Benjamin! I'm *so* glad you're the one they sent!" I cried as the poor man staggered backward and came to a stop.

A growly voice behind him said, "Ain't you glad about me, too, Miss Daisy?"

Shocked, I barked, "For heaven's sake, what are *you* doing here?" at Mr. Lou Prophet, who stood behind Doc Benjamin. Indeed, he's probably the one who'd stopped the good doctor from falling on his back. As ever, he looked like a gunman out of the old west and grinned like a demon.

With a laugh, Dr. Benjamin said, "Sam telephoned my office. Lou was there for an appointment, so Sam asked that he come along with me."

The doctor's words sobered me, and I squinted at Mr. Prophet. He looked just the same as he ever did, which wasn't awfully good. He was old and ragged and rugged, had one leg and a peg, gray hair and so many wrinkles, he eyes nearly got lost when he smiled. Or smirked, which was what he was doing then. "What's the matter? Are you sick?" He was one of the men in my life who drove me nuts most often, but I liked the old goat and didn't want anything bad to happen to him. Anything *else* bad, I should say.

"Just gettin' the old arm checked," said he, walking into the room behind Dr. Benjamin. I guess Mr. Browning had hurried off in another direction—I suspected to the nearest powder room in order to throw up.

"And Sam asked you to come, too?"

"Wouldn't be here otherwise," Mr. Prophet said. "Ain't fond of weddings, but I'm s'posed to guard the door while the doc checks the body."

"Ah." That made sense. Nobody who wanted a peek at the corpse would dare argue with Mr. Prophet in order to do so. Mr. Prophet appeared too mean to mess with. That's because he could be too mean to mess with at the drop of a hat. "I'm so glad you're here!"

He turned his head, lifted a skeptical eyebrow and said, "Yeah?"

"Yes! We need you!"

"If you say so." The old reprobate snabbled a stray chair standing against an upstairs wall and set it in front of the door. I suspected he aimed to sit in it as the doctor examined the body.

Oh, and the reason he'd been to Dr. Benjamin about his arm is that his upper left arm had been creased by a bullet a few weeks prior. He seemed all healed up now, but Doc liked to keep an eye on it. I don't think he trusted Mr. Prophet to keep the wound clean and bandaged. If that were the case, he did the man an injustice. Since he'd ended up in Pasadena, after a brief stint as a consultant for a couple of western flickers, he'd been taken in by Sam. And me, but mostly Sam.

Mr. Prophet now acted as caretaker of the home Sam had bought, and he came in *extremely* handy when someone required subduing with a firearm or throttling with a rope. Or even if you needed a cook in a hurry. His meals weren't fancy, but they were tasty.

Beckoning at me to follow him, Dr. Benjamin entered the room. Although I didn't much want to see that body again, I did as he'd mutely asked. Mr. Prophet shut the door behind me, and I heard the chair squawk as he sat in it.

Kneeling beside the body, frowning at the gaping mouth over-flowing with blue and white flowers, Dr. Benjamin said, "How odd."

"Yes," I agreed. "It is."

I hung back from the body and pressed my back against the door. As I stood there wishing I could leave, I heard a male voice, rather loud, say something to Mr. Prophet. Then I heard Mr. Prophet say something back to the other voice, and then I heard footsteps retreating to the staircase.

Nobody ever argued with Mr. Prophet. Well, except me sometimes, but that was mostly in fun. I wouldn't want to get on his bad side. The man was invariably armed to his dingy old teeth.

THREE

"Daisy," said Dr. Benjamin, gesturing at me. "Will you come here, please?"

"Do I have to?"

With a chuckle, Doc said, "Yes. I know it's unpleasant, but I want a witness to what I'm doing here."

"Lucky me."

"Right. Can you take notes by any chance?"

"Take notes? Not really. I mean, I can write things down if you tell me what to write, but I don't take shorthand." I had absolutely no useful skills, in truth, but the people who hired me only wanted me to do the impossible, so my paucity of marketable skills didn't matter.

I think that might be a sad commentary on the state of the world, but I'm not sure.

"Take my notebook, find a pencil, and write down what I tell you. You can do that, right?"

"Yes, sir," I said, taking the notebook. Then I peered around the room for a pencil. Bother. I didn't see one, and I didn't want to open drawers or anything for fear I might mess up a clue.

A hard rap at the door nearly made me squeal. I whirled around and saw the door being shoved open by none other than my occasionally irritating fiancé, Sam Rotondo.

He scowled at the room. "You all right in here? Need anything?"

"A pencil," I said. "Doc wants me to take notes as he examines the body."

"Why you?" asked Sam.

"Nobody else seems to be available, Sam," said Dr. Benjamin from his crouch next to the corpse. "You don't mind, do you?"

Instantly I bristled. Why was the doctor asking *Sam* if he minded if *I* assisted? Did he think a *man* would do a better job, or that I needed a *man* to give me permission?

"Hell, no," said Sam, smoothing my prickles before I could make them known. "Just wondered, was all. Yeah, I have a pencil." He reached into his inside coat pocket. "In fact, take two in case the lead breaks. I don't have a pen knife with me, but you probably won't need one."

Eyeing the two stubby pencils Sam had handed me, I said, "No, I probably won't."

"All right. Lock this door, will you? I've posted Lou outside, but I don't want anyone to enter this room until Doctor Benjamin examines the body and I get a crew in here to dust for prints." He peered around the room and expelled a big sigh. Shaking his head, he said, "Which is probably going to be impossible."

"I was thinking the same thing," I admitted. "But thanks for the pencils, Sam."

"You're welcome." And he turned. I heard the door lock, and knew he and Mr. Prophet exchanged a couple of grumbled remarks, but I didn't hear the words clearly.

"Okay. I'm ready now, Doctor," I said, returning to where he knelt on the floor, grimacing at the body.

"How the devil did somebody stuff a bouquet into his mouth?" he asked softly.

I shrugged, which he couldn't see, so I said, "Don't know. Is that what killed him?"

"I doubt it, but I'll have to start there, I guess. I at least need to get these flowers out of the way so I can investigate for bodily trauma, et cetera."

"Mind if I sit while I write?"

"Not at all."

Therefore, I went to the dressing table, elbowed the dainty chair into a position where I could see the doctor and what he was doing and hear him clearly. I didn't want to add any of my fingerprints to the back of the chair, which was why I used my elbow. It probably didn't matter, but I was being careful.

"Very well," said Dr. Benjamin. "What we have here is a young man lying on his back with his arms straight and at a slight angle away from his torso."

"I should write that down?"

"Yes. Just write everything I say from now on. Stop me if you have questions or if I talk too fast."

"All right."

"Did you get that description of the body?"

"On his back with his straight arms at a slight angle away from his torso," I read from the doctor's notebook.

"Very good. Now I'm going to begin removing the flowers." He shook his head. "This is a new one on me." He swiveled his head to face me. "You don't have to write down that part."

I nodded.

"We have here…" He squinted at the jumbled bouquet that had been so beautiful only an hour or so earlier. Now all the petals were crushed and bruised. "Hydrangea, I think. Are these hydrangea blossoms?" Dr. Benjamin held up a stalk that used to have a full flock of petals on it.

"Yes. The light blue ones growing in clumps are hydrangeas. The darker blue spiky ones are hyacinths. The little white ones are baby's breath."

"Thanks, Daisy. Boy, you couldn't ask for a more lethal bouquet if you wanted one. Well I guess you could add a few oleander sprigs and lily of the valley."

"Oh, my. I knew about hydrangeas and hyacinths, but I didn't know baby's breath was poisonous, too."

"Yep. Do you have all those written down?"

"Yes, sir."

"Good. Um…" Dr. Benjamin looked around, and I realized he was trying to find a place to put the ruined bouquet so that it could be taken to the police station without being manhandled further.

"Here," I said, handing him the lace doily from the dressing table. I hoped it didn't hold any evidential significance.

"Thank you." He carefully laid the messy pile of flowers on the doily and set it aside. "All right," he resumed, rubbing his hands together. "What do we have here? It wasn't the flowers that killed him. I can tell that already."

After scribbling down what he'd said, I asked, "Really? How can you tell?"

"Because he shows all the signs of suffocation, but he could have spat those flowers out. There's something else caught in his throat."

"My goodness!" Although I was surprised at his words, I didn't neglect my duty. I wrote a note saying something else was stuck in the young man's throat besides flower petals. Which reminded me of something.

"Do you know who he is?" I asked.

"Nope."

"But he's a young man, right? Not a middle-aged man or an old man?"

"I'd say so, but I'll have to look closer to make sure."

"Poor fellow."

"Right." Dr. Benjamin swiveled, still on his knees, and withdrew a small tubular thing from his black bag. "Now, let's take a look here." Darned if the tubular thing wasn't a pen light! Or whatever doctors use to observe things in people's throats. "For goodness' sake."

"What is it?"

"Not sure." He turned off his light, set it gently beside his bag and reached into the dead man's throat. After a grunt or three, he sat back, a scowl on his usually genial face. "Can't get it out of there. It'll require tools I don't have with me."

"Can you tell what it is?" I asked.

"Not for certain, but it looks like a tennis ball."

"A *tennis* ball?" I echoed, astounded.

Nodding, he repeated, "Yes. A tennis ball."

Ew. "Can you do anything else before you have to get the ball out of his throat?"

"Yes. Please continue taking notes. Write down that I'm undoing the fellow's tie."

"Got it."

The doctor continued removing clothes from the young man until he was almost nude, dictating notes as he went. "Seems to be a man in his late teens or early twenties. Well-nourished. Brown hair. Brown eyes. Fair skin." He picked up a hand, inspected it, put it down, then picked up the other hand and did likewise. "Doesn't work with his hands, although he may play tennis." He glanced up at me. "Don't write this next part down, but it's ironic if he does play tennis. Wonder if he beat someone at a match who was annoyed by it."

"Whoever it was would have had to be *really* annoyed. I can't imagine killing someone because I lost, say, a game of gin rummy to him or her."

"Me either, but some of these youngsters these days are complete wastrels. In my day, a lad generally had work to do and couldn't afford to play games all day."

That was true of youngsters in my day, too, but I didn't say so. I think each generation resents the next generation for one reason or another. And face it, if you were born when Queen Victoria was alive, you'd probably look upon today's so-called "flaming youth" with horror. I was of the "flaming youth" generation, and I still looked upon some of my contemporaries with horror. And disgust. And even revulsion.

Back to the death room. "Can you help me turn him over, Daisy?" asked Dr. Benjamin.

"Sure." Laying the notebook and pencil on the vanity table, I carefully walked to the body. It looked pathetic, all white and nearly naked. Well, except for its blue face. "What part of him do you want me to take?"

"You shove his shoulder, and I'll shove his posterior," said Dr. Benjamin.

I got into position beside the pathetic flesh, and glanced at the doctor. "Ready?" I asked.

"Ready. On three. One, two, three, and *heave*."

We both heaved, and the corpse sort of splatted onto its front. I have no idea when rigor mortis sets in after death, but this guy hadn't been dead long enough for rigor to start. He was, basically, a container of flesh and bones and a heck of a lot heavier than I'd expected.

With a half-smile, Dr. Benjamin said, "Don't get any help from dead people if you want to move them, do you?"

"No, you sure don't. I didn't realize how heavy he'd be."

"And yet he's not an overweight fellow."

I stood with a creak that shouldn't have been there since I'd been exercising quite often lately. What good was that idiotic exercise class if I still creaked when I stood up?

Never mind. "No, he wasn't overweight. Well, he is now. I guess he wasn't when he was alive."

"Right." Dr. Benjamin chuckled.

A knock sounded at the door, and Sam's voice said, "Are you ready for the meat wagon?"

The *meat wagon*? Good Lord.

"Almost," said Dr. Benjamin. "I want to examine the fellow's back, although lividity is settling in."

"What's lividity?" I asked.

"Let me know when you're ready," said Sam.

"Will do," said Dr. Benjamin to Sam. To me, he said, "When you die, the blood travels down and settles into the lowest part of your body. Since this man was flat on his back, you can see the blood has begun to settle in his back, under arms, lower legs, and so forth. In corpses, that discoloration from blood gathering is called lividity. See what I mean?"

I saw. Then I scurried back to the vanity, sat down, and picked up my pencil and notebook again. "So shall I write that lividity is taking place?"

"Yes, please."

So I did.

"In life, this fellow was around five feet, ten inches tall."

I wrote down that he'd been five-ten.

"He's got bruises on his shoulders," the doctor said.

I wrote down that the corpse had bruises on its shoulders. *His* shoulders. Gah.

"No sign of attempted strangulation. Wonder what those bruises mean, though."

I couldn't offer a suggestion, but I wrote down his words.

Fortunately, Doc's perusal of the dead man's body didn't last too much longer.

FOUR

The stretcher bearers were carrying the corpse of the unknown young man down the stairs. From there, they'd make their way out the back door and stick the body into the morgue truck, which sat in the way back of the Browning drive. Before they could get to the back door, the front door to the house burst open to reveal Robert Browning's giggly cousins, Madge and DeeDee.

"There are police everywhere!" said one of the cousins, eyes wide. "What's going on?"

"What happened?" asked the other one.

"Never mind," said Mr. Browning, rushing up to the girls, taking an arm each, and attempting to steer them in a direction away from the staircase.

But the girls, evidently accustomed to working as a team against restraint, wrenched their arms from Mr. Browning's grip and raced to the stretcher. They looked pretty much alike, so I'm not sure who reached for the sheet covering the body. Neither man doing stretcher duty could smack her hand away from it, and there was no policeman—or me—nearby to do it for them.

One of the bearers said, "Hey!" but the girls remained undeterred.

Madge—unless it was DeeDee—whipped the sheet off the body, dropped it to the floor, pressed her hands to her cheeks, opened her mouth, and gasped in what looked like abject revulsion.

DeeDee—unless it was Madge—stopped short beside her... sister? Honestly, I didn't know what relationship the girls were to each other. Anyway, she stopped beside her companion, peered, goggle-eyed, at the corpse and shrieked, "Cecil! It's *Cecil*! Oh, my God, what *happened*?"

Before she'd ended her question, Sam arrived, placed a firm hand on the gasper's shoulder. Lou Prophet, who had finished his duty as door guard upstairs and come downstairs again, grabbed the other one's shoulder. Both men yanked the young women away from the stretcher. Officer Stephen Doan, a fellow who'd worked with Sam before, picked up the sheet from the floor, and gently spread it back where it belonged.

One of the stretcher men said a gruff, "Thank you," and the two men continued their interrupted journey to the back door of the Browning home.

"Come with me, you two," growled Sam.

The young woman whose shoulder he gripped glanced up at him, saw him glowering at her, and didn't argue.

"Put a cork in it," growled Mr. Prophet to the other damsel. She took one look at him and opened her mouth to speak again, but a guttural snarl from him made her think better of it.

"Madge! DeeDee! What are you two bellowing about?" Mr. Fitzgerald had heard the commotion—it would have been difficult not to—and rushed into the living room. The stretcher fellows finally managed to make it through the back door of the house, and a young man in a formal suit closed the door behind them before joining the hubbub in the living room.

"What's going on?" the young man in the formal suit asked, skidding to a stop before the two girls, Sam, and Mr. Prophet.

"Who are you?" asked Sam, none too gently.

"Me?" asked the young man, pointing at his chest. "Me?"

After thumbing through his notebook, Officer Doan said, "That's Mr. Ferrell Hawley."

"Ferrell," said Mr. Fitzgerald in a pleading tone, "Will you please help these poor men subdue the girls? They're in great distress and are being rather... unruly."

The young man I now assumed to be Ferrell Hawley said, "Of course." He glanced at Sam, lifting a hand for some reason or other but, after seeing the frown on Sam's face, dropped it to his side again. "Um... may I help, Officer?"

"Yes," said Sam. "It's Detective Rotondo. Are these two your sisters?"

For the record, both women had taken to sobbing, one still in the grip of Sam, and the other still in that of Mr. Prophet, who looked as if he'd just as soon grab his Colt revolver and shoot the both of them. However, he now lived in the civilized confines of Pasadena, California. He no longer worked as a bounty hunter in the good old days of the Wild West, so he couldn't. I understood his urge, however, although I know that's mean-spirited of me. For all I knew these two poor girls were related to the dead man. It wasn't their fault they were young and... well, kind of silly.

As soon as Ferrell spoke again, I felt guilty. Not a new feeling, unfortunately.

"I'm sorry, Detective," Ferrell said. "Madge was engaged to Cecil. This must have been a terrible shock to her. And they're my cousins, not my sisters. My Uncle Charlie and Aunt Maud's two girls."

"Oh, my," I said, feeling even guiltier. "I'm so sorry."

I don't think Madge heard me. Neither sister acknowledged my sentiment, at any rate.

"Will you please come with us, Mr. Hawley?" said Sam. "Let's go to another room. Maybe your presence will make your cousins feel more comfortable. I have to ask questions of them."

Mr. Ferrell Hawley, who was, I think, about twenty-four or –five, frowned at Sam but didn't object. I wouldn't have objected either. Sam put up a formidable front, but it was nothing compared to the formidability of the rest of him. Perhaps Mr. Hawley sensed Sam's strength of character and purpose.

Whatever he did or didn't sense, Mr. Hawley said, "Yes, Detective, of course," and reached for one of his cousins. I still didn't know which one was whom. Who? Whatever it's supposed to be.

Mr. Browning, whose feathers still seemed a trifle ruffled after having been rebuffed by both Madge and DeeDee, scurried up to Sam and said, "Here. You may use this room. It's the room Mrs. Browning uses for her activities."

"Thanks," said Sam, steering the girl whose arm he held through the space revealed when Mr. Browning opened the door, and into a pleasant room at the side of the house.

Pretty, subdued floral wallpaper covered the walls in Mrs. Browning's activity room, and the room contained a dainty roll-top desk, an appropriate desk chair, a chaise lounge and two comfy-looking chairs, all upholstered in pastel fabrics that went well with the wallpaper. If I'd still held Dr. Benjamin's notebook, I'd have taken notes about the room's décor. I'd be decorating my own home soon, after all.

But Dr. Benjamin had taken himself and his notebook away with him. I do believe he aimed to follow the coroner's truck to the morgue in the basement of Pasadena City Hall and conduct a proper autopsy. I have no idea if Mr. Cecil Whoever's next of kin had been notified of his demise.

Rather than lead the maidens to the chaise, as I'd half-expected him to do, Sam plopped the young woman whose arm he held into one of the pretty chairs in the room. Mr. Prophet deposited the other one on the other chair, then stood with his back against the closed door and his arms crossed over his chest, as if daring anyone to try to escape from the room.

Because I didn't know what else to do, I perched myself on the desk chair. This move on my part wasn't sheer chance. The desk and chair sat in a corner on the far wall from the chaise and chairs, and I chose this chair because I didn't want Sam to notice my presence and tell me to leave. As it turned out, as soon as he saw me shrinking into my corner, he gave me a good glower, but he didn't eject me from the room. Whew!

"All right. First of all, I'll need your names. You first." He pointed at one of the young women.

The two girls looked a good deal alike, but they weren't twins. They both stood approximately five-feet, five inches—a trifle taller than I—had blonde hair marcelled to within an inch of its life, and each had a few spit-curls decorating her forehead. I wasn't a big fan of spit-curls, and not merely because they had a disgusting name. I was an old widow-lady of twenty-five, and these two lassies were clearly attempting to give Clara Bow a run for her money in the flapper department. I had to dress soberly and with dignity because I had a position as Pasadena's best spiritualist-medium to uphold.

Not that I'm saying anything against the two girls, whom I didn't know at all. They certainly weren't the only young ladies in those days trying to emulate Clara Bow. Heck, I'd tried my best to adopt an Anna May Wong look myself a year or so ago. Failed miserably, and not merely because I'm neither Chinese nor out-and-out gorgeous.

"My name is Madge Hawley." She sniffled. "This is my twin sister, DeeDee."

So much for my powers of observation. But they weren't identical, so maybe I can be forgiven my faulty assumption. Probably not, huh?

Anyway, Sam wrote in his own notebook and asked, "Is Madge a nickname or a shortened version of a longer name?"

"Margery. My full name is—"

"Spell it, please."

"W-what?"

Sam didn't even huff. He merely said, "Please spell your first name. I've seen various spellings of the name, Margery."

"Oh. M-a-r-g-e-r-y."

"Thank you. Your full name?

"Margery Ann Hawley."

"Spell your middle name, please."

"Ann?"

It hadn't seemed like a difficult question to me, but Sam didn't even blink. Solid; that was my Sam.

"Yes. How do you spell your middle name? With an E or without an E?

"Oh. A-n-n. No E."

"Thank you," said Sam, writing this fascinating information in his book. Because Madge continued to drip tears, he reached into a back pocket and produced a handkerchief. "It's clean," said he before Madge could protest or ask about its state of sanitation.

Out of curiosity, I looked at Madge Hawley's ring finger, but as she wore gloves, I didn't see a ring. I did see a bump under her glove, so I figured she was wearing an engagement ring.

Sam always carried extra hankies with him for occasions when he'd be questioning people, although I was kind of surprised he'd carried extras to a wedding. Perhaps he'd expected more tears of joy than had been shed or something of the like.

"Age?"

"Age?" Madge repeated, again as if trying to come up with an answer to a difficult question. The poor thing was clearly taking the death of her fiancé hard, something I could understand and sympathize with.

"Yes," said Sam. "How old are you and your sister?"

"Oh," said Madge. "N-nineteen."

Only nineteen! My empathetic heart ached for her. Stupid heart.

"And you said you were engaged to the now-deceased young man?"

"Y-yes," stuttered Madge. "Mr. Cecil Darlington and I were engaged to be married." She gave another shuddering sob and resumed crying, so Sam turned to DeeDee.

"Your full name?" He asked her.

"Deborah Ann Hawley."

"Deborah with an O and an H, and Ann with no E?"

She contemplated his question for several seconds, ultimately answering, "Yes."

Perhaps their parents lacked imagination if the two girls had been given the same middle name. Or maybe there was a wealthy aunt, Ann, hovering in the background, and the parents wanted her to know she was appreciated. Hmm. That meant Madge was a MAH, and DeeDee a DAH. Wondered if that meant anything.

I told myself to stop creating fantasies and pay attention.

"You knew this fellow, Cecil Darlington, too?"

"Yes," said DeeDee, squeezing another teardrop or two from her swollen eyes. I don't think she was as upset by Mr. Darlington's passing as was her sister. Which made sense. It had been her sister who'd loved the dead man enough to become engaged to marry him.

"Thank you," said Sam, busily writing. "When was the last time you saw Mr. Darlington?"

DeeDee glanced quickly at Madge, then said, "Um, before the wedding started."

"How long before the wedding started?"

"How long?" Again DeeDee shot a peek at Madge, who sniffled, wiped her eyes, and answered for her sister.

"We just went upstairs to wish Regina good luck, and we met him in the upstairs hallway."

"I see. You've known Miss Regina Petrie for some time?"

"Well, yes. Kind of. I mean, we came to the wedding with Mr. Fitzgerald, because we were neighbors, and his wife was ill and couldn't accompany him."

"I see," said Sam. "Do you live in Oxnard, too?"

"Um, well, no," said Madge. "Mr. Fitzgerald picked us up from our parents' home in Pasadena before driving us all to the Brownings' home. Our mother and Susan Petrie are friends, and Mr. Fitzgerald used to live next door to us before he moved to Oxnard."

Aha. So Mr. Fitzgerald hadn't had to drive them all the way from Oxnard. That was nice for him.

I beg your pardon. I didn't mean to be mean. It's just that neither of these two young women seemed to be a sparkling conversationalist. Not that I knew it for a fact. I'd only noticed them giggling before the wedding and crying since they'd come back from the train station. For all I knew, they were both geniuses and kept up with all the latest news and so forth.

"All right. Now Deborah, how long have you known Mr. Darlington?"

"Me?" DeeDee seemed puzzled. Then—I swear, you could see the light dawning upon her—she said, "Everybody calls me DeeDee."

Sam sighed faintly. "All right. Now DeeDee, how long have you known Mr. Darlington?"

"Me? How long?" DeeDee repeated. She sounded confused. It didn't seem like a difficult question to me, but perhaps I'm being a grumpy old widow-woman. However, after receiving a nod from her sister, she said, "About a year or so. Isn't that right, Madge?"

"Yes," said Madge. "About a year."

"I'm speaking with your sister now, Miss Madge," said Sam in a voice so firm, it would have been made from cement if anyone had wanted to memorialize it. "I'll conduct my interview with you after I talk to your sister."

"Oh. Well." Madge sounded a little frightened. Sam could do that to a person without half trying. "All right then." Madge spoke no more and resumed wiping her tear-stained face. There was no mirror handy, but she evidently knew where her mascara would drip, because she did a fair job of ruining Sam's handkerchief with Maybelline's formerly caked product.

"So, Miss DeeDee Hawley, you have known Mr. Cecil Darlington for about a year?"

"Yes," said DeeDee, after getting a nod of approval from her sister.

"Did he live in Pasadena, too?"

"Um... Yes. He lives on Madison Avenue. Near Washington."

"And do you know his age?"

"Um... I'm not sure. Madge knows him better than I do. Did. Oh, dear." And she began weeping again.

Fortunately, Sam had another hankie in his back pocket. Also fortunately, Madge seemed to be over her own bout of sobs. Therefore, after handing DeeDee a handkerchief, Sam turned back to Madge. "All right, Miss Madge Hawley. While your sister composes herself, let us chat." Chat. That was one word for it. "What is your address, Miss Hawley?"

"Which Miss Hawley?" asked Madge in a voice sounding suspiciously snippy.

"You," said Sam in a voice that would have made a stronger specimen of humanhood than I suspected either Hawley sister of being sit up and take notice. "And your sister, too, if you live in the same home."

Without further ado, Madge recited the address of the Hawley family on North Los Robles Avenue.

"Thank you. How did you and Mr. Darlington meet?"

"How?" Madge repeated.

"Yes. How did you meet?"

These weren't tough questions. I wasn't sure why the two Hawley ladies seemed so confused about answering them. On the other hand, I remember being wretchedly miserable, unhappy and... well, in a fog, I guess, after my own darling Billy died. When that thought struck me, my battered heart went out to poor Madge.

"At a party at the Pasadena Golf and Tennis Club."

My heart returned to its accustomed position, my nose wrinkled of its own accord, and my sympathy for Madge suffered a slight dent. I'd had a terrible experience during a Christmas party at the Pasadena Golf and Tennis Club, which seemed to me to be populated by the snobbiest set of people in my fair city of Pasadena, California.

When that thought whizzed through my brain, I knew I couldn't stay in the room any longer. I'd begun judging these two young women for no good reason. Trying to be inconspicuous and failing, I rose from my chair and walked softly to the door.

"Leaving so soon?" asked Mr. Prophet with supreme sarcasm.

"Ask Mr. Fitzgerald if he'll come to this room, will you, Daisy?" asked Sam with no sarcasm at all.

"Absolutely." And I skedaddled out of there happily and with a mission to accomplish. I accomplished it admirably, escorted Mr. Fitzgerald to the interview room, knocked, and when Mr. Prophet opened the door, left Mr. Fitzgerald to his tender mercies. Then I went back into the living room, wishing that, if somebody *had* to murder Mr. Cecil Darlington, he or she couldn't have chosen a better occasion. This was a lousy way for a day that should have been restricted to joy and happiness to end.

Ah, well. Life never seems to do what I want it to do when I want it to do it.

FIVE

Thanks to the as-yet unknown person who'd murdered Mr. Cecil Darlington, Sam, Mr. Prophet, and I didn't get home until almost dinnertime. I'd telephoned to let my mother, father and aunt know we'd be late and the reason.

"A *murder*!" Pa exclaimed. "I swear to goodness, Daisy, I don't understand why you keep finding dead people!"

His words hurt a bit, but not a lot. He spake only the truth, darn it. If I didn't know myself to be innocent of any evil intentions toward any—make that most—of the murder victims with whom I'd been involved, I might wonder if I was a mass murderer in disguise. But I wasn't. Unlucky, I guess is what you might call my proclivity for finding bodies. And confoundedly annoying. I was nearly starving to death by the time we finally got home. Not really, but I was darned hungry.

Sam pulled his big black Hudson into my parents' driveway, got out and came around to open the door for me. That's because I had my hands full of Regina's wedding dress, wedding shoes, and my handbag. Under normal circumstances, I'm fully capable of opening car doors for myself. Also, Sam is a gentleman, no matter how hard he tries to hide it.

"Lou and I are going across the street to get out of these monkey suits. We'll be back as soon as we can be," he told me.

"That's not a monkey suit," I said. "A monkey suit is a tuxedo. At least I think it is. That's your Italian count suit."

The light on that fair early-June day hadn't faded, so I saw him lift his gaze to the sky briefly.

"Stop rolling your eyes at me. You look extremely handsome in that suit."

"Yeah? Well, it's uncomfortable, so I'm going to change into something else."

"Yeah," said Mr. Prophet from the back seat. "I been wearing this fancy suit and my peg all day long, and my stump hurts, dammit."

Golly, before that moment, I'd never thought about whether he sometimes removed his peg leg due to discomfort.

"I'm sorry," I said to Mr. Prophet. "You may not look like an Italian count, but that suit you're wearing makes you look…" Dang I hadn't thought out my sentence before beginning it. "Like a dashing and respectable Pasadena gentleman."

"Well, hell, now I've *really* gotta get out of it," muttered Mr. Prophet.

"That was supposed to be a compliment," I told him.

"Yeah. I feel much better now," he said in a withering tone of voice. "Thanks."

"You're welcome," I said, withered.

Chuckling, Sam said, "Need any help getting that stuff into the house?"

"I could use you to hold the wedding gown. Thanks, Sam. I'm afraid I'll crush it or drag the hem on the ground or something if I try to carry everything myself."

"Sure." He took the padded clothes hanger upon which the gown hung, lifting it up so that it couldn't have touched the ground if it had wanted to.

"Thanks." I slid out of the car, carrying Regina's wedding shoes and my handbag. I would have been carrying Regina's wedding bouquet if someone hadn't stuffed it down Mr. Cecil Darlington's throat. I'd thought about bringing home a stray flower to press, but the notion vaguely repelled me, so I didn't.

Trudging across the lawn to the front porch, Sam and I carried our burdens. Spike had already begun his happy greeting cry when we walked up the front steps. I loved Spike. A black-and-tan dachshund, I'd finagled Spike for my late husband, Billy. Finagled, because I'd asked Mrs. Bissel for one of her darling dachshund puppies as payment for ridding her basement of a ghost.

That probably sounds odd, but it's the truth. It's also a whole 'nother story I won't go into now.

Before I could begin juggling Regina's shoes to get at my handbag and dig for the key, the front door opened, and my smiling father stood there. "Welcome home, you two. Where's Lou?"

He took a step out onto the porch, looking around as if he suspected Mr. Prophet of hiding in the bushes. To be fair, Mr. Prophet liked his quirlies—cigarettes—and he'd been known to take a break to smoke one or two. Or three or four.

"In the Hudson," I told him. "He and Sam are going across the street to change for dinner."

My father laughed a little. "Change for dinner? Isn't that an old Victorian custom?"

"Probably," said Sam, carrying Regina's dress into the house. I'd already laid her shoes and my handbag on the table next to the front door so I could kneel down and greet Spike properly. "In this case, we're going to dump our formal wear and put on something comfortable. We've been in these formal duds all day long, and we're both sick of them."

"Makes sense to me," said Pa.

I rose from my knees—without a creak this time—and grabbed my handbag and Regina's shoes once more. "Okay. Spike, heel."

Spike, who had come in first at the Pasanita Dog Obedience Club's training class about three summers earlier, heeled. What a great dog. To my surprise, Sam heeled too, and we walked through the living room, through the dining room, and through the kitchen —which smelled like heaven—greeted my aunt and my mother, and went to my room, which was directly off the kitchen.

By rights, Vi should have the bedroom off the kitchen, but Billy and I took it because he'd been gassed and shot in the war and couldn't climb stairs. There was a charming two-room suite upstairs. We'd planned to live there until he'd come home from the war in a wheelchair with his lungs eaten away by mustard gas.

Ask me how I like Kaiser Bill. Go ahead. I dare you.

Just kidding.

Actually, I'm not. It's probably best not to get me started. As soon as we entered the room, I told Spike to sit and stay, which he did. It was *so* nice to know there was at least one sentient male being in the world who always obeyed me.

Sam carried Regina's dress into my bedroom and looked around. "Where do you want me to put this thing?

"Good question. How about you hang it from the curtain rod on the door to the back yard?"

He couldn't hang it in my closet, because my closet was stuffed to more than capacity with my own clothes. I'm not a spendthrift, but I had a lot of clothes. That's because I made every single garment hanging in that closet using my mother's knee-pedal White Sewing Machine. I loved to sew. It was my one true skill. I don't count acting the spiritualist as a real skill; spiritualism was more of a meal ticket. It also paid a heck of a lot better than sewing. Probably not for Coco Chanel or Paul Poiret, but I wasn't either of them.

At any rate, Sam hung Regina's dress on the curtain rod, and I dumped her shoes and my bag on the bed, Spike wagging gleefully at our feet. I looked down at him. "Okay, Spike!" "Okay" was our word signifying he could stop doing what I'd commanded of him and be a plain old dog again.

Relieved of his burden to behave, Spike jumped up on the bed and sniffed Regina's shoes. While Spike was no longer a puppy and prone to chew up shoes, I decided the bed was a bad place for anyone's shoes so, to his disappointment, I picked them up again and put them in my closet, the floor of which was relatively clutter-free. Spike sighed and jumped down from the bed. He didn't have far to jump, in case you're worried about his back.

Then both Spike and I walked Sam to the front door, and he—

Sam, not Spike—gave me a kiss on the cheek before departing to fetch his car and drive across the street to his house. It would soon be *our* house, by golly!

After Sam had left through the front door, Spike and I turned to see Ma, Pa, and Aunt Vi standing in a row in the archway between the living room and dining room, staring at me.

"Your father tells us you found another body today, Daisy," said Ma. "At a *wedding*, of all places!" She sounded as if she thought I'd killed Mr. Darlington just so I could find his body.

Shaking her head, Vi said, "I don't know how you keep doing this, Daisy."

"I don't, either," said Pa. "What is it? A gift? A talent? Like sewing and reading tarot cards?"

When I glanced down at my dog, he had a disapproving frown on his muzzle, too.

"If it's anything, it's a darned curse!" I cried, feeling beleaguered. "Why is my own family turning on me? It's not my fault. I went upstairs to get my handbag and the wedding bouquet—Regina threw it straight to me—and there was a guy dead on the floor! It was awful! What's even worse was that whoever killed him shoved the bouquet down his throat, so I didn't even get to bring it home!"

Pa came up to give me a hug. "We know it, sweetheart. It's just so… odd, that you keep finding dead people."

"I know, and I hate it," I said into his shirtfront. Then I bethought me of possible makeup stains I might be making on his shirt and withdrew. Fortunately, at least for Pa's shirt, the day had been hard and long, and any powder I'd daubed on my cheeks was long gone. I never wore much makeup anyway. I had a subdued and respectable persona to maintain.

"It's all right, Daisy," said Ma, coming over to me to and taking over the hug from Pa when he let me go. "Only it seems to happen so often."

"I know it does," I said dismally.

"Well, I don't know how you do it," said Vi in a crisp voice. "But if you could come on in and set the table, I'd appreciate it. Peggy's been helping me in the kitchen."

"Will do, Vi. Just have to take off this finery and slip into a more comfy dress." And shoes. My feet were *killing* me. They weren't made for pointy-toed shoes, my feet. But pointy toes were what the fashion dictators sold to us ladies, so if we wanted to look appropriate for a formal occasion—like, for instance, a wedding—we wore them.

"Thanks, sweetie," said Vi, and she turned and strode back to her realm. Queen of the kitchen was my wonderful aunt.

I followed her, limping a trifle. I wasn't sure, but I thought I had a blister on the little toe of my left foot. As soon as I entered my room and plopped on my bed—Spike leapt up and did likewise instantly—I shoved off the left shoe with the right and sure enough, my poor left pinkie toe was all red and had a blister on it. Great. What was one supposed to do for a blister on one's little toe? I think we had some adhesive bandages in the bathroom. Perhaps I could cut one of those down and tape it to my poor toe.

But that would have to wait. I was already five or six hours late coming home from the wedding. So I took off my wedding apparel and threw on my old green day dress. Then I put on some thick stockings, slid my aching feet into my sloppy bedroom slippers, and joined everyone in the kitchen.

"Whatcha making, Vi? It smells wonderful."

"Just some ham steaks with a cheese soufflé, which is about ready to come out of the oven. Stuffed tomatoes. English peas. Nothing fancy."

"Ha! Nothing fancy, the woman says. I could no more make a cheese soufflé than I could fly to the moon. Or stuff a tomato. I'd probably burn the ham and make mush out of the English peas, too." I headed to the dining room and began setting the table.

"Raisin pie and custard for dessert."

"Now I *know* I can't make a raisin pie or custard," I said, trying to sound chipper. In truth, my kitchen failures troubled me. I'd be a married woman soon, and my poor husband was liable to starve to death if I had the running of the kitchen. I hoped Sam liked cornflakes. Even *I* couldn't ruin cornflakes.

"Nonsense," said Vi, laughing. "You just don't concentrate."

"You're always telling me that, and it doesn't help. I still can't cook."

"Neither can I," said my mother under her breath, although she didn't have to. We already know she couldn't cook any better than I.

"You ladies have other talents," said Pa, heading to the front door, probably because Spike was already there and setting up his usual happy, friends-are-here barking frenzy. "Spike, quiet," said Pa.

Spike, marvelous hound that he was, stopped barking. His tail still wagged so fast, it stirred up a heavy air current. Good thing he was so close to the ground, or the wind he created might have knocked the papers off the table next to the door.

Naturally, I'd expected to see Sam and Mr. Prophet when Pa opened the door. Therefore, when I saw Dr. Benjamin standing on the front porch with his black doctor's bag in his hand, I was surprised.

So was Pa. "Doc! What brings you here?" Fearing he might have sounded ungracious, he instantly said, "Not that we aren't happy to see you. We're always happy to see you. And I'm sure there's plenty of food, so please stay and take some dinner with us."

Quickly recalling the evening's menu, I decided Pa was right, so I said, "Let me take your hat, Doc. It's good to see you again."

"You might not think so after I tell you what I discovered today," said Dr. Benjamin, sounding grim. "But thank you for the invitation. I'm starving, and Dorothy's at her sister's place for a couple of days." He let out a small groan as he slipped off his coat. Guess I wasn't the only who made noises when he or she did things.

"That doesn't sound good," I said, taking his hat. "I mean about your news. I'm glad Mrs. Benjamin is enjoying some time with her sister."

"I guess," he said. "I miss her, though."

Aww. I thought that was sweet. As I hung it on the coat tree on the other side of the front door from the table, Dr. Benjamin knelt to say hello to Spike. He was a good man, by golly, and one who didn't shirk small, important things like greeting other people's dogs.

Sam and Mr. Prophet showed up before we could close the door behind Dr. Benjamin. So I rushed to the dining room to set another place for the doctor and tell Vi I hoped she'd prepared enough food for seven people.

As I might have expected, she had. Vi loved feeding people.

SIX

Dinner was spectacular, as usual. I particularly enjoyed Vi's stuffed tomatoes which, she told me, were scooped out and filled with smashed cracker crumbs, cheese, some of the scooped-out tomato bits and a variety of herbs and spices. She didn't bother telling me which herbs and spices since, when it comes to the kitchen, it's as if she's speaking a foreign language when she tries to explain things to me.

As we ate, I asked, "What was it you discovered that troubles you so much, Dr. Benjamin?"

He glanced up from his plate, dangling a bite of ham from his fork. "It would probably be better if we saved my news until we've all eaten."

"That bad, huh?" I asked, dismayed.

"Just not suitable dinner-table conversation," he said with a smile, and stuck the forkful of ham into his mouth.

Very well, so much for chatting about the corpse. "I felt sorry for that poor girl. Madge? I think that's her name," I said, scooping out some tomato stuffing. "She was engaged to the poor fellow who died."

"Is that so?" asked Dr. Benjamin, appearing interested.

"Yes," said Sam, saving me from talking with my mouth full or making Doc wait until I swallowed. "Margery Ann Hawley is her full name. Her twin sister is Deborah Ann Hawley."

"Their middle names are both Ann?" asked Ma, as if she disapproved. "Why did their parents give both of them Ann as a middle name?"

"I wondered the same thing," I told her. "My middle name is Anne, but you spelled it with an E on the end. The twins' Ann has no E. I kind of figured there's a wealthy Aunt Ann hiding somewhere in the woodwork."

Mr. Prophet, who sat across the table from me, cackled. "Makes sense to me."

"Daisy Gumm Majesty, what a cynical thing to say," said Ma, her tone at least as disapproving as it had been when she'd mentioned the two girls' middle names both being Ann.

"Why else would they give them both the same middle name?" I asked. "Lack of imagination?"

"I favor the rich-aunt scenario. I can't think of another reason to use the same middle name for both girls, unless it's a family tradition," said Pa, surprising me. He didn't always take my side when Ma expressed disappointment in me. I grinned at him to let him know how much I appreciated him.

"Odd tradition," said Vi, whose own name was Viola Melba Gumm. Well, her maiden name had been Peach. Viola Melba Peach. Maybe that's why she'd become a cook. Perhaps she'd been destined for the kitchen from birth. Probably not.

"Maybe it's a family name?" suggested Sam.

"Ann? There's at least one Ann, with or without the E, in almost every family." I turned to peer at Sam, who sat next to me. "Do you have any Anns in your family?"

Tilting his head as he chewed, Sam thought. Then, after swallowing, he said, "Well, Renata's middle name is Andreina."

"That's a lovely name," I said, wishing Sam's sister Renata liked me better. But it wasn't my fault Renata's son, Frank Pagano, had tried to kill me. I had done nothing to incur this odd behavior on Frank's part, either. "Are there any other 'Ann' names Italians use?"

Another spate of thought on Sam's part eventually produced, "I suppose Andreina, Angelica, Angelina, and Annetta might be kind of like Ann."

"They're prettier than Ann," I said. "Especially when you say them in Italian."

Sam turned to look at me. "Say them in Italian? I just recited a list of names. How would *you* pronounce those names?"

"Well, I wouldn't roll my R's so much. Italian is such a pretty language. I mean, English is so blah. Andreina sounds much nicer than An-*dreen*-uh."

As Sam continued to stare at me, Mr. Prophet laughed outright. So did Doc Benjamin, Ma, Pa and Vi.

I sniffed and lifted my chin. "Well, *I* think the names sounded beautiful when Sam said them. With my Pasadena-American accent, they... sort of lost something."

"Daisy, you're such a caution," said Vi, still chortling.

Whatever a caution was, I seemed to be one quite often around Vi. I guess that wasn't a bad thing.

Dr. Benjamin stopped laughing and said, "Anyhow, you say one of those girls—did you say their last name is Hawley?"

"Yes." I nodded.

"One of those Hawley girls was engaged to the deceased Mr. Cecil Darlington?"

"Yes. Madge. Why? Do you think one of *them* did him in?" I asked, probably too avidly.

"Daisy," said Ma in *that* voice again.

"Just asking," I said. "But we can discuss it after dinner." Then and there, I decided *my* children would be allowed to talk about anything in which they were interested around *our* dinner table. Unless it was totally disgusting, of course. Turning to Sam, I said, "If we have a daughter, may we name her Andreina? It's such a beautiful name."

After almost choking to death on a bite of ham—I had to pound him on the back a few times—Sam said, "Why don't we discuss chil-dren's names after we finally tie the knot, Daisy?"

"Oh, all right," I agreed, frustrated. Evidently, conversational topics of interest to me were *verboten* at our dinner table. Sorry I used a German word. I generally avoid anything remotely Germanic for reasons already mentioned.

"How was the wedding?" Ma asked. "Before the murder, I mean."

Aha! Here was a topic about which I could elaborate forever. "It was lovely," I told everyone. "Robert's parents held it in their back yard, which is beautiful. They either already had a gazebo, or they built or rented one. Either a florist or a bunch of ladies had deco-rated the white gazebo with pink and white roses with tiny blue flowers interspersed here and there. They might have been forget-me-nots. Anyway, it was gorgeous."

"It was," Sam agreed. "In fact, the wedding was really nice, for a wedding. Too bad about what happened after it. But at least the married couple managed to get away before Daisy tripped over the body."

"I didn't trip over the body!" I snarled. "I—"

"Just joshing," said Sam, interrupting me, which was probably just as well.

"It sounds lovely," said Ma wistfully. "We have a pretty back yard, too, thanks to you and your father."

Pa and I liked gardening.

Aha! There was another thing I was good at: gardening. So that meant I possessed three useful skills: sewing, gardening and spiritu-alist-mediuming. I often despaired of my overall uselessness, but I wasn't totally without merit.

Ahem. Back to the dinner table.

"I'd love to have our wedding in our back yard," I told Ma. "In fact, I'd love to have it in the back yard across the street, even. All of my wealthy clients are after me to have the wedding at one of their homes, but if I choose one of them, I fear the others will be miffed." I contemplated my words for a second. "Although, it might be nice to have the wedding at the Castleton place."

"The *Castleton* place!" Ma exclaimed. "Do you know Miss Castleton as well as all that?"

The Castletons were a fabulously wealthy family in Pasadena. Mr. Castleton was, according to his daughter Emmaline, a former robber baron who had made his fortune on the backs of Irish and Chinese immigrants when he was building railroads across the country. After he'd clawed and bullied his way into great wealth, he began spreading it around. Kind of like Andrew Carnegie, who'd sponsored libraries all across the country after he'd made his millions. Mr. Castleton now had a hospital and a huge hotel named after him here in Pasadena.

"Emmaline Castleton and I are friends," I said. "She's offered her father's house and grounds, and evidently he's said it's all right if we want to hold the wedding there. The catering would probably be easy, since he also owns the Hotel Castleton."

"Nuts to that," said Mr. Prophet. "I ain't one for grandeur. I think it would be better for you and Sam to get married right here." He tapped the dinner table with his finger. Probably his trigger finger.

"I agree," said Sam.

"Me, too," said Pa.

"Actually," I said, "I do, too. Anyway, Harold has told me not to worry about the venue. He'll work with whatever we decide. He's doing the flowers," I added.

Harold Kincaid, Mrs. Pinkerton's son, was one of my very best friends. Sam had disapproved of our friendship for quite some time because Harold wasn't what you'd call a man's man. In fact, Mr. Prophet had called him "one o' them lavender cowboys," but without disparagement. I had yet to detect an ounce of bias or prejudice in Mr. Prophet, mainly because he didn't care what color or religion people were as long as they left him alone. He'd told me that, too, which is how come I know.

"Well, let's talk about the wedding later," said Vi, standing up from her chair at the head of the table. "Daisy, will you please clear the table? I'll bring out the pie and custard."

"Pie and custard?" Dr. Benjamin exclaimed. "If I'd known

there'd be pie and custard, I wouldn't have eaten two of those delicious tomatoes."

"Yes, you would have," said Vi, who'd known the doctor for decades.

With a laugh, Doc said, "Yes, I would have."

So Ma and I both rose and began collecting plates and bowls and so forth and taking them to the kitchen. To my surprise, Sam collected all the silverware, bless him. I thanked him appropriately, then got out dessert plates and forks and set them at Vi's place at the table. I rinsed and stacked the dishes while Ma dealt with leftovers. Then Ma and Sam went back to the table and sat. I brought the bowl of custard and a serving spoon, which I also set it Vi's place, and Vi brought out her masterpiece of pie-making.

We all ate raisin pie with custard sauce and then sat at the table, looking at each other, most of us too full to move.

After I don't know how long, but it seemed like hours, I nobly rose to the occasion. Standing with a subdued grunt, I said, "I'll clear off the dessert stuff and get the dishes soaking. Don't anyone talk about the murder until I join you in the living room."

"Thank you, Daisy," said Vi. "I'll let all of you go to the living room and talk about the murder. I've been on my feet all day, and I want to go upstairs, soak my feet, and go to bed."

"Sensible woman," said Dr. Benjamin with a smile.

"'Night, Vi," the rest of us said. More or less. A couple of us thanked her again for the lovely meal.

I always did the washing up after meals, and she appreciated me for it. But the way I figured it was that she cooked all day at the Pinkertons' place, then came home and cooked for us. Ma worked as the head bookkeeper at the Hotel Marengo up the street from our house all day and then came home and needed to rest. Pa used to work as a chauffeur and a mechanic for rich Pasadenans. He couldn't do that any longer because he had an iffy heart. Doc Benjamin was a busy doctor. Sam was a busy detective.

Mr. Lou Prophet was a… Well, I'm not sure what he was these days. He'd been a successful bounty hunter in the olden days, and he still made himself useful quite often. At this juncture in his increasingly long life, he acted as caretaker for the house across the street and lived in a small cottage behind the main house. Overall, the arrangement was darned efficient. Besides all that, he was old.

So I washed dishes. Figured I should.

After I'd set all the dishes to soak, I joined everyone in the living room. By golly, they'd actually waited for me before they began discussing the murder! That was so nice of them. I joined Sam on the piano bench. Ma and Pa sat on the sofa with Spike sprawled half on and half off Pa's lap, and Mr. Prophet and Dr. Benjamin took the other two chairs in the room.

"You said you wanted to tell us something you learned after examining the body?" Sam asked. As soon as I plunked my weary bottom down on the piano bench, he took my hand, and I felt less weary. Odd how that happens.

"Yes," said Dr. Benjamin. He'd fetched his black bag from where he'd set it on one of the benches in the inglenook. Settling the bag on his lap, he opened it and fished around in it for a second or two. "Have any of you ever seen this before?" He held up what appeared to be a platinum or white-gold ring sparkling with maybe a pound or three of diamonds.

"May I see it?" I asked.

"Sure." Doc handed the ring to Sam—whom he could reach—and Sam handed it to me.

I peered at it closely, turning it in my fingers. It was clearly an expensive ring. It was also pretty, if a little more elaborate than I liked. It had a big round cut diamond nestled in a bed of smaller diamonds sort of stacked on top of each other. I think jewelers called these "pyramid-shaped" rings. It wasn't my personal favorite style, but I tried to maintain a subdued, non-ostentatious persona to the world. Nobody would hire a flashy spiritualist. Or maybe they would; I'd never tested the possibility, mainly because I don't care for flashy stuff in the first place.

When I compared the massive glittering pyramid to my own perfectly gorgeous gold ring with the emerald flower embedded in its golden leaves, I remained more than satisfied with my ring, thank you very much. Sam's father had crafted it for me, even though he hadn't wanted to. More about that later.

"Wow. This is some ring," I told Dr. Benjamin. "Where'd it come from?"

"The late Mr. Cecil Darlington's stomach," said the doctor.

"*Argh!*" Horrified, I dropped the ring. Fortunately it was too heavy to bounce away and get lost or anything. It just sat there, on the living-room rug, winking at all of us in the lamplight.

SEVEN

When Ma said, "Daisy," this time, the word lacked conviction as a chastisement. That's partly because the look of horror on her own face was unfeigned. I noticed Pa's arm tighten around her shoulder, and he seemed appalled, too.

"I'm sorry, folks. I should have said where it came from before I showed it to you," said Dr. Benjamin, sounding as if he meant his words sincerely. I'm sure he did. As a rule, he wasn't a practical joker.

Bending over to pick up the ring, Sam sat back and turned it in his fingers thoughtfully. "This must have cost a bundle," said he, who knew all about rings and so forth, because his family had been in the jewelry business for generations.

"It's... really gaudy," I said, ashamed of my initial reaction. The ring had been cleaned and polished since it had come from the late Mr. Darlington's stomach, after all. Still...

"It's in the latest style," said Sam. He held it out to my parents.

Pa took it. Ma looked as if she never wanted to see it again, and actually turned her head so she wouldn't have to see it. "It's big. Wonder how many carats are in this thing," muttered Pa.

"Haven't a clue," said Doc.

"Lemme have a look," said Mr. Prophet, holding out a hand. So Pa handed the ring across Ma, and Mr. Prophet took it and eyed it. The glorious diamond ring looked strange in his gnarled, sun-bronzed fingers. "Never saw one like this before."

"Did you see many engagement rings in your line of work?" I asked, honestly curious.

Handing the ring to Dr. Benjamin, Mr. Prophet said, "Naw. Only fancy stuff I ever saw was made by Injuns. Silver with turquoise, mainly. Didn't see too many diamond rings in the old days, and sure never saw one like *that*." He sounded as if he disapproved of the ring. His opinion didn't wound me. I didn't like the garish thing, either.

"So you've never noticed a ring like this on the finger of anyone you know, Daisy?" asked Sam.

I shook my head. "No. Not that I recall. And I'd probably recall an ostentatious ring like that."

"You really don't like it?" asked Sam, as if he truly wanted to know.

"No," I said firmly. "It's too ornate and... I don't know. Kind of tasteless. At least it's not to my taste." I gave him what I hoped looked like a loving smile, because it was meant to be one. "The one you gave me is absolutely perfect for me." I held up my hand and showed everyone. Not that they hadn't seen it before.

"I can get you diamonds, if you want diamonds," Sam said.

"We've been through this before, Sam Rotondo. I don't even *like* diamonds. I love the beautiful emerald in this beautiful ring, and that's enough about us." I turned to Doc. "How do you suppose the ring ended up in that poor man's stomach? Did he swallow it? Well, I guess he had to have swallowed it, didn't he?"

"Yes, but he didn't want to."

"What do you mean?" asked Sam, reaching into the inner pocket of his jacket to fetch his notebook and pencil. After frowning at his pencil, he turned to me. "Got a pencil or a pen anywhere? This one has no lead left, and I gave my others to you."

So I turned around on the piano bench and picked up a pencil from the music stand. I'd been practicing the day before and making notes. "Here."

"Thanks." After giving me a very nice smile—Sam doled out his smiles sparingly—he turned back to Dr. Benjamin. "Now, what do you mean, he didn't want to?"

"His trachea was scratched, and the ring seemed to have been shoved down his throat forcefully, along with a length of some filmy material, a tennis ball, and the wedding bouquet."

"It *was* a tennis ball?" I asked, feeling vaguely sorry for the dead man, whom I'd never met. At least I didn't think I had. It's possible we'd been introduced at the wedding, but I sure didn't remember it if we had.

"Yes," said Dr. Benjamin. "It was a tennis ball. It got stuck going down."

"It came to a glottal stop!" I said brightly. Then, feeling abashed and impolite, I said, "I'm sorry. That just kind of slid out."

"Daisy!" said Ma.

Mr. Prophet laughed.

Actually, so did Pa, Sam, and Dr. Benjamin. The doctor went on to say, "You might put it that way. Whoever stuffed the ring down his throat followed it with the filmy material, the tennis ball and the flowers."

"He didn't just stand there and let someone kill him, though, did he? I mean, didn't he put up a fight?" I asked.

Sam turned to frown at me, and I decided to stop asking questions.

"Yes, he did fight back," said the doctor. "Remember when I told you about the bruises on his back?"

"Yes. I wrote about them in your notebook."

"You did, indeed. Well, from what I can deduce from examining the body, someone held him still while someone else stuffed things in his mouth. He tried to fight. There was skin under his fingernails."

Ew. "You mean, he scratched his attacker?"

"Yes."

"Do you have any idea how that could be done? The holding and stuffing process, I mean," asked Sam, so I didn't have to.

"As far as I can figure it—and I'd like you to check this out for yourself, Sam—the young man was backed up against the footboard of the bed in that room while someone else stood on the bed, holding him in place as well as possible, and another person or persons did the stuffing. At least two people were involved in killing the fellow, because one person couldn't have accomplished the deed."

"So he was killed in that room?" Sam said. "He wasn't moved?"

"No. He wasn't moved. As far as I can tell, as soon as his attackers figured he was dead, they let him drop to the floor, and there he stayed until Daisy found him."

"Lucky me," I said glumly.

"However," the doctor continued, "I'd like you to visit the morgue and the room in the Brownings' home again before I make my final report, Sam. I telephoned the Brownings after I made my initial findings. They weren't happy about it, but they said they'd leave the room untouched until we can both take another look at it."

"I left a man to guard it," said Sam. "I figured I'd want another look after I found out how the fellow died." He heaved a Sam-sized sigh. "What an experience for the Brownings."

"You're right," said Ma. "A terrible thing to happen after such a joyous occasion."

"The manacled pair got off before the murder was discovered," said Mr. Prophet. "At least that part went all right."

"Manacled pair?" I stared at Mr. Prophet.

He gave me a cynical grin. "Might as well wear handcuffs as a wedding ring. That's always been my motto. One of 'em, anyway."

"It's probably something you've never had to worry about," I said. "Not everyone shares your unique outlook on life."

"That's the truth," he said, grinning more broadly.

My mother and father were holding hands on the sofa. Spike still sat next to them with his head on Pa's thigh. Spike didn't care about manacles or wedding rings or people's opinions. He was a happy hound.

I grinned back at Mr. Prophet. "I, however, am happy to be getting manacled to Sam here."

Still writing in his notebook, Sam grunted, "Yeah. Likewise."

How sweet.

Sam stopped writing for a second and glanced at me. "Did you notice a ring on the Hawley girl's finger when we talked to them?"

"She was wearing gloves," I said. "But I noticed a bump on her ring finger I assumed was her engagement ring."

"Huh," grunted Sam, recommencing his note-taking.

"Will you be going to church tomorrow, Sam?" asked Dr. Benjamin.

"I imagine so, unless something else comes up," said Sam.

My family and Doc Benjamin and his Dorothy, when she was in town, all attended the First Methodist-Episcopal Church on the corner of Marengo and Colorado in our glorious city of Pasadena. "If you do, maybe we can detour past the Browning place, and then go on to the morgue."

"Oh, but come to dinner at our house first, Doctor. With Dorothy away, you'll need a good meal you don't have to fix yourself."

"Fixing good meals isn't a specialty of mine," said Doc. I knew the feeling. "I'll be happy to have dinner with you."

We always had dinner at noon on Sunday. I'm not sure why. Tradition, I suppose.

As for Sam, he sat next to me on the piano bench, finished writing in his notebook, and then stared into the middle distance as he contemplated the morrow. Then he shrugged. "Yeah, why not? We can meet up at church, have dinner, and then deal with murder." He wrinkled his nose. "I'd rather skip that last part."

With a sigh, Pa rose from the sofa, dislodging Spike, who appeared disgruntled for approximately three seconds, then curled up into a shiny black cinnamon roll and resumed sleeping. Ma rose a second or so after Pa did. "We should get to bed." Ma glanced at me. "You, too, Daisy. You'll have to sing tomorrow morning."

Did she think I didn't know that? Every now and then my mother could be painfully obvious. She didn't want Sam and me to do any canoodling after she and Pa went to bed, although she'd never say anything so overt.

Dr. Benjamin chuckled and headed for the front door.

Snickering, Mr. Prophet also rose from his chair. Only then did I recall his peg leg. Shame on me!

"Is your leg still aching, Mr. Prophet?" I asked kindly.

"Naw. It's fine. But it'll be good to hit the hay."

"I thought you said it hurt from you having to stand for so long at the Brownings' house."

"Probably did say that," said he.

"But your leg didn't hurt?"

"Yeah, it did."

"Oh. Well, I'm glad it doesn't hurt any longer."

"Thanks."

"Don't pester Lou, Daisy," advised Sam. "You know he's an ornery cuss."

"Who, me?" Mr. Prophet artfully arranged his wrinkles into an expression of hurt dismay.

"Oh, brother," I said.

Mr. Prophet gave one of his not-quite-evil chuckles. "Thanks for the sympathy, Miss Daisy. Appreciate it."

"Sure you do." But I giggled. Couldn't help it. Mr. Prophet occasionally drove me nuts, but I'm glad he'd ended up in Pasadena.

"I'm going to take off now," said Dr. Benjamin. "Thanks for feeding me."

"You're welcome to dine with us any time, Doctor. You know that," said Ma. Easy for her to say. Neither she nor I ever cooked meals. Well, he'd have been welcome even if we did, but he wouldn't thank us for feeding him.

"Yes," said Sam. "It's time we got across the street."

"Be sure to come for breakfast," I told him.

"Of course," said Sam, who'd lived a precarious bachelor's existence since the death of his first and dearly beloved wife, Margaret, who had died about two years before my Billy did. She'd been a victim of tuberculosis, unlike Billy, who'd been a victim of war.

"C'n I come, too?" asked Mr. Prophet plaintively.

Planting my hands on my hips, I said, "That depends. Are you coming to church with us?"

"Hell, no!" said Mr. Prophet, horrified. Sam had dragged him to services on Easter Sunday, but he preferred not to darken the doors of churches if he could avoid them.

"Well, then…" I let my words trail off ominously

"Daisy!" said Ma. "Of course, you may come to breakfast, Mr. Prophet!"

Sometimes I wished my mother had a sense of humor. She's a wonderful woman, and I wouldn't trade her for anyone else, but every now and then I kind of wished she'd been gifted with imagination and a sense of humor along with her ability with accounting.

"She's joking, Peggy," explained my father, taking my mother's arm. "You're always welcome to take meals here, Lou. You know that."

"Just like to rile Miss Daisy every now and then," said the old sinner, chuckling evilly.

"Likewise, I'm sure," I told him.

"Cut it out, you two," said Sam, rising from the piano bench and stuffing his notebook into his jacket pocket again. "Come on, Lou. I'm bushed."

"Yeah. Me, too."

"Good night," said Ma as she led Pa across the living room.

"Night, all," said Pa, happily being led.

"Spike and I will escort you to the door," I told the three leftover men. Spike had jumped down from the sofa and stood on the living room rug, gazing up at the four of us and wagging his tail uncertainly. To him, I said, "Yes, you may come outside with us and make a deposit on the hydrangeas." I remembered the hydrangeas in the late Mr. Cecil Darlington's mouth and shuddered slightly.

Putting an arm around my shoulder, he said, "Cold?"

"No. Just thinking about hydrangeas. There were some hydrangeas in that bouquet."

"Ah."

The men got their hats from the rack beside the door, plopped them on, went outside and stood on the porch. Spike dashed out ahead of them, raced down the porch steps and, sure enough, dived into the hydrangea bushes. About a second later, Samson, the

Wilsons' cat, shot out of the hydrangea clump as if he'd been shot from a gun rather than rousted by a smallish black-and-tan dachshund. The Wilsons were our neighbors to the north.

"Good night, all," said Dr. Benjamin, heading to his car.

"Night!" we all chorused.

Rustling noises came from the bushes beside the front porch. Spike.

"I admire that dog's assiduity," said Sam.

"Yeah," said Mr. Prophet. "Me, too, whatever the hell that means."

"Persistence," I said. "Firmness of purpose." Then, having been struck with a brilliant thought, I stuck my finger in the air and said triumphantly, "Doggedness!"

"By gawd. No shit?"

"No… kidding," I said.

Sam laughed as he kissed me on the cheek. "See you tomorrow, love."

I gave him a kiss, too. Had to stand on my tiptoes to do it, Sam being a good deal taller than I.

Mr. Prophet's rusty chuckled lingered in the air as the two men crossed the road to Sam's house.

I eventually managed to pry Spike away from his diligent pursuit of cats and other interesting critters of the night—not to mention odors—and get him into the house. He followed me around the house as I locked every door. We never used to lock our doors. Events at the first of the year changed our opinion on the matter, and I never wanted to go through anything like it again. So Spike and I went all over the house, locking doors, and making sure windows were securely fastened.

Except for the one in my bedroom. It had been a warm day, and I wanted the slight breeze to blow over Spike and me as we slept. This was especially true since one of our lemon trees was in bloom, and the fragrance, while not as powerful as when all the orange trees in Pasadena bloomed in early spring, was sweet and pleasant, and Spike and I loved it.

We slept sweetly, too. I like to think we did, anyway.

EIGHT

I love to sing. Hmm. Maybe that's another one of my few talents. The only problem is that I sing alto. Mind you, my voice is pretty good. In fact, I sang the role of Katisha in Gilbert and Sullivan's *The Mikado* a year or so prior to that Sunday.

Being an alto, however, precluded me from singing any but the final verse in that day's anthem, "Come, Holy Ghost, Our Souls Inspire," which had a tricky tune that sounded downright ancient. At least Medieval. At all odds, it was a strange hymn. Our choir director, Mr. Floy Hostetter, was having the baritones and basses sing the first verse, the sopranos sing the second verse, the baritones and basses sing the third verse, and then all of us sing the last verse. So I didn't get to stretch my vocal chords a whole lot. Lucille Zollinger, a soprano with whom I sang duets quite often, enjoyed herself, so that was nice.

After the church service, I hung my choir robe in the closet of the choir room, and decided to take my music folder home with me so I could practice next week's anthem, "One Holy Church of God Appears." "One Holy Church" also has an interesting tune, although, unlike "Come, Holy Ghost," one could hum it if one wanted to. I aimed to practice it on the piano and sing it a lot. I felt a little cheated that Sunday.

But enough whining. My family, Sam and Dr. Benjamin skipped tea and cookies in Fellowship Hall after church, and went directly to our house. Vi had dinner pretty much ready to dish up. She'd fixed a ham-and-bean soup with yesterday's leftover ham, and had already made some cornbread to go with it. It wasn't a fancy meal, but it was mighty tasty.

Then Sam and Doc Benjamin vanished and didn't take me with them. Men!

However, shortly after they'd gone and I was feeling sorry for myself, the telephone rang. Because telephone calls in our house were almost always for me—and most of the time from Mrs. Pinkerton, who couldn't seem to survive without my spiritualist advice—I hopped it to the kitchen to answer the instrument of torture.

Hoping against hope the caller wasn't a wailing Mrs. Pinkerton, I picked up the receiver and said (as ever), "Gumm-Majesty residence. Mrs. Majesty speaking." Then I withdrew the receiver from my ear in case Mrs. P was in shrieking mode.

"You can put the receiver against your ear, Daisy. It's just me. By the way, are you going to remember to call yourself Mrs. Rotondo if you ever get married?" the caller asked.

"Harold! I was afraid your mother was calling! I'm so glad it's you!"

"As well you should be. Say, Daisy, are you available this afternoon?"

"Yes. For what?"

"I want to show you some color images of a few china patterns I think you'll like," said Harold. "I just got them from a pal of mine."

"I'd love it!" I said, happy to have something enjoyable with which to while away the remaining hours of the day. "Want me to go to your place, or are you coming here?"

"I'll be at your place in about fifteen minutes. Then we can plan our shopping spree for next Monday, too."

"Thanks, Harold!"

"I'd rather go this coming week, but I have to work." Harold sounded disgruntled.

"I think I'll spend the week sewing. I have to stitch up all the clothes people will wear at my wedding."

"I can help if you need me to," offered Harold.

"Thanks, Harold, but I think I'll have plenty of time to get everything made if I don't get too many other calls on my time this coming week."

"Good. Then I'll be there soon, and we can plan our outing for Monday next."

"Thanks, Harold!"

Oh, boy! Harold knew *everything* about china and flatware and home furnishings. He worked as a costumer at a studio in Los Angeles, and his taste was exquisite. That's probably because he... um... well, he was a lavender cowboy, or would have been if he'd been a cowboy rather than a costumer. In fact, he lived with a gentleman named Delray Farrington in a beautiful mansion in a city called San Marino, just a little south and east of Pasadena. Perhaps this is the best way to describe Harold and Del: if they were a man and a woman, they'd be married. But they were a man and a man, and they couldn't get married if they wanted to. In fact, I think they might be persecuted, if not prosecuted, if anyone wanted to make an issue out of their relationship.

It didn't matter to me what folks did in their own homes.

And Harold was coming over to show me china patterns and plan for our trip to downtown Los Angeles next Monday! I thought about taking the telephone off the hook, just in case Harold's mother called in a blind panic and said she *needed* me, but I decided that to do so would be cowardly.

Naturally, not two minutes after I'd hung up from chatting with Harold the phone rang again. I'd barely made it into the living room, where I planned to practice next Sunday's anthem on the piano, when I had to turn around and go back to the kitchen. There I lifted the receiver from its cradle, held it a few inches away from my ear in case the caller was Mrs. P in a tizzy, and gave my patented greeting.

"Daisy?" said a subdued woman's voice. I didn't recognize the voice.

Puzzled, I put the receiver against my ear and said, "I'm so sorry. I didn't hear you."

"Daisy?"

It sounded like Mrs. Pinkerton. But how could it be Mrs. Pinkerton if she wasn't screaming into the telephone? The only times she ever called me was when she was in a flutter about something and wanted to avail herself of my spiritualist services. Cautiously, in case I was wrong, I said, "Mrs. Pinkerton?"

"Yes, dear. It's Madeline. And I'm calling to invite you to a luncheon in your honor on Tuesday, the twenty-eighth, at one p.m. *Do* say you can come, dear! Griselda will be there, and several other of the ladies you serve so well. I'll send you a formal invitation as soon as you tell me the date and time fit into your schedule. I know how busy you are." She giggled.

Mrs. Pinkerton *giggled*!

"And I'll even find some young people to join us. Because your wedding will take place in September, I want to be the first to invite you to a pre-bridal luncheon!"

So stunned was I to be speaking to a Mrs. Pinkerton who seemed neither alarmed nor insane, I couldn't make myself talk for a second.

"Daisy?" Mrs. P asked uncertainly.

"Yes! Yes, thank you, Mrs. Pinkerton. It is I, Daisy."

Mentally, I shook myself and demanded my internal fortitude to reassert itself.

"Well?" she asked, still sounding tentative.

"What a lovely invitation, Mrs. Pinkerton!" I cried, trying to sound overjoyed. In truth, I was stunned, but that was mainly because I seldom spoke to Mrs. P unless she was in a frenzy of emotional agony.

Oh, and Griselda is Mrs. Bissel, breeder of Spike and other magnificent examples of dachshund-hood, in case you wondered.

"Wonderful! I'm *so* glad, dear. I'd invite Harold, because I know you two are fast friends, but it really should be a luncheon for ladies only."

Well, that let me out.

Just kidding. Honestly, though, I was so surprised to hear Mrs. Pinkerton in a good mood, I wasn't quite sure how to respond. My normal mode of dealing with her was soothingly spiritual, and I invariably tried to ease her battered soul. In fact, this was the first good mood I could remember her being in since her daughter was arrested for trying to kill me. She did other things for which she was arrested, too, but I was particularly peeved about her having tried to kill me.

"This is so sweet of you, Mrs. Pinkerton," I said, thinking madly. "Thank you so much for thinking of me."

"My dear, I *always* think of you." A pause erupted, and I didn't know how to fill it. Most unusual for me when dealing with clients. Only in this case, Mrs. P wasn't being a client. She was being a friend. The notion almost made me cry. Fortunately, it didn't quite.

"You're so kind to me, Mrs. Pinkerton. And to my aunt. I know she adores cooking for you." I didn't truly *know* that, but Vi never complained, so I said it.

"Your aunt is a treasure, and so are you, Daisy. I wish I had a daughter like you. But it's too late for that."

"I'm sorry, Mrs. Pinkerton." And again I lost the power of speech. She wanted a daughter like *me*? Perhaps she should talk to my mother. "Um... Have you been in touch with Stacy lately?" One of Stacy's trials was coming up soon, and I did feel sorry for Mrs. P.

"I haven't talked to her for months," said Mrs. P, a bite to her voice. "She's gone so far off the path of goodness, I despair of her. That fellow you know, Captain Buckingham? Do you remember him?"

Did I *remember* him? Good grief. "Johnny Buckingham. Yes. He and his wife are both good friends of mine. More than that, they're both truly good and kind people."

"I guess they must be. When Stacy first joined the Salvation Army, I thought she'd gone 'round the bend, but Captain Buckingham is the only person who still seems to care about her. She wouldn't see him for a long time, but he kept going to the jail and eventually she agreed to talk to him."

"How did you find out about his visits?" I asked, flummoxed, mainly because I couldn't imagine Mrs. P having many connections to the Pasadena Police Department. Well, except through me, but we never talked about police business unless it involved her ghastly daughter.

I heard an audible gulp on the end of the wire. Then Mrs. P said in a strangled voice, "He telephoned to tell me she had accepted a Bible from him and allowed him to pray with and for her."

The man deserved a medal for fortitude! Not to mention persistence. "Captain Buckingham is an *extremely* kind soul."

"He told me he was only doing his job. Can you imagine it? Visiting criminals being part of your job? Then he said God had called him to that particular ministry."

Again a spate of nothing filled the air. I knew Johnny believed he'd been called from "the gutter to do God's work," as he expressed it. I figured he did more good in the world than most of the other people I knew (including me), and I honored him and his darling wife, Flossie, for it.

However, I wasn't about to tell Mrs. P, born to wealth and status, that Johnny had been so damaged by his service during the so-called Great War that he'd tried to drown himself in a bottle of booze and credited the Salvation Army for saving not merely his soul but his very life. She wouldn't understand.

"Yes. He believes it to be true," I said at last. "He and Mrs. Buckingham are loving, giving, happy people. They're expecting their second child. They already have a little boy they named after my late Billy."

"How lovely. I... understand from Captain Buckingham that the Salvation Army was founded in Great Britain to try to reach people who aren't"—again she gulped audibly—"welcome in more conventional churches. I... didn't know that. I just thought they dealt with the dregs of society because... well, I didn't know why. But I've begun to see the Salvation Army as a truly deserving institution if lovely folks like your friends are involved and still care about people others have given up on."

By golly, I'd wronged the woman. She *did* understand!

After I'd swallowed the pesky recurring lump in my throat, I said, "Yes, indeed. It's a worthwhile institution, and Flossie and Johnny are marvelous people."

"Yes. Well, thank you, dear. I didn't mean to get maudlin. I mainly wanted to invite you to luncheon on the Tuesday after next. We should have a good time, and I'm sure everyone will be happy to wish you the very best in your married life."

"Thank you. It sounds lovely. You're awfully kind."

"And... well..."

Here it comes, thought I. She wants me to read the Ouija board for her. Or lay out the tarot cards. "Yes?" I said. I said it amiably, too, darn it!

"Well, um, I'd like to make a donation to the Salvation Army Church your friend belongs to. I thought I'd give it to you, if you wouldn't mind taking it to Captain and Mrs. Buckingham for me."

Again, I'd wronged the dear woman. Boy, I had some work to do on myself, I reckon. "I'll be happy to transport your donation, Mrs. Pinkerton. I'll be sure to tell Flossie and Johnny it's from you, too."

"There's no need for that, Daisy. You may give it anonymously. It's so seldom I meet genuinely good people. You're one. Father Frederick is one. Algie is one. And your friends, the Buckinghams. They're expecting their second child, you say?"

"Yes, probably in November or December."

"Good. Then I'll double my donation. For years and years I had believed all men to be like Eustace, who was a horror." Eustace Kincaid, Mrs. P's first husband had, indeed, been a horror. I'd long ago decided Stacy inherited her evil streak from him. "And then Stacy turned out so... so awful." She sobbed a little, and my heart hurt for her.

"Stacy's not your fault, Mrs. Pinkerton. Remember Harold. He's a prince among men, and you reared him, too."

After several sniffles, Mrs. P said, "Thank you, Daisy. But you know I was weak. I didn't discipline Stacy as I should have."

"Stacy chose her own path, Mrs. Pinkerton," I told her sincerely. "There are people in the world who are born into dreadful circumstances and who really don't stand a chance to rise in life. Like Flossie Buckingham! Flossie grew up in a dreadful New York slum, and now she helps to direct the Pasadena Branch of the Salvation Army! But Stacy's not one of the Flossies of this world. She had everything, and she threw it away. Eagerly and with both hands."

"I suppose you're right. I do feel guilty about how horribly she's turned out, though."

"Perhaps the Buckinghams will work some of their kindly magic on her," I suggested, not believing my words for a minute.

"I hope so," said Mrs. P.

Spike, who'd become bored with my gabbing several minutes before this, began yapping at the front door in his joy at greeting a friend. I could tell this was a happy bark. "But I think Harold has just arrived at the door, Mrs. Pinkerton. He's bringing me some pictures of china patterns and so forth."

"Please give the dear boy my love," said the dear boy's mother.

"I will. And thank you again for the luncheon invitation. You're awfully kind to think of it."

"Nonsense."

Spike's volume rose significantly. "But I really must run. I'm sure Spike has spoiled my father's nap."

"Oh, dear. I'm so sorry, dear."

I thought about telling her it wasn't her fault I had an ill-behaved pet, but didn't want to waste the time. "Thank you again!" I called through the receiver. Then I plopped it into the cradle and ran for the door.

NINE

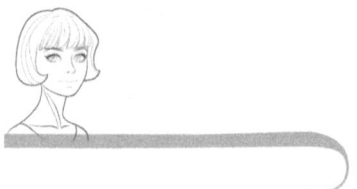

Fortunately, Spike's barking didn't seem to awaken any of the nappers in the house. I swung the door open to find Harold, a stack of cards in his hands. He shoved them at me so he could kneel to give Spike the greeting he deserved. Harold had his priorities in order, for the most part.

When he straightened, Harold said, "Okay, where do you want to go through these?"

"Dining room table," I said. "We have to be quiet because everyone's napping."

"Fine by me," said Harold. He marched through the living room arch, into the dining room, and gestured for me to put the cards on the table. Hmm. I think that's a gambling term. I didn't mean it as such then. At any rate, I put the cards on the table. Then I shut the door to the hallway, so as not to awaken anyone should Harold and I get rowdy. Not that we would, but we did make each other laugh a lot.

"Before we begin, I have some stuff to tell you. Did you hear that Mr. Cecil—"

My fascinating tidbit of gossip met a quick death when Harold interrupted me.

"Darlington. Somebody finally put the world out of its misery and killed him. Yeah, I heard. About damned time, if you ask me."

I stood there with my jaw flapping—not really—for a second or three. Then I said (and brilliantly, too), "Huh? He wasn't a nice person?"

"Nice person!" Harold whispered his exclamation, but I heard both it and its accompanying horrified denial. "The man was a sot and a lecher! Lord, Daisy, where have you been all your life?"

"Here?" I said weakly.

"You don't have to deal with the worst elements of the upper echelons, do you?"

"If Darlington was one, I guess not," I said.

"He was a louse and a drunk. His friends are all the same. And I take it back. He's not of the upper-upper echelons. He just wanted to join us there. But he'd never have made it, even if somebody hadn't put an end to him before he could try some more."

Golly, Harold never—well, hardly ever—spoke of himself and his friends in terms of class in our supposedly classless society, no matter that he and I knew precisely where we all fit into the caste system of Pasadena, California. "You'll have to tell me more," I said. Then I took a chair next to him and prepared myself to listen avidly.

"Ugh. I don't want to talk about him. Just take it from me that he considered himself the greatest catch on earth and tried to convince as many silly women as he could to think likewise. He also drank like a fish—which is a silly term. Fish don't drink or they'd drown in the water in which they live, wouldn't they?"

"Of course, fish don't drink. But I want to know about Cecil Darlington!"

"You don't, either. Trust me. You're lucky never to have seen him in life."

"I'd have been luckier if I hadn't had to see him in death," I muttered.

Harold glanced up from the cards he'd been sorting and stared at me. "Don't tell me *you're* the one who found him? Good God, Daisy, did you trip over another corpse?"

"I didn't trip over him," I said grudgingly. "But yes, I found his body. I didn't want to, believe me."

"Oh, I believe you. I just don't understand this gift you seem to possess of finding dead people all over the place."

"It's more like a curse," I grumbled.

"Suppose so. Well, I'm not going to tell you anything else about that wretched Darlington creature, so just prepare to be enchanted by these china patterns I brought for you to look at."

So, although I thought Harold was being mean by not revealing more about the evidently scandalous career of the late Mr. Cecil Darlington, I only sighed and looked through the cards as he handed them to me. "Oh, my," I said at one point. "I can't wait to see some of these in person."

"You will. These are my favorites."

"They're marvels of artistry."

"Only the best for *my* pals," said Harold.

"I love them all," I said, "Oh, and speaking of love, your mother called and sends her love to you. I meant to tell you that earlier."

"Oh, gawd. Spare my digestion, please."

"But she wasn't crying or screaming or anything," I told him. "She was perfectly sane and normal."

"If she was sane, she wasn't being normal, Daisy Gumm Majesty."

"Harold!" I said in a scolding voice. "She was subdued and nice and even said she's going to make a donation to the Salvation Army because evidently Johnny Buckingham is the only person in Pasadena who's still speaking to Stacy."

"Better him than me," grumbled Harold.

"Well, I think it's nice of her to make a donation, even though she wants me to take it to them. I wonder why."

"No you don't," said Harold. "You know damned well she wouldn't set foot in a Salvation Army Church. She's too uppity for that."

"Well, I think she was being extremely nice," I said stoutly. "And I believe she genuinely appreciates Johnny and Flossie for not giving up on Stacy. I know I gave up on her years ago."

"As well you should have."

"But still, I think your mother is being swell, Harold."

"Applesauce," said he. "Let's go through these again."

As he patted the cards back into some kind of order—I think Harold had sorted them as we'd looked the first time—my parents walked into the dining room.

"Good afternoon, you two," said Pa. "Whatcha doing?"

Being a well-bred gentleman of the Brahmin caste, Harold rose and held out his hand to my mother first then, after she shook it, to my father. "I'm just showing Daisy some of the china patterns I want her to think about. Join us, why don't you?"

"May I sit in and look, too?" asked Vi, who entered the dining room through the kitchen door just then.

"Of course!" I said.

Harold, needless to say, also shook Vi's hand. Then we all sat around the dining room table, and Harold handed out one card after another, announcing the pattern's name as he did so. I got them all mixed up in my brain, but I do recall the brands Shelley and Spode being attached to a few I especially liked. We must have sat at that dining room table for an hour or more, oohing and aahing over china patterns. My head had begun to spin by the time Harold patted his stack of cards together again.

"But I don't know how I'll select only one among them all," I said as Harold rose from the table. I felt like smacking myself on the head in an effort to make all those patterns clatter into some kind of order, but I didn't. It was probably just as well. My mother would have accused me of being dramatic or something.

"My goodness," said Ma. "I had no idea there were so many patterns to choose from."

"Nor did I," said Vi.

"Glad I don't have to choose," said Pa.

"When you see some of these in person, you'll be able to decide," Harold told us all.

"Do you really think so?" I asked, doubt plain to hear in my voice.

"Yes. And don't forget that I'll be with you. I won't allow you to make a mistake."

"Thanks, Harold," I said without sarcasm. I meant it.

"Happy to help. I love doing stuff like this! So on Monday, the twenty-seventh. I'll pick you up at... when? Tennish?"

"Tennish will be swell," I said faintly. I'd *never* be able to select one or two china patterns from all those gorgeous examples; I knew it.

TEN

After Harold left and my parents and Vi had gone to bed, it was a weary and confused Daisy Majesty who took Spike out front to sniff around. I hoped Sam and Mr. Prophet would come back and tell me all sorts of interesting things they discovered about the case before I became too fatigued to remain upright and fell into bed. Unfortunately, Spike got tired of sniffing before the men returned.

Frustrated, I let Spike back inside the house, but not before squinting across the street to see if Sam's Hudson was parked in his drive. It wasn't, which was a good thing. I'd have been irked if he'd not reported to me before retiring.

Just as I was about to give up and go to bed, Spike zoomed to the door. Because I frantically told him, "Spike, quiet!" he didn't begin barking, but his tail was going a mile a minute. Sure enough, when I looked through the peep hole, I saw Sam and Mr. Prophet standing on the front porch.

I must have looked as exhausted as I felt, because Sam asked, "What's the matter, Daisy? You look down in the dumps." He had to stop and pet Spike before I could answer.

"Yeah. What's wrong, Miss Daisy? You look like you swallered a toad."

"Swallowed a *toad*?" I said, distracted enough to allow all the pieces of china swirling in my head to crash to the ground and smash into smithereens. "Do people swallow toads?"

"Not as a rule. Gen'ly if a critter messes with a toad, it'll end up foaming at the mouth. The critter, not the toad."

"Good heavens," I said, my voice still faint, but perking up some. "Why do they foam at the mouth?"

"Toads' skin got something on it that poisons the critters. Gen'ly the critters don't die. They just foam at the mouth for a while."

"I had no idea," I said.

"Didn't think so," said Mr. Prophet.

Both he and Sam had entered the house by that time.

Sam gave me a little hug. "What's wrong, Daisy? You looked unhappy when you opened the door."

How sweet he could be!

"Nothing's wrong. And I'm not unhappy. It's just that Harold just came over with some pictures of china patterns, and they keep running together in my brain and I'm kind of... frustrated and confused, I guess. He's taking me to Bullock's in Los Angeles a couple of Mondays from now. He said that's the best place to shop for stuff like china and so forth."

"Shee-oot," said Mr. Prophet, barely scraping by without uttering a naughty word. "You gotta buy all that stuff, Sam? She's gonna empty your pocketbook before you even get hitched."

"No, I won't," I said. "Harold said I'm going to sign what he called Bullock's 'registry,' telling them the patterns I've chosen. Then other people will buy pieces of china and silverware. According to him. I've never heard of anything like that in my life."

"That's big in New York," said Sam, letting me go, darn it. "Our shops have registries for brides, too. So does Tiffany and Company."

"I've heard of Tiffany's," I told him.

"Most folks have," said Sam.

"I haven't," said Mr. Prophet.

I wasn't surprised. "Did you learn anything interesting when you went to the morgue and the Brownings' house?" I asked, ever hopeful.

"No," said Sam. "And if we had, I couldn't tell you about it."

I heaved a gigantic sigh. "What a frustrating day this has been. Not only did I not get to sing much this morning, but I'm totally confused about china patterns, and now you won't tell me anything about the murder inquiry."

"Ain't nothin' to tell," said Mr. Prophet.

"Nertz," I said, thinking he was just trying to be annoying.

"It's the truth, Daisy," said Sam, smiling at me. I think it was supposed to be an affectionate smile. "We only stopped by on our way home to tell you we're back. And now it's late, and we're heading across the street. I'm bushed." He bent and kissed me on the cheek. Better than nothing, I guess.

"Thanks, Sam. Good night, you two."

"Yeah," said Mr. Prophet, limping away.

"Sleep well, sweetheart," said Sam. This time I *know* his tone was affectionate, because I heard it.

By the time Spike and I hit the hay that Sunday night, I was exhausted. I also dreamed about people throwing teacups at me all night long. Stupid dreams. I woke up, exhausted from dodging expensive china, but I had to get up and face the day because I really did want to get my wedding dress made during the week. I'd carefully refused anyone wanting my services just so I could have this week to myself.

Therefore, I dragged myself out of bed and used the bathroom, checking myself in the mirror for bruises. There weren't any, of course.

A cup of coffee, some bacon, eggs, toast (thanks to Aunt Vi), and an orange later, I felt much better. I felt even better after Pa gave me the crossword puzzle to do. The *Pasadena Star News* and the *Herald Examiner* had begun printing crossword puzzles every day not long back, and I loved solving them. So Pa and I sat happily at the breakfast table, Pa reading, me writing, and Spike, ever hopeful, sitting on the floor between us, waiting for somebody to drop something. His hopes were often fulfilled, although I did try to watch his waistline. If I allowed Spike to get fat, neither Mrs. Pansy Hanratty nor Mrs. Bissel would ever forgive me.

Oddly enough, the first day after that hellish weekend murder passed pretty much as I'd hoped it would: peacefully. I fashioned my own wedding gown, not following any particular pattern. Because this was a second marriage for both Sam and me, I had decided to keep my gown simple. I made the under-slip of ecru satin with an overdress of filmy ecru silk fashioned in a drapey style. The neck was rounded, and the train only came to a little below the hem of the dress in back. Because I didn't care for the modern fashion of huge wedding hats, I aimed to wear a simple bandeau around my bobbed red hair, crafted of the same ecru satin and silk.

The only ornamentation was a thin, beaded, braid of fabric in the same ecru color that draped slightly below the waist and came together with a circlet of beads and emeralds at the side, which effectively drew the robed overdress together. It was simple, elegant, and I loved it. Harold had approved the design, too, so I knew it was all right.

The telephone rang at approximately nine-thirty, startling me out of my happy sewing daze. Fiddlesticks!

Pa called from down the hallway, "Want me to get it?"

With a sigh, I set aside the piece of silk I'd been gently gathering —the gathered fabric would go around the gown just below the waist and clasp on the side—and said, "No thanks. It's probably for me."

"Probably," agreed Pa.

I walked from the sewing room to the kitchen, where the telephone hung on the wall, and picked up the receiver. "Gumm-Majesty residence. Mrs. Majesty speaking."

"Oh, Daisy!" said Mrs. Pinkerton. I hadn't thought to hold the receiver away from my ear, but it didn't matter, because she wasn't screeching. How odd.

"Good day to you, Mrs. Pinkerton. May I help you?"

"Yes, dear, if you wouldn't mind."

Still no shrieks. And what was this *if I wouldn't mind* business? She'd never cared if I minded before. Heck, maybe she actually *had* reformed. We'd see. "I'll be happy to help if I can," I said. I'd learned long ago that it was wise to be careful what I said to Mrs. P and not agree unconditionally to anything she wanted to do until I knew more about it.

"You probably know I've been sending out invitations to your bridal luncheon on Tuesday, the twenty-eighth."

"Yes, and it's so kind of you," I murmured.

"It's only what you deserve, dear. Before I could think better of it, I sent one to Ethel Darlington, the poor woman whose son was so foully done to death at the wedding of your librarian friend."

I perked up slightly.

"I didn't realize you knew the Darlingtons. Yes, it was a shame about his demise." Except that he was a scoundrel and a cad and a loathsome creature, so who basically cared except Miss Madge Hawley? Well, and his mother.

Perhaps. All I knew is what Harold had told me. Maybe Harold had been wrong.

Naw. Harold was never wrong about people.

"Yes. We've been friends for quite a while through the Shakespeare Club and the Pasadena Woman's Hospital Board. Her children are younger than mine, so they didn't mix at school or anything."

Good. Stacy hadn't had a chance to corrupt him. Although evidently someone had. Unless he had been born a rascal. "It was terrible what happened to the fellow," I said, not quite sure I meant my words.

"Yes, well, that's where you come in, if you're able."

"Oh?"

"Yes, I told Ethel all about you, dear, and she'd love it if you could hold a séance and try to get in touch with poor Cecil. Perhaps he might even be able to give you the name of his killer."

Aw, fudge. I hated when clients wanted me to get in touch with murdered people. I was a phony, for crumb's sake. Oh, well. Money was money, and I earned mine by lying to people, so I said, "I can certainly attempt to do that, Mrs. Pinkerton. You know, though, that sometimes it takes quite a while for a soul to adjust to being on the Other Side. It might be too soon for Rolly to find Mr. Cecil Darlington."

"But you could try?" she asked, a pleading note to her whine.

"Yes. Depending on the day, I can try. I'm busy this entire week." Besides, if Mr. Prophet and Sam had come up with any interesting tidbits of information during their discussions at the police department, I might even have something useful to tell the séance attendees. Probably not, but you never knew.

"Bless you, dear!" Mrs. P cried joyfully. Better than when she cried woefully. "You say you're not available this week? What day will you be available?"

"Let me see. I'll consult my calendar."

I didn't have a calendar, but I let clients think I needed one. "Ah. Here we are. I have choir practice on Thursday evening, and a commitment on Friday." My Friday commitment was sewing and ironing, but Mrs. P didn't need to know that.

"What about Saturday? Can you hold a séance on the evening of Saturday, the eighteenth? I hate to rush you. And I know what a conscientious church-goer you are, what with singing in the choir and all, so I'll make sure everyone leaves before ten, if that isn't too late for you."

This was extremely strange behavior on Mrs. Pinkerton's part. She didn't used to care about anyone's time but her own. I guess Johnny and Harold and Father Frederick were all doing her some good.

"Ten o'clock is all right, and this coming Saturday will be fine." Something occurred to me. "What about a funeral service for the poor fellow? When will it be held?" He'd only died a couple of days ago, for pity's sake.

"They're holding his service on Thursday, the sixteenth," said Mrs. Pinkerton in a sad voice. "I hope Ethel will be recovered enough to attend a séance for him on Saturday night."

"Perhaps you should get in touch with her on Friday evening

and let me know," I suggested. I'd be home Friday night. At least I thought I would be. Besides, even if I wasn't back from the Buckinghams' by then, someone would be here to take a message.

"That's a good idea. I'll attend the funeral. It's being held at St. Mark's Episcopal Church in Altadena. You know the one. It's right across the street from Griselda's house."

"Yes, I know do know it. Father Frederick is the priest there, isn't he?"

"Yes, the dear man."

Father Frederick had been a friend of Mrs. Pinkerton's since before I'd first known her. And, from all I'd been able to gather, he was indeed a dear man. He used to be one of the priests at All Saints Episcopal Church, but had transferred to St. Mark's.

"Very well, then, if you believe Mrs. Darlington is not too upset by events and the funeral, let me know. I'll be happy to perform a séance at your home on Saturday. If Mrs. Darlington is too upset, or if Saturday is too soon for her, we can decide upon another date."

"Thank you, dear. Shall we set the time at eight? That will give me plenty of time to cancel, should it be necessary."

"Perfect," I said. "I'll get there at seven-thirty to set up the room properly."

"Wonderful!"

We said our polite good-byes, and I hung the receiver on the hook. When I turned around, it was to find Pa seated at the kitchen table, grinning at me and eating an orange. "Another séance?" he asked.

"Yes. Mr. Cecil Darlington's mother is hoping I'll be able to chat with him and maybe discover who murdered him." I shrugged my shoulders in a helpless gesture.

Wrinkling his nose, Pa said, "And will you be able to do those things?"

"Of course not." I sighed, pulled out a kitchen chair and flumped into it. Spike instantly put his paws on my knees, so I petted him.

"I have to say, Daisy, that you have the strangest job I've ever even heard about. And you're my own daughter! Who'd'athunk it?"

"Not I, certainly. Well, until I was ten and Vi brought home that stupid Ouija board."

Pa laughed, got up from the table, and headed to the hall. He was probably going to nap for a while. He'd been taking more naps in recent months, and I feared the reason for his naps had to do with a worsening of his heart condition.

And then the blasted telephone rang again. Glumly, I answered it.

However, when I gave my standard welcoming statement, darned if Harold wasn't on the other end of the wire. "Harold!" cried I, surprised

"I know, I know. I hadn't planned to bother you until next week, but my new car just came in, I'm on my way to pick it up, and I want to show it to you before I go to work."

"You got your new car?"

"Isn't that what I just said?" Harold sounded the tiniest bit sarcastic.

"Sorry, Harold. I've been sewing, and I got kind of lost in fabric and so forth for a bit."

"Wedding paraphernalia?" he asked.

"Gown," I told him.

"Perfect. You can show me sometime during the week. Won't have time this morning."

"Happy to, Harold. I'm sure Pa will want to look at your car, too. But I thought you'd bought a new Stutz."

"I did, but I decided I liked this one better."

"Oh." Must be nice to have tons of money. "I'm sure Pa will be delighted to see your new automobile."

"Of course, he will. Everyone will. It's special, Daisy."

Harold sounded so delighted, I laughed. He didn't mind. "Be there soon, sweetie."

"Okay! I'll warn Pa."

Fortunately for Harold and me, Pa hadn't begun to nap. In fact, when I neared his bedroom door, it opened and he emerged with a book in his hand. I told him Harold's news.

"He bought a new automobile?" If there was anything Pa loved more than books, it was cars.

"Yup. And he's bringing it by for us to exclaim over."

"Sounds like a brilliant plan to me."

Therefore, Pa was even happier than I—I'd personally rather sew than look at automobiles—when Harold's knock smote our ears. Pa opened the door, and Harold gestured for the both of us to take a gander at the monument to modern-automobile-engineering residing at the curb in front of our modest house on Marengo Avenue.

Mind you, Harold had bought a brand new, bright yellow Kissel 45 Gold Bug not long back, but Sam's rotten nephew had driven it into a ditch and crunched it to death. Therefore, Harold had bought a new Stutz. Then, evidently, he'd ordered a new automobile to be made.

And what a car it was! Extremely long and extremely red, it had a silver-looking something-or-other as a hood ornament. It fairly screamed opulence, at least to my plebeian ears.

"Boy, Harold, you don't spare the pocketbook, do you?" said Pa. "That's a Hispano Suiza H6B, isn't it?"

"Good call, Mr. Gumm. It is indeed. Ordered it from Paris, and it arrived over the weekend. I had my mechanic pick it up for me and go over it."

"I've never seen one of these in person," said Pa reverently. We'd walked out to the street by this time. You've heard the expression, "Feast your eyes" on something? Well, my father exemplified the expression as he perused Harold's new automobile.

"Feel free to examine it to your heart's desire," said Harold with a theatrical gesture at the car.

"It's red," I said. "Like your old Stutz."

"This is a different red, though," said Harold. "More subdued. That's a bow to Del."

"It doesn't look awfully subdued to me. What's that hood ornament? It looks like a loon diving into a lake for a fish."

"That, my dear, is a stork," said Harold.

"Oh. Why'd they use a stork as a hood ornament? I think of

storks delivering babies in Victorian times, not hanging out on the hoods of fancy automobiles. And why do they call it a Hispano-Suiza if it's made in France?"

"Shut up, Daisy," said Harold.

I shut up.

"This is some machine," said Pa, getting behind the wheel. I knew he'd love to drive the thing, but his driving days were pretty much over. As already mentioned, his tricky heart had been bothering him more and more in recent weeks. He caressed that silly car's interior, though, as if it were something living. A beloved pet like Spike, maybe.

"It's nice to know *somebody* around here has good taste," Harold said. He much preferred Pa's reverence to my utter ignorance.

Still and all... a stork? "It's really pretty," I said, hoping to make up for my lapses.

"Beautiful," said Pa, climbing reluctantly out of the automobile. "I'd have loved to drive one of these when I was still driving. Maybe you'll let me look at the engine one of these days. Daisy tells me you need to get to work today, though."

"Happy to let you investigate the engine all you want, Mr. Gumm. But yes, I do have to get to the set now. It's in Alhambra, so I don't have to drive too far."

"Well, that's lucky," said Pa.

"Indeed," I said. "And I want to get back to my wedding gown."

"Don't forget I want to see it before the nuptials," warned Harold. "Don't want you making any serious blunders."

"Harold Kincaid! I'm as good at this fashion nonsense as you are!"

"Well." Harold sniffed meaningfully. "Perhaps. I still want to see it. And the bridesmaids' dresses, too."

"You may," I told him. "And Ma and Vi's dresses, too."

"Good Lord," said Pa. "I don't remember all this fuss around your first wedding, Daisy."

I heaved a sigh. "No, there wasn't any fuss. I'd just graduated from high school, and Billy'd just joined the army. We were both so young and stupid."

"Well, I don't know if I'd put it precisely like that," said my kindhearted father.

"At least you're not young any longer," said Harold in a brisk voice. "I'll give you a call sometime this week, Daisy. We need to select your flatware and glassware, too."

"Oh." My voice wasn't at all brisk.

ELEVEN

Only when Harold was safely planted behind the steering wheel of his new toy and delightedly steering it down Marengo Avenue did I wonder what Pa thought of Harold and the delight he took in china, flatware patterns and home decorations in general. Most of the men Pa knew were like him. They loved cars and baseball and wouldn't know a cream jug from a gravy boat. I'd never asked him, but I think Pa knew about Harold's preference for men over women, but he didn't seem to care. Nor did any of my other family members, bless them.

The rest of that week passed peacefully enough. Mrs. Pinkerton only called me three or four times, and she wasn't upset during any of our telephone visits. Wondered how long she could keep up this calm exterior. I truly hoped her exterior was a mirror of her interior, but I didn't hold out too much hope for that. In the however many years I'd known her, she'd been in a flap about one thing or another pretty much all the time.

On Wednesday afternoon I had to interrupt my sewing marathon to attend the exercise class I'd had the poor judgment to join, and I actually enjoyed choir practice on Thursday evening. Other than that, though, the week was totally, marvelously uneventful. I about had my entire wedding ensemble prepared by Friday afternoon.

Feeling as though I'd actually accomplished something worthwhile, I hung my unhemmed wedding gown in the sewing room and went into the hall to find Spike curled up and sulking. I'd had to banish him from the sewing room, poor baby.

"Spike, my sweetheart!" I said when he leaped to his feet—sometimes it was difficult to tell if he was standing or lying down against the dark pattern of the hall runner—and wagged at me. "I'm so sorry I've had to leave you out of the sewing room for so long."

"Afternoon, sweetie," came my father's voice from the kitchen. So Spike and I toddled into the kitchen and found him snapping beans at the table. Pa liked to be useful, and we had a *gigantic* crop of Kentucky Wonder Beans growing in the kitchen garden.

"Hey, Pa. You're doing something good for the whole family. I've just been making my wedding dress." Naturally, I felt guilty.

With a chuckle, Pa said, "I'm through here. I'm just going to stick this bowl of beans in the Frigidaire. I figured I'd better harvest them because there were so many of them. Your aunt might want to preserve some of them."

"Ah, yes. I'll help her." I hated preserving vegetables and so forth, but I figured it was my duty, so I did it. "Before that happens, want to take Spike for a walk with me?"

Pa shoved the big bowl of freshly snapped beans in the Frigidaire. As he shut the door of same, he said, "I was just going to ask you the same question."

So Pa and I took a happy Spike—he never sulked for long, being a dog and not a person—for a nice long walk. It felt good to be out in the open air, even if it was relatively warm air. I'd been cooped up in the house most of the week. Spike said he had been, too, and he didn't appreciate his enforced coopage. Don't tell me dogs can't talk. They may not use words, but they can tell you what they're feeling.

All three of us felt better after we got home from our walk to discover Aunt Vi in the kitchen, beaming at the bowl of snapped beans in the Frigidaire. She made excellent use of them, too.

That evening after dinner, Ma got out the hem marker. I went to the sewing room—leaving poor Spike out in the hall—and donned my wedding gown. Carefully. The outer fabric was filmy, and I didn't want to snag it on anything. When I walked into the dining room, everyone smiled at me. Even Ma, in spite of her first question.

"This dress is beautiful, Daisy. It's quite plain, though. Is that what you intended?" Ma didn't sound disapproving, just curious.

"It's precisely what I intended, Ma. This is a second go-round for both Sam and me, and I didn't want to wear white or frills or anything. I'm also not going to wear one of those new-style wedding hats."

"The ones that cover your whole head?"

"Yes."

"I'm glad of that. Um... So your veil will be beige, too?"

"It's not beige, Ma. It's *ecru*. I think that's a French word for beige. But yes, it will be the same color as the dress. I found some white veiling I believe I can stain with tea so that it'll be about the same color as the dress. The only color will be the green and gold of the side fastener and the green and gold in my ring. And, of course, the green and gold on the bandeau I aim to make."

"Oh, my. Well, it sounds lovely. What colors will your attendants wear?"

"Daphne's dress will be emerald green." Daphne, my older sister, said she'd be my matron of honor. I'd asked Flossie Buckingham if she'd be my MOH, but she'd declined the offer, telling me, "I'll be as big as a house by the time of your wedding, Daisy!" She'd sounded rather shocked that I'd even asked, so I didn't press the point. "And Polly and Peggy will have mint-green dresses."

"So your wedding will be mostly greens?"

"Yes. Except for you and Vi."

"Oh?" Now Ma sounded the least little bit worried.

"Don't worry. The colors will look wonderful. Your dress will be in a light rose color, and Vi's will be a little darker rose. I think the light will go better with your coloring, and the darker with Vi's."

"What shoes will you wear with your lovely gown?"

"I don't know yet. Maybe I'll ask Harold what he thinks. I'm kind of hoping I won't have to wear squishy toes and high heels, but Harold will know for sure. He's my arbiter for all thing fashionable." I laughed.

"My goodness. You have this whole thing planned out, don't you?"

"Pretty much. I'm a little worried about Harold taking me to find china patterns on Monday, but I'll probably survive. At least there won't be the tiniest possibility that Vi will get flour on her dress during the wedding reception, because Harold is having the Castleton cater the affair."

"He is? That must be costing him a fortune."

"It probably is. He's the best friend anyone ever had. He's also managing the flowers. I asked him not to, but Harold says I'm worth it. I don't agree, but there's no arguing with Harold."

"You're more than worth it, Daisy. After all the time you've spent caring for his mother and being nearly murdered by his sister, I imagine Harold figures he owes you."

"Well, he *did* take me to Egypt, don't forget."

"How could I forget?" Ma shuddered slightly.

Our trip to Egypt had been harrowing in spots. And *hot*? Merciful heavens, I don't think I've ever been so hot in my life. And that's only partly because I was sick and had a fever for several days.

Ma slipped the last pin in the gown—I'd purchased special pins for silk fabrics that wouldn't snag the fine threads of the cloth—and I walked to my bedroom to look at the result in the cheval glass mirror.

"What do you think?" I asked Ma, who'd followed me.

"I think you're going to be a beautiful bride," she said wistfully. "Again."

"Thanks, Ma." I sniffled a bit, thinking of my ecstasy when I'd married Billy almost ten years earlier. Didn't seem that long somehow. And I wasn't exactly ecstatic this time. Life had knocked both

Sam and me around quite a bit in the years between 1917 and 1925. At least we'd survived. Lots of people hadn't, which is why we'd both had to bury spouses.

But I didn't want to think about that.

So I again retired to the sewing room for a bit. I hemmed my wedding gown and contemplated whether or not I should attempt to find appropriate shoes when Harold took me to Bullock's the next Monday.

However, when I imagined tramping all over the store, I decided not to package too many things into one single day. I could make a trip to Nash's Department Store, where there was always a good selection of footwear, and if I couldn't find anything there, I'd ask Harold where to find shoes. There was plenty of time, after all. Our wedding wasn't going to be held until sometime in September, after all.

Sometimes I amaze myself with my own naivety.

TWELVE

O n Saturday, I helped Vi and Ma preserve four quarts of string beans, ten quarts of tomatoes, five quarts each of apricots and beets, and I was so hot and sweaty, I despaired of ever managing to look decent for the evening's séance at Mrs. Pinkerton's house.

"What time do you have to be there?" asked Ma when I wiped my forehead with my apron and moaned about perspiration.

"Seven-thirty."

Vi glanced at the kitchen clock. She was even sweatier than Ma and me, because she's the one who womanned the kitchen range and boiled all those jars before and after they were filled. I was mostly in charge of chopping things and pouring paraffin. Ma placed the rubber rings on the jars, did the capping, and filled the rack to put in the steam-pressurized pot Vi used for preserving foods. She favored Ball jars over Mason jars, but I don't know why.

Wiping her own brow, Vi said, "It's only four o'clock, so you'll probably recover, Daisy. We got a lot done here today. Good work, you two." She beamed at Ma and me.

I, for one, beamed back. I couldn't cook, but I could preserve the heck out of foodstuffs from the garden.

Then Vi said, "I think you should take a cool bath, Daisy, and just rest before you have to conduct your séance."

"I'll take a cool bath first, if you don't mind," said Ma. "Then Vi, and then you, Daisy. That way you'll be fresher when you have to go to Mrs. Pinkerton's place."

"Sounds like an excellent notion to me," I told the most important women in my life. "Right now, I'm going to my room to take off these old sweaty clothes and hang out with Spike for a bit." And if I could catch a few winks, so much the better.

"Wonderful idea," said Ma, and Vi nodded.

Spike, who had not been underfoot all day, although he could have been had he not been so well trained, liked the idea, too.

Therefore, as Ma and then Vi soaked in the tub, I disrobed down to my combinations and then, feeling a great sense of satisfaction because I'd actually done something useful that day, flopped on top of the quilt on my bed. Spike joined me, and we were soon sawing logs.

About an hour later, I rose from the bed and made my way to the bathroom, where I glanced in the mirror and was aghast at the mess those beets had made of my hands and parts of the rest of me. It looked as if I'd dipped my hands in blood and then splattered myself with it, for crumb's sake! Good thing I'd worn an apron, or I'd have looked even more like a murder victim than I already did.

I used some of the bubbly bath salts Harold had given me. After washing my sweat-dampened hair, I scrubbed my hands really well with my loofah—grown in our own back garden, by golly—and my blood-red hands turned pink again. The other red blotches were on my front, so I scrubbed those, too, and they mostly washed off.

My pinkish hands wouldn't matter. I'd wear gloves when I arrived at Mrs. P's house and only take them off when the séance began and the lights were out so nobody'd see my beety hands. The loofah performed miracles on my fingernails, too, as well as the rest of me. It was a well-scrubbed Daisy Gumm Majesty who climbed from the bath and slathered healing cream, also gifted to me by Harold, on her body.

Then I retired to my bedroom with Spike again—he'd declined

bathing with me, silly dog—put on a clean and comfy day dress, and buffed my nails until they were as shiny as shiny could be. A glance at my bedroom clock told me I'd better decide what to wear that evening. As I gazed at my overstuffed closet, I decided, as the day still seemed awfully warm—although that might be partially a result of our preserving efforts—to wear a light-weight dress.

Oh, in case anyone wondered, Regina's wedding gown was safely covered with a sheet and hanging upstairs in Vi's closet, which had room for it, unlike mine.

Spike and I spent about fifteen minutes going through my closet and deciding which séance gown would be best for a warm July evening and still look somber enough for the mother of a murder victim. I decided upon a light gray scalloped dress I'd copied from a Chanel model I'd seen in *Vogue Magazine*. It had a rounded neck, scallops from top to bottom, and was sleeveless. I'd made it of cotton voile, so it was incredibly comfortable, but it looked sophisticated. A belt of the same gray voile tied loosely right below the waist, so its tails fluttered when I walked. I could wear my black low-heeled shoes and take my black handbag. Feeling not merely warm but daring, I decided to wrap a necklace of black beads around my dark red hair, thereby achieving a measure of coolth (I just made up that word) while being fashionable at the same time. I laid out my dress and the beads on the rocking chair and gazed at them with some satisfaction.

There. My outards would be perfect. Still wasn't sure about my innards. I guess the state of those would depend on how Mrs. Darlington felt about her departed son, how she reacted to the séance, and how believably equivocal I could be. Stupid job.

Along about six-thirty, Vi knocked at my door.

"Daisy? You'd better come out and eat something before you have to go to Mrs. Pinkerton's place."

Lordy, I'd forgotten all about food. Most unlike me. Guess all that steam heat had fogged my brain.

"Thanks, Vi. Will do."

"Just sandwiches for supper, I fear. I'm too bushed from canning all day long."

"I'm sure you are. But you don't need to make a sandwich for me. I can make my own sandwich."

"Piffle. I've already prepared chicken sandwiches for everyone."

"Thanks, Vi. I didn't know you'd cooked a chicken."

"I cooked this chicken last year and bottled it, but it's pretty tasty mixed with mayonnaise, chopped celery, diced onions and some of my dill pickle slices."

"You're a culinary genius, Vi," I said. Deciding not to abuse my feet any more than I had to, I stuffed my feet into my carpet slippers. If I'd known I'd encounter Sam and Mr. Prophet sitting at the kitchen table along with Ma and Pa, I might have worn socks and shoes. Oh, well. Too late now.

"Hey, guys," I said to the assembled diners.

"Your mother tells me you're going to conduct a séance for the Darlington woman tonight," said Sam, getting right down to business.

"Yes, Mrs. Pinkerton called and asked me to, so I said I would."

"I'd like to sit in on one of your séances one of these days, Miss Daisy," said Mr. Prophet with an ironical glint in his eyes.

"I'm sure you would. You'd probably disrupt the thing by laughing."

"Might," he agreed.

"Well, I'm going to join you tonight," said Sam, surprising me.

"Why?" I asked, vaguely alarmed.

"Just want to see who shows up, is all," he said. "I won't mar your séance with my presence. I'll just drive you there, sit and wait, and then drive you home again."

"Oh. In that case, I'm sure it'll be fine. Except for Mrs. Pinkerton and Mrs. Darlington, I don't know who'll be there. Wonder if the Hawley sisters will be invited."

"I want to know that, too," said Sam.

"But sit down and eat, Daisy," said Vi, sticking a plate in front of me with a delicious-looking sandwich. She'd added celery sticks and a couple of slices of dill pickle on the plate to even things out, I guess.

"And don't worry about the dishes," said my wonderful mother. "I'll do the dishes while you dress for your evening."

"Thanks, Vi and Ma." I glanced at the kitchen clock. "Fiddle-sticks. I'll have to eat quickly—"

"Don't gobble," warned my mother. "It's bad for your digestion."

"I won't gobble," I promised. "But I won't be able to stick around for seconds or anything. I've got to get my spiritualist togs on and make myself look mysterious."

My mother shook her head, as if in despair. Mr. Prophet chuckled his evil chuckle. Pa, Sam and Vi laughed. Spike just wagged.

For the record, Vi's preserved-chicken sandwiches were deli-cious. I'm sure the fact that she also baked the bread, made the mayonnaise and turned some of last year's crop of cucumbers into dill pickles also helped. As I rose from the table and retired to my bedroom to dress, I vowed I'd make at least one more stab at attempting to cook something more difficult than toast. Of course, it would help if I could slice an even piece of bread, but I'd work on that, too. Poor Sam deserved better than me.

However, I could sure look good when I tried to! After I'd brushed my teeth and dabbed cologne in my armpits—nobody wanted a stinky spiritualist, and warm nights were iffy—I went back to my bedroom and put on the outfit I'd laid out on the rocking chair. I hadn't quite dared lay it out on the bed for fear Spike might jump up on the bed and snag the voile fabric. He wouldn't do this out of malicious intent, because Spike wasn't that sort of dog. He was, in fact, the best-trained hound in the city of Pasadena. However, he still had claws on his feet, and those claws could snag filmy voile even if he didn't want them to.

When I gazed at the end result in the mirror in my bedroom, I smiled. Thanks to bubbles and my loofah, no one would ever know I'd only earlier in the day managed to get beet juice all over myself. The black beads circling my head were a glorious touch, too. And to think I'd almost passed over this voile when it was on sale at Maxime's Fabrics! It was gray, for glory's sake, and gray is dull. But it made for an absolutely *perfect* gown for a spiritualist-medium bent upon coaxing a murdered man out of his grave.

I didn't mean that. The real, honest-to-God ghost of a murdered man actually *had* shown up at one of my séances once. Scared me nearly to death. Didn't do much for the séance attendees, either. Worse, the mother of the murdered man then asked me to investigate his death, which had been labeled suicide by the medical examiner. I never wanted to go through anything like that again. In fact, I'd already vowed to myself that, if it *did* happen again, I'd be out of the spiritualist biz like a light!

Sorry for the diversion.

When I again emerged from my bedroom clad in my spiritualist's togs, everyone nodded and said I looked great. That was nice. I'd patted a little pale rice powder on my face and used a tiny bit of eyebrow pencil and mascara, but my lips were devoid of color. Pale and interesting. That was the image I strove to achieve. According to reports, I achieved it that night.

Sam and I drove to Mrs. Pinkerton's grand mansion in Sam's big black Hudson. He parked it in the circular drive in front of the gigantic porch, escorted me up the porch steps, and he clapped the brass lion's knocker on its brass knocking plate.

Featherstone, Mrs. Pinkerton's marvelous butler, answered the door, looking as sober as a funeral director, which was appropriate. Featherstone was a prince of a butler. He even had an English accent. He'd also sustained an injury to his knee a month or so prior to this séance, but he showed no signs of limping. I considered asking about his state of health, but didn't. Featherstone didn't stray from his butlerish ways unless compelled to do so by dire circumstances.

As for Sam, he again wore his Italian-count suit and we looked perfect together, if I do say so myself. Even Mrs. Pinkerton appeared impressed. She also remembered Sam's last name. Triumph!

"But let me introduce you to Mrs. Darlington, Daisy," said Mrs. P. Glancing at Sam, she said, "Um, would you mind, Detective Rotondo? I'll only borrow her for a minute or two."

"Please, feel free," said Sam, sounding less gruff than usual.

My Sam could act the gent when he chose to, by golly! It helped that Harold was there, sitting in a corner near the fireplace. When he saw Sam and me, he moseyed over, and he and Sam went back to Harold's corner so as not to interfere with all the feminine emotions hovering in the air, along with the heat. Mrs. P had several electric fans turned on, so the heat wasn't too overpowering.

Aha. I spotted Madge Hawley, along with her sister and a woman clad in black, drooping on a sofa against a far wall. Sure enough, Mrs. P led me over to the trio. When we approached, it appeared to me as if all three ladies had been crying. I felt sorry for them.

"Ethel," said Mrs. P softly. "Please allow me to introduce you to Mrs. Majesty, who will be conducting our séance this evening."

Mrs. Darlington lifted a tear-streaked face to me. Madge and DeeDee appeared thunderstruck.

Madge said, "You? *You're* the medium?"

"Good heavens," DeeDee said faintly.

Ignoring as best I could the cries of the two younger women, I knelt beside the sofa, gently took one of Mrs. Darlington's hands, and said, "Mrs. Darlington. I'm so sorry to have to meet you under these unfortunate circumstances."

Wiping her drippy eyes—if she'd once worn any makeup, it was long gone—Mrs. Darlington squeezed my hand. Hard. Ow. Good thing my joints hadn't yet been claimed by the rheumatics. "Oh, Mrs. Majesty, thank you so much for doing this."

"Doing what?" asked DeeDee, clearly confused.

"Attempting to discover Cecil's killer, of course," said Madge, who sounded more sarcastic than sorry. "I thought your name was Daisy," she said to me.

"It is."

"Her real name is Desdemona," said Mrs. Pinkerton, who still didn't understand I'd adopted the name Desdemona in my tenth year. At this point in my life as a spiritualist-medium, about all I could say about my adopted cognomen was that it was slightly better than Ophelia. Or Medusa.

"Oh," said Madge. "You were Regina's matron of honor."

"Yes. Mrs. Browning and I have been friends for many years," I said. Turning my attention back to Mrs. Darlington, I rose, with her still holding my hand. Feeling like a total louse, I said, "I will do my best, Mrs. Darlington. However, as Mrs. Pinkerton has probably already told you, it often takes a spirit some time to adjust to the Other Side, and I may not be able to get the results for which you hope."

Mrs. Darlington sniffled. "Thank you for trying, Mrs. Majesty."

Madge shot me a little frown. Although she spoke under her breath, I heard the words she spoke: "How convenient."

Well! What was *her* problem?

"But come along, Daisy. I'll take you to the séance room, and you can set it up."

"Thank you, Mrs. Pinkerton."

I felt Madge Hawley's disapproving gaze as if it were a flaming arrow as I walked away from Mrs. Darlington and went with Mrs. Pinkerton to her dining room. Sam noticed us and joined us in the hallway.

"Those two Hawley girls," he said, "will they join the séance?"

"Miss Madge Hawley will be joining us," said Mrs. Pinkerton. "I'm not sure about DeeDee. Madge was engaged to Cecil, you know. She's almost as crushed by his death as poor Ethel."

"Yes," I said. "So I see." But why was she irked at me? I didn't ask.

We entered Mrs. Pinkerton's dining room. I really hated this room. It had a balcony on the far end from where I would be sitting, and it loomed over the room like a gallows. It was probably built to allow musicians to play while the rich folks dined, but it served no purpose that evening except to give me the willies. Images of people tossing bodies over the balcony and onto the séance table flitted through my mind and, as much as I attempted to banish them, they wouldn't go away. Great. Just what I needed. A murdered man's mother, his fiancé, and images of dead bodies falling through the air.

All things considered, I'd rather have my mental images haunted by people flinging teacups at me.

THIRTEEN

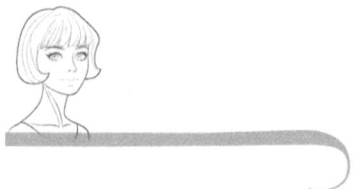

The séance was not precisely a disaster, but it came close. The ghost of Cecil Darlington didn't show up, thank God, but Rolly wasn't his usual helpful self, either. In fact, he was a brat. Perhaps he sensed the vague hostility radiating from Miss Madge Hawley.

Yes, I know. That's a stupid thing to say. Rolly was me. Perhaps *I* sensed Madge's hostility. Still and all, I could generally control Rolly better than I did that evening. I couldn't account for Madge's hostility, either, which confused me and probably contributed to the Rolly problem.

The séance began as all my séances did, with me sitting at the head of an oblong table with one cranberry glass candle holder in the table's center. Inside the cranberry globe a single candle flickered.

I called for Featherstone to turn off the lights. He did.

I called for anyone who was wearing them to remove their gloves. They did.

I called for silence. Silence almost ensued. When it comes to a group of human beings, complete silence is impossible. Somebody always sniffles, coughs, moves his or her chair, etc.

After the room was as silent as it was going to get, I said, "Please join hands."

I presume everyone joined hands. It was dark, and I couldn't tell, but I figured they'd do as I demanded since this was a séance, and *everyone* knew hands were held during séances. And then I sat still and silent until I bowed my head slightly to one side and went into my "trance."

"What's she doing?" asked a person. I think it was Madge Hawley.

Mrs. Pinkerton, who could be positively ferocious when it came to my spiritualistic self's well-being, whispered, "Shhh. She's going into a trance. You *must* be quiet."

"Huh." I think that came from Madge Hawley, too.

A few minutes into my trance-state, I spoke to Rolly. "Rolly? We're here this evening to attempt communication with the spirit of a young man named Cecil Darlington. Has he reached the Other Side and settled in yet?"

Rolly was slow to answer, darn him. Finally he said (in a tone an octave or so lower than my speaking voice), "Och, my love, Mr. Darlington is not settled here."

"No?"

"Nae. And from what I've heard, he may never settle here."

Huh? I wanted to tilt my head and slap it to get the junk out. Why had Rolly said that? I didn't mean him to.

"I... don't understand, Rolly. What do you mean?"

"That young man was a wrong 'un, my love. He may never settle anywhere."

Good grief. What did this mean?

"Wh-what do you mean, Rolly?"

"I mean what I say. Wickedness has no place here with us peaceful souls."

Wickedness? For the love of God, why'd Rolly say *that?*

A heavy sob smote my ears. It came from one of the séance participants seated to my right. I figured it came from Mrs. Darlington, and I felt ratty.

"I... I still don't understand, Rolly. Whatever do you mean?" As soon as the question passed my lips, I wished it unsaid. Too late.

"The young Darlington fellow wasn't a nice person, my love. I don't want to grieve his poor mother, who didn't know about his ways. She's not to blame for anything he did. Or anything he didn't do."

"Oh, but Rolly, surely you don't really mean it?"

"Oh, but I do, my darling."

"But he was so *young*."

"So was Caligula."

Rolly! Why was he introducing an insane Roman dictator into *my* séance?

"Rolly, please stop saying unpleasant things about the late Mr. Darlington. His mother is here, and she's attempting to find out what happened to him."

"His enemies did him in," said Rolly, blast him!

"His enemies?"

"He might have been young," said Rolly through my mouth, "but he was old in the ways of sin."

More sobbing and a furious whispered, "No!" ripped through the room.

Okay. That was it for me. Mrs. Darlington was weeping in earnest, it sounded as if Madge Hawley was about to rebel and upend the table, and I couldn't take any more. What the heck was *wrong* with me that night?

Trying my best to wrench control of the séance from the entity I'd invented, I forced Rolly to say, "But he might come 'round one day. He might well join those of us here and happy on the Other Side. Eventually." Dang. I hadn't meant that *eventually* to sound so much like a hurried addition, but it did, probably because it was.

And then, by all that's holy, I felt a shaft of pain pierce my body. I cried out in agony. Actually, it wasn't so much of a shaft as it was a bomb blast, and it hit every single inch of me. When I collapsed more deeply into my chair then, it wasn't an act. It was a result of excruciating pain. I moaned, "Aaaaah," and thought my body might explode. The sensation was truly hideous.

I don't know how long I slumped there, whimpering, but eventually somebody turned on the dining-room light, and the pain gradually left me. It left me a wreck, but it left me.

"Daisy!" cried Mrs. Pinkerton. "Oh, Daisy, what happened?" She hurried from her chair to the head of the table where I still gasped in leftover agony.

Although I tried to speak, my voice wouldn't work. Wish it hadn't worked during the séance, but oh, no. It had to leave me now, when I needed it, and after it had imposed a world of sorrow upon at least one grieving woman.

"She's *wrong*!" shrieked Madge Hawley. "She's *wrong*!"

Mrs. Pinkerton, bless her heart, said, "Stop that this instant, young woman. *She* didn't say a word. Her spirit control did the talking."

If only that were so.

"Oh, my God," whimpered Mrs. Darlington. "It can't be true."

Although I couldn't yet open my mouth, I could open my eyes. As I forced myself to sit upright, waiting for another crushing pain to fell me, I saw Madge Hawley lead a doubled-over Mrs. Darlington from the room. I knew Madge was furious, because she was red as a tomato and shooting invisible bullets of hatred at me.

Then Sam showed up. He stomped into the room, scattering loose séance attendees as if he were a bull running on the streets of Pamplona, Spain, and they were fleeing peasants. Harold scurried after him.

"Daisy!" bellowed Sam. "Daisy, what the devil is going on? I heard you scream and somebody else holler, and… Why are you hunched there like that?"

"Oh, God," said Harold, "Cecil didn't show up, did he?" Harold had been at the séance where the ghost of the murdered Eddie Hastings had spoken through me. That séance had been worse, in its way, than this one, but not by much.

"Something happened to her," said Mrs. Pinkerton. Then *she* started blubbering.

Oh, Lord, what had I done?

The last pangs of anguish finally exited my body. I swear I felt them crawl from my pores like invisible ants. Invisible *biting* ants. At any rate, when I managed to open my mouth, I whispered, "I don't know. Rolly said all sorts of awful things about Cecil Darlington, and then a huge pain hit me."

"Come with me, Mother," said Harold, latching onto Mrs. P's arm and lifting her off me. That might have assisted in easing my pain, but I don't think so. The pain that had whacked me was from another source entirely. I saw Harold lead his mother from the room, then dart back in and slam the door behind himself, locking it for good measure.

Sam said, "Huh?"

Tentatively, worried that any second the noxious ants would return, I sat up straight. No daggers of fire. Good.

"I'm not sure what happened," I told Sam, not expecting him to believe me because why should he? I fully acknowledged myself to be a phony spiritualist-medium, at least to him and my family. And Harold, of course.

"Something *did* happen, Detective," said Harold. "She's not lying or making it up. It was as if all the demons from hell attacked her at once, and she collapsed. In terrible pain, if I'm not mistaken." Harold squinted at me for verification.

I whispered, "Yes."

"Damn," said Sam. I was glad no one was in the room except Harold and me. "How did that happen?"

"I don't know," I whimpered.

"She's telling the truth," said Harold. "I was in the room." To me he asked, "Did Rolly get away from you again?"

"Y-yes."

"I'm so sorry," said Harold, full of sympathy, bless him.

"That's nuts," said Sam.

Harold said, "It probably is nuts. It's also the truth. I was at another séance where something like this happened."

"The hell you say!" Sam turned to glare at Harold, who only shrugged. Although Sam was big and Harold wasn't, Sam didn't intimidate Harold.

"Not my fault," said Harold. "As I said, it's the truth. I think she might be wise to attempt another line of work after you two are married."

"No kidding," said Sam.

"I'd better go out there and see if I can smooth ruffled feathers," I said. I never wanted to face that group of people again in this lifetime. Especially Mrs. Darlington and Madge Hawley.

"To hell with that. I'm taking you home," said Sam. And darned if he didn't scoop me up from my chair.

I tried to struggle but couldn't. That explosion of pain had hit me kind of like the Spanish Flu had hit millions of people, but I didn't die. Rather, I was so weak, I could barely hold my head up. In fact, I couldn't. Harold shoved it onto Sam's shoulder when he realized my predicament.

"Don't worry about the séance crowd, Daisy," said Harold, nobly. "I'll speak to them and explain what happened."

"How can you explain it when even *I* don't know what happened?" I managed to whisper through dry lips.

"Kincaid's smart," said Sam. "He'll think of something."

"Yes, I am, and I will," said Harold. "Why don't you carry her down the hall and right out the front door, Detective? I'll escort you and then go into the drawing room and try to calm everyone down. I expect my mother's in a full-blown tizzy by this time, too. And Mrs. Darlington and that idiot, Madge."

An idiot, was she? Interesting. I didn't say so. More to the point, I *couldn't* say so.

"Call us later and tell us what happened, will you?" asked Sam of Harold. Sam had long since been won over to my conviction that Harold had not chosen to be the way he was, but had been born that way, so he no longer tried to avoid him.

Besides that, Harold had shot a man in Turkey in order to save Sam from a gang of antiquity thieves who'd kidnapped him. Yet another story I won't go into here. But still, Sam actually kind of owed his life to Harold.

"Will do. Now let's get Daisy to your car."

"Thanks, Kincaid," said Sam.

"Thanks, Harold," whispered I.

"Happy to help," chirped Harold. "With any luck, by the time I'm through in the drawing room, all those people will go straight home and write you sympathy cards."

Somehow I doubted it.

So Sam carried me down the hall and out the front door, which Harold obligingly held open for us, I presume because Featherstone was otherwise engaged. Probably fetching possets for fainting females, poor guy.

And it was all my fault. I turned my head until it was buried on Sam's shoulder and didn't open my eyes even after Sam gently sat me in the passenger side of his Hudson. I sat there, slumped, eyes still closed, until Sam got behind the wheel, started the engine, and began making his way down the long, long drive of the Pinkerton Palace.

After he went through the big wrought-iron gate, opened for us by somebody who wasn't Jackson—Joseph Jackson had been Mrs. Pinkerton's gate guard since before I met her—and turned onto Orange Grove, Sam said, "All right. Are you ready to tell me what happened in there?"

I heaved a small sigh. "I'll try. Rolly didn't behave well tonight, and—"

"What do you mean, he 'didn't behave well'? You invented him, didn't you? He's a figment of your imagination, isn't he?"

I sat in silence as I attempted to gather my wits. They didn't want to be gathered.

"Well?" Sam demanded.

"Yes," I said upon another sigh, which came out as a whoosh of breath and sound. "Yes, I invented him and his story when I was ten years old."

"Well, then?"

"Every so often, my creation gets away from me," I said lamely. "I mean, sometimes, Rolly says things I don't mean him to say. I had meant him to be sweet and comforting to poor Mrs. Darlington and Madge Hawley, but instead of being comforting, he was a beast."

"Huh?" Sam's gaze only left the road for an instant when he looked at me.

"He was awful," I said, beginning to regain some strength. It was about darned time. "He said hateful things about Cecil Darlington. He even called him wicked and sinful. Poor Mrs. Darlington was devastated." After a second or two, I added, "So was I. Madge Hawley was outraged."

"Why'd you do that?" asked Sam. It would have been a reasonable question if I'd had any control over my invented spiritual control.

"I didn't do it. Rolly did. He got away from me."

"Daisy, that doesn't make any sense."

"I know it doesn't. It's true all the same."

"You said you were in pain?"

"Yes. At the end, when I tried to get Rolly to be nice about Mr. Darlington, a massive... I don't know. A cramp? A spasm? A horrible pain struck me, and I collapsed."

By the light of the street lamps, I saw Sam shake his head. Silent seconds slipped past. At last Sam said, "Maybe Kincaid will be able to make sense of this for me."

"I hope he can," I told him. I doubt I'd ever been so sincere in my life.

FOURTEEN

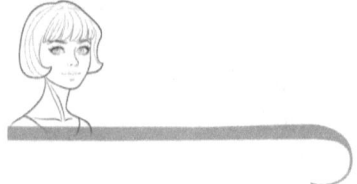

I had rather hoped that when Sam pulled into the driveway of my parents' tidy little bungalow on South Marengo Avenue, everyone would have gone to bed. Unfortunately, the lights in the living room were on, which meant someone was still up and about. Darn.

"Do you need me to carry you inside?" asked Sam

"No. I expect Pa is still awake because the light is on. I don't want to alarm him, so I'll walk on my own."

With doubt in his voice, Sam said, "*Can* you walk on your own?"

"Absolutely."

I spoke before attempting to stand, which I did as soon as Sam opened the passenger door for me. Sucking in a huge breath and girding my loins—I actually don't know how to do that—I stood. And instantly sat back down again. I said, "Oh, dear."

"Come on. I'll carry you."

"No," I said firmly. "Pa will be upset if you have to carry me inside, and I don't want anything to strain his heart."

"All right," Sam said glumly. "Want to try again?"

"Yes. Thanks, Sam."

This time before I tried to stand, I made sure my feet were

firmly planted on the driveway. Then, taking my time and using Sam's arm and the Hudson's door jamb as supports, I stood. I said, "Very well."

"Can you walk?"

"Let me try. I'll hold on to your arm until we get to the front door, if that's all right with you."

"For God's sake, of *course* it's all right with me!"

"I'm sorry. Thanks, Sam."

So, with exquisite care, Sam assisted me to walk across the lawn until we got to the front porch steps. I climbed them one at a time. By that, I mean I placed one foot on the step and then the other foot on the same step before attempting to make my way to the next step. Sam helped. By the time we achieved the three whole steps to the porch, I needed to pause and rest for a few seconds.

"I don't want anyone to open the door until I know I can walk on my own," I told Sam.

"Well, hell, then, try to walk. I'll be right here."

"Thanks, Sam."

And, by golly, I *walked*. Slowly but surely, I traveled the approximately one and a half feet to the front door. Because I figured someone was inside, I hoped the door was unlocked. It was. Thank God.

Putting on the sprightliest front possible, I nodded to Sam, who pushed the door open. Then we both walked through it together, Spike frolicking at our heels. Good thing we had a wide front door.

"Spike. Down," said Sam.

Poor Spike quit frolicking, but his tail still wagged as he sat at our feet. I wanted to lean over and pet him but feared I'd fall flat on my face. Sam sort of bent sideways and petted him, and that seemed to suffice. Spike was a wonderful friend.

Sure enough, Pa and Lou Prophet had set up the card table in the living room and were playing what I hoped was gin rummy. Having come to know Mr. Prophet, it wouldn't have surprised me to learn they were playing poker, but I doubt Mr. Prophet would have taken money from my father if it *was* poker they were playing. Not that I didn't think my father could play poker as well as the hardened ex-bounty hunter.

Very well, that last part was a lie.

The two men glanced at us as Sam and I entered the house. Pa frowned a little. Oh, dear. I should have asked Sam if I looked presentable before facing my father. Unfortunately, I hadn't.

"You look kind of pale and sickly, Daisy. Are you all right?" asked Pa, rising from his chair and peering at me with concern.

After taking a squint at me, Mr. Prophet also rose from his chair. He gestured to my father to sit again and walked over to Sam and me, frowning up a storm.

"I'm fine, Pa," I said, aiming for vivacious and almost achieving it. "The séance was kind of difficult because Mrs. Darlington kept crying, poor thing."

"Well... If you're sure," said Pa.

"Oh, yes. I'm sure."

"She's fine, Joe. Just a little tired," said Sam. "The Darlington woman and the Hawley girl who was engaged to Cecil Darlington were there, and they started weeping and wailing. They upset Daisy a little bit."

Under his breath, Mr. Prophet growled, "What the hell happened?" To my father, he said, "I've gotta talk to Sam for a minute, Joe. Be right back."

"All right."

A sudden inspiration made me say, "I'm going to make some cocoa, Pa. Would you like some?"

"Sure. That'd be nice. Thanks, Daisy."

The night was too warm for cocoa, but Pa didn't catch on to my ploy, thank heaven.

With Mr. Prophet holding one arm and Sam the other, we walked through the dining room and into the kitchen, where Mr. Prophet pulled out a chair. Then he and Sam positioned me to sit. I sat.

"Now," said Mr. Prophet, standing back, fists on hips, scowling, "tell me what the hell happened."

"Daisy'll have to do that. I don't have a clue," said Sam, pulling out another chair and taking a seat.

"Crap. I'll make the cocoa," said Mr. Prophet, who began doing just that. Fine with me. If I'd attempted to make cocoa that night— or any other night, probably—I'd have boiled the milk to oblivion and ruined the stovetop with encrusted milk, sugar and cocoa powder.

The telephone rang. Sam instantly rose from his chair and, with one giant step, got to the telephone on the wall and yanked the receiver from the cradle. "Kincaid?" he growled into the receiver.

Mr. Prophet put a pot full of milk on one of the burners and lit the fire beneath it. As he reached into the appropriate cupboards for the cocoa powder—the sugar resided in a bin built into the counter —he glanced back at Sam, who nodded at him.

So, as Mr. Prophet continued cocoa preparations, Sam talked to Harold in a soft voice. I could kind of make out the conversation, even though I only heard one side of it, and that almost whispered. It sounded to me as if Harold explained precisely what had happened during the séance and then reported about what he'd done after Sam and I had left Mrs. Pinkerton's home.

"That doesn't make any sense," Sam said at one point. He still spoke softly so as not to disturb anyone else in the house. I saw his gaze pay a visit to the ceiling, so I knew he rolled his eyes when Harold explained further. At last Sam said, "Cripes. Well, thanks. And thanks for calming everyone down."

Harold must have said something else, because Sam then said, "Right. Ten o'clock a.m., on Monday, the twenty-seventh. Right. I'll tell her. Thanks again."

Receivers on both ends of the wire were then replaced—of course, I'm only assuming Harold replaced the one on his end—and Sam turned and frowned at me. Fortunately, by that time Mr. Prophet had finished preparing the cocoa, and he poured four cups of the brew. "I'll take this to Joe, but I want to hear all about what happened tonight."

"All right," I said faintly. I still felt faint, dadgummit.

"I'll go with you and tell Joe you and I have to talk about something. Maybe he'll go to bed, and the three of us can figure out what the hell went on during that stupid séance, and if we have to do anything about it," said Sam.

I was glad they both left the kitchen. Their absence would give me more time to recover from... whatever had happened in that horrible dining room with the looming balcony. By then I hated the room even more than I'd hated it before.

About ten minutes after the two men had left me to nurse my own cup of cocoa, which was actually quite refreshing even if the night was a warm one, they returned to the kitchen with Pa in tow. I smiled brightly at them.

"Hey, Pa," I said to my father.

"Sam said you turned your ankle getting out of his car. You okay, sweetie?"

Bless Sam's loving heart. Golly, I'd never have even *thought* about such a sensible lie. "I'm okay. It just hurts a little bit. I'm sure it isn't actually sprained, because the pain's beginning to go away already."

Pa walked over and gave me a peck on the cheek. "All right. I don't like to think of my little girl hurting." He chuckled softly. "Thanks for the cocoa. I'm turning in now. It's past my bedtime."

"Mine, too," I said, grinning what I hoped was a passable grin. "Soon as I drink my own cocoa, Spike and I will hit the hay."

"Okay." Pa looked concerned again. "Will you be able to walk to the choir room if we take the automobile to church tomorrow? Don't want you to really injure that ankle."

"I'll be fine, Pa. Thanks."

My father left the room, visited the bathroom, and then walked down to his and Ma's room. As soon as the three of us heard the bedroom door close softly, Mr. Prophet looked straight at me and said, "All right, what the hell happened? You looked as if a vampire had nipped your neck and drained all the blood from your body when you walked inside the house."

"Good Lord, did I really?"

"No," said Sam.

"Yes," said Mr. Prophet.

I just hunched in my chair and looked at Sam. "What did Harold tell you?"

"He said Rolly—"

"Who the hell is Rolly?" Mr. Prophet said, interrupting.

"Cripes. You explain, Daisy."

"I made up Rolly to be my spirit control—"

"What's a spirit control?"

After sighing heavily, I explained. "A spirit control is the fake entity through which a spiritualist-medium communicates with dead people."

"Hellkatoot."

"Something like that," I said. "Anyhow, I invented Rolly when I was ten. As I already said, the spirit control is supposed to communicate with the medium during a séance and chat with dead people, tell the medium about the chat and, through her, report to other séance attendees what's going on over there."

"Over where?" Mr. Prophet's bushy gray eyebrows almost met over his nose.

"In heaven. Or the other side of life. Whatever people want to call it," I explained.

After several seconds, I presume needed to digest what I'd just told him, Mr. Prophet said, "No shit?"

"No… fooling," I said. "So," I said to Sam, "what happened after we left Mrs. P's house? Did Harold say?"

"Yes. He said he attempted to soothe Mrs. Darlington's nerves." He stopped talking for a second, then pinned me with a narrow look. "Why do women always have *nerves*, anyhow? You never hear about men having fits of nerves."

"*I* don't have fits of nerves," I said sharply. "But many rich women don't have anything else to do, so they get emotional a lot. Like Mrs. Pinkerton."

"Oh. Well, anyway, Kincaid said he had more trouble with the Hawley girl—Madge, I guess. She's the one who was engaged to the Darlington kid, right?"

"Right," I said.

"She was upset, according to Kincaid, and she was still angry that you said he was a bad person and so forth. Did you really say that?"

Aw, jeez. "Yes. Those words came out of my mouth, but they were spoken by Rolly."

Both Sam and Mr. Prophet stared at me as if they thought I was speaking Arabic or something.

"I mean, they were *supposedly* spoken by Rolly. I spoke the words."

"Why'd you do that?" asked Sam. It would have been a good question if I'd had a good answer.

I shrugged. "I honestly don't know. I swear, I don't, Sam. I didn't mean to. It was—you're going to laugh hysterically at this—but it was as if Rolly were speaking through me."

"I think maybe it's time to retire Rolly," Sam muttered.

"Rolly, eh?" said Mr. Prophet. "How the hell did you come up with the name Rolly?"

Another shrug. "I was ten years old. What did I know about anything? Heck, I called myself Desdemona. If I'd known better, I'd have chosen another fictional heroine. Preferably one who wasn't murdered by her husband."

As Sam shook his head in wonderment or bewilderment or some other word meaning incomprehension, Mr. Prophet said, "I'll be damned."

"I don't doubt it," I said.

"All right," said Sam. "Now that we know Kincaid tried to smooth ruffled feathers and Lou's up-to-date on who Rolly is—I mean *what* Rolly is—tell us what else happened at the séance to ruffle the feathers in the first place."

Feeling not quite so much as if I was going to fall down and splat into a puddle of leftover human being on the floor—that cocoa had done some kind of magic, I guess—I described what had happened during the séance to both men. Then I sat there and my gaze went from one man to the other, both of whom gawped at me rather blankly.

It was Mr. Prophet who broke the silence. "You wearin' the charm that Voodoo woman give you?"

For a second I didn't understand what he'd asked. Then I slapped my chest. My juju wasn't there! "Oh, my God, I forgot to put it on!"

"Shhhh," said Sam.

I hadn't meant to speak so loudly. When I spoke again, my voice was a whisper. "I mean, I couldn't have worn it around my neck with this dress on, but I'd meant to wrap it around the belt. I forgot."

"You don't wanna forget that thing again. In fact, it'd probably be a good idea if you stopped messin' with them spirits altogether. I don't expect Sam to believe me, but I been around enough Injuns and Cajuns to know how messin' with spirits can upset 'em. And they don't take kindly to bein' upset."

Both Sam and I stared at Mr. Prophet.

Sam said, "Are you serious?"

"Serious as smallpox," said Mr. Prophet, referring to a disease that had killed thousands of Indians in the last century because the U.S. Army had given them blankets contaminated with whatever germs carry smallpox.

"Good God," said Sam.

"You're right," said I. "I meant to take my juju with me and forgot."

"Don't ferget it again," warned Mr. Prophet.

"I won't."

I felt like *such* a fool. Now I know this doesn't make any sense, and I don't expect anyone except Mr. Prophet to believe me, but I'd had experience with my juju. It didn't work all the time, making it a most unreliable "charm," as Mr. Prophet had called it. However, it had worked often enough—by heating up and nearly searing the flesh from my chest—that I knew it held some kind of occult power. Plus, it had been created for me by Mrs. Jackson, a Voodoo Mambo from New Orleans, Louisiana. She was Joseph Jackson's mother. Joseph Jackson, as mentioned previously, had worked as Mrs. Pinkerton's gate guard for at least as long as I'd been cluttering up this earth.

"Crumb. I knew this evening's séance wasn't going to be any

fun, but I meant to bring along my juju. And don't talk to me about how stupid jujus are, Sam Rotondo!" Not that he'd been going to, but he had opened his mouth, and I wanted to prevent any unkind words to issue therefrom. "Your own personal juju heated up and burned your skin every time you were in the vicinity of the awful student who'd murdered that poor librarian a year or so back!"

Sam lifted his arms and let them fall, softly, onto the table. "Looks like I'm outnumbered here."

"You are," said Mr. Prophet and I together. We didn't sound as musical as we might have, but we got our point across.

"Take that juju and put it under your pillow when you go to bed," Mr. Prophet commanded of me.

"Very well," I said meekly. "I shall."

"Let me wash the cups and saucers," said Sam, shocking me nearly out of my gorgeous voile dress.

I attempted to leap to my feet and couldn't. About halfway out of my chair, I plopped back onto it again. Guess I hadn't quite recovered completely yet. I said meekly, "Thanks, Sam."

"You're welcome." He added, "Don't move," for good measure.

I didn't move.

"I'd like to meet this Rolly character someday," said Mr. Prophet, eyeing me with avid interest. "I ain't seen no magic in a quarter-century or more."

His statement surprised me into saying, "Good Lord. I haven't even been alive for a quarter-century yet." Then I wished I hadn't. Said it, I mean.

"Yeah," said Mr. Prophet, sounding grumpy. He got up from the table and dried the teacups and saucers Sam washed.

As all this was going on, a woebegone Spike sat at my feet sulking because no tidbits had fallen on the floor for him to eat. I gazed down at my adorable pooch. "I'll give you a treat before we go to bed, Spike," I promised.

He wagged his thanks at me.

Sam and Mr. Prophet left Spike and me alone in the kitchen a very few minutes later. Sam quizzed me about my health, and was eventually satisfied I could get myself safely to bed with Spike, although it was Sam who reached into the Frigidaire and got a piece of formerly canned chicken for Spike's treat.

"Thanks, Sam."

"You're welcome. Need me to tuck you in?"

"I don't think so." This time when I attempted to rise from my chair, I did so slowly, and used the table as a lever. And I stood! "I think I'm fine now. Thank you."

"We'll lock the front door on our way out." Sam must have seen me open my mouth to ask him to check on the other doors in the house, because he added, "And we'll make sure the rest of the doors are locked, too."

"Thank you."

He kissed me on the forehead, grabbed Mr. Prophet by an arm, and the two men left the kitchen. I heard them softly checking all the doors in the house and then heard the front door shut and latch before I took my dog and me to bed.

Sure enough, there was my juju on the bedside table. I swear it twinkled at me.

After giving it a good scowl, I hung up my lovely voile dress and Spike and I went to bed. I stuffed my juju under my pillow, just in case.

FIFTEEN

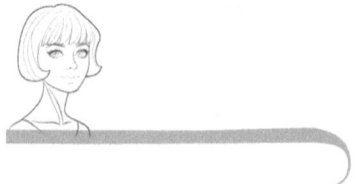

When Spike and I awoke on Sunday morning, memories of the preceding evening's séance assailed me. Hard. Fortunately the ghastly pain didn't. I must not have moved much during the night, because when I got out of bed and began to make it up, I was momentarily surprised to find my juju under my pillow.

Then I remembered why I'd put it there. "I'll never leave the house without you again," I told it. It didn't answer me. Figures.

Enticing smells followed me as I went to the bathroom to wash up and prepare to dress for church. Spike had already gone outside to the back yard to do his duty as a dog, and he, not requiring special help in the looking-good department, went directly to the kitchen when he returned to the house. No dummy, he. He knew precisely where the food resided.

I didn't think too hard about what I'd wear. The day would be hot, so I chose an extremely lightweight floral print dress. I'd still be hot, because Mr. Hostetter would require us choir members to wear our robes, but at least I'd dry out quickly when we disrobed.

Oh. That's where that word came from, isn't it? Because men used to wear robes. Women didn't, but nobody ever names anything after women, unless it's a word with a negative connotation.

Please pay no attention to me.

I wore my juju, which fitted nicely around my neck and couldn't be seen under my dress. There. If anything bad happened to me that day, it wouldn't be *my* fault. Well, it might be, but maybe my juju would help. Probably not, but you never knew.

Anyhow, breakfast, as always, was delicious. We decided to take Sam's Hudson to church because the weather was already too warm for walking. Although Mr. Prophet ate breakfast with us, he declined our invitation to church, preferring to visit a lady friend who lived down the street. At his age, I figured more power to him. The randy old goat.

Lucy and I did a great job on the second verse of "One Holy Church of God Appears." That's not mere boasting on my part. Several members of the congregation told us we'd done splendidly, so I decided to believe them.

When we got home, Vi served us an easy lunch of chicken salad. It was delicious, especially if you plopped some of it on a slice of Vi's delicious bread and topped it with another slice, thereby making a sandwich! Vi cut up a couple of oranges, so we had chicken salad (or, in my case, a chicken sandwich) with oranges on the side. She served us tapioca pudding for dessert.

We Gumms, this Majesty, and Sam Rotondo were *so* lucky to have Vi feeding us. Mr. Prophet would have been lucky, too, had he not been cavorting with his lady friend.

So far the day had passed peacefully enough. Then, as if absolutely *no* day could pass entirely without incident, the telephone rang right after Vi served us our tapioca pudding. Naturally, everyone looked at me. So, with a deep and heartfelt sigh, I set my spoon on my plate, rose and answered the blasted instrument.

"Gumm-Majesty res—"

"*Daisy!*"

Crumb. I'd become so accustomed to Mrs. Pinkerton not shrieking at me, I'd neglected to hold the receiver away from my ear. I feared she might actually have punctured my eardrum that morning. I yanked the receiver from my ear, shook my head hard, and said, "Mrs. Pinkerton. How are you this afternoon?"

"I? How am *I*? How are *you*? Oh, Daisy! Harold told us how that horrid dead fellow sent villainous spirits to pierce your body! Poor Ethel was crushed! Those two Hawley girls were being brats and saying Harold was lying, but I know you, and I know Harold, and I knew Harold wasn't lying! Besides, as gently as he could, he told both Ethel and those silly girls that Cyril had been a cad."

"Cecil," I said softly.

"Whatever his name was. Harold *knew* him, and he knew about his wicked ways, and he *told* us!"

Well, I'll be darned. Bless Harold for a saint. "My goodness. I wish I'd known about him before I tried to reach him," I said, lying through my teeth. Harold *had* told me, but I hadn't expected what he'd told me would affect the séance so dramatically. "I'd only been feeling sorry for Mrs. Darlington and Madge. Madge was engaged to Mr. Darlington."

"Huh," said Mrs. Pinkerton, reminding me oddly of Sam. "She was wickedly deceived. Harold said he was a horrid fellow and that, as sorry as he was for Mrs. Darlington, the Harlow girl had a lucky escape."

"Hawley," I muttered.

"Whatever her name is."

"My goodness." Wasn't sure what else to say.

"I just wanted to make sure you were recovered today, dear. I had *no* idea what that young man was like, or I'd never have asked you to conduct the séance."

"It's all right, Mrs. Pinkerton. Neither you nor I had any idea he wasn't a nice fellow, and what happened at the séance wasn't your fault."

"You're so kind and forgiving, Daisy. I should strive to be more like you and that lovely Captain Buckminster fellow."

"Buckingham," I said upon a tiny sigh.

"Of course. Captain Buckingham. Are you sure you're well today, dear?"

"Yes, indeed. Thank you, Mrs. Pinkerton. I'm just fine. In fact, Mrs. Zollinger and I sang a duet during our choir's anthem this morning. I'm sure that soothed any remaining tatters in my soul."

Whoo boy. Was I laying it on thick, or what? Oh, well. Mrs. Pinkerton liked that sort of thing.

"Wonderful! I'm *so* relieved!"

See? Told you.

"I felt *terrible* after you left. I wanted to telephone you last night, but Harold wouldn't let me."

Bless Harold for *two* saints, by crikey!

"I do appreciate your concern," I said, belatedly recalling I was in the kitchen and my family was listening to my side of the conversation. Drat. "But I'm just fine. All well and hale and hearty." Bother. I wish I hadn't told her I was hale and hearty. Spiritualists were supposed to be wispy and wafty.

"I'm so glad, dear. And relieved." She released a gust of breath that just about took out my other eardrum.

"Thank you for calling," I said, trying to sound chipper and spiritualistic at the same time.

"You're welcome, Daisy. And I'm *so* sorry about that awful man's ghastly spirit!"

"Everything is just fine, Mrs. Pinkerton. Thank you again for calling."

"That relieves me a good deal, dear. Harold said he's taking you to Bullock's in downtown Los Angeles tomorrow so you can select china patterns for your new life as a married woman."

"Yes, he is. It's extremely kind of him. He's much better at selecting tasteful china and so forth than I am." Should I have said that to Harold's mother? Oh, why not? If she didn't realize precisely what Harold was, at least she knew him to have impeccable taste.

"I'm sure that's not true, dear. Although, I do know what you mean. Harold is forever telling me how to arrange my furniture and which tea set I should use for what function and so forth and so on."

"He needs to have a good eye for such things, or he wouldn't be so successful as a costumer for the moving pictures," I said, thinking I'd hit upon a salient point.

"Yes. I suppose you're right. I'm still just a *tiny* bit sorry you and Harold aren't tying the knot, but at least Harold tells me your detective friend has good taste." She tittered. "As Harold told me, he chose *you*, didn't he?"

Oooh, boy, I'd be sure to tell Sam how good his taste was. "Thank you, Mrs. Pinkerton."

"You're probably with your family, aren't you?"

"Yes. We're just finishing up our luncheon, in fact. We're so fortunate to have Aunt Vi cook for us."

"Yes, you are. So am I. Your aunt is a miracle worker."

"Indeed, she is," I said, hoping she'd hang up the stupid telephone so I could go back to the table and eat my tapioca pudding.

"Very well." Mrs. P sounded relieved. "Have a wonderful day, dear, and have a lovely time tomorrow. Harold said he's going to wear you out at Bullock's, so prepare yourself."

"I'll be sure to do that. Thank you, Mrs. Pinkerton."

"Farewell, dear." And she hung up. Thank God.

Ma, Pa and Aunt Vi were huddled in a clump at the table, and Sam was speaking softly to them when I turned from the telephone. I'd intended to march back to the table and finish my dessert without bothering to explain why Mrs. Pinkerton had telephoned, but I halted, puzzled.

"So you see, everything is all right. A little misunderstanding was all. She's perfectly fine and healthy," Sam said, clearly explaining why Mrs. Pinkerton called me in a tizzy this morning seemingly worried about my health.

Bless Sam for a saint, too.

I rejoined the group and tried to be invisible when I sat in my chair. Because I'm a corporeal entity, I failed. The expressions of puzzlement on the faces of my family made my heart hurt a trifle.

"Are you sure you're well this morning, Daisy," asked Ma. "Sam said there was some unpleasantness at last night's séance."

"Um…" Fiddlesticks. I didn't know what Sam had told them, so I wasn't sure how to respond.

"I just explained about the Hawley sisters being angry that you couldn't summon the spirit of the dead Darlington fellow," said Sam. "And that Mrs. Darlington was upset when Harold explained —gently—that her late son hadn't been the soul of propriety."

Good job, Sam! I could work with that. "Yes. I feel sorry for Mrs. Darlington. And Madge. She and her sister are both pretty silly. Well, they're awfully young," said I, the elderly widowed lady.

"They sound like a couple of spoiled brats," Pa said, dipping his spoon into his tapioca bowl. I noticed everyone had waited for me. How nice they all were!

"Joe," said Ma, not quite admonishing my father for rudeness, but coming close.

"No, Peggy," said Sam. "He's correct. Both of those girls are silly, spoiled creatures. Kincaid said they'd been pampered all their lives and have never learned manners."

"That might be a little harsh," I said, not meaning my words. "They're both extremely young."

"Nertz," said Sam. "I'll bet anything that when you were eighteen or nineteen, you weren't giggling and screaming and disrupting wedding receptions and séances."

Oh, my word, this was *great*! Good for Sam. "Of course, you're right," I said, trying to sound kind. "But my circumstances were different from those of the Hawley girls."

"That's no reason for them not to have been taught good manners," said Ma, having switched sides in a jiffy. Bless her, too.

Vi shook her head. "Some young people these days have no concept of courtesy or politeness. Look at Stacy Kincaid, for example."

This statement brought the conversation to a halt, it being virtually impossible to find a worse example of human being-ness than Stacy Kincaid. I was glad of it, not eager to remember the preceding night's doings. We all finished our tapioca pudding, Ma and I cleaned up the luncheon dishes, and the rest of the day passed in peace and quiet.

Mr. Prophet returned from his lady friend's house in time for supper (more chicken salad, only this time we all had it in sandwiches) along with carrot sticks and radishes (both plucked in whole vegetable form that morning from the rich earth of our kitchen garden). Not only was he in time for supper, but he'd brought with him two delicious cakes baked by the cook in the house down the street. That house, by the way, was the biggest and fanciest in the entire neighborhood, and it had been bought not too long back by (gasp!) a scarlet woman.

In truth, this particular scarlet woman, Mrs. Evangeline Mainwaring—at least her last name was Mainwaring in 1925 (it tended to change from man to man)—owned the largest and most profitable orange grove in the entire city of Pasadena. In those days, Pasadena was home to many, many orange groves. The fact that the most profitable one was operated by a female made me happy. I didn't let on. The neighborhood had been faintly touched by scandal earlier in the year, thanks to Mrs. Mainwaring, but I liked her anyway. For the most part. And no one, no matter how biased in favor of one race or another, could deny the beauty of Mr. Prophet's lady friend, Li Ahn, who had been born in China.

At any rate, Mrs. Mainwaring employed a cook, a Negro lady named Hattie Potts, who was almost as talented as Aunt Vi. The delicacies Mr. Prophet brought us that evening were two of her apricot pound cakes. We'd eaten this confection before, and... Well, I don't know what to say, except that Mrs. Potts's apricot pound cakes rivaled Mrs. Jackson's beignets and my own Aunt Vi's coconut cakes and floating island.

That's saying a whole lot. In fact, I ate two slices, and hoped nobody would get up to snack on pound cake during the night, because I wanted more for breakfast.

SIXTEEN

L uck favored me on Monday morning, and I don't think it had anything to do with my juju, although I still wore it. But there was an entire apricot pound cake still extant when Spike and I rolled out of bed and staggered into the kitchen to see what was cooking. Well, we could smell bacon, the ethereal aroma of which permeated the entire house.

At the stove, tonging bacon strips onto butcher's paper—Aunt Vi was fast friends with the butcher at Jorgensen's, Mr. Larkin, and he kept her well supplied with butcher's paper—Vi turned and grinned at me. "Bacon and apricot pound cake for breakfast, young lady, although you'd best dress quickly if you want to make sure there's some pound cake left. The ravening horde will descend upon the kitchen soon."

It took me a minute to figure out who comprised the "ravening horde," but that's only because I wasn't fully awake yet. She meant Sam and Mr. Prophet, of course.

"I'll hurry!" I told her, and scuttled to the bathroom to prepare myself for the day, which I expected to be tiring, what with Harold dragging me to Los Angeles. Well, I don't suppose "dragging" was the appropriate word. I wanted to go. Sort of. I still wasn't sure I'd be able to select china patterns from the dozens Harold promised were awaiting my perusal at Bullock's.

Sam popped by the house in a rush and only managed to snabble a piece of bacon. "I've got to attend a meeting at eight-thirty this morning," he said. "I'm sure they'll have sinkers and Joe there."

"Well, at least take this piece of pound cake with you!" said Vi, thrusting a thick slice of apricot pound cake at him.

"Thanks, Vi," said Sam, grinning. He stooped to kiss my cheek, because I was at the kitchen table chewing, and said, "Have fun with Harold today."

"Thanks, Sam. Have fun at your meeting," I told him.

"Oh, yes. I'm sure I will." "Sardonic" best described the tone of his voice. He left us, stuffing apricot pound cake into his mouth.

"Wonder where Mr. Prophet is," I said as Spike moped back into the kitchen. He'd frolicked at Sam's feet to the front door, and looked a bit depressed not to have been allowed to go with him. "You wouldn't like it at the police department," I said in order to cheer him up. My words didn't do much for his mood, but the little piece of bacon I tossed him perked him right up.

"Who knows?" said Vi. She removed her apron, hung it on the hook on the service porch, and went to the bathroom to ready herself for work. She and Ma walked back into the kitchen together, with Pa bringing up the rear.

Quickly downing the last of my breakfast and taking a last swig of coffee, I rose from the table, aiming to drive Ma and Vi to work because the weather remained warm, and I didn't want them to have to walk.

That deed done, I drove back home, and Pa and I took Spike out for an abbreviated walk. The day was already hot, and I didn't want to be drippy when Harold picked me up at ten, which he did on the dot, by golly.

"So what do you plan for us to do at Bullock's? Is this trip strictly for china-picking?" I said when his fabulous new Hispano Suiza idled on Colorado Street—being gazed at in awe and wonder by passers-by—while Harold waited for a bunch of other cars to pass by so he could turn left and head down Fair Oaks Avenue. "Nash's Department Store wouldn't be just as good? And I know I saw fancy china when I went to Arnold's Jewelers."

Harold took his attention from the traffic to turn and stare at me for a second. Probably not more than that, because nobody honked. "You *must* be joking," he said.

"Am not. What's wrong with Arnold's, if you're too snooty for Nash's?"

"We live on the west coast, Daisy, and Bullock's is *the* place to go for fine china and silverware."

"Do they have everyday dishes, too?" I asked, my voice small. I honestly didn't think I needed a million-dollar set of dishes, especially since I couldn't cook. Mr. Prophet had fed us baked beans and bacon on toast for breakfast once when Vi had been kidnapped, and they'd tasted really good. However, they sure didn't need to be served on a hundred-dollar plate, if you know what I mean.

"Daisy, my darling, I know you've lived a Spartan existence, but haven't you mingled with the upper crust of Pasadena society long enough to understand a woman needs everyday dinnerware, formal dinnerware, a tea set or two, a coffee set, a cocoa set, and perhaps a set of luncheon dishes? Then there's the glassware and silverware."

"Yeah," I said. "I've mingled with a lot of upper-crusties. Most of them aren't quite as... um... rattled as your mother—"

Harold interrupted my almost-polite statement with a roar of laughter. "Daisy, my dear, my mother is a nitwit!"

"Well, I didn't want to say that. Besides, except for when she called me yesterday, screaming about that wretched séance, lately she's seemed perfectly subdued and quiet and... well, kind and nice. But do all rich women have all those dishes? *How* many sets did you say?"

"We'll start with casual, everyday china," said Harold. "I don't want to overwhelm you on your first outing."

"Thanks, Harold."

"You're welcome. But you're going to have to select a formal set, eventually."

"Goody."

Harold only snickered at me.

After driving for about forty-five minutes through bare country-side, little communities and a couple of tunnels, we got to Los Angeles proper, if anything about Los Angeles could be called proper. I doubt my aunt or my mother thought so, the behavior of so many moving-picture people being so scandalous and all.

Eventually Harold pointed to a gigantic building sitting on the corner of Seventh Street and Broadway in downtown Los Angeles. I hadn't been to Los Angeles very often, although sometimes Ma, Vi, and I liked to take a red car to downtown L.A. and visit some of the stores, making a day of it. It was fun. Bullock's had always seemed too ritzy for us, but according to Harold, it wasn't. I aimed to reserve my own personal judgment.

"All right," said Harold. "Let's go to the Broadway entrance and see if I can find a parking place. We need the sixth floor. That's where the fine china is."

"How about the not-so-fine china?" I asked meekly.

"*All* the china," said Harold, his voice firm. "Will you stop worrying? You know so many wealthy people, you'll probably have received a service for twenty-four in three different patterns by the time you and Sam tie the knot. Have you set a date yet, by the way?"

"We're thinking early- to mid-September. Then we'll head to New York to visit his family and then Massachusetts to visit mine. Sam said the leaves will be turning colors then, and it will be beau-tiful in New England."

"If you enjoy looking at trees," Harold muttered.

Then he let out a cry of glee and swooped into a parking place just vacated by another fancy car. I squinted at it and decided it was a Rolls-Royce. When Harold opened my door for me and I stepped out and looked around, I noticed the street was lined on both sides with cars that had probably cost more than my parents' modest bungalow on Marengo in Pasadena. Ah, well. It was fun to visit fancy places sometimes.

The innards of the store were beautiful. I had no idea where anything was, but Harold didn't suffer from my problem. He walked me directly to a bank of elevators and pressed the button. Several well-dressed ladies stood waiting for elevators, too. A couple of them wore fox fur stoles, which I thought excessive for the heat of the Los Angeles July day, but I didn't much like the notion of killing animals for their fur in the first place.

The costume I'd chosen that day was a pearl-gray chiffon number with lace around the square neck and the lowered waist. I wore a double strand of pearls (real ones, gifted me by Mrs. Pinkerton), short-heeled black shoes with a Louis heel, and I clutched a black bag. On my shingled dark red locks, I'd plunked a lightweight cloche hat covered in the same pearl-gray chiffon as my dress, and decorated with a band of the same lace as decorated my dress. I fitted right in with the rich ladies, once Harold told me to stop fingering my pearls. Not wanting Harold to be ashamed of mingling with a person from the hoi-polloi, I obeyed.

"Sorry," I muttered. "They're real, and I'm a little scared to be wearing them in public."

"I know they're real. I bought them for Mother to give to you. But stop fingering them. You might break the string, and then there would be pearls rolling around on Bullock's floor forever."

Instantly, I let my hand drop to my side. Because I held my handbag in my left hand, Harold hooked my right elbow, thereby making it impossible for me to touch my pearls again.

"Thanks, Harold."

"You're welcome."

An elevator came to a rumbling halt, and we allowed the ladies who'd been waiting longer than we to enter the carriage before us. The elevator lad wore a snappy livery and seemed to take everyone's floor requests in his stride. Of course, he probably stopped at every floor anyway, so it would have been difficult for him to make a bad blunder. Well, unless he halted the carriage above or below the floor level so people would trip and stumble getting out.

No such catastrophe occurred, and we eventually arrived at the sixth floor. Harold escorted me from the elevator carriage and started walking as if he knew where he was going. "You know where the china department is?" I asked, not surprised.

"Of course. I shop here all the time. People insist on getting married and moving into new homes and so forth. Can't stay away from the place. Sometimes—recently, for instance—I've come to browse just to see what's available with you in mind. I've ordered several place settings to be set aside for your perusal."

"Oh. Thank you! I didn't know you could do that."

"All you need is money, my dear, and you can do pretty much anything. You of all people should know that by now."

"Yeah, I guess you're right."

A tall, stick-straight woman in a black dress, with pepper-and-salt hair pulled back in a tight bun at the back of her neck, spotted Harold from several yards away. She'd been looking down her nose and speaking to a clump of equally dismally clad women, but when she saw Harold, she said something to the young women, and left them to approach us.

I squinted at the clot of women, and thought I recognized one or two of them. Because we were in Bullock's in downtown Los Angeles, being borne down upon by a woman who looked as much like a witch as made no matter, I didn't veer off to see if I actually *had* recognized any of them. It seemed they were annoyed by their clerk's abrupt departure, because they frowned at Mrs. Grundy's back as she approached Harold and me.

Aha. Then I recognized two of the abandoned women. The Hawley sisters. They transferred their frowns from Mrs. Grundy to me. Oh, joy. This should be fun.

"Mr. Kincaid," said the woman—I'm sure her name wasn't Mrs. Grundy, but since I don't know what it was, Mrs. Grundy will do. "I'm so happy to see you again."

She didn't look as if she were happy about anything.

"How do you do, Mrs. Maxwell? This is the young lady I was telling you about, Mrs. Majesty."

"How nice," said the woman I now knew to be Mrs. Maxwell, who offered me a smile that looked as if it cracked a stony surface.

I held my hand out (Harold had let go of it). "How do you do, Mrs. Maxwell?"

"Very well, thank you, Mrs.... Majesty, did you say?" She gave my hand two brief, limp pumps.

"Yes." I stiffened until I felt like Mrs. Maxwell looked. She'd sounded snide. I don't approve of snidity, although I often find myself guilty of it, so I shouldn't criticize.

"Mrs. Majesty, as I believe I told you, Mrs. Maxwell, is a widow. She aims to be married in September, and I've brought her here today to look at some of the china patterns I asked you to put aside for us."

"Of course, Mr. Kincaid." Ignoring me, Mrs. Maxwell turned and headed back toward the cluster of young women still standing at a counter looking peeved.

"Mrs. Majesty!" Miss Madge Hawley said, rather too loudly for Mrs. Maxwell's comfort to judge by the stiffening of her shoulders, which I hadn't known could get any stiffer until that instant.

"Miss Hawley," I said sweetly, holding out my gloved hand. She and her sister smirked unkindly at me, and they each shook my hand, Madge first. As already mentioned, they were clad in proper mourning black. Because I wasn't altogether sure what to say to a recently bereaved woman who'd been ugly to me on Saturday night, and who was evidently attempting to cheer herself by going on a shopping spree, I said, "I hope you're feeling a little better today."

"Feeling better?" Madge said, as if she didn't know why she should be feeling anything at all. Then apparently she recalled her dead fiancé, and said, "Oh, yes, thank you. DeeDee and Alma and I decided to visit Bullock's and look at all the fine china I'd hoped to have soon. Not that *you'd* know about that, after the spectacle you enacted on Saturday night."

"I fear Rolly was a trifle unruly on Saturday," I said before thinking better of it. "You already know Mr. Harold Kincaid, who kindly brought me here today."

"Yes," said Madge. "We know Mr. Kincaid."

The two Hawley girls held their hands out for Harold to shake, which he did with obvious reluctance. "Madge and DeeDee," he said and gave each girl's hand a perfunctory shake.

"Mr. Kincaid," said Alma, a dark-haired girl with fine brown eyes and thick eyelashes. Her eyes and eyelashes were about the only part of her upper face one could see, because she wore a black silk scarf puffed up around her neck and nearly covering her chin, and her black cloche hat covered her forehead. I personally didn't care for huge cloche hats. They were hot and uncomfortable. And what was going on with that scarf? "How nice to see you again." She didn't mean her words. Both Harold and I could tell.

"Miss Jervis," Said Harold with his usual aplomb. He bowed slightly, since Miss Jervis didn't hold out her hand for him to shake. "Good to see you again."

All three women nodded at him, then at me, and then at Mrs. Maxwell.

"Would you like to see the china I set aside for you, Mr. Kincaid?" asked Mrs. Maxwell in a voice of ice. Difficult to achieve in the depths of a hot Los Angeles July, but she managed.

"Please don't let us interrupt you," said Madge nastily.

Because Mrs. Maxwell annoyed me even more than Madge Hawley did, I said, "I think it's the other way around. I think we interrupted you." I gave Madge, DeeDee, and Alma another tepid smile.

"I'll be with you ladies in a minute," said Mrs. Maxwell in a stern voice. "Over here, please, Mr. Kincaid and Mrs. Majesty." She turned and stalked off.

"Have a good day," I told the three women, as Harold took my arm and headed after Mrs. Maxwell. I didn't care if they had good days or not, but I was polite anyway.

I got a bunch of finger waves in return for my courtesy.

SEVENTEEN

"I have arranged five place settings, Mr. Kincaid," said Mrs. Maxwell, sticking to business. "Here they are. Of the examples you suggested I chose Wileman Orange Daisy, Copeland Spode Wicker Dale, Shelley Black Leaf, Royal Albert Wild Rose, and Royal Copenhagen Blue Fluted Half Lace pattern."

"Oh, my," I said, taking in the gorgeous china settings. They were more formally placed than anything I'd ever seen on our dinner table at home, although I'd dined with enough of my wealthy clients—including Harold—to know this was the way china was *supposed* to be laid out. "They're all beautiful."

"Well, you can register for all of them if you want," said the ever-practical Harold. "But let's look them over. Also, don't forget your husband will be dining off whatever you choose, too, so don't choose anything too pink."

"And Mr. Prophet," I muttered, thinking about his wrinkled, old gnarled fingers, which would exclude some of these delicate teacups with the crimped ears.

"He'll be living with you?" Harold turned his head and gawked at me.

"He already does," I said. "Well, not *with* us, but he's the caretaker for the property Sam bought across the street from us. You know that. Heck, you've *seen* his little cottage!"

"No, I haven't. I guess I just knew it was there. There's an orange grove between Sam's house and that so-called cottage, don't forget."

"It's not an entire orange grove, and it's not a *so-called* cottage. It's adorable. Just right for an old bachelor. Or a mother-in-law, although I hope to heaven Sam's mother will never have to live there." A grim thought struck me, and I said, "Although maybe Ma will. But not for years and years and years."

"This isn't the time to get maudlin, Daisy. Let's look at the china. And, although I'm not altogether sure why, we'll eschew crimped teacup ears."

"Every time anyone says 'eschew,' I want to say, 'bless you,'" I told Harold.

"Very funny. Now look!"

"If you'll notice," said Mrs. Maxwell, standing next to Harold and looking like a Royal Danish ice queen, if there was such a thing, "you'll see I placed a cup and saucer of a slightly different pattern next to a couple of the Shelly patterns. And the Copeland Spode. I've set out a teacup and saucer of Chelsea Garden next to Fairy Dell. Although you didn't ask about Wedgwood or Minton, I did set out a cup and saucer of Wedgwood's Chinese Legend and Pagoda patterns and one or two of the Minton."

"Thank you, Mrs. Maxwell. Perhaps Daisy will enjoy the Wedgwood and Minton."

I gathered from the tone of Harold's voice, which was polite, that he didn't much enjoy Wedgwood or Minton.

"Thank you, Mrs. Maxwell." I didn't want this old battleaxe looming over Harold and me while Harold explained the ins and outs of fine china to me. She made me feel stupid just by being there. "Please feel free to help the Misses Hawley and Miss..." I couldn't remember Cloche-hat's name.

"Alma Jervis. Yes, that's a fine idea," said Harold.

I'm pretty sure Mrs. Maxwell wouldn't have gone away at my bidding alone, but Harold had boocoo bucks, and people, especially those in subservient positions (like me, for instance), paid attention to people with money. So Mrs. Maxwell stalked off.

"Thanks, Harold. I didn't want that ice queen judging me. Not my fault I don't know beans about fine china."

"True. But I shall educate you."

So Harold educated me. I'm sure my eyes were as glassy as the superb china placed on the table by the time the two Hawley girls and Alma Jervis wandered over to join us. I glanced at them and wanted to tell them to go away but didn't.

"Is someone you know getting married?" asked Madge Hawley as if she didn't much care.

DeeDee suddenly gasped. "Oh! Are *you two* getting married?" She, on the other hand, sounded excited.

Alma Jervis said nothing. I saw she still had her scarf pulled up and her hat pulled low. She also wore a dress with three-quarter sleeves, but I noticed what looked like several big bruises on her right arm when she lifted it to adjust her scarf. Poor thing must have had an accident. Although... I squinted, trying not to look as if I were staring.

I was right, though. Those bruises had been made by a human hand or hands. I'd seen bruises like those on a woman whose husband had nearly beaten her to death. I suddenly felt intense sympathy for Alma Jervis, even though I didn't know her.

"No," said Harold, answering DeeDee's question. "Daisy is going to be wed in September."

"How lovely for you," crooned DeeDee.

"I thought you were already married," said Madge.

"I'm a widow," I said, thinking the young woman impolite and rude. Then again, maybe I was being too sensitive. Naw. She'd been rude and impolite at that horrible séance, too.

"Huh. I didn't know that," said Madge.

Because I was curious and because Madge had been nosy, I decided to ask my next question. "I'm a little surprised to find you here. Had you found a china pattern already, or were you just browsing? I'm sorry about the loss of your fiancé."

Madge Hawley said, "Of course, you are. We discovered that last Saturday night."

DeeDee appeared confused for a second, and then said, "Oh, yes. Poor Cecil!" She patted her sister's shoulder in a comforting gesture.

Madge dropped her disapproval-of-me act, bowed her head and lifted a hankie—I guess it had been stuffed up her sleeve or something—to what looked like a couple of dry eyes.

Alma adjusted her scarf to hide a little more of her face, and I again noticed those hand-made bruises. "Yes," she said. "Such a tragedy."

I smelled something fishy in the air. Or maybe I didn't and was just making a mystery out of nothing. Then again, the Hawley sisters *had* been inappropriate at Regina's wedding and at the séance.

Nertz. What did I know about modern manners? Nothing. That's what. And that thought made me feel really old.

"Have you decided on a china pattern, Mrs. Majesty?" asked DeeDee, sounding almost interested. Well, she hadn't had as large a stake in Cecil Darlington's death as her sister, which perhaps accounted for her relative lack of malice toward me.

"There are so many to choose from," I said, bewilderment fuzzing my brain once more. "But I think I've narrowed down my choices."

"Really?" said an avid DeeDee. "Which ones do you prefer? I noticed Mrs. Maxwell had set out a bunch of dinnerware patterns and wondered who they were for."

Whom, I didn't say. Rather, I shared a glance with Harold, and he rescued me. It felt to me as though we'd been looking at china patterns since the beginning of time, and they'd begun to blend together in my mind. Fortunately for yours truly, Harold's mind is much better organized than mine. He said, "Daisy is particularly fond of a couple of the Shelley patterns."

"My favorite is the Wileman Orange Daisy pattern, but I think the ears on the teacups are too small. My fiancé is a large man."

"Wileman?" asked DeeDee, sounding almost as bewildered as I.

"They changed their name to Shelley," said Harold, fount of all china information.

"Oh, I didn't know that. When I was looking before, I adored the Coalport Pembroke and Shelley Chintz Oleander set," said Madge.

"Oleanders are poisonous," I said because I couldn't help myself.

"All the better," muttered Alma.

"Well, the Coalport Pembroke is pretty, too. I didn't know that about oleanders," said Madge, wrinkling her dainty nose a bit.

"I like Shelley's Syringia Gardenia, quite well," I told her. "And it would look swell in the dining room."

"Or in the china cabinet in the dining room," said Harold with a touch of cynicism. He was well acquainted with my cooking skills. Not that he's ever attempted to eat anything I'd cooked, but he'd heard the (not unsupported) rumors.

"Yes," I said, elbowing him lightly. He elbowed me back, not lightly.

"Well," said Madge, lowering her voice and sounding a little sad. "We only came here today to take one last peek at china patterns. I love looking at china. I'd registered for Spode Buttercup, but they'll just have to take my name off the registry now." Out came her hankie, and she again dabbed at her eyes.

"You're better off this way," said Alma.

"Oh?" I didn't understand her comment, which had been too cryptic for this spiritualist-medium.

"Pay no attention to Alma," said DeeDee, giggling. "She's off men. At least for a while."

"Forever," said Alma in a voice that made it clear she wanted no argument from DeeDee. Or anyone else, most likely.

"I'm sorry," I said, thinking about her bruised arm.

"Don't be," she said and repeated, "It's better this way."

"Are you going to register for a pattern?" said Madge, sounding almost interested.

"Am I?" I looked to Harold for counsel.

"We're going to get a bite to eat and discuss the matter," said

Harold with all the authority of one who knows what he's doing. Glad one of us did.

"How nice," said Madge, somewhat wistfully.

"Yes," said DeeDee, likewise affected.

"Yes," said Alma. "How nice." I didn't believe her for a second.

Harold and I again walked to the bank of elevators. This time when a liveried elevator operator stopped at the sixth floor, Harold said, "Eight," as we got in. Even in my short and comfy Louis heels, my feet ached from standing so long.

"What's on the eighth floor?" I asked, hoping I wouldn't have to look at silverware now. My brain was still clattering with china patterns, and they'd begun to blur together. I couldn't even remember the names of the ones I'd especially liked. Good thing Harold was with me.

"The Palmetto Room. We can have a bite of lunch there. It's too hot for the soup bar downstairs."

"I should say so."

The Palmetto Room was a magnificent place. In fact, the entirety of Bullock's was magnificent. It was the fanciest store I'd ever been in, and I loved it. In fact, I almost wished Pasadena could get a Bullock's of its own.

After a liveried host led us to a table next to a window that gave an excellent view of downtown Los Angeles's bustling Broadway Street, I sat with a sigh when the host held a chair for me. "Thank you," I said when he handed each of us a menu.

"You're more than welcome. Your waitress will be with you shortly."

And, with a bow worthy of Featherstone himself, he turned and walked back to his post at the front of the room. I leaned across the table and said, "Who the heck is Alma Jervis, and why is she hanging around with Madge and DeeDee and covering herself from head to toe? Did you see those bruises on her arm? I fear the poor thing was roughly handled by a man. Small wonder she's 'off men,' as DeeDee said."

Lowering the menu he'd been studying, Harold squinted at me.

"You just met her, and you already have her being beaten to death by a brutal man? You ought to take up writing novels, Daisy."

"Not funny, Harold. Don't forget who hid Mrs. Bannister for those few horrible weeks when the police thought she'd killed her husband! Men beat up women all the time, and you know it."

"How," asked Harold sternly, "could I *ever* forget hiding Mrs. Bannister in the upstairs bedroom of my own home? I thought the whole lot of us were going to be carted off to prison! If you ever do that to me again, Daisy Gumm Majesty, I'll stop being your friend."

"Harold! You helped save the woman's life! Anyway, who's Alma Jervis? She was bundled up as if it's midwinter instead of midsummer, and I *saw* those bruises on her arm. They were made by a person, Harold!"

"You met her at the wedding, didn't you? Your librarian friend's? She was there, according to Madge and DeeDee."

"I don't remember her from the wedding. But you know Madge and DeeDee, too, don't you?"

"Not by choice," said Harold drily. "They're daughters of one of my darling mother's friends."

"Well, then, you know Madge's fiancé was murdered after the ceremony, which is why your mother wanted me to perform that stupid séance."

"Yes, dear. I know all about it. According to Madge and DeeDee, Madge's *beloved* fiancé was killed. Not sure why she was so irritated with you about it, but she was sure a brat at the séance."

"You sound awfully mean about someone losing a loved one, Harold Kincaid, even if he turned out to be kind of a horrible person."

"Get a grip on yourself, Daisy. Those three idiotic girls don't know what love is. And anybody who'd become affianced to Cecil Darlington is a lame-brain to begin with. They ought to be cheering, not sobbing. Not that they were doing much sobbing on séance Saturday. They were bitching and moaning on séance Saturday."

"Stop calling it séance Saturday. That was an awful séance. Most of my séances aren't that bad."

"Whatever you call it, they were mad as hell then, not sobbing. They weren't doing much sobbing today, either."

"No, they weren't, were they? In fact, what the heck were they doing in Bullock's china department anyhow?"

"How the devil should *I* know? Un-registering Madge, according to her," said a clearly cranky Harold. "Choose what you want for lunch, and let's talk china."

"Very well. But I'm wildly curious to know why they were all here, and why Miss Jervis was all bundled up and bruised. And why was Mr. Cecil Darlington such a rotten catch for a wealthy young woman, by the way? Was he really as bad as you claim?"

Pointing a finger at my nose and making me go cross-eyed, Harold said, "Select your luncheon and forget those foolish girls. Think *china*, dammit."

"Yes, sir," I said, sitting back in my chair and looking at the menu. "I don't want anything hot."

"The ham salad sounds good to me," said Harold. "Ham salad and rolls and butter will see us through your momentous decision."

"And lemonade," I said.

"Iced coffee for me," said Harold.

"They put ice in coffee?"

After staring at me only briefly, Harold shook his head and said, "You really ought to get out more, Daisy."

"I get out plenty," I said, only slightly miffed. I didn't really like coffee all that much, and it would never occur to me to put ice in it.

"If you say so."

After we'd finished our delicious luncheons, Harold took me back down to the sixth floor. The Hawley sisters and Miss Jervis had left the area by then. I was glad of it. So Harold and I thought long and hard and looked and looked until we'd made Harold's final decision—I mean *my* final decision—on china patterns.

Therefore, for Sam's and my everyday china, I registered for Copeland Spode Wicker Dale. Harold also made me register for a formal set, so I decided on Shelley's Syringa Gardenia, which was kind of dainty, but it wasn't pink. It was slightly more formal than Wicker Dale, although it wasn't swirling with gold rims. I figured it was better that way, given my way with dishes and so forth. Although I must admit, I was more ruinous to food than I was to tableware. Anyway, Syringa Gardenia was also perfectly gorgeous. It was colorful enough to suit me and not too dainty for Sam and Mr. Prophet. And it really *would* look beautiful in our dining room. Or in our dining room hutch.

Most importantly, the teacups of both sets didn't have crimped ears. Some of the patterns I especially loved, most made by Shelley, had little crimped handles on the cups, and I could envision them smashing on the kitchen floor daily. At least the men in my life would have a chance to drink their coffee or tea with ease if they sipped it from either a Wicker Dale or a Syringa Gardenia cup.

Mrs. Maxwell, friendlier now that she'd made what she presumed would be a lofty profit from this day's work, carefully packed a cup and saucer from each set, set them neatly in a bag, and handed them to Harold. She handed *my* china to *Harold*!

It's all right. I'm sure she dealt with wealthy people all the time and knew from the start I wasn't one. I have the same ability. It comes from close observation of one's fellow humans, and I've had plenty of opportunities to observe.

I felt limp as a rag when Harold drove us back to Pasadena.

EIGHTEEN

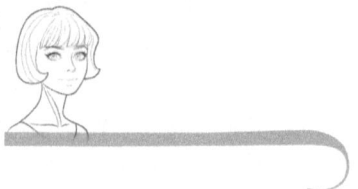

As luck would have it, the telephone began ringing as soon as Harold and I entered my parents' bungalow. I sighed heavily, said to my leaping hound, "Be right back, Spike," and headed for the kitchen.

"What about me?" asked Harold indignantly, although he did stoop to greet Spike.

"I'll be right back with you, too." I picked up the receiver, wondering if I dared hold it to my ear, and took a chance. "Gumm-Majesty residence. Mrs. Majesty speaking."

For once—actually, two or three times by then—I was in luck. "Daisy," said Flossie Buckingham. "I called earlier, and your father said you were out with Mr. Kincaid looking for china patterns at Bullock's in downtown Los Angeles. That must have been fun!"

"It was," I told Flossie, feeling guilty for absolutely no reason whatsoever. However, Flossie and Johnny Buckingham didn't have fine china and never would. I'd bet any amount of money on it, if I did anything so foolish as to place bets.

"Did you find anything you liked?"

"Oh, Flossie. It was grueling. I know I'm lucky to be able to register for fine china and so forth, but they all began to look alike after a while."

"But you found a pattern you especially liked?" Flossie sounded wistful. Then and there, I decided Flossie was going to get a set of china. I wasn't sure how I'd pay for it, but I made good money conjuring up and chatting with people's dead relatives, and I'd put some of it aside for Flossie and Johnny.

"Yes. Next time I see you, I'll show you. There were some lovely patterns I didn't even consider because the ears to the teacups were pinchy. Can you imagine Sam or Mr. Prophet trying to drink out of a teacup in the ears to which they couldn't insert a finger?"

With a laugh, Flossie said, "No. Especially Mr. Prophet."

"Exactly."

"But Daisy, Mr. Prophet is one of the reasons I telephoned you today."

"He is?" How odd.

"You know how much little Billy loves that wrinkled old man."

"I do, indeed." It had come as an almost stunning shock to me when Flossie and Johnny's little boy had taken a shine to Mr. Prophet. Of course, the first time he espied the man he'd been scared so badly, he'd hidden his face on his mother's shoulder. But Mr. Prophet had demonstrated hidden depths to his personality that day and had eventually charmed the socks off the kid. Ever since their first meeting, little Billy had loved the stuffing out of him. So to speak.

"Well, Johnny and I want you and Mr. Prophet to come to lunch one of these days. The ladies of the church are so excited about you and Sam marrying, they want to host a luncheon on your behalf. It won't be on a grand scale like the luncheons some of your clients are, I'm sure, going to put on for you, but it should be fun."

"How sweet! I'd love that. Thank you, Flossie!"

"You may mostly thank Hilda Schwartz, whose last name is now Gibson, for initiating the idea. She's never forgotten it was you and Miss Emmaline Castleton who allowed her to remain in this country even though she hails from Germany."

"Oh, but she saved my life!" I said, trying to forget the fact I'd initially hated Hilda because I suspected her of being from Germany rather than Switzerland, as she'd claimed. "She has no reason to be grateful to me. I should be throwing a shindig for her!"

"Nonsense. She adores you, and she's thrilled you and Sam are getting married. So don't argue. According to Sam, you're going to a luncheon at Mrs. Pinkerton's house next Monday."

"Boy, Sam is blabby. I don't even remember telling him about it."

"Word spreads, Daisy. You know that better than most people."

"I guess, although I'm not sure why a luncheon for me at Mrs. Pinkerton's place should spread to the Salvation Army."

"We have our ways," said Flossie, sounding as if she were trying to emulate an international spy. Then she laughed, and so did I.

"Well, Miss Mata Hari, if you're sure, any old time will be good."

"Wonderful. Are you free this coming Friday?"

"Yes, I do believe I am."

"Perfect. I'll check with the ladies and get back to you, although I'm pretty sure Friday is a good day. And you *must* bring Mr. Prophet, even if Sam has to work. Bring your father, too, and anyone else you'd like to bring. Your mother and aunt, if they're not working. There will be plenty of food. It will probably be a covered-dish luncheon, with people bringing all sorts of different dishes."

"Thank you, Flossie. You're so kind to this person who lies for a living."

My comment provoked a huge laugh from Flossie. "Applesauce! You help people who want to be comforted. In my book, and Johnny's, you're doing a good thing."

"If you say so, I'll try to stop feeling guilty about my line of work," I told her, knowing I'd feel guilty forever, if not about my living, then about all my other failings as a human being. I contemplated telling her about Mrs. Pinkerton's upcoming donation, but decided against it. Mrs. Pinkerton's heart was in the right place—most of the time—but she wasn't precisely dependable.

Flossie and I said our good-byes, and I walked back to the living room, thinking how nice it was to have a private telephone line. I used to have to shoo our party-line neighbors off the wire if I wanted any privacy. Even then, most of them heard more than I wanted them to. One of them in particular, Mrs. Barrow, had spoken with the most ghastly New York accent I'd ever heard. My Sam didn't have that hideous an accent.

By the time I'd made my way back to the living room, Harold and Spike had taken up residence on the sofa. "Bring me something to drink, will you, Daisy? I'm tired and thirsty," said Harold. "Hauling you all over Bullock's wore me out."

"It wore me out, too. Let me say hi to Spike first."

Spike seemed pleased with my greeting, but he didn't bother getting too excited. He was comfy. So, after petting him a little, I went back to the kitchen, still feeling rather like a worn-out washrag. Nevertheless, I looked in the refrigerator, faintly hoping, and lo and behold, some kind soul had put a pitcher of lemonade in there! I suspected my darling father, who did things like that. So I took a couple of chunks of ice out of the freezer compartment, which looked as if needed to be defrosted soon, dumped them in two plain old glasses—Harold said we'd select glassware later, a threat that filled my heart with dread—filled the glasses with lemonade, and dragged myself back to the living room. I took a couple of coasters with me so we wouldn't mar the furniture with our frosty glasses.

"So," said Harold, after he'd thanked me for fetching him lemonade, "when do you want to go back to Bullock's and select silverware and glassware?"

Sitting on the piano bench facing Harold, I took a slug of lemonade and felt my fearful heart slither down into my pretty Louis heels. Which reminded me that my feet were aching to beat the band, so I shoved the shoes halfway off until they dangled from my toes. "Never. Why don't you choose for me?"

Still petting Spike with one hand and holding his lemonade glass with the other, Harold feigned shock so well, I almost believed him. "*I* can't do that! Shame on you for even saying such a thing! The china, flatware and glassware you select now will be used by you and Sam and your children and grandchildren for generations to come!"

Lowering his tone a trifle, he said, "Next week sometime. I know your pal Mrs. Buckingham will be throwing a party for you—"

"How did you know *that*?" I demanded. "I only heard about it when I answered the telephone after we got home."

Harold tapped his head. "You're not the only psychic in town, my dear."

"Jeepers. I feel as though my life is the hot topic of conversation in Pasadena at the moment. Flossie knew about your mother's luncheon for me on Monday, and you evidently knew about the Army's Friday covered-dish luncheon for me before *I* did! Has some rogue Hollywood reporter decided I'm worth writing articles about?"

"Lord, no. Your life is boring as hell."

"Hunh," I said, disgruntled. I drank more lemonade and noticed my father, looking pleased with himself and the world, enter the living room. I scanned his face for signs of the heart problems that occasionally caused his skin to take on a muddy cast, but he looked healthy. That made me happy. "Hey, Pa! Thanks for making the lemonade," I said, rising to give him a kiss on the cheek.

"You're more than welcome. I figured two people who spent their day exploring the depths of the china department at Bullock's in Los Angeles would probably need a cold drink when they got back to civilization."

"You were right." Then I understood all. Well, almost all. "Oh! *You're* the one who told Harold about the Salvation Army wanting to give me a bridal luncheon on Friday, aren't you? And I'll bet you told Flossie about Mrs. Pinkerton's luncheon for me next Monday, too, huh?"

"Guilty as charged," said Pa, laughing. He sat on one of the living room chairs.

"Aw, heck, Joe," said Harold. "I was trying to convince her I was psychic."

"Sorry, Harold," said Pa, jovial as ever. Turning to me, he added, "Harold said you chose two beautiful patterns for your everyday and formal china, Daisy. Lah-di-dah. Your mother and I never had formal dinnerware. We come from the working classes."

"So do I," I told him, deciding Ma and Pa would get some fine china, too, before I was through with this china-selecting nonsense. "And at least everything you have matches."

"More or less," said Pa with a laugh.

"More or less," I agreed. "That awful store clerk packed up a cup and saucer from each set for me to take home. Want to see them?"

"Why don't you wait until dinner time? Then you can show all of us." Pa stood from his chair with a little grunt. "Think I'll take Spike for a stroll around the neighborhood. We won't be gone long. Your mother and aunt will probably be home soon, and I'm sure you're too bushed to walk that animal."

That animal leaped from the sofa as soon as the word "walk" hit the air. Then he gamboled and danced around Pa as if he were being released from some sort of ghastly imprisonment. Silly dog.

"Don't walk too far," I told my father. "Exercise is good for you, according to Doc Benjamin, but don't overdo."

"Yes, Grandma," said Pa. "Don't worry. If I feel the least bit faint, I'll slip a couple of pills under my tongue and bring Spike home."

"All right." It worried me that he'd begun having to use nitro-glycerine tablets, but at least modern medicine was working in his favor. I don't know what people did in, say, the Middle Ages if they had heart problems. Dropped dead, I guess.

After Pa and Spike had gone, I rounded on Harold. "Okay, Harold Kincaid. Tell me why Mr. Cecil Darlington was such a poor choice as a groom for Madge Hawley! I mean, besides being a sot, which I guess is bad enough."

"He was a poor choice for any woman anywhere, not just Madge, although she, DeeDee and Alma are especially idiotic."

"Why?"

"Why what? *I* don't know why they persist in being idiotic!"

"Stop being annoying, Harold Kincaid! Why was Cecil Darlington such a poor choice as husband material?"

"Why do you care? The man's dead and no longer a menace to anyone."

"Because somebody *killed him*, darn you! Maybe one of those silly girls did it. I'm sorry. That was mean of me. I didn't mean to call them silly."

"Why not? They are silly."

"Miss Jervis didn't seem as silly as the Hawley sisters," I muttered.

"Trust me. She's just as silly. Maybe even sillier than the other two, because she takes herself so seriously."

"If somebody had been beating her—and those *were* man-made bruises on her arm, Harold—maybe she has reason to take herself seriously."

"Pah. They're all young and giggly and annoying as hell."

"They're young. Give them a year or two to grow up some." Recalling what Aunt Vi had said about modern young women not being taught good manners, I wondered about my words.

Harold didn't suffer from my qualms. "Give them all the years you want. Those girls will be silly when they're fifty."

"You can tell the future, can you?"

"Sometimes. Take those silly girls, for instance."

Frowning at Harold, I said, "I'm going to tell Sam about you. He'll arrest you for fortunetelling."

"Nonsense. Anyone with half a brain can foretell the futures of those three. They're childish, shallow, and don't have a lick of sense among them."

"Why do you say they have no sense?"

"For one thing, Madge was engaged to Cecil Darlington."

"Harold Kincaid, if you don't tell me this instant why he was such a horrible catch, I'm going to stab you to death with a hat pin!"

As I spoke those dreadful words, the front door opened, my mother walked in, and she stopped and stared at me. "Daisy Gumm Majesty, what a terrible thing to say to Harold!"

Wouldn't you know it? Harold, after setting his empty lemonade glass on his coaster, stood politely and went to the door to assist my mother with her lightweight summer sweater. "Think nothing of it, Mrs. Gumm. Daisy's always picking on me. I'm used to it."

"I am not!" I said, stuffing my aching feet back into my shoes, irked at both my mother *and* Harold. My mother knew Harold was probably my best friend, and best friends tease each other. "It's just that Harold is being ridiculously evasive about a matter there's no reason to be evasive about."

"Still, it's not nice to tell people you'll stab them to death. Haven't you found enough dead bodies to know that?" said Ma.

"You're right," I said, giving up the battle.

"Anyway, I'm not being evasive," said Harold, carefully hanging Ma's sweater on the rack. "I was just about to tell Daisy about the late Cecil Darlington being a secret sot and a care-for-nobody who played around with all the girls he could and then bragged about his conquests at his club."

"Goodness gracious!" said Ma, shocked. "He sounds like an awful person."

"Yes," I agreed. "He does." Taking a page from my mother's book I added piously, "Although I'm sure it's not *my* place to judge anyone."

Ma shot me a poisonous look. "No, it isn't."

"Why don't you scold Harold, then?" I demanded.

"Because," said my mother, whom I'd seldom seen exhibit a sense of humor, "it's not *my* place to discipline someone else's child."

"Good one, Ma!" I said, impressed.

Harold and my mother laughed. Ma followed Harold and me back into the living room after she'd shut the front door. "So how did your shopping expedition go today?"

"Really well," I said, subsiding again onto the piano bench. Harold held a chair for Ma, and she gratefully sank into it. "I'll show everyone the two patterns Harold forced on me at dinner time."

Squinting at me, Ma said, "He *forced* on you?"

"She's trying to be funny, Mrs. Gumm," said Harold. "But she had nitpicking requirements, especially for her teacups."

"I wasn't nitpicking! I just want Sam to be able to use the cups! He could never fit one of his fingers into one of those squinchy teacup ears."

"If you say so," said Harold.

"You two are a caution," said Ma, standing again. "Where are your father and Spike?"

"They went for a walk," I told her.

"Well, I'm going to slip into something more comfortable. I'm glad you had fun today," said Ma.

"Thanks," Harold and I said together.

Then Harold asked, "What's a caution?"

NINETEEN

"I have no idea what a caution is, but evidently we're both cautions. Vi's always telling me I'm a caution."

"Well," said Harold, "I can understand it of *you*."

"And just what do you mean by that?"

"You not only keep stumbling over dead bodies, but you think every woman you meet is being beaten to death by some man." He rose from his chair and stretched. "I've got to go. Roy is fixing lamb chops for dinner, and I need to rest up. You wore me out."

Roy Castillo, Harold and Del's efficient houseboy, had been taught to cook by none other than my aunt, Viola Gumm, the best cook in the world.

"You wore *me* out," I retorted.

"This conversation is getting downright salacious," said Harold as he headed to the door.

"Harold Kincaid, if you're not the most—"

But I didn't get to finish my sentence because the front door opened to reveal Aunt Vi, closely followed by Mr. Prophet and Sam. Sam held a large cardboard box. Pa and Spike brought up the rear.

Leaping aside, Harold said, "Good evening, folks! Need any help? I was just going to take off."

"Thank you, Harold dear," said Vi. "I think these big, strong men can handle dinner for us." She hooked a thumb over her shoulder. "It's in that cardboard box."

Harold took a long sniff. "Hmm. That smells heavenly. Maybe I should stay here for dinner."

With a laugh, Vi said, "There's plenty for everyone." My blessed aunt absolutely loved feeding people.

"Thanks, Mrs. Gumm, but I'd best be off. Your niece wore me out today. She hauled me all over Bullock's until I thought my feet would fall off!"

"Harold!" I squeaked from behind him.

But everyone only laughed, and Harold took himself off in his beautiful new Hispano-Suiza.

"So, ya had fun today, did you?" Mr. Prophet said, limping into the house and hanging his hat on the rack.

"We did, but it was kind of exhausting." My feet gave a particularly painful twinge. "In fact, I haven't even changed my shoes yet."

As Sam carried the cardboard box into the kitchen with Vi following him—she was on her feet all day, every day, but she wore sensible shoes, and I guess her feet were used to all that standing—I started making my way to my bedroom off the kitchen.

"Spendin' all that money tired you out, did it?" said Mr. Prophet.

Peeved, although I know the man took delight in teasing me, I said, "I didn't spend a dime. The people who buy the china will spend *their* money."

"They goin' to spend it on you and Sam?" he asked, sounding skeptical.

Although I'd been wondering the same thing, I only said, "Harold claims they will."

"He's prob'ly right. Folks in this town got more money than's good for 'em."

"You're only mad because they don't spend more of it on you," I snapped just as I disappeared into my room. Spike didn't tag along because he wanted to stay in the kitchen along with the good cooking smells. My feelings were only slightly dented. Whatever was in the cardboard box smelled *good*.

I heard my mother's correctional, "Daisy!" but pretended I didn't. When I exited my bedroom in my comfy housedress and sloppy slippers, I felt *much* better. So I decided to set the table.

"What dishes should I put out, Vi?" I asked. "Soup bowls? Plates? Both?"

"Just stack regular old plates at my place and put a napkin in a basket for the rolls," she said, already standing over the stove and stirring something. I noticed another pot next to the big one she was stirring.

"One plate or two?"

"A plate and—well, I guess stack some bowls at my place, too."

So I did. "Need any help getting stuff on the table, Vi?" It was only about five-thirty, but I didn't want to join the lazy men in the living room unless I knew Vi didn't need my help. After all, I'd been out frivolling all day, and she'd been working like a slave and was still working.

"I'll call you when I need you to put food in serving dishes," she said. "Go on and sit in the living room with everyone else while I finish this up."

"You work too hard," I told her.

"Don't I know it," said she. "But I do love feeding people."

See? Told you so.

"We love you feeding us, too."

So I slouched into the living room, where Ma and Pa sat on the sofa with Spike, Mr. Prophet sat on a chair, and Sam sat on the piano bench. He patted the place beside him, so I sat there.

"Joe says you didn't get home until after four this afternoon," said Sam. He was smiling, so I didn't take his comment amiss.

"He's right. I swear to heaven, Sam, I didn't know there were so many china patterns in the entire universe! How many rich people are there that manufacturers need to produce so much china?"

"Beats me," he said.

"You don't really need to be rich in order to have pretty good china," said Ma, surprising me. "You don't have to buy your dinnerware at Bullock's. There are places where they sell good dinnerware for much less money."

"Honestly? I didn't know that. I've never done this before." And that simple statement brought back such a flood of memories, I feared to open my mouth again lest sobs emerge.

Ma sighed.

Pa said, "You and Billy were so darned young."

Ma said, "But your father said you have a cup and saucer to show us."

I cleared my throat and when I was sure I wouldn't cry, I said, "Yes, I do. Two cups and two saucers. I'll show you at dinner. I want Sam and Mr. Prophet and Pa"—boy, was I glad I remembered my father—"to pick up the cups and see if they can stick their big fingers in the ears."

Mr. Prophet stuck a finger in his ear, wiggled it, and said, "Ain't no problem, Miss Daisy."

Ma giggled.

"The ears of the teacups," I explained, although I know he already knew that. Then I remembered the three girls. "Oh, Sam! Have you learned any more about Mr. Darlington's murder?"

Frowning, my beloved said, "No. Why? And don't forget I can't tell you about the case."

"I know. I know. But the two Miss Hawleys and a young woman named Miss Alma Jervis were lounging around the fine china department in Bullock's when Harold and I got there today."

"Yeah?" Sam sounded curious so, encouraged, I went on.

"Yes. And they didn't look awfully darned heartbroken, although Miss Jervis had bruises all over her arms. She was covered from head to toe in scarves and a huge cloche hat, even though it was hot as an oven today, so all I could see were her arms. They were made by hands, those bruises."

"How do you know that?" demanded Sam.

"I've seen bruises like those before."

"You have?" Mr. Prophet.

"I have." Me.

"She has." Sam. With an accompanying sigh. "Don't forget we're talking about Daisy here."

"Oh," said Mr. Prophet. "Yeah. I fergot."

"It's not my fault," I said indignantly. "Oh, and Harold said Mr. Cecil Darlington was a cad and a drunken lout, and he made a habit of seducing young women and then bragging about his conquests at his club."

Silence prevailed, although my mother's face showed her disapproval of such callous behavior.

"F. Scott Fitzgerald has a lot to answer for," I muttered, thinking about all the so-called flappers, drinking and smoking and running wild in these modern times.

With a soft chuckle, Sam said, "You just never gave yourself time to be a youth. You and Billy got married right after you graduated from high school, and you've been working since you were a kid. It's natural for young people to want to have fun."

I peered up at my fiancée, dumbfounded. "You mean you *approve* of young people drinking and smoking and visiting speakeasies and that sort of thing?"

"Of course I don't," said Sam. "But youngsters want to have a good time." He shook his head. "It's too bad they want to have fun in such destructive ways."

"Indeed," said Ma. "In our day, we'd have dances in the town hall or the high-school gymnasium, and everyone just had fun."

"I suspect some kids got up to more than mere fun at some of those shindigs," said Pa. "In fact, I remember Chuck Hollis. He always brought a bottle to the dances, and his cronies would gather outside and drink themselves silly."

"I don't remember that!" said Ma, shocked.

"You're kidding!" I said, also shocked.

"Nope. It's the truth. Naturally," he said with an air of pure innocence, "I never participated in such goings-on."

"That's probably because I'd have killed you," said Ma. With a sigh, she went on, "I know you're right. I just never thought about things like that back then."

"I ain't sayin' a thing," said Mr. Prophet.

Pa said, "You fought in a war when you were a kid. You should know about taking on responsibilities when you're too young for them."

My father's comment surprised me, although it shouldn't have. Sometimes I forgot Mr. Prophet hadn't been born a hardened reprobate.

"Accordin' to Miss Daisy, I fought on the wrong side o' that war," said Mr. Prophet, squinting at me.

"Yes," I said, squinting back. "But you were young and probably didn't know better. I'm sure you didn't own any slaves."

"Slaves? Lordy, gal, it was all we could do to keep food on the table when I was a sprout. Then some fat politicians up north said we had to change our wicked ways. At the time I didn't *have* any wicked ways. All's I thought about was somebody from up yonder tellin' us folk in Georgia we couldn't live the way we wanted to, so I got my gun and went to war." He stopped speaking and his face took on a musing cast. "Come to think of it, we got paid some money to sign on with the Confederate Army. So I gave that money to my Ma and went to war." He shook his head. "Didn't have no home left when I tried to go back to it after the war was over. Never did take a hankerin' to Yankees after that. Present company excepted."

"Of course," I said.

"Of course," he said, and he gave me one of his wicked grins.

"Anyhow, I met me a lot of buffalo soldiers and black cowboys when I got to the west, and they was no more stupid or ignorant than any of the white folk I ever met. Injuns might be another matter—them folks's smart—but the gov'ment pretty much wiped them out."

We sat solemnly for a few seconds. Don't know about anyone else in the room, but I was thinking about the history of the United States, and how much of our great land was yanked away from other people with violence. I finally said, "F. Scott Fitzgerald isn't the only one. We all, as a culture, have a lot to answer for."

"Don't talk to me about it," said Sam. "Let me show you something. I've carried it around for years just for the heck of it." He rose from the piano bench, reached into his back pocket and pulled out his wallet. From it he extracted an old, yellow clipping and handed it to me.

I read it aloud, headline first, "'NO ITALIANS ALLOWED. On May 28, 1888, council passed a resolution to the effect that parties receiving the contract for paving E. Washington St. shall bind themselves not to employ any Italian labor.'"

My mouth fell open. "Sam! This is terrible!"

He shrugged. "It just is. I doubt there's a single community of people anywhere in the world that hasn't been discriminated against at one time or another." He cocked his head and grinned at me. "Maybe except for you lily-white folks."

I recalled another time he'd said something to this effect, and my heart pinched. "We just can't get along with each other, can we? I mean, unless other people look just like us, we don't want anything to do with them, huh?"

Oddly enough, it was Mr. Prophet who broke the glum silence prevailing. "Don't know about that. Lookin' around this room, I see a few lily-white people, a big Italian feller and me. And what with you and Sam gettin' hitched, your whole family will be full of mutts pretty darned soon." He glanced at Spike. "Sorry, Spike. You'll always be a thoroughbred."

"Purebred," I corrected him. Then I laughed. "You're right. We're going to produce mutts! Oh, Spike, will you speak to our children?"

"Dogs don't care," said Pa. "And neither do we. I'm sorry about that article, Sam. But I remember seeing the orange-packing plants with signs saying 'No Chinese Need Apply'. And that was in Pasadena."

"In New York City, it used to be that way with the Irish *and* Italians," said Sam.

"That's so unfair," I said, thinking suddenly and perhaps tangentially about Miss Emmaline Castleton. "Emmaline Castleton said her father and the other railroad barons imported the Chinese and Irish because they'd work on the railroads for low wages. After the railroads were built, we didn't want them anymore. That's pretty... awful."

"In Los Angeles, there was a massacre of Chinese by whites and Mexicans in the 1870s," said Sam.

My eyes fairly bulging, I asked him, "What? How do you know that?"

"I like to read about history," he said simply. "And in Tulsa, your friend Mrs. Browning's hometown, the white population massacred an entire prosperous section of town where Negros had built a thriving community. They even bombed the place."

"When?" I asked, incredulous.

"1921. Four years ago. I suspect that's the main reason the Tulsa contingent of Mr. Jackson's family followed him to Pasadena."

Have I mentioned that Mr. Jackson was Mrs. Pinkerton's gate-keeper? Probably, huh?

"Good heavens," I whispered. "I'll bet you're right. I remember reading about what they called 'race riots' in the newspapers, but that doesn't sound like any race riot to me. It sounds like... like... like a war." I fingered the Voodoo juju Mrs. Jackson, Mr. Jackson's mother, had crafted for me. She'd made one for Sam, too, when he got shot a while back. That had been a perfectly ghastly time.

"Sounds like a pretty dam—er, darned one-sided war to me," opined Mr. Prophet. "More like a massacree."

"You're right," I agreed.

"Dinner's ready!" came Vi's cheery voice from the kitchen. "Daisy, will you please help me fill the serving dishes?"

I handed Sam back the yellowed newspaper clipping. "Sure will!" I called back to Vi. To Sam, I said, "I'm sorry."

"It's all right," he said with fake solemnity. "I forgive you."

So I whacked him on the shoulder and went to the kitchen to help Vi.

TWENTY

In case anyone wondered, all the men in my life except Spike could easily pick up and hold on to both the Copeland Spode Wicker Dale and the Shelley Syringa Gardenia teacups. Everyone loved the patterns, too, although I got the distinct impression Ma had hoped I'd select something fancier, or at least with more gold on it, for my "best" china. Ah, well. I'd get her something fancy later.

After a tiring day—and all I'd done was select china patterns—I slept well Monday night. I did have one disturbing dream in which Mr. Prophet aimed his shotgun at Sam and said something derogatory about Italians, but that's all I could remember of it when I awoke Tuesday morning. I didn't like the dream. It was unfair to both Mr. Prophet and Sam, and it left me with a gloomy feeling.

After I'd been to the bathroom to do my morning ablutions, gone back to my bedroom to change into comfortable clothes, and put on shoes that gave my poor beleaguered feet room to move, I felt better. I felt even betterer (that's not a word, but what the heck) when I left my bedroom and found Ma, Pa, Sam and Mr. Prophet all sitting at the kitchen table. Vi stood at the stove, stirring something. The fragrance of breakfast sausage filled the air. I was darned near elated when I greeted my family. Well, and Mr. Prophet, who might as well be family. I'd already said a hearty good-morning to Spike.

"Want me to drive you guys to work today?" I asked Ma and Aunt Vi.

After only a second or two's thought, Ma said, "That would be lovely, dear. It's already pretty warm out there, and it's not fun walking in the heat."

"Great. I want to go to the library. Anybody have any books you want me to pick up?"

"Anything new by Zane Grey or Edgar Rice Burroughs," said Pa.

"Let me think about it," said Sam. "I like reading about history."

"I know you do," I said. "For some reason, your interest in history surprised me."

"Huh," said Mr. Prophet. "Sam here's a font of information about lots of things. Care for the company of a crippled old man, Miss Daisy?"

"Sure!" I said. I enjoyed Mr. Prophet's company, even if I disagreed with many of his opinions, especially about women.

"Any new detective novels you can find," said Ma. "And if that Sabatini fellow has written any more rip-roaring adventure yarns, I'd love to read them."

"I hope he has," I said.

"Here Daisy," Vi said from the stove. "I'm dishing out breakfast for everyone, and you can carry the plates to the table."

"Happy to," I told her, and walked to the stove. There she dished out potato patties—made from leftover mashed potatoes from last night—sausage patties, and individual omelets. "My good-ness, Vi, you're a marvel! This is a feast, and then you get to go and prepare feasts for the Pinkertons."

"This isn't a feast, you silly thing. This is merely sensible use of leftovers."

If she said so.

Anyhow, I carried plates to the table, Ma and Pa first, then I went back and got full plates for Sam and Mr. Prophet. And then I picked up my own plate, carried it to the table, and Vi did likewise with hers. Someone—I suspect Sam—had already filled mugs with coffee. We always had a bowl of oranges on the kitchen table, because we always had oranges on one of our two trees. And now Sam supplemented our orange supply with fruit from his own trees across the street.

Pa said a short prayer, and we all dug in. Best breakfast I'd had since the last time Vi fixed breakfast for us. I tell you, the woman is a wizard in the kitchen.

As we ate, Sam suddenly said, "I know! See if you can pick up any books about gardening in this part of the world."

"Gardening?" I asked, once again surprised by my fiancé's variety of interests.

"Yes. There's a lot of ground across the street, and I'd like to see if we can grow something besides orange and lemon trees. I'd like to know if other kinds of trees do well here. And different flowers. And vegetables."

"I'll be happy to," I said. I meant it, too. I enjoyed gardening. The prospect of Sam and me having a lovely garden across the street seemed magnified that morning.

"I think you should get one o' them rose bushes that have the little pink flowers on 'em. Don't know what they're called, but they climb all over the place at... another house around here."

The house to which he referred belonged to Mrs. Emmaline Mainwaring, former scarlet woman and now queen of the orange-growers in Pasadena. Mr. Prophet's primary interest in the Mainwaring residence was, as mentioned previously, Li Ahn. Or maybe her name was Ahn Li. Anyway, she and Mr. Prophet had known each other in Tucson in the bad old days, and they'd become reacquainted earlier in the year. However, Mrs. Mainwaring also possessed a magnificent garden with a Cecile Brunner rose that cascaded over the archway leading to her house.

"Cecile Brunner," I said to Mr. Prophet.

He squinted at me. "Thought his name was Darlington. Anyhow, what's that owlhoot got to do with little pink roses?"

"The dead man's name is Cecil Darlington. Cecile Brunner is

the name of the rose you're talking about, and even though the rose has an E on the end of its first name, it's pronounced the same as the dead man's first name. Cecil."

"Huh," said Mr. Prophet.

"What's an owlhoot?" asked Ma.

Because I'd been taking notes of Mr. Prophet's interesting old-west sayings, I replied for him. I wasn't being rude. His mouth was full. "An owlhoot is a bad guy. In the wild west."

"Oh," said Ma, and she resumed eating.

I noticed Sam and Pa smiling between bites. That's probably because Mr. Prophet had discovered my little secret and had begun recording modern-day slang in his own notebook. Turn-about's fair play, I reckon. At least that's what folks say.

Breakfast was soon over, and I carried the dishes to the sink. I aimed to wash them after I took Ma and Aunt Vi to work, even though that would have interrupted the flow of the day I'd planned. Listen to me. "Interrupted the flow" of my day? How pompous can one fairly young widow sound? The only things I'd planned to do that day were visit the library and do a little sewing and ironing.

It turned out I didn't have to interrupt anything because Pa said, "I'll do the dishes, Daisy. You take your mother and aunt to work, and then you and Mr. Prophet can visit the library."

After taking a good, long look at his face, I said, "Thanks, Pa."

He shook his head. "I swear, Daisy, you'd think I was an inch away from dying, the way you keep track of me."

"Just don't want you to overdo," I said, feeling as though I'd been caught committing a crime. But I didn't want him to die! There's nothing wrong with that, is there?

"Lemme go across the street and pick up the books I borrowed last time I went to the library," said Mr. Prophet.

"Okay. You can just leave your books on the table by our front door if you want to. That's where we put all of our already-read books to be returned to the library."

He nodded at me, said, "Thanks, Miss Daisy," and walked to the front door.

"I don't know why he hasn't already started doing that," I mused as Sam helped me finish cleaning off the breakfast table.

"Probably because he didn't know he was permitted to," said Sam.

"Golly, if I'd known he needed a formal invitation, I'd have given him one months ago," I muttered.

"Lou's an odd duck," said Sam with a chuckle. "He doesn't like being what he called himself. You know, old and crippled. I get the feeling he's still about thirty years old inside."

"Golly, I'm not even thirty years old now."

"Give yourself five years," said Sam, who would have his thirty-first birthday in August.

"Okay, then. I will."

He stooped to kiss me, and then he took off for the Pasadena Police Department.

"Ready to go, ladies?" I asked as Ma and Aunt Vi entered the kitchen.

"Yes, indeed," said Ma. "Is Mr. Prophet back?"

As she voiced her question, Mr. Prophet appeared at the side door to the house, which led to a porch and down to the driveway where we kept the Chevrolet parked.

"You takin' my name in vain?" he asked through the screen door.

"Of course," I said.

"Good." He nodded.

When we all got to the motorcar, I suggested Mr. Prophet sit in the front and hold the books. So he opened the car's back doors for Ma and Aunt Vi, maneuvered himself into the front seat, and I stacked the books on his lap. Then I backed the car down the driveway slowly—backing up wasn't one of my tip-top skills— sighed with gratitude when I made it down the drive and on to Marengo, then backed up a little more, turned the wheel left, and drove north on Marengo until we got to the Hotel Marengo, where Ma worked. Then I drove up to Orange Grove, turned left, and motored to the magnificent mansions lining Orange Grove once you got past, say, Fair Oaks Avenue.

When we arrived at the Pinkerton place, I made a right turn into the drive, stopped at the gatehouse, exchanged pleasantries with Mr. Jackson, who opened the wrought-iron gate for us, and continued up the deodar-lined drive. I bypassed the turnoff to the circular drive where guests entered and parked and drove Vi to the kitchen entrance.

"Want me to pick you up later, Vi?" I asked as she trundled to the door and opened it.

"No, thanks. I'll just take the bus if Sam doesn't drop by to pick me up as he did yesterday."

"Okay." I never had asked Sam why he'd driven Vi home the day before. So, as I drove back down the long, long tunnel that was the Pinkerton place's drive, I asked Mr. Prophet. "How come you and Sam picked up Vi yesterday?"

"Sam had to talk to Mrs. Pinkerton about her lousy daughter."

"Why'd he have to do that?"

"Trial's comin' up. You'll have to testify, you know."

"Yes," I said. "I'm not looking forward to it."

"Neither's Sam. Neither am I. Neither's Mrs. Pinkerton, from what Sam told me. She doesn't even want to be at the trial. I think she's finally washed her hands of that rotten kid of hers."

"Huh," I said inelegantly. "When I talked to her a week or so ago, she said pretty much the same thing. And she wasn't even in a tizzy about it. Gee, maybe she won't need me any longer."

"Worried about losing a paying customer?" asked Mr. Prophet.

"No! I'm glad of it. She screeches when she's upset about Stacy, and Stacy doesn't deserve the amount of hand-wringing and heart-wrenching Mrs. P's done over her through the years."

"I agree with you on that one," said he. "Hell... Uh, heck, the only reason I met Sam and you was because I was after the curly wolf who tried to stick you with that knife, and the Kincaid brat was behind his doing it."

"I haven't forgotten, believe me," I said and shuddered slightly. "And that particular curly wolf turned out to be Sam's nephew. Poor Sam."

"Sam can take care of himself and a dozen scrawny kids like that nephew o' his."

Mr. Jackson had left the gate open for us, and both Mr. Prophet and I returned his wave as we left the Pinkerton mansion. "Mr. Jackson's son plays the horn at the Ambassador Hotel's Cocoanut Grove. They make him enter through the kitchen, though, because he's not white."

"Yeah. People are stupid. I've met pretty much every color and creed in my long life, and there ain't one race better than the other that I've ever been able to tell."

"I agree with you."

He shifted a little in his seat. He had a gigantic stack of books on his lap and I suddenly felt a sting of compunction. Yes, I know it was a little late. "Do you want me to pull over and put those books in the back seat?" I asked.

"No. Why'd you want to do that?" he asked, as if he thought my question a ludicrous one.

"Just didn't want the weight of all those books to hurt your leg, was all. You don't need to get miffy with me."

"Oh," he said. "No, I'm just fine, thanks. I'll need your help to get 'em off my lap and into the library when we get there."

"Of course. I'll be happy to help you."

"Thanks, Miss Daisy. Sorry I barked at you."

I briefly took my gaze off the road in front of me and looked with amazement at Mr. Prophet. I couldn't recall him ever apologizing for anything before.

"It's all right," I told him. Then I contemplated saying something else and decided I'd better not. Didn't want to spoil the mood.

"Gonna be different in the library with your friend not there."

"Yes," I said with a big sigh. "It will be."

"She quit her job when she got married?"

"I'm not sure. She didn't say anything to me about quitting, and I was afraid to ask for fear she'd tell me she had. She's been my favorite librarian for years."

"Yeah, I know. Nice lady."

"Yes. She's a good friend."

"Shame what happened after her wedding."

"Yes, it sure was."

Mr. Prophet said, "Huh."

"Pretty soon, we'll all be going to the brand-new library," I said, my heart crunching a trifle. I'd been a patron of the Pasadena Public Library since almost before I could remember. I'd seen plans for the new building, and it looked nice, but it sure wouldn't be the same.

"They gonna keep the park and the pond?"

"I didn't see them when they printed the plans in the newspaper," I said, and my heart sank a trifle lower. I loved our gorgeous library with its beautiful green park and pond and the gazebo, where you could sit and read a book, or just sit and do nothing if you wanted to. "We're getting a new city hall pretty soon, too."

"Yeah, Sam told me."

"I like the looks of the new city hall better than the looks of the new library."

"Yeah?"

"Yes. Our city hall now is small and kind of dingy. And the back of it holds the police department and the few jail cells we need in Pasadena, too."

"They gonna build a new police station, too?"

"I... don't know. Huh. I should have asked Sam. He'll probably know."

"I expect he does."

"The newspaper article said they're moving the children's section of the library to Lamanda Park now that it's been annexed to the City of Pasadena. I guess the city fathers decided they'd need a library there since it's now part of the city." I contemplated Lamanda Park for a second or two and said, "Better a library than a speakeasy."

"Eh?" Mr. Prophet turned his craggy old head and stared at me. "What were you doin' in a speakeasy, Miss Daisy?"

Contemplating the experience I'd had in that dreadful place and not much wanting to, I said, "I'll tell you later. The police swept up a bunch of bootlegging gangsters there." And Flossie and I had been nearly buried under concrete dust when one of the gangsters began shooting up the place with his Tommy gun.

It was lucky for me that I pulled up in front of the library just then, or Mr. Prophet might have dug for more information. Although, come to think of it, he didn't generally pry into other people's business. I could probably learn that trick from him if I weren't so blasted nosy.

Ah, well, we all have our faults. Some of us have more than we want to admit to.

TWENTY-ONE

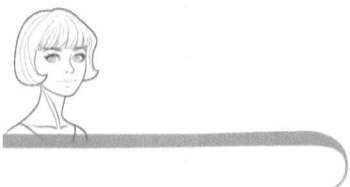

I helped Mr. Prophet carry the big pile of already-read books up the library steps and into the main room. I opened the door for him, and I know he didn't like that I had to do so. After the active life he'd led, being old and one-legged bothered him. Made sense to me.

Wouldn't you know it? The first people we saw when we entered the main library hall were the two Hawley sisters and Miss Alma Jervis. They saw us at the same time we saw them, and one of the Hawley sisters smiled broadly and began making her way to us. Then I suspect she realized I was with the tall, rough-looking, peg-legged man who looked just like what he was: a character out of the old wild west, who hadn't yet been tamed in spite of living in Pasadena and consorting with a police detective's fiancée.

Because the three young women stood before the check-out and returns counter, Mr. Prophet and I had to walk over to them. They scooched a little farther down the long counter, peering at us with fascination, if I were to judge. I smiled at them, figuring why not?

After Mr. Prophet and I had deposited our books on the counter, I whispered, "Good morning, Miss Hawley, Miss Hawley and Miss Jervis. May I introduce you to Mr. Lou Prophet? Mr. Prophet is a

178

friend of the family, and he was kind enough to come to the library with me today. The Misses Hawley might recall him from the day of the wedding."

I got a squint from Mr. Prophet, but the three women seemed to relax once they knew Mr. Prophet wasn't there to shoot up the place. He probably could have if he'd taken it into his head to do so. He always kept his Colt pistol tucked somewhere on his person. I'd asked him once why he always went everywhere armed. He'd told me some habits were hard to break.

Very well then.

"Oh," said one of the Hawley sisters. I think it was Madge. "How nice to meet you."

"Yes," said the other Hawley.

Miss Jervis said a languid, "Good morning," and held out a limp hand to be shaken. She'd managed to cover herself with scarves again today, and her hat brim curved around her cheeks. Covering her bruises? I suspected so.

Whatever her motive in dressing so conservatively, Mr. Prophet obliged her, shaking first Miss Jervis's hand and then those of the two Hawley sisters.

"I don't believe I've ever seen you at the library before," I whispered to the threesome by way of making conversation.

"We don't come to the library very often," admitted a Hawley. "But we wanted to see where Regina worked."

"Let me show you," I said, leading the way to the desk Regina generally occupied.

Today a woman I didn't know sat there. She appeared every inch the grim librarian just longing for someone to speak loudly, so she could say, "Shhhh."

But I'd wronged the woman. When the five of us gathered around her desk, I introduced myself and said, "Good morning. I'm Mrs. Majesty. Mrs. Browning and I are good friends. Are you filling in for her while she and Mr. Browning are on their honeymoon?"

"Oh, Mrs. Majesty, it's so good to meet you!" said the woman, surprising me. She held out her hand for me to shake, "I'm Miss

179

Miller and I am, indeed, filling in for Mrs. Browning for a few weeks. She's told me so much about you."

"She has?" I said, astounded.

"She has. She said you're a brilliant seamstress who not only designed her wedding gown, but those of her bridesmaids and her aunt, too."

"Oh. Well, yes, I did, but I enjoy sewing, so it wasn't any trouble," I said as I felt heat creeping up from my neck to decorate my face. The trouble—one of them—with being a redhead is that one tends to blush too blasted often. I had patted a little rice powder on my cheeks that morning, but probably not enough to hide my pink cheeks.

"Sewing is such a useful skill," said Miss Miller, beaming at me. Then she said, "Mrs. Browning left some books for you and your family."

"She did? How kind of her!" Golly, I hadn't expected Regina to think of my family during the most exciting couple of weeks of her life.

"She did." Miss Miller bent down and lifted three books onto the desk. Then she did it again. "Whew! She asked me to give you these six books."

"My, my. Aren't you special?" said Miss Jervis, sounding snippy.

"Yeah," said Mr. Prophet. "She is." Then he pinned her with a look that made her shrink back against one of the Hawley sisters.

"How nice for you," said one of the Hawleys; DeeDee, I think. Her voice sounded almost placating, as if she didn't want any unpleasantness to erupt. That was all right by me. And why was Miss Jervis such a wet blanket, anyhow? Ah, well. Mine was not to reason why, as some poet once said. I don't care for the rest of the poem.

"Pa is going to love these westerns, and the rest of us will love the mysteries. And we'll all enjoy the book by Mr. Wodehouse." I clutched to my breast *Grey Face*, by Mr. Sax Rohmer; *Carry On, Jeeves*, by Mr. P.G. Wodehouse; *The Carolinians* and *Fortune's Fool*, by Mr. Rafael Sabatini; *Hired Guns*, by Mr. Frederick Faust; and *The Long, Long Trail*, by Mr. George Owens Baxter. "What a haul!"

"Are you really going to read all of those books?" asked another Hawley sister. Madge, I think. I still hadn't quite figured out which one was which.

"Oh, my, yes. I love to read and so does everyone else in my family," I told them.

"Mrs. Browning said to tell you that Mr. Earl Derr Biggers should have another Charlie Chan book out early next year."

"Wonderful!"

We were whispering, by the way, in case you wondered.

"Good grief," said Alma Jervis. "I haven't read that many books in my entire life."

Giving her another baleful squint, Mr. Prophet said, "Mebbe you should start. Learn something useful."

I guess Miss Jervis had gathered courage from her friends, because she gave him a sneer and said, "Whatever can you learn from westerns and mystery stories?"

"Mebbe you could learn some manners, fer one thing," said Mr. Prophet.

The sneer on Miss Jervis's face vanished.

I hurried to say, "My fiancé loves reading about history, and he also asked if there was a gardening book you might have that will explain which plants, trees and flowers grow well in our soil. We have orange and lemon trees, but he'd like to plant other fruit trees. And I want to get a Cecile Brunner rose, too, but I know you don't sell roses here." I feigned a giggle, thinking as I did so that I would be a dismal failure as a comedienne.

"According to my mother," said a Hawley. Madge. I'm sure it was Madge. "The best place to get plants and so forth is Liljenwall's Nursery."

"Yes, I agree," I told her. "That's the one we use most often. My aunt has her own compost pile at the back of the garden. Unfortunately, my dog occasionally tries to excavate it."

"What's a compost pile?" asked Alma Jervis.

"Basically, a compost pile is where you throw out all your vegetable and fruit peelings, coffee grounds, tea leaves, and so forth. You can put pretty much anything except meat products into a compost heap. It'll rot, and then you can use it as fertilizer."

"Doesn't it stink?" asked Miss Jervis, wrinkling her nose.

"That's why it's in the back of the garden," said Mr. Prophet, who had clearly taken a dislike to Miss Jervis.

"Exactly," I said. "My father finally had to build a container for ours because of the dog. He loved to drag out old potato peels and munch them."

"Goodness," said Madge Hawley. "What kind of dog do you have?"

"A liberty hound," I said, not wanting to get into the "dachshund" dilemma. After the Great War, some people had actually *killed* dachshunds and German shepherds and other so-called "German" dogs. Spike wasn't German. He was born in Altadena, California. People amaze and appall me with their stupidity and malice sometimes.

Because I wanted to forestall more questions, I said, "That doesn't always stop him, though. I got a sack of bone meal from Liljenwall's because I was planting a couple of rosebushes along the side of the house, and darned if I didn't turn around and see Spike waltzing off with the sack in his mouth! I guess dogs like bone meal as much as roses do."

"Good Lord," said Miss Jervis sneeringly. "I'm glad we have a gardener."

"I love to garden," I told her with a sweet smile.

"You garden, sew, read, prepare compost heaps, and I understand you're also a medium," Miss Jervis said, still sneering.

"Indeed. I do all of those things."

"Don't you run an exercise class, too?" asked Madge (I think) Hawley.

Wondering how she'd heard about that but not wanting to get involved in a long discussion, I said, "Yes. One o'clock at the fellowship hall of the First Methodist-Episcopal Church on Marengo and Colorado. Every Wednesday afternoon. I don't precisely lead it."

"Good Lord. You sew, garden, read, summon the dead *and* exercise?" Alma Jervis again. And, again, sneering.

"Yes." I still smiled sweetly, although doing so was something of a strain.

"Can you do anything?" asked Mr. Prophet.

"Yes," she said in a disagreeable voice. "I'm quite accomplished. I play the piano and sing, for instance."

"So does Miss Daisy," said Mr. Prophet. "I think she's got you beat by a mile." He turned to Miss Miller. "So can you show us to any gardening and history books?"

Miss Miller started slightly. Guess she'd been interested in the gently whispered battle being waged between Miss Alma Jervis and me. For the life of me, I don't know what Miss Jervis had against me, unless the Hawley sisters had told her about that lousy séance, and that wasn't my fault. I'd threatened before to fire Rolly; maybe I should actually do it. Most people didn't hate me on sight. It took them at least a few hours.

Just kidding.

"Oh, yes. I can help you with history and gardening. Do you have a particular area of history in mind?"

Peering at Mr. Prophet, I asked, "Mr. Prophet? Has Sam mentioned any areas of history he's especially interested in?"

He surprised me by saying, "Yeah. He's interested in India. He's curious about how the Brits got in there and took it over."

"Oh," I said. "How interesting. I'd like to read about that, too."

"You can read it after he does," said Mr. Prophet with a wicked twinkle in his eye.

"Wonderful!" said Miss Miller, sounding more exuberant than I considered the history of India warranted. On the other hand, I'm sure people who lived there had a different perspective on the matter. And British people too.

"Gawd," said Miss Alma Jervis.

"Why don't you gals mosey off?" suggested Mr. Prophet in a voice and with a sideways glance that would have withered me. "You don't have interest in much of anything, 'pears to me. Why don't you go out and buy a dress or something?"

"Oh, no!" said Madge—I think. "We don't mean to sound uninterested." She elbowed Miss Jervis, who straightened up and lifted a hand to her slouchy hat. When she did that, I saw the bruises on her arm again.

Mr. Prophet saw them, too. Reaching out and lifting Miss Jervis's arm, a move that shocked her speechless and motionless, he said, "How'd you come by these? They look like some feller got mad at you. Them's hand-made bruises."

Jerking her arm from Mr. Prophet's grip, Miss Jervis said, "That's none of your—"

"How kind of you to ask," said Madge—I'm pretty sure it was Madge—Hawley. "Miss Jervis was in an accident last week."

"You can call it an accident if you want to," said Mr. Prophet, eyeing the three women askance, "but I know when a woman's been beat up by a feller. And when a ring's been jerked off a finger."

"What?" My gaze shot to Miss Jervis's left hand and, sure enough, before she could tuck it into her fluttery scarf, I saw scratches on her ring finger. "You poor thing! How did that happen?"

"It's a personal matter," said Miss Jervis repressively.

"Alma doesn't care to talk about it," said Madge. She bowed her head and looked sad. Taking her cue from her sister, DeeDee did, too. I finally figured out—took me long enough—that Madge was the leader of the duo, and DeeDee followed her example. For the heck of it, I looked at Madge's left hand, just to see if there was a ring mark there. As she wore gloves, I didn't see her left finger at all, although the bump I'd noticed after Regina's wedding was now gone.

"I'm so sorry," I said, meaning it. Those bruises and that scratched finger signaled something intimate and painful to me. Poor girl probably got jilted by some horrid man. I could envision her tearing the ring off her finger and flinging it him. I got the impression she'd get mad before she got sad when people did mean things to her.

My thoughts stopped dead for a second, and then began swirling. Could the man have been Cecil Darlington? Harold had told me he was a womanizer and a show-off. Perhaps he'd fooled *two* of these three young women. The cad!

"Yes, well, the problem is solved now," said Miss Jervis, sounding almost conciliatory for once.

"We'd best be going," said Madge—I'm *sure* it was Madge, because DeeDee never spoke unless Madge spoke first. "We have a couple of other errands to run. It was nice to see you again, Mrs. Majesty. And... uh, Mr. Prophet, it was lovely to meet you."

Mumbles from DeeDee and Alma.

Mr. Prophet said, "Yeah. Likewise, I'm sure."

When the three young women were out of hearing range, he turned to me. "There's somethin' goin' on there I don't like."

"What do you mean?" I asked, surprised, although I'm not sure why. I'd already learned that Mr. Prophet was a shrewd judge of people.

Miss Miller cleared her throat. "Um... would you like me to show you the gardening and history books now?"

Merciful heavens! I'd forgotten we were in the library. Silly me. "Oh. Yes, thank you."

"We'll talk later," said Mr. Prophet.

He wanted to talk to me! Probably about the late Mr. Cecil Darlington and the three weird sisters. Well, two formerly giggly sisters and one weird friend. "Yes, please. Let's talk later."

Miss Miller found a book called *Curry and Rice*, by Mr. George Francklin Atkinson. When she handed it to me, she said, "This will give you an idea about how the British lived in India. I'm not sure we have any books about the history of the British Raj."

"The British what?" asked Mr. Prophet.

"The British Raj," repeated Miss Miller. "That's what they call the British government in India."

"Huh." Mr. Prophet didn't appear especially satisfied with Miss Miller's explanation.

"To tell the truth," said Miss Miller, sounding hesitant, "I think your best bet might be back issues of *The National Geographic Magazine*. I believe there were a few articles in October and November of last year's issues that dealt with India, although I don't know if they covered the British government's involvement in the country."

"That's a good idea," I said, wishing somebody would start writing about the British Raj, which I hadn't even known existed until that day. "Sam has a subscription to *The National Geographic*, and I know he keeps all the issues."

"Yes," said Mr. Prophet, sounding kind of glum. "He does."

"His house has plenty of room to hold them all," I pointed out.

"Yes," said Mr. Prophet, still sounding glum. "It does."

I spared a moment to wonder what Mr. Prophet had against *The National Geographic*, but my attention was again caught by the librarian.

"Excellent," said Miss Miller, obviously considering her India-history search complete. "Let's look for books about gardening in this neck of the woods." She stopped talking and lifted a finger to her cheek. "Actually, there's another magazine to which you might consider subscribing. *Sunset* has been publishing since, I think, the late eighteen-hundreds, and it gives nothing *but* advice about planting things in California."

"Wonderful!" I said. "May we see a few issues?"

"Certainly, although, of course, we don't lend magazines because they tend to fall apart if people handle them too much."

So she led us through the periodical room until we reached the stack featuring *Sunset* magazines, and she was right! "This is wonderful. I'll need to subscribe to this for Sam as soon as I get home." I copied down the information about how to subscribe to the magazine. After I checked out all the books, Mr. Prophet and I left the library carrying several books and lots of good ideas.

I also carried with me an unsettled feeling about the Hawley sisters and Miss Alma Jervis.

TWENTY-TWO

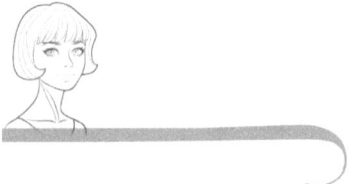

"There's something wrong with those three females."

We'd loaded the books into the back seat of the Chevrolet, Mr. Prophet had maneuvered himself into the front passenger seat, and I'd just settled myself behind the steering wheel when his comment jarred me out of happy contemplation of magazine subscriptions.

"I beg your pardon?"

"You saw the bruises on the snotty one's arm. You talked about 'em yesterday when you said you saw those same three females at that fancy store."

"Yes, but... well, what do her bruises have to do with something being wrong with her?"

"Not sure. But it ain't just her. There's something wrong with all of 'em. Mebbe it's only when they get together. Kind of like a pack of dogs. They're probably not dangerous one at a time."

"*Dangerous*? How can three youngish women not yet out of their teens be dangerous?"

Mr. Prophet stared at me fully long enough for me to get nervous. I started the Chevrolet.

"Well?" I asked as I began sliding the car carefully into traffic on Walnut Street. "Why do those three girls bother you so much?"

"Lemme talk to Sam about it first."

Heck and darnation! "Mr. Lou Prophet, you drive me *nertz*! Why'd you even bring up the subject if you don't aim to do anything but tantalize me with possibilities?"

"Just like gettin' your goat, Miss Daisy. You ought to know that by now." The old sinner smiled at me.

"So you don't really think they're dangerous?"

"Oh, yes, I do. Like a pack-of-coyotes-near-a-baby-bunny dangerous."

"But you won't tell me why you think so."

"Got it in one," said Mr. Prophet.

"And I'm not a baby bunny!"

"Huh."

I'd have liked to bop him with a book, but the books were all in the back seat. Besides, I'd never treat a book so roughly. Mr. Prophet was another matter.

We'd been traveling slowly in the Walnut Street traffic, when Mr. Prophet spoke again. "C'n you drop me off at the police station? I want to talk to Sam."

"I can, but maybe I won't."

He shrugged. "Mebbe you won't. My notions will keep."

I was being ridiculous. The police department was about three feet away from us, on the corner of Walnut and Fair Oaks Avenue, behind the soon-to-be-replaced city hall. Very well, it was more than three feet, but it sure wasn't far. "Never mind. I'll drop you off. You don't want me to come in with you, do you?"

"No, I don't. I want to talk to Sam before you get involved. I just have a feeling you might be in some kind of trouble."

"Trouble? Me? *What*? What kind of trouble?"

"Don't know, but I want to talk to Sam and toss a few ideas around with him. If he thinks I'm on to something, we'll tell you."

"How kind of you both," I said, sounding every bit as snide and cranky as Miss Alma Jervis.

"Yeah, ain't we?"

Because I recognized Sam's big black Hudson in the parking lot of the city hall/police station, I figured I was safe in letting Mr. Prophet off at the entrance to the building. I wouldn't have wanted to leave him Sam-less, even though I was annoyed with him. But he'd have had quite a hike to a red car stop, and I didn't want the crippled old goat to suffer. Much.

Therefore, as soon as he left the vehicle, and because I was still seething with impotent anger, I decided to inflict myself on Flossie Buckingham and little Billy. Flossie always made me feel better. Not sure if the reverse was true.

Flossie welcomed me with open arms. So did little Billy, who was a trifle sticky, but I didn't mind.

"Mr. Pwophet?" said he, clearly hoping I'd brought the antiquated bounty hunter with me.

"I'm sorry, Billy," I said, accepting the damp rag Flossie handed me and wiping my face and the front of my dress, glad I'd opted for comfort over fashion that day. "He'll see you on Friday, though." I hoped.

"Fwiday?" Billy frowned up at his mother, as if asking what in the world a Friday was.

"Today is Tuesday, Billy," said Flossie with such loving patience, that pesky lump lodged itself in my throat again. "Do you remember the days of the week? There's Sunday, Monday, Tuesday, and do you remember the rest of the days?"

Wrinkling his little brow, Billy said, "Wenzday, Turzday"—He suddenly smiled a brilliant smile—"an' *Fwiday!*"

Flossie bent and scooped Billy up. "Yes, indeed. You'll see Mr. Prophet on Friday. At least I hope you will. That's only three days away."

"Twee days," said Billy with satisfaction.

"You two are so adorable together, I think I'm going to cry," I said around my lump.

"Come into the kitchen. I was just making some sandwiches for Johnny and me for lunch. I'll make some for you, too. We have ham and cheese, thanks to the good ladies of the church."

"Thank you! I just came from the library with... uh... Billy's friend, the old scoundrel, and he made me so mad, I decided to visit with you, because you always make me feel good."

"My goodness, you'll have to tell us all about it. I think I hear Johnny coming."

Sure enough, the kitchen door opened, Billy ran into his father's arms, and Johnny swung him up into the air. Billy squealed with glee.

"Daisy! Good to see you!" said Johnny, tossing his son up in the air and getting another squeal for it.

"Careful," Flossie admonished. "He just downed a ham and cheese sandwich, a molasses cookie and a big glass of milk."

"Whoops," said Johnny, quickly depositing his son on the kitchen linoleum lest Billy get sick from the sky-bumping. "Better the floor than me."

Flossie and I laughed. And, perhaps fortunately for all of us, Billy kept his lunch down. Flossie then carted him off for his after-lunch nap. The kid didn't even cry. The Buckinghams made me happy, and I was so glad I visited.

"May I help you with lunch?" I asked when Flossie returned to the kitchen, mainly to be polite. Flossie knew about kitchens and me.

"Would you mind slicing a couple of apples for us? We can eat them with our sandwiches."

It was just like Flossie to give me a task even I couldn't ruin so as not to make me feel like an inept fool. So I washed, cored and sliced two apples and set them on a plate. Then Johnny and I sat at the table, Flossie set a plate of sandwiches on the table next to the plate of apple slices, and handed out smaller plates for Johnny and me.

It shouldn't have surprised me when both Flossie and Johnny each reached for one of my hands, but it did. I tried not to show it, and bowed my head like the good Christian wench I tried to be as Johnny said a short prayer of thanks over our lunches.

We had a nice chat as we ate. I told them both about Mrs. Pinkerton's altered opinion of the Salvation Army, the nearly catastrophic séance, and also about Mr. Prophet's suspicions about the Hawley sisters and Miss Jervis. I added, "I have *no* idea how he came up with the notion they were dangerous. They're not even twenty yet. At least... well, I know the Hawley sisters aren't. I'm pretty sure Miss Jervis isn't, either."

"That old man's pretty perceptive," said Johnny. Then he took a bite out of his sandwich.

Puzzled, I asked Johnny, "You mean he perceived they're dangerous in a pack. A pack of three? How'd he do that? How dangerous can they be?"

"Don't know," said Johnny after he'd swallowed. He grinned and said, "You should ask him. He must have formed an opinion somehow. He's not one to pull rabbits out of hats unless he knows somebody stuffed a few rabbits in the hat beforehand."

"I did ask him," I said bitterly. "He wouldn't tell me."

"Guess you'll have to possess your soul in patience, then," said Johnny, his grin broadening. "I know how much you adore being patient."

Johnny Buckingham knew me too well, dang it. As Mr. Prophet might say. Only he'd have used a word other than "dang."

"Maybe he and Sam will let you in on his suspicions this evening," said Flossie in an attempt to make me feel better.

"I doubt it," I muttered.

Both Buckinghams smiled.

"Have any séances coming up?" asked Johnny.

"No, thank God. After the last one, I don't want to conduct any more séances. Anyhow, Mrs. Pinkerton hasn't been in a tizzy for ages, thanks to you. You're ruining my business, Johnny."

Johnny and Flossie both laughed. So did I.

"Sorry about your business," said Johnny, "but the poor woman really needs to stop fretting about Stacy. Stacy's paying all by herself for the mistakes she made all by herself."

"Yes, evidently you've convinced even Mrs. Pinkerton of the truth of your observation."

"And you did, too."

"I did?"

"Yes. You and Rolly."

"Well, nertz. I'm doing myself out of my own job!"

Again we all laughed. Then Flossie went and spoiled the mood. "Are you ready for our exercise class tomorrow, Daisy?"

"I'm *never* ready for our exercise class, but I'll be there."

"I think it's kind of fun to get out of the house and do something different," said Flossie.

"Hmm. I'd never thought about it like that. Maybe you're right."

"It's probably more fun for me than you. You get out a lot more than I do," said Flossie.

"That's for sure," said Johnny. "Poor Flossie is stuck here at the church organizing various things. When she's not organizing, she's with the baby and dealing with people coming in and asking for help all the time. I'm generally out on the street with the band, so Flossie gets to handle everything else."

My gaze slid between the couple for a second. "I never even thought about you being stuck at home, Flossie," I said, feeling stupid. "If you ever have the urge, just come on up to our house. Pa and I may not be very entertaining, but I'm sure Billy would like to go for a walk with Pa and Spike and you and me."

"Thanks, Daisy. I might just take you up on your offer one of these days."

"Flossie said you made yourself a new pair of gym bloomers. She told me you didn't like the ones with red polka-dots on them." Johnny snickered.

"Yes," I said grumpily. "I finally got some white cotton percale and sewed up some dignified gym bloomers. Well, as dignified as gym bloomers can be."

"Does the woman who screams all the time still attend the classes?" he asked then.

Flossie and I exchanged a glance. I felt guilty. Flossie had no reason to, since she'd cared for an ailing Miss Betsy Powell after she'd been sick at our very first exercise class. I'd wanted to run away from the mess, but not Flossie. These two people were so good, and I was so... not. Ah, well.

"Yes. Oddly enough, she still comes, even though it was another of her gentlemen friends who helped kidnap Vi."

"I get the feeling she's kind of a poor lost soul," said Flossie in her gentle way. This way was *miles* away from the way she'd talked when I'd first met her, although she'd been a gentle soul then, too. I just hadn't recognized her as such. For that matter, neither had she. Which just points out I could learn as much from the Buckinghams as could Mrs. Pinkerton.

"Maybe you're right," I said, trying not to sound resentful. "But so many of her gentleman friends have been *so* horrid, and a couple of them even tried to kill me. She needs better man-hunting skills."

"Flossie told me she's a middle-aged woman," said Johnny in a neutral tone. "Perhaps she doesn't think she's attractive enough to get herself a good man, and just grabs anyone who pays attention to her. I'd venture to guess the pickings are fairly slim at your church." He grinned at me.

"You're right. We're all old married folks, soon-to-be married folks, or widows and widowers."

"She might snag herself a widower," Flossie opined. "Didn't your other friend do that?"

"Lucy Spinks? Yes, she married Mr. Zollinger, who was a widower. You may be right, Johnny! Too bad the only widower I can think of right off the top of my head is old Mr. Dundas. I think he's at least a hundred and three."

"Ripe old age," said Johnny, grinning.

"Old, anyhow," I agreed.

"She should attend church services here," said Flossie, surprising me. "Many of our male members have been through some mighty tough stuff and hard times, but most of them are now men of good character. Some of them are middle-aged. Some of them are old. They've all seen too much of the world, as nearly as I can tell. Just like me." She gave me a beaming smile.

"And me," said Johnny, also beaming.

"What a good idea," I said, meaning it. "Now, if we can only pry Miss Betsy Powell away from the Methodist-Episcopals and get her to the Salvation Army, her pickings might be much better. Another positive angle to this church-change is that, when she's alarmed, she'll scream here and not there." I peered at Johnny and

Flossie, who both looked at me askance. "Sorry," I said, feeling guilty. "I didn't mean it."

Both Buckinghams burst out laughing yet again. "Yes you did!" cried Flossie. "And I don't blame you!"

"I understand her screams can shatter glass," said Johnny.

"Well, our Methodist-Episcopal stained glass has survived quite a few of her screams, but I think my eardrums are shot," I told him.

Shortly thereafter, I left the love and comfort of the Buckinghams and drove home.

TWENTY-THREE

Spike was overjoyed to see me. He met me at the side door, bless him. As soon as I'd set my pile of books on the dining room table, I knelt to greet him properly.

"I don't know what I'd do without you, Spike."

He said he didn't know what he'd do without me, too, but I didn't believe him. *Everybody* loved Spike. He'd have no lack of care-takers if I kicked the bucket.

What a dismal subject. How'd I manage to get on it?

Picking up the books once more, I deposited them on the hutch in the dining room and moseyed into the kitchen, intending to go to my room and change into my floppy slippers. Pa sat at the table eating an orange, and I stooped to kiss him on the cheek, then flumped into a kitchen chair.

"Want a sandwich?" Pa asked.

"No, thanks. I went to see Flossie and Johnny after I left Mr. Prophet at the police station. He wanted to talk to Sam. Anyhow, the Buckinghams fed me lunch."

After swallowing an orange segment, Pa said, "Why'd Lou want to see Sam?"

My feeling of grievance came back with a vengeance. "*I* don't know! We met the two Hawley sisters and Miss Alma Jervis at the library."

"Do they go there often? I mean, do you see them there often?"

"I've never once seen them there before today."

"Then it seems a little peculiar that they should show up at the library, doesn't it? When you're there?"

"They wouldn't know I'd be there," I pointed out. "We don't keep in touch."

"Unless someone told them you'd go there today."

"Who'd do that?"

"I don't know."

"I don't, either."

Pa swallowed a piece of orange. "In that case, it seems *quite* peculiar that they'd show up there and then, doesn't it?"

"I guess so. Miss Madge Hawley said they wanted to see where Regina worked."

"They were in her wedding procession, right?" said Pa.

"No. They just attended. I think they're Robert's relations, not Regina's. I think the only relatives Regina has—well, that she's willing to acknowledge—are her aunt and uncle."

"Wonder why they wanted to see where Regina worked."

"Beats me. They made it clear they don't read for fun. Or probably for anything else."

"What do they do to pass the time?" Pa said, probably wondering, as did I, how a person could live for years and not read anything except periodicals.

"I have no idea. Maybe they read movie magazines. Anyhow, Mr. Prophet seems to think their behavior is not merely strange, but that there's something dodgy about the three girls."

"Huh. That sounds odd," said Pa, frowning.

"I think so, too."

We just looked at each other for a couple of seconds. I didn't know what to say, and Pa seemed to suffer from the same problem as regarded me. Then he said, "But if you're not too tired from library-ing and socializing, want to go with you-know-who and me for a w-a-l-k?"

By that time in his doggy life, Spike could spell almost as well as I could. Instantly he began jumping up and down and letting out joyful yips. Then he ran to the service porch where his leash hung.

"We'll figure out another word to use," Pa said.

"I don't think it will matter. Anytime anyone says, 'Do you want to go,' Spike can figure out the ending."

"Smart dog."

"Yes, he is. Let me change into something more comfy and put on my walking shoes, and I'll be right with you."

"I'll try to keep Spike from eating the leash while you change."

"I'll hurry."

So I hurried, and then Pa, Spike and I took a nice walk around the neighborhood. The July day had turned from hot to breezy and mild. The pepper trees lining both sides of Marengo Avenue had grown into a canopy over the street. The trees had tiny greenish-white flowers on them. The red berries would grow in the autumn. I loved the trees, but they were sure messy. Walking during the fall and winter months could be a crunchy experience.

Not that day. That day was perfect. Spike thought so, too. He busied himself sniffing bushes and rocks and people's fences, and marking them as his from beginning to end.

Only then did it occur to me that Spike might have a problem after Sam and I married. He'd always have a home, but which home? Would he move across the street and live with Sam and me (and Mr. Prophet a whole lot of the time)? Or would Ma, Pa and Vi want him to remain in their bungalow? I'd originally procured him for my late husband, but now he was a certified family pet, and he definitely was a comfort to Pa when everyone else in the house had gone to work.

But what would I do without Spike? I couldn't bear the notion of not having my dog live with me. Then again, it was probably more important for Pa to have Spike as a companion.

Bother. Why did I seem always to borrow trouble?

Spike didn't have a clue about my muddled thoughts. He trotted along, tail in the air and wagging, nose to the ground, and often with one of his hind legs lifting as he watered a plant here or there. We had a good time.

When we got home again, Pa chose *The Long, Long Trail* from the books on the dining-room hutch, then went into the living room to read it. I decided I'd wasted enough of the day and that sewing would be self-indulgent, so I donned an apron. Then I carpet-swept the living room carpet and the rug in the dining room, dusted the furniture and dust-mopped the floor.

After my chores were done, and I didn't feel guilty about being a slacker any longer, I went through the library books neatly stacked on the dining-room hutch. Then I, too, selected one of them to read. I chose *Carry On, Jeeves*, joined Pa in the living room, and was giggling like mad when Sam, Aunt Vi, and Mr. Prophet strolled into the house via the front door. Again, Sam carried a cardboard box containing something that smelled heavenly.

Spike had already raced over to greet the incomers, so Pa and I joined him. Sam carried the cardboard box into the kitchen, so I relieved my wonderful aunt of her hat and handbag and went to set them neatly at the bottom of the stairs to her room.

"Thank you, Daisy," she said as she followed Sam into the kitchen.

"You're welcome," I said, and began to walk through to the kitchen only to encounter Sam—a rather large obstacle—and Mr. Prophet standing at the doorway I'd intended to use.

"Hey, Sam," I said cheerfully.

Looking serious and worried, Sam said, "Come on outside with Lou and me for a minute, Daisy."

And darned if he didn't take my arm and steer me down the hall to the dining room and out the side door to the porch. We'd put pots of flowers out there, including an amazing one in the shape of a dachshund, painted white with bright flowers. Mrs. Pinkerton had given it to me after I'd been hit by a car on New Year's Day. The thing was perfectly frightful by itself, but I'd planted some trailing lantana in it, and the plant's flowery stems pretty much covered up the hideous painted blunders.

When we were outside and Sam had carefully shut the doors

leading into the house, I said, "What's the matter, Sam? Why do you look so somber?"

"Lou said the Hawley twins and that other female—Jarvis?"

"Jervis. Alma Jervis," I said.

"Whoever she is. Anyhow, Lou said those three were at the library when the two of you got there."

I glanced at Mr. Prophet, who was leaning against the porch wall and rolling himself a quirley. That's a cigarette, in case I forgot to mention it before. He was considerate about his nasty habit. He never smoked inside our house, which I appreciated because the smoke got into the fabric of the furniture and made it stink. He gave me a curt nod before sticking the coffin nail in his mouth and snapping a wooden match against a gnarled thumb's nail to light it.

"Yes. They were there. Miss Jervis isn't awfully nice, but the Hawley sisters seemed to be doing pretty well, considering Madge lost a fiancé only a couple of weeks ago."

"That's what Lou told me. Listen, Daisy, I don't know what's going on. So far, the Pasadena Police Department is stumped as to how Darlington got all those things stuffed down his throat. All we know is that it would have taken more than one person to do it, and he had an unsavory reputation. I don't like the way those females keep showing up where you are."

"But..."

"Told her already. There's somethin' weird about 'em," said Mr. Prophet.

"I agree with you, especially about Alma Jervis, but how could they know I'd be going to the library today? Or to Bullock's downtown yesterday?"

"I have no idea," said Sam. "But I want you to tell me if you see them again. All right?"

"Sure. I can do that." We all three stood there for a couple of seconds as I pondered Madge and DeeDee Hawley and Miss Alma Jervis.

"Alma Jervis reminds me of one of the witches in Macbeth," I said.

"Did the witches kill anybody?" asked Mr. Prophet.

"Did you ever have to read *Macbeth* or see a production of it?" I asked him back.

"Saw the play once in San Francisco."

"Wow. You really got around, didn't you?" I said, marveling. I swear, the man must have been in his late seventies or early eighties, but he was still ramrod-straight, if a little contorted by the rheumatics, but he'd pretty much gone everywhere and done everything in his misspent life.

"Yeah. I got around a lot."

"Then you know the witches didn't kill anyone."

"Those gals ain't the witches in *Macbeth*, and they're up to no good. I kin feel it, and I've lived long enough and hard enough to trust my feelings."

"One of my all-time favorite lines comes from that play," I said with total irrelevance. "'Light thickens, and the crow makes wings to the rooky wood.' I just love that line."

"Good to know," said Sam sardonically. "I'll have it engraved on something for you. What I want you to do now is let me know if you see any or all of those women anywhere else you go. If they start turning up everywhere you are, I *really* want to know about it."

"You make them sound sinister," I said, shivering slightly, and not from the cold, because there wasn't any.

"They might well *be* sinister. Given the nature of the late Cecil Darlington, it wouldn't surprise me much if we find out a herd of wild women conspired to kill him."

"A herd of wild women?" I repeated in awe and wonder. "You've been spending too much time with Mr. Prophet. I can see *him* being surrounded by a herd of wild women angry enough to do him in, but Cecil Darlington was in his early twenties, wasn't he?"

"Hey," said Mr. Prophet. "That herd o' wild women after me didn't have killin' on their mind." He gave me one of his more fiendish grins. "They were only out for a bit o' fun."

"Good Lord," I muttered. "Very well, Sam. I'll let you know if they show up in my vicinity again."

"Good. Thank you, Daisy." After shooting Mr. Prophet a glance, he said softly, "This might only be one of Lou's fancies, but humor us, all right?"

"All right. I'll humor you."

"Good." He stooped to kiss me on the cheek then opened the door so we could go inside the house.

Before we trekked indoors, I noticed Mr. Prophet drop his cigarette on the ground, mash it with his peg, then stoop to pick it up. Wow. Somehow, somewhere, the man had been trained not to litter. I was impressed.

He saw my impressedness and grinned again, evilly. "I been taught manners, Miss Daisy. Never had to use 'em much until I came to this stuffy damned place."

Before I could react to his condemnatory statement about my beloved Pasadena, Sam shoved me into the house. He was chuckling, blast him.

The rest of the evening passed peacefully. Vi'd prepared chicken croquettes with a nice cream sauce, peas, carrots, and a delicious apple salad. Ever since I'd been forced against my will to teach a cooking class to needy immigrant ladies at the Salvation Army, I'd held a minor grudge against croquettes. That's because I'd had to make so many for us to eat at home before daring to attempt to teach other women the art of the croquette. I'm sure it comes as no surprise to anyone that Vi's croquettes were miles and miles better than any croquette I'd ever made.

I didn't allow myself to become discouraged about my lack of domestic usefulness, however. After all, I'd cleaned the house before everyone except Pa had come home, so I couldn't accuse myself of slothfulness.

After dinner, Harold called. I was so happy it was he and not his mother or another wealthy woman in distress about one thing or another, he accused me of sounding perky. Harold didn't care for perkiness in people, believing most of the time, if a person acted perky, he or she was... well, acting.

"I'm not perky," I told him. "I'm just glad it's you and not your mother or another rich woman in misery."

"I can understand that. It's about time they all understood you actually have a life outside of spiritualism and my mother's daft needs."

"Your mother's needs aren't entirely daft," I said in defense of Mrs. P, who hadn't shrieked at me for at least a couple of weeks by then. Well, except for the day after that ghastly séance.

"Nertz to that," said Mrs. P's loyal son. "Are you free to go to Bullock's again on Thursday? I want to get your flatware patterns chosen and get you on the register for dining implements. Then we'll have to select glassware and stemware."

"Um..." I contemplated Harold's question. The notion of another drive in his magnificent new automobile appealed, but the notion of trudging all over that huge store and trying to decide upon one pattern of flatware *or* glassware made my feet hurt. And my head, too.

"Um, what?" said Harold, impatient.

"Um, I don't suppose you could select the patterns for me, could you? I chose the china. You're good at this picking stuff. You'll know better than I what look will look good with both sets."

"Daisy Gumm Majesty, a person would think you had no interest in your own wedding!"

"I do have an interest in it, but I've got to go to that wretched exercise class tomorrow, choir practice is Thursday night, and a luncheon on Friday. If I go to Bullock's during the day Thursday, I'll be dead from exhaustion by the time choir practice starts."

"You and that stupid church," muttered Harold. "You're as bad as Del and his precious Saint Andrews. If Saint Andrews knew about Del and me, poor Del would be barred from the lousy church's doors. They'd probably have him arrested. And me, too."

"That's so unfair."

"Tell it to God."

"It's not God who makes up those stupid rules. It's men claiming to speak for God."

"Whatever you say."

"You know, Harold," I said tentatively, afraid he'd get mad at me, "I honestly wouldn't mind if you chose a couple of—or three or four, maybe—patterns of flatware and glassware, and just let me choose among the few you choose. I mean, I don't think flatware and glassware are as... um... personal and important as, say, the china. Everybody notices the china. People just use the flatware to eat with and they drink from the glasses, you know?" My voice had begun to run out of steam toward the end of the last sentence.

"Daisy, you're terrible."

"Am not."

TWENTY-FOUR

After a significant pause, during which my heart beat so hard, I feared I'd developed Pa's heart condition, Harold said, "Actually, that's not a bad idea. I have costume fittings for a couple of flickers coming up, so I'm busy. I also have a pretty good idea about which silver and glassware will go well with both of your china patterns."

After giving one ecstatic leap, my heart resumed its normal beat.

"Oh, Harold, that would be so nice of you!" Something else occurred to me. "Speaking of fittings, I have to finish all the dresses for my own bridal party. That's going to take some time."

"Oh, you can do that in a couple of days," Harold said. "I know you. You'll whip up dresses for the bridesmaids and your sister and the mother-of-the bride gown and a gown for your marvelous aunt, and have time left over to make a tuxedo for Spike."

"I'd never make Spike wear a tuxedo! Besides, he's already wearing black."

"True. Anyway, I guess I can help you out without dragging us both back to Bullock's."

"Thanks, Harold. I appreciate you *so* much for choosing some flatware and glassware patterns."

"You'll still have to make the final decisions," he said firmly.

"I don't mind. I just... can't quite face selecting from several hundred flatware and glassware designs. When I had to choose from all those china patterns, I nearly lost my mind—"

"What little is left of it," said Harold, rudely interrupting.

"Applesauce. I'm not your ordinary rich society debutante, you know, Harold Kincaid. I have a job and work for a living."

"All right, all right. But be prepared. I'll show up at your house at seven-thirty tomorrow evening."

"That soon?" I asked, confused—which was becoming my normal state.

"Sure. I know which ones you'd like and which will go with the china patterns you selected."

"You knew which china patterns I'd like, too, because you had Mrs. Grundy set out place settings for me to look at!"

"Her name is Mrs. Maxwell, and yes. China was the most important decision. Tomorrow at seven-thirty. Be home. I'll be there bearing flatware and glassware. Or at least photos thereof."

"Thank you, Harold," I said humbly. "I truly appreciate this."

"As well you should. You're welcome. And here comes Roy with dinner. See you tomorrow."

"Thanks again, Harold," I said as the receiver on his end of the wire clicked into its cradle.

I felt like I'd dodged a bullet after Harold's call. If I were actually a perky person, I might have jumped up and down and clapped or something. Instead, I knelt to give Spike a thorough petting. Spike had nothing against perkiness.

On Wednesday morning, after I'd washed up the breakfast dishes, Pa and I took Spike for the requisite first walk of the day. Spike appreciated it. So did Pa and I.

When we got home, I decided it would be a good time to wash some windows. So I did, starting with the living room. I got through the dining room before I had to put the vinegar and rags away and have a bite to eat before going to the exercise class.

"Just a light lunch," I told Pa. "I don't want to throw up during the exercise class."

"That sounds reasonable," Pa said.

So my wonderful father made one and a half chicken sandwiches—the half was mine—for the two of us, using the chicken Vi hadn't needed for her croquettes. I always loved when my father made the sandwiches because I couldn't cut the bread straight. If I tried to cut a slice of bread, it would be bigger on one side or the other, or the bottom would peter out into a wafer-thin sliver of bread that wouldn't hold a feather, much less a piece of chicken with mayonnaise and lettuce and tomatoes.

"So you're going to your exercise class at one?" Pa asked as we sat at the kitchen table munching on chicken sandwiches and leftover apple salad Vi'd stored in the Frigidaire from the night before.

Hmmm. Maybe I could make apple salad. Couldn't be *too* hard, could it? It didn't require anything to be cooked, so I couldn't burn it if I tried. And, except for bread, I could slice and chop things, because Vi had taught me, putting heavy emphasis on always having my knives sharp. Not even I could mess up an apple salad. Probably.

"Daisy?" said Pa. "You daydreaming about Sam or something?"

I jumped slightly in my chair. "Oh. I'm sorry, Pa. No. I was actually thinking I could probably fix an apple salad without killing myself or anyone else, as long as I held the knife properly. And yes, I'm going to the exercise class. For some reason unknown to me, Lucy Zollinger says she needs me there to help her lead the class because she's too shy to do it on her own."

"I'm sure she's telling the truth. I know people who suffer terribly from shyness." He winked at me. "You never did."

"No. That's one problem I've never had."

That salad was *so* good. I took my fork and started spreading it around on my plate to see what was in it. I saw apples, celery, skinny green onions, and... were those walnut pieces? I think they were. So I'd only have to worry about the dressing. Mayonnaise and... My mind went blank. The salad dressing wasn't made merely with mayonnaise. There was other stuff mixed with the mayonnaise.

And why was I thinking *merely* mayonnaise? I didn't know how to make mayonnaise. I'd watched Vi make it quite often. It required several minutes of whipping with a whisk, and it contained eggs. Or maybe just egg yolks. And... lemon juice, I think. Unless it was vinegar. What else? Piddle, I couldn't remember.

"You off in dreamland again?" asked Pa mildly.

"Oh! Sorry. No, I was wondering how to make mayonnaise."

With a lift of an eyebrow and a tilt of his head, Pa said, "I'm sure Vi can write down the recipe for you."

After heaving a deep sigh, I said, "I'm sure she can, too. I'm not sure I can follow the recipe. I'm such a dud in the kitchen."

"You just need to practice," said Pa soothingly.

"That's what Vi's always telling me. That and, 'You only need to concentrate, Daisy.' Well, I've practiced and concentrated, and I still can't cook."

"You have other useful skills."

"Maybe, but I can't, say, sew up a tasty breakfast."

With a chuckle, Pa said, "True, true. But didn't Sam say he aimed to hire Mrs. Rattle to cook and clean for you?"

"I can clean for myself. If she could cook for us, it would be wonderful."

"I'm sure your aunt would love it if you continued to take your meals here," said Pa.

"She probably would, but I'd still feel like an incompetent wastrel."

"Daisy, stop talking about yourself like that," said Pa, sounding almost stern, for him. Pa was probably the world's nicest person, and he didn't sound stern often. I can't imagine how he managed to make Walter, Daphne and me behave during our childhoods, but he'd done it admirably, and almost always without shouting or spanking.

Walter and Daphne are my older siblings, by the way.

"Sorry. Sometimes I just get to feeling useless."

"Nonsense. You have talents some of us will never be able to master."

Nobody'd want to, probably. I didn't say that, because I didn't want to grieve my marvelous father. With a sigh, I took my last bite of apple salad feeling wistful and inept, and began gathering up the dishes to wash.

"I'll take care of the dishes, sweetheart," said Pa. "You get ready for your class."

"Thanks, Pa. Oh! I almost forgot. Harold will be here at seven-thirty this evening. He's going to bring pictures of silverware and glassware patterns, bless him. That way, I won't have to go to Bullock's with him tomorrow and wear myself out before choir practice."

"Sounds good to me."

"Me, too. I couldn't even bear the thought of another trek to Bullock's."

Pa smiled and finished clearing the table. Then, as I went to my bedroom to change for the exercise class, Pa washed the dishes.

It was perhaps silly of me to be surprised when I found not merely Lucy Zollinger, Flossie Buckingham, Miss Betsy Powell, and the rest of our usual exercise group members, but also the two Hawley sisters and Miss Alma Jervis waiting for me when I arrived at the church. Not that I was late. They were early.

Very well, perhaps Mr. Prophet was correct about those three. If they weren't actively malevolent, they were at least creepy. I felt as though they were following me around. Only they always seemed to be where I was going before I got there. Can you anticipate someone around? Oh, dear. I wondered if I should call Sam.

Naw. I'd wait until after the class. Then you bet I'd call him. I wish I hadn't walked to the church from home, because that meant I'd have to walk home again. With those three women stalking me, I was kind of afraid to be alone on the sidewalk.

That was silly. I'd made it here alone, after all.

Maybe. But now they knew I was here. Bother. Oh, but I'd bet Flossie would be glad to drive me home.

Pretending not to be startled to see the threesome, I said, "Good afternoon Miss Hawley, Miss Hawley and Miss Jervis. Good to see you here. Let me introduce you to the rest of the class."

"Thank you," said Madge Hawley. Her two coven members nodded.

Alma Jervis, I noticed, wore a loose, long-sleeved shirt with her athletic togs. Didn't want anyone to see those bruises, I opined to myself. She also wore athletic socks that came up to her knees, and her gym slip's hem fell below the knee. All three women wore sleeker gym costumes than the rest of us. Mine were the puffy variety girls wore at the high school I'd attended. These three had probably gone to an expensive, snobby private school.

Shame on me!

After I'd introduced everyone, I said, "Just stand any old place. Stay far enough apart that you won't strike each other when we do lunges, and we'll get this show on the road."

We exercised to Miss Betsy Powell's radio, which she'd already tuned to a station that played the latest hit tunes along with some older melodies. A faithful member of our exercise class, in spite of a few unfortunate incidents during our very first class meeting, she brought that radio with her every week and then took it home again. It was a superior radio, an RCA Radiola, and I do believe it had originally been stolen, but not by Miss Powell, so I personally had no objection to her keeping it. Nice of me, eh?

It was probably unkind, but I was pleased to see the Hawley sisters and Miss Jervis gasp for breath and sweat in the middle of our program when we undertook some of the more strenuous exercises. Even our most strenuous exercises weren't very, however. I thought these women played tennis. If they played tennis, a few stretching exercises shouldn't knock the wind out of them, should they? Maybe they didn't play tennis, but only belonged to the Pasadena Golf and Tennis Club in order to socialize. I know the place had get-togethers, dances, parties and the like.

At the end of approximately forty-five minutes, I said, "All right. Let's do some simple stretches to cool down some."

We did simple stretches and cooled down some, although not much, the day being warm.

My three shadowers came up to speak with me after the class. Lucy smiled at them. I would have, too, except I saw Flossie grabbing her bag into which she'd flung her towel—we all brought towels to wipe away perspiration should there be any—and I startled her and the other women nearly to death by lunging after her and grabbing her arm. She squeaked in surprise.

"I'm so sorry, Flossie, but could you drive me home?"

"Sure! Happy to," said the ever-helpful Flossie. She joined Lucy, the three oddities and me at the front of the fellowship hall, where we always held our exercise class. Miss Betsy Powell unplugged her radio and waved as she carried it off. I waved after her.

Miss Betsy Powell had proven problematical over the years, but at least I more or less knew what to expect from her. I hadn't a clue about these three adherents. If that's what they were.

I decided to ask.

TWENTY-FIVE

"My goodness, but I seem to see the three of you everywhere I go these days," I said, smiling up a storm so as not to let on that they made me nervous.

As Miss DeeDee Hawley and Miss Alma Jervis gazed blankly at me, Miss Madge Hawley smiled a happy smile. "We were intrigued when we met you in the library and you told us about this class, so we decided to visit."

"And you were at the library only because you wanted to see where Regina Browning worked?" I asked, trying not to sound suspicious.

"Of course," said Madge, still smiling.

"And you were at Bullock's in order to remove your name from the bridal register?"

"Yes," said Madge, her smile fading slightly, probably because of her purpose in going to the store.

"Why else would we be there?" asked Miss Jervis.

"I don't know. That's why I asked."

"Do we bother you?" Miss Jervis asked, her mouth tilting into a line that looked more like a sneer than a smile.

DeeDee elbowed her, but Miss Jervis just rolled her eyes. *She's the one who bothered me most. Miss Jervis, not DeeDee.*

"Yes, actually," I said, opting for honesty. "I met the two Misses Hawley at Regina and Robert's wedding, then saw them again the Saturday after the wedding. I'd never seen you before you were at Bullock's when Harold Kincaid and I were there."

"I was at the wedding, too. I wasn't asked to participate," said Miss Jervis, sounding downright hostile about having been left out of the bridal party.

"I beg your pardon. I neither saw nor met you there," I said with, I believe, becoming friendliness. "And then you three showed up at Bullock's and at the library."

"You're the one who showed up," Miss Jervis observed snidely. "We were already there."

"Yes. That's true," I said. "But it does make me nervous when three people I didn't even know this time two weeks ago seem to appear wherever I'm going to be."

Miss Jervis opened her mouth, probably to say something else nasty, but DeeDee actually kicked her. Miss Jervis said, "Ow," and turned to scowl at DeeDee.

This gave Madge the chance to say, "We don't mean to make you uncomfortable. It was pure chance we met at Bullock's and the library. And when you mentioned this class, we thought it might be fun to attend."

"I see. Did you have fun? I never do."

"Daisy!" said Flossie and Lucy together.

"Well, I don't," I said. I said it with a smile, though.

"No," said Miss Jervis, stepping away from DeeDee, I guess in case DeeDee decided to punch her next time.

"Well, then. See you somewhere else soon, I reckon." My smile was so broad, my cheeks felt as if they were going to crack.

"I reckon," snarled Miss Jervis through her sneer.

"Thanks for letting us come!" said a perky Madge. Only then did I understand why Harold didn't care for that word. Madge was clearly acting. She didn't want to be at that class any more than Miss Jervis or I did.

"Right. Bye," I said as the three turned and stalked off.

"Daisy!" whispered Lucy. "Why were you so rude to those young women?"

"Because they give me the creeping willies. Everywhere I go, they're already there. *Everywhere*. I don't know why, but I do know two—well, according to Miss Jervis, all three of them—were at the wedding where that young man was murdered. The two who look kind of alike. They're the Hawley twins. The other one, Miss Alma Jervis, might have been at the wedding, but I didn't see her there. In fact, she didn't show up in my life until two Mondays after the murder. She had bruises all up and down her arm and a ring finger that looks as if someone had ripped a ring therefrom."

"My goodness!" said Lucy.

"It's the truth. I'd never met any of them before, and now it seems as if I'll never stop seeing them, whether I want to or not. Mr. Prophet and Sam think they're following me around for some fell purpose."

"Golly, really?" said Flossie.

"Good heavens!" said Lucy.

"Yes. I can't imagine why they'd want to do anything to me. I didn't witness anything the day of the wedding or afterward, except when Sam questioned them. The Jervis wench reminds me of one of Macbeth's three witches, though."

"Is that why you wanted me to drive you home?" asked Flossie with sudden understanding.

"Yes. I know I only live a few blocks down the street, but I didn't want to walk that stretch by myself. Marengo is such a shady, private street in some ways."

"Oh, Daisy!" said Flossie. She gave me a hug, which was extremely kind of her under the current perspirational circumstances. "I'll always be available if you need me. Or Johnny will be. And Sam and Mr. Prophet will always guard you if you need guarding."

"That's really weird, Daisy," said Lucy. "I wondered why those three suddenly showed up today. Do you think they were really interested in the exercise class?" She said it doubtfully.

"I don't know, Lucy, although I doubt it. I'm just nervous about them. That Jervis creature actually frightens me."

"I don't blame you," said Lucy. "She gave me the creeps."

"Come on, Daisy. Let's get you home," said the marvelous Flossie.

"See you tomorrow night?" asked Lucy, as if she feared I might shy away from choir practice because of the three women.

"Yes, indeed," I told her. "I'll be there with bells on."

"You can leave the bells at home," said Lucy with a giggle.

"If you insist," I said.

Flossie not only drove me home, but she accompanied me from the curb in front of our house to the front porch. I was reaching for my key—we never used to need keys—when the door opened. I probably jumped a foot and a half, the notion of the three witches having made it to my home before me having pounced into my addled brain.

"They show up?" asked Mr. Prophet, who'd opened the door. As usual, when he spoke to me, he frowned, but his frown tipped upside down when he saw Flossie. "How-do, Mrs. Buckingham. Thanks for bringin' our Miss Daisy home."

"Of course. I'm always happy to help out," said Flossie, meaning it.

"Well?" said Mr. Prophet. "Did they show up?"

"Yes," I said to him.

He said, "Huh," reminding me of Sam.

Flossie and I entered the house as Mr. Prophet stepped aside to let us in. He closed the door behind us.

"Want to come in for some water or orange juice or something?" I asked Flossie. "Something wet to make up for the perspiration?"

"I didn't perspire much. The exercises aren't that strenuous. I get a better workout chasing Billy around the house."

"I'm sure you do. And I agree. I get more exercise walking Spike. Those three oddballs made me sweat more than the stretches, although they were all three dripping. I thought they played tennis, but I guess they don't."

"Why'd you think they played tennis?" asked Mr. Prophet. Flossie had opened her mouth, probably to ask the same question.

"Because the Hawley sisters told me they met Mr. Cecil Darlington at a dance at the Pasadena Golf and Tennis Club."

"Huh," said Mr. Prophet.

"Hmmm," said Flossie.

"I'll walk Mrs. Buckingham out to her buggy, Miss Daisy. You go call Sam. He's pretty much expecting your call."

"Why?" I asked, surprised.

"Tell you later," said he.

"Bother."

But, as Mr. Prophet walked Flossie out to her car, I dutifully called Sam at the Pasadena Police Department.

When the switchboard operator connected my call to Sam's desk and he answered, I said, "Mr. Prophet said you're expecting me to telephone you and tell you those three young women showed up at the exercise class."

"And did they?"

"Yes."

"Huh," said Sam.

"Why were you expecting this call from me?" I asked, wildly curious.

"Tell you later," said Sam, and he hung up the receiver on his end.

Well!

"I did some checking on the Hawley sisters and Miss Jervis," said Sam at dinner that evening. As soon as I'd made it home securely, and after seeing Flossie to her and Johnny's old Model-T Ford, Mr. Prophet had left the house, probably so he wouldn't have to listen to me pester him about the three witches.

"Are those the names of the three girls who've been showing up everywhere Daisy goes?" asked Pa, whom I'd regaled with my tale about being stalked by the strange threesome.

"Yes," I said.

"Three girls show up everywhere you go?" said Ma, bewildered.

"Yes."

"How odd," said Aunt Vi.

"It's unnerving," I said.

"Yes, well, it turns out both Miss Madge Hawley and Miss Alma Jervis believed they were engaged to marry Mr. Cecil Darlington," said Sam.

"What?" I said, fairly stunned.

"You heard me," said Sam.

"Ya know, I only saw that feller after he was dead, but I didn't see the attraction," said Mr. Prophet. "Seemed like a scrawny lad, and pasty-faced, to boot."

"When I first saw him, his face was blue, and his tongue was sticking out of his mouth," I said. Then I shuddered, remembering.

"Daisy!" said my mother.

"Well, it's true," I said.

Sam sat next to me at the dinner table, and I felt his shoulders shake. When I looked at him, I saw he was trying not to laugh.

"I didn't think it was funny at the time," I said sulkily. "At the time, it was awful."

"Sorry, sweetheart," said Sam. "But you and Lou should take your show to Vaudeville."

"There's a thought," said Mr. Prophet, tipping me a wink. "Probably make lots o' money if we work up some comedy routines. Only I don't think Miss Daisy gets the jokes half the time."

"You're right," I snapped. "So, Madge and Alma were both engaged to the same man, and he's the one who ended up dead, with an elaborate engagement ring having been shoved down his throat. Followed by a tennis ball."

"Correct," said Sam.

"And some filmy fabric," added Mr. Prophet.

"Oh, that's right," I said. "I forgot about the filmy cloth."

"And now Miss Hawley and Miss Jervis and another person named Hawley are following you around?" said Ma, trying desperately to grasp the situation. She saw no humor in it at all. Neither did I, truth to tell.

"To be fair, they seem to be everywhere I'm going before I get there," I said, wanting to be perfectly clear.

"How do they know where you're going?" asked Ma.

"I have absolutely no idea," I told her.

Only then did I realize Pa was holding up his hand as if he were a kid in a school class. I looked at him.

"I think," said he, "Sam was going to explain the matter when he was interrupted."

"True," said Sam. "Want me to continue?" He looked at me. *Me!* As if I were the only one who'd said anything to stop the flow of his explanation.

Rather than get huffy, I said mildly, "Yes, please." Then I looked across the table at Mr. Prophet and stuck my tongue out at him. He returned the favor.

My mother said, "You two are awful!" At least I wasn't alone in her chastisement that time.

I swear, though, you'd think we were in the second grade!

TWENTY-SIX

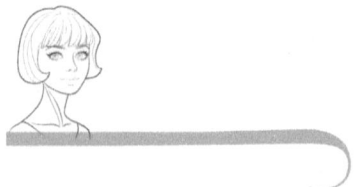

"Very well," said Sam after everyone had settled down again and we'd resumed eating Vi's tasty salmagundi salad, which was a perfect meal on a warm evening, "Miss Jervis and Miss Madge Hawley both believed themselves to be engaged to Mr. Cecil Darlington who, as I believe you mentioned, Daisy, had an unsavory reputation for being a..."

While Sam searched for an appropriate word, I plopped in, "Cad."

"Daisy!" said Ma.

"Actually, Peggy," said Sam. "Daisy's correct. He had a reputation as a cad and a fellow who cared only about his own pleasure."

"Sounds pretty good to me," muttered Mr. Prophet.

With a chuckle, Sam said, "Yes, I suppose so, but this is Pasadena in the twentieth century, not the Old West in the nineteenth."

"Indeed," I said, squinting at the old villain. Mr. Prophet, I mean, not Sam. "Pasadena is a civilized city. It's not like Tucson in *your* day."

Mr. Prophet shook his head sadly. "Yeah, that's the truth."

I pinched my lips together so as not to smile. Nobody else bothered to contain their mirth.

"Ahem. To get back to the subject," said Sam, "a check of local jewelry stores found two rings, precisely the same—just like the one Dr. Benjamin found in the dead man's stomach—were purchased by Mr. Darlington on the same day—May fifteenth of this year—from Arnold's Jewelers."

"Interesting," I said. "That looked like a really expensive ring, even if it was too gaudy for my taste."

"It was expensive," said Sam. "What's even more interesting is that Mr. Darlington requested Arnold's make paste copies of them that same day. He picked up the paste ones and the real ones the week after the order was placed."

"How many fakes did he ask them to make?" I asked, thinking Mr. Darlington was not only a cad, but nuts to boot.

"Three."

"*Three?*" I exclaimed. "But why would any man, even a lout, want five engagement rings?"

"I think Sam was going to tell us, Daisy," said Pa, grinning at me.

I got the hint, but I asked, "Was that a genuine diamond ring in his stomach?" because this story fascinated me.

"Oh, yes. I would have told you if it was paste," said Sam, whose family had dealt in precious gems for probably a hundred and fifty years.

"Did he give the copies to other women?" asked Mr. Prophet, who seemed to be taking a renewed interest in the conversation.

"Don't know," said Sam. "Also don't know if he gave both Miss Hawley and Miss Jervis genuine diamond rings, or if he gave the Hawley woman genuine diamonds and Jervis the fake one, or vice versa. I didn't think to ask to see her ring when I was questioning her. It didn't seem relevant at the time."

After mulling over the matter for a second or two, I said, "Hmmm. If he gave Alma Jervis a fake diamond ring, I guess I can understand her being mad at Madge Hawley, although it was Cecil's fault. But how could she know?"

"Beats me," said Sam. "Lou said her ring finger looked bruised."

"Yes," I agreed. "She had bruises on her arm and her ring finger looked as if a ring had been painfully removed therefrom."

I took another bite of my tasty salad, then noticed something distinctive about this particular salmagundi salad that made it different from other salmagundi salads Vi had served us on other warm evenings. "There's something special in this salad, Vi. It's not just chicken and eggs and bacon. It's... special. And really good."

"I wondered if anyone would notice," said Vi, who seemed pleased. "Yes, Daisy, you are correct. There's a little chopped salami in this salmagundi salad. I thought about tossing in some chopped olives, too, but didn't feel like pitting them."

"Salami!" Ma said with alarm. "I thought she was a woman in the Bible."

"That's Salome, Ma," I said, grinning—well, we all were, except Ma, who still appeared horrified. "This is salami. Totally different. Salome's the one who danced for Herod and got John the Baptist's severed head on a silver platter for her efforts."

"Good Lord!" said Ma. "I don't think you should talk about such things at the dinner table, Daisy."

"Well, you asked. Or maybe you didn't. You thought Salome and salami were the same things, and I only pointed out the difference."

"In a rather graphic manner," said Ma, indignantly.

I shrugged.

"Dang. I gotta read me some of the Bible," muttered Mr. Prophet.

Sam cleared his throat and then spoke rather loudly. "Yes. Salami is a type of sausage. It's a hard Italian sausage," said Sam with justifiable pride. "I think Jews perfected pastrami, but salami is Italian."

"What's pastrami?" asked Ma in a weak voice.

"It's cured meat. It's not hard, like salami," said Sam. "It's more like roast beef, if you slice it thin, only it's tastier than plain roast beef."

"Jorgensen's has pastrami as well as salami, if you'd like to try pastrami one of these days, Peggy," said a happy Vi. She just loved introducing the family to new foodstuffs. New to our family, I mean. Clearly, people had been eating salami and pastrami for... well, probably centuries. Just not us folks on the west coast of the United States. Vi had introduced the family to chorizo sausage, which is a Mexican invention, a year or so earlier, and my very own Sam had introduced the family to real, honest-to-goodness Italian red sauce.

"Does salami taste like pastrami?"

"No," said Sam. "Pastrami is delicious, but it's different from salami."

"What does it look like? The salami, I mean," asked Ma, peering into her salad bowl, as if trying to find an interloping bite of salami.

"It's the dark meat that isn't bacon, Ma," I said in an attempt to help her out. "It's spicy. Not hot-spicy, but interesting-spicy."

My mother looked at me as if I'd lost my mind.

"Daisy's right, Peggy." Darned if Vi didn't reach into her own salad bowl and pluck a piece of chopped salami out and show it to my mother. "This is the salami. I'm surprised you didn't notice it before. You usually won't eat anything the least bit unusual."

"I didn't know it was unusual until Daisy said something," said Ma. Now she sounded a trifle peeved.

"Nertz, Ma. If you didn't even notice it, you liked it," I said.

After tilting her head to one side and thinking about it for a few seconds, Ma, a scrupulously fair woman, said, "I suppose you're right, Daisy." To Vi, she said, "I'm sorry, Vi. I'm not an adventurous diner, as you well know by this time."

"My goodness, I certainly do," said Vi with a laugh.

We all went back to munching our salads. To Sam, I said, "Sorry I interrupted, Sam."

"That's all right. Gave me time to eat instead of talk."

"But I still don't know why those three women anticipate my every move and show up wherever I'm going before I get there."

Holding up a finger, Sam swallowed and said, "We may have an answer to that question, too."

"Good grief, really?"

"Yes. Possibly." He hesitated, as if he wasn't sure he should go on.

I didn't have his qualms. "Well? Tell us. Please."

"You won't like it."

"How come?"

"Because it involves Pudge Wilson."

"*Pudge?*" I cried. "What's Pudge got against me?"

"Not a thing," said Sam. "As far as I know, he still adores you from afar."

Pudge Wilson was the scion of the Wilson family, who lived just north of my parents' bungalow. They're the ones who owned Samson, the cat Spike liked to chase. Pudge was about twelve years old by this time, I guess, and he'd been sweet on me for years. And nobody knows why anyone decided to call him Pudge, because he's as big around as a pencil.

"What does he have to do with the three witches, then?" I demanded.

"Daisy," said Ma.

"They scare me, Ma," I told my mother to keep her from scolding me. "It's unnerving to see the three of them staring at me every time I turn around." Turning to Sam, I said, "What about Pudge?"

"You know he's a Boy Scout."

"Yes, of course. He tries to get his good deed out of the way early in the morning, so he can have the rest of his day to himself."

"He the one who makes the gawd-awful noise on that bugle?" asked Mr. Prophet, who had darned near shot Pudge once when Pudge had decided to practice his bugle-playing without warning. I think that, at the time, Mr. Prophet thought we were under attack by savages. To give him his due, Pudge's bugle-playing had been mighty rough at the time.

"He's improving," I said in Pudge's defense.

"Thank God," said Mr. Prophet, sounding not the least bit reverent.

"Anyway," said Sam, loudly, "Pudge is in the same Boy Scout troop as a kid named Reginald Jervis. Reginald has an older sister named Alma. Reginald's cousin, Jeffrey Jervis, is the leader of the scout troop."

I gasped.

"It seems Pudge likes to talk about you, Daisy, and his pal Reginald is quite interested."

"So Reginald is the one who snitches to his sister or maybe his cousin on my every movement, and whichever one it is gets his information from Pudge? That's incredible!" So shocked was I, I could only stare at Sam for a second or three. Then I got angry. "Darn Pudge Wilson!"

"Won't get an argument from me," said Mr. Prophet, who'd never forgiven Pudge for the bugle incident.

"To be fair, I haven't checked to be certain yet," said Sam. "So don't get mad at Pudge yet. For all we know, Miss Alma Jervis listens in on the scout meetings or asks either Jeffrey or Reginald to find out about you. Or whatever. I don't know yet. All I know for sure is that Pudge Wilson and Reginald Jervis are in the same scout troop, they're good pals, and the troop leader is Jeffrey Jervis, Reginald's cousin. And Alma Jervis is Reginald's sister."

"How old is this Jeffrey character?" I asked, beginning to loathe the entire Jervis clan.

"Jeffrey is twenty years old. He attends Pasadena Community College, and is a member of De Molay."

"What the heck is De Molay?" I asked.

"It's a fraternal service club for fellows from ages twelve to twenty-one. Have you heard of the Masons? Or the Freemasons?"

"I've heard of them. I guess some men like belonging to the Masons, but I don't know anything about them."

"I don't, either, but evidently if a kid wants to belong to the Freemasons when he's an adult, he might join De Molay as a youth. And the Masons are like the Rotarians, Lions, and Kiwanis Clubs. Maybe the Shriners. I think the Shriners are part of the Masonic organization, or an offshoot of the Freemasons, too, although don't quote me on that. Anyhow, De Molay is a service club. Like the Odd Fellows."

A loud guffaw from Mr. Prophet diverted everyone's attention to him. "Don't talk to me about the Odd Fellows," he growled. "I ended up at their so-called Home of Christian Charity after I lost my leg. They were odd, all right, but I can't say as to how Christian they were."

"Yes, I remember," I said. Poor Mr. Prophet. Sam and I had sprung him from the Odd Fellows Home of Christian Charity almost a year ago. "Mr. Brimstone wasn't very nice, and he was supposed to run the place."

Mr. Prophet guffawed.

With a laugh, Sam said, "I think his name was actually Crimstone."

"Brimstone suited him better," I said, feeling snarly on Mr. Prophet's behalf.

"Daisy," said my mother.

"Nertz, Ma. You didn't see that place or meet that awful Brimstone character."

"Let me just say here and now that I'll owe Sam and Miss Daisy for the rest of my life for springing me from that joint. It was awful."

"I got the feeling they didn't like you much, either," I said, trying not to smile at Mr. Prophet.

"I should hope to hell—I mean heck they didn't. Didn't want 'em to."

"You succeeded admirably," said Sam with a big grin. "What a gloomy place that was."

"I'm sorry, Lou," said Pa.

"No worries now, Joe," said Mr. Prophet.

"I'm so sorry you had to endure such an awful experience," said Vi, gazing with sisterly—I hoped—fondness at the wrinkled old reprobate.

Holding up both of his hands, Mr. Prophet said, "Didn't mean to interrupt. Go on with your story, Sam. You say this Jervis kid is in that weird-sounding group and that's why he's leading the scout troop? How come is that?"

"The De Molay organization, as I said, is a service club. The members of De Molay do good works in the community. Leading the scout troop is, I presume, one of Jervis's good deeds."

"Hmmm," I said. "Maybe more people should join it. The world could use more do-gooders in it."

"Mebbe," said Mr. Prophet. "But some folks join them organizations just to make themselves look good."

"You may be right," I said. "What's the Eastern Star Organization? I think Mrs. Bissel is an Eastern Star, but I don't know what that is. It's another... what did you call them? Service clubs?"

"Yes," said Sam.

"It's another service club, I guess. They collect money for various charities, from what I've gathered from Mrs. Bissel. And I think they also offer a yearly scholarship to a deserving girl if she wants to go to college. I'm not positive about that, but I'm pretty sure I heard Mrs. Bissel and Mrs. Hanratty talking about a scholarship fund."

"I think it's another branch of the Freemasons," said Sam, "but don't quote me on that, either. I get all these organizations mixed up. Italian Catholics weren't generally recruited for any of them when I was a kid." His expression was wry.

"Neither were good old Georgia boys," said Mr. Prophet.

"I guess I could have been a Mason," said Pa. "If I'd wanted to be one, but I didn't. All the rituals they go through always seemed kind of silly to me."

"No sillier than some of our church rituals, probably," I said musingly.

My mother said, "Daisy!"

TWENTY-SEVEN

Deciding not to pursue the subject, I asked Sam, "So how do we find out if Pudge is telling either Reginald or Jeffrey Jervis about me? Do we ask Pudge? I don't want him to think I'm mad at him, even if I kind of am."

"If he's the source of information about you, you can bet anything he's not telling anyone out of malice. I think he still wants to marry you."

"He'll have to wait until you croak," I said.

Ma said, "Daisy!"

But Sam, Mr. Prophet and Pa all laughed.

"Isn't the Boy Scout motto 'Be prepared'? Maybe he's preparing a way in advance," opined Sam.

"Or maybe he's preparing your demise," said Mr. Prophet.

Ma didn't "Mr. Prophet" *him*!

"If you're all through with your salads and silly talk," said Aunt Vi, attempting to regain control of the dinner table, "will you please pick up the plates, Daisy, and I'll get dessert."

"Happy to," I said, getting to my feet, glad to oblige even though I didn't think the conversation had been all that silly. Pudge Wilson, of all people. Dear Lord.

"I'm going to dish out dessert in here," said Vi when I set the dinner plates on the draining board of the sink and began rinsing them. "Then you can take them out individually."

"That's fine. What are you making?"

"Hot fudge sundaes."

I turned from rinsing dishes to stare at my aunt. "What in the world is a hot fudge sundae?"

"Your pal Harold told me about them. Hot fudge sundaes are vanilla ice cream served in a fluted dish with hot chocolate sauce poured over them, sprinkled with nuts, and topped with whipped cream. The hot chocolate sauce slightly melts the ice cream, and the ice cream turns the hot chocolate sauce hard. Like fudge."

"Merciful heavens! I've never heard of anything like that before, but it sounds delicious."

"It is," said Vi with a sneaky grin, as if she loved springing new treats on the family. Well, I know she did. "Harold told me there's an ice cream shop in Hollywood called C. C. Brown's. Harold credits Mr. Brown for coming up with the recipe."

"And Mr. Brown just handed out his recipe to Harold Kincaid for the fun of it? I thought chefs and famous cook-type people tried to keep their recipes a secret."

"I sincerely doubt Mr. Brown *gave* Harold the recipe, but Harold is quite resourceful, you know."

Thinking about past escapades I'd shared with Harold, I said, "Yes. He's extremely resourceful."

My mouth watered as I finished rinsing the dishes. Then Vi handed me two fluted glass bowls loaded with vanilla ice cream, hot chocolate sauce, what looked like chopped roasted almonds with a big dollop of whipped cream on top. "Take these to your father and Mr. Prophet," said she.

Although I wasn't sure why Mr. Prophet took precedence over Sam, I did as she'd requested. The folks in the dining room emitted several ooohs and aaahs as I set the magnificent desserts at Pa and Mr. Prophet's places at the table. I turned to go back to the kitchen only to find Vi heading into the dining room with two similar bowls. She set one at Sam's place and one at my mother's, and I felt better about life. So I rejoined her in the kitchen, and she and I each brought out our own hot fudge sundaes. I suppose we could have used a tray and carted them all at once, but this was a weeknight family dinner so we didn't bother.

"Dig in," said Vi happily, demonstrating.

So the rest of us followed her example and dug in.

Oh, my goodness, I don't think I've ever tasted anything so delicious in my entire life! All chitchat around the table ceased as we ate our sundaes.

For the record, my mother only stared at her dessert for a second or two before she took a tentative bite. Then her eyes opened wide, and she became as piggy as the rest of us.

"This is amazing, Vi," I told her between bites. "I'm so glad Harold told you about it."

"Me, too," said Pa. "Harold knows his onions."

"And his ice cream," I said.

Vi only laughed.

"I've never eaten anything like this before, Vi," said Sam. "I'd begun to think all the good recipes in the world originated in France, Italy or New York City, but I see I'm wrong. Again." He added the "again" as an afterthought. He didn't want to be murdered in his fiancée's house, I suspect.

"Harold said this one was invented in Los Angeles at Mr. Brown's ice cream store," said Vi. She was forever showing Sam a thing or two about fabulous cuisines. If a hot fudge sundae fits into the "cuisine" category.

"Glad he's a friend of the family," said Mr. Prophet, scooping out a bite that seemed to have some of everything on it.

"Me, too," I mumbled between bites.

As if someone had choreographed us, we all finished at the same time, sat back in our chairs, and let out fulfilled sighs.

After several silent, satisfied seconds, I said, "Mind if I pick up the dishes and wash them after we've discussed what to do about Pudge? I don't think I can move quite yet."

"Just get him over here to eat one of these things," said Mr. Prophet, gesturing at his empty bowl. "He'll answer all your questions and do anything you tell him to do. Hell... uh, heck, he'll follow you to the ends of the earth if you bribe him with one of these things."

A bevy of startled glances passed from person to person around and across the table—if you know what I mean.

"By golly, you're probably right," I told Mr. Prophet, attempting to straighten in my chair and almost succeeding. I was *so* full of spectacular food.

"What do you call these things again?" asked Mr. Prophet, clicking his spoon against his empty ice-cream bowl.

"Hot fudge sundaes," said Aunt Vi. "Harold told me about them and somehow or other, he got the recipe for the fudge sauce from the fellow who created it."

"Amazing," said Pa.

"Wonderful," said Ma.

"Do you have any ice cream and sauce left?" asked Sam. "If you do, maybe Daisy can go over and ply Pudge with an invitation to try out a new dessert."

"Me?" I asked, considering the state of my over-stuffedness.

"He's madly in love with you," said Sam. "He'll do anything you ask of him."

Squinting slightly at my beloved, I said, "I wouldn't necessarily call Pudge's infatuation being *madly in love*. I'd call it a schoolboy's crush, or something of the sort."

"Whatever you call it, he adores you."

"True," agreed Mr. Prophet. "No accounting for taste."

I gave him the stink-eye, but he only honored me with one of his more devilish grins.

"It doesn't really matter what you call it," said Vi, sounding and looking as satisfied as the rest of the family. And Mr. Prophet. "I don't have any more of the sauce. I can certainly make some more, but I think it would be nicer to invite the entire Wilson family over for a new dessert. Maybe tomorrow? In fact, we can invite them to dinner."

"That's a good idea, if you don't mind," I said. My aunt was such a marvelous person.

"Don't mind at all. I love feeding people. Let me see. It will be a Thursday night. Oh!" She sat up straight in her chair. "You have to go to choir practice tomorrow night, don't you?"

"Yes, but that's not until seven."

"We dine at six," said Vi. "But I don't suppose it matters. You can still go to choir practice, and Sam and Lou can talk to Pudge."

"But I want to know what they say to him," I cried. "And I want to know what he says back!"

"We'll tell you," said Sam.

"Promise? You won't keep anything back?"

"Promise. Joe can sit in on the interrogation to make sure we don't leave anything out when we tell you about it."

"I'll keep 'em honest," said Pa with a wink for me.

"Well..." I didn't like this idea at all. Sam seemed to delight in keeping information from me.

"Daisy," said my mother in her disapproving voice. "You really should trust your father, Sam and Lou to tell you the truth about their discussion, for heaven's sake."

"They've kept important things from me before," I said, noticing my voice had gone a trifle sulky. And then I remembered Harold! "Oh, shoot! Harold's coming over at seven-thirty to show me glassware and silverware patterns! I'd better get the dishes washed and put away, or he'll be here before I finish!"

"I'll help you," said Sam, rising from his place beside me at the table.

"You've had to work all day, Sam Rotondo," said Ma. "It's women's work, and I'll help Daisy."

"Nuts on the 'women's work' notion, Ma," I said, nettled. "You've worked all day, too."

"Daisy!" Now poor Ma sounded shocked.

"You go to the living room and rest, Peggy, Vi and Joe. You, too, Lou. I'll help Daisy with the dishes."

When Sam wanted to, he could sound quite authoritative. He did then.

Therefore, my mother and father rose from the table and set off for the living room.

Vi said, "I'm going up to my room to plan tomorrow's meal. We can't eat only hot fudge sundaes."

Bet I could. I didn't say so.

Vi tapped her chin with a finger. "Perhaps a chicken dish I can cook on the stovetop so I won't have to use the oven and heat the whole house. Or a small ham! I have some wonderful salads that will go perfectly with a cold ham." She wandered stair-wards, thinking about tomorrow's meal. I could hardly think at all, due to today's dinner still resting heavily in my tummy. My aunt was absolutely amazing.

Oddly enough, it was Mr. Prophet who helped Sam and me clear dishes from the table and carry them to the kitchen.

"Thanks, Lou," said Sam.

"Yes. Thank you," I said.

"No bother," said Mr. Prophet. "Ain't like I had anybody to wait on me my whole sorry life. Besides, I want to hear more about what you learned today, Sam."

I stopped dead in my tracks, a bunch of spoons clutched in one hand and a stack of glass bowls in another. "You haven't told me everything?"

"Not yet, but I will," said Sam, eyeing Mr. Prophet with some peevishness. "Cripes, Lou. You know I'll tell you all about it."

"You were going to tell him, but you weren't going to tell me?" I asked in high dudgeon. I finished taking spoons and glasses to the sink and set them down. Then I put the plug in the sink, added some soap powder, and turned on the hot and cold water taps. Bubbles began filling the sink, and I turned to glare at Sam.

"I'll tell you both! Cripes!" said Sam. He went back to the dining room, lifted the tablecloth from the table, took it to the side porch, and shook it out. When he brought it into the kitchen, he was eyeing it closely. "Do you think this thing needs to be washed before you use it again, Daisy?"

He was tall enough and his wingspan was wide enough that he could display the entire tablecloth. I peered at the tablecloth closely. It was pretty stained in spots. "Better put that one in the laundry basket. I can use another one tomorrow. If the Wilsons are coming, we probably ought to use a clean tablecloth anyway."

"Sounds good to me." Sam crumpled up the tablecloth and took it to the laundry basket on the service porch.

"How many o' them things do you have?" asked Mr. Prophet, sounding honestly curious.

"Oh," I said. "Dozens. I make 'em, you know, just like I make everything else. We have enough tablecloths and napkins to set a hundred tables, probably."

"Shoot," said Mr. Prophet.

"Please don't," I said.

"Aw, hell, you spoil all my fun."

"And don't swear."

"Hellkatoot."

"Children, children," said Sam, laughing as he rejoined Mr. Prophet and me in the kitchen. "Let's get these dishes out of the way, and I'll tell you the rest of what I found out."

So as I washed dishes and Sam dried and put them away, Mr. Prophet sat at the kitchen table and waited patiently. It didn't take us long to get the dishes conquered. Sam and I joined Mr. Prophet at the kitchen table when we were finished.

Sam had just finished telling us the tale of Cecil Darlington and his various conquests when a knock came at the door, and Spike tore out of the kitchen, barking madly and heading to the door.

"Harold," I said.

"Good. I want to ask him if he thinks the Darlington story is true or just a bit of braggadocio."

"A bit o' what?"

"Showing off," I told Mr. Prophet. Sam and I went to answer the door as Mr. Prophet veered off to join my parents in the living room. When I glanced into the living room, I saw Ma and Pa both yawning, so I doubted they'd be with us very long. That evening, I mean; not in the overall scheme of things.

The notion of anything bad happening to either one of my parents gave me a sick feeling in my stomach.

Spike hadn't fibbed. Well, I don't suppose dogs ever do, which makes them vastly superior to most of the human beings I've met in my life. Anyhow, it had been Harold who'd knocked at the door. He now stood in the evening light, holding what looked like an entire ream of paper in his hands.

"Evening, folks," said Harold, grinning at Sam and me. There had been a time when Sam had disliked Harold for no good reason, but Harold had always found Sam amusing. Even when I didn't.

"Hey, Harold. Do I have to look through every one of those pieces of paper?"

"Come in, Harold," said Sam. "Pay no attention to Daisy. You're doing her a huge favor, and she shouldn't whine about it."

"I'm not whining!" I said.

"Yes, you were," said Harold, stepping into the house and handing Sam the sheaf of papers. He took off his hat and coat, stooped to pet Spike, regained the papers, greeted my parents and Mr. Prophet, and headed to the dining room table, where the light was better than in the living room.

Because Sam offered no opinion on the matter of glassware or flatware—although he remained by my side through the whole ordeal—he didn't object when I finally selected William Rodgers & Sons' Triumph silver-plated flatware. Selecting glassware was much more difficult, because all the pictures Harold showed me looked as if they were made to hold wine or other spirits.

"You can use these as water glasses, Daisy," he told me, exasperated.

"I'm not accustomed to drinking water out of stemmed glasses. It's not my fault I wasn't born rich, Harold Kincaid."

"All right. You're going to register for this one," he said at last, holding up a sheet of paper with photographs of glassware on it.

So the way things ended up, I'd register for William Rodgers & Sons' Triumph silver-plated flatware and Fostoria's Rose Garland glassware. If people wanted to give us wine glasses, I guess I could just stick 'em in a cupboard. Sam's house across the street had a whole lot of storage space. "And I guess I can get used to drinking water out of a stemmed water glass," I said, feeling numb.

"Of course, you can," said Harold, stacking his papers again and thumping them on the table to get the edges straight. "It's easy."

Then Sam called Mr. Prophet to come to the dining room. My parents had already gone to bed by then.

Once we were all gathered around the table, Sam asked Harold if the rumors he'd heard about the late Mr. Cecil Darlington were true. Harold confirmed them all. Crumb. What a bad man Cecil Darlington had been! Don't tell anybody, but I was glad someone killed him before he could ruin any more young women's lives.

"He was truly awful," Harold confirmed. "I don't know what girls saw in him, although most of the ones he seduced were too young and stupid to know what was happening to them. They had no idea he was using them as tools in a cruel game."

"They were probably young and naïve," said Sam.

"Exactly," Harold said.

"Huh. Never met no females like that in my life," said Mr. Prophet.

"Not even when you were young?" I asked, thinking he must be exaggerating.

"Nope. I was a kid when I went to war, and by the time I got out, I'd already discovered I liked loose women better than tight ones."

"You are impossible, Mr. Lou Prophet!" I declared.

He only winked at me.

"I suspect any of the women you hung around with would have skewered Mr. Cecil Darlington over hot coals and let the buzzards pick at his bones," said Harold.

"Probably," said Mr. Prophet. He sounded reminiscent, the wicked sinner!

Then it was I decided it didn't matter if I told my innermost thoughts, so I said, "I'm glad somebody bumped him off."

"You and a whole lot of other people," said Harold, rising from the table.

"I'm only sorry because I have to find out who did it," said Sam.

"Guess it's your job," said Harold. "I'm kind of sorry, though. His killer deserves a medal."

"Good Lord," I said.

"You know it's true," said Mr. Prophet.

After thinking for about a split-second, I said, "You're right."

Sam, Spike and I walked Harold to the front door and waved him off.

As I locked the door behind Harold, I told Sam, "I didn't have to go through this rigmarole when I married Billy."

"I did when I married Margaret," said Sam. "Only not quite so much of it."

"I'm not sure I like it."

With another chuckle, Sam stooped to kiss my cheek and said, "You'll probably get used to it. Don't forget we're living in what people are beginning to call the 'roaring twenties,' and Harold knows what brides are supposed to 'need' to begin their married lives."

"I hadn't met Harold before I married Billy, and please don't tell Harold, but I'm sort of glad of it. Billy would have pitched a fit about all this 'registering' for china and flatware and glassware and so forth and so on."

With a shrug, Sam said, "Guess I'm used to it. My family owns jewelry stores. Besides, New York is home to the Rockefellers, Astors, Morgans and, according to the *Times*, at least four hundred other too-wealthy people."

"I remember reading about Mrs. Astor's four hundred," I said with a sigh. "But the Gumms and Majestys weren't among them."

"Neither were the Rotondos. We only catered to them."

"Who were the four hundred, anyhow?"

"I don't have a clue."

"I thought you catered to them."

"We did, but their servants did the shopping. Doesn't matter anyway," said Sam. "If you want some regular old stemless glasses, you can always pop into Nelson's Five and Dime and pick some up. Harold doesn't have to know."

"Thanks, Sam. I never imagined a time when I'd be afraid to eat off my own plates and drink out of my own glasses for fear of breaking something that cost somebody else a fortune."

"We can get cheap plates, too, if you want them."

"I love you, Sam," I said, throwing myself at him.

"Think I'm gettin' sick," said Mr. Prophet, turning around.

He needn't have worried. Sam gave me a good hug and a quick kiss, then said, "I love you, too, but now I've gotta go home and get some sleep. Busy day tomorrow. Have to be in court at nine for a preliminary hearing."

"What kind of hearing is that?" I asked, a trifle worried. Sam had been targeted by some pretty nasty people not long back. Well, so had I.

"It's the hearing they have to decide if a crime has been committed."

"Who's the one who committed the supposed crime?"

"Mrs. Gaulding. The lady who shot me."

"Oh, I hope they hang her."

"California uses the electric chair. Besides, she didn't kill me. Anyhow, this isn't that trial. This is the preliminary hearing for her having abetted Percival Petrie and Leo Bannister in kidnapping and smuggling children into the country to act as slaves to perverted men."

"Disgusting people," I muttered. Then I frowned. "Why wasn't I called to testify at this hearing? I was there when the horrid woman shot you and Petrie tripped over my body and fell down the basement stairs."

"You weren't there when they discovered the kids. This is that trial."

Mr. Prophet grimaced. "Wish I'd'a been there. I'd'a shot the whole gang."

"Then I'd have had to arrest you," said Sam.

"You were bleeding on the floor, and I'd never have told on you, Mr. Prophet," I said.

"Thanks, Miss Daisy."

"Cripes," said Sam.

"When's the one for when she shot you scheduled?" I was getting confused.

"Don't know yet."

After heaving a huge sigh, I muttered, "All right."

I felt a little sad when I walked him and Mr. Prophet to the porch steps and couldn't follow him down them and across the street to what was going to be our house soon.

When I considered how evil Mr. Cecil Darlington had been, I sank farther down into the dumps. Spike cheered me nominally when he and I finally got to bed. He never held a grudge against anyone.

TWENTY-EIGHT

Because we were having guests for dinner that night, I spent Thursday morning tidying up the house, dusting, dust-mopping, and completing the washing of windows. Of course, Pa and I took Spike for the requisite walk before I began my marathon cleaning spree. I was in the middle of washing the last windows—those in the kitchen—when the rotten telephone rang. With a sigh, I stepped down from my stool and walked across the room to answer it.

"Gumm-Majesty residence. Mrs. Majesty speaking," said I in my low, soothing spiritualist's voice. As I felt cranky about being interrupted, assuming my image was more of an effort than usual.

"Good morning, Daisy," said a voice I didn't mind hearing. I heaved an internal sigh of relief.

"Good morning, Mrs. Bissel." Mrs. Bissel had always been easier to deal with than Mrs. Pinkerton, mainly because she didn't get into tizzies. Also, she'd given me Spike.

"I understand last Saturday's séance wasn't awfully pleasant, dear," said she.

Shoot, I'd almost forgotten about that. "Yes, indeed. It wasn't. Rolly was a little rough on poor Mr. Darlington."

"Poor Mr. Darlington is undoubtedly burning in hell as we speak, Daisy. Don't waste any sympathy on him. I feel sorry for his mother and all the poor girls he duped, but not him."

I felt my eyes pop wide open. "You know about his philandering ways?" I asked, surprised.

"Oh, of course. The only people who didn't know about his black heart were poor Ethel and the silly girls he fooled."

"My goodness."

"Goodness was a quality distinctly lacking in that young man," said Mrs. Bissel with a sniff. "But that's not why I telephoned, dear. I called to ask if you could hold a séance some upcoming Saturday evening. I know you're busy planning your nuptials, but I'm hoping to get in touch with the late Mrs. Baskerville again."

"Didn't we call her up two or three years ago?" I asked, wondering what the heck Mrs. Baskerville might have learned whilst having been dead for several years.

"Yes. But I have another question for her."

"Oh? What question would that be?"

"I want to know if there's such a thing as a piebald dachshund and, if there is, will the American Kennel Club recognize it as a standard color pattern any time soon."

How the heck was I supposed to find out if there was such a thing as a piebald dachshund in the world? What *was* a piebald dachshund? I decided to ask.

"What in the world is a piebald dachshund?"

"Well you might ask," she said darkly. "Piebald dachshunds are primarily white with splashes of red on them."

"A spotted dachshund?" I looked down at my black-and-tan dachshund, Spike, in amazement. "I can't quite picture such a thing."

"You shouldn't have to," said Mrs. Bissel in a sternly meaningful voice. "Piebald dachshunds shouldn't exist. If somebody wants a hound with different colors in its coat, that somebody should get a basset hound."

"Oh. I never thought about basset hounds having coats with splashes of red and white on them, but I guess they do. I haven't seen very many basset hounds, to tell the truth. Actually, I don't think I've ever seen one in the flesh. I still have a book my parents bought me when I was a little girl that has pictures of different dog breeds. Basset hounds are adorable."

"I don't know about how adorable they are," said Mrs. Bissel with a sniff. "But they're *supposed* to have coats with different colors on them. Dachshunds are *not* supposed to have variegated coats. They're supposed to be solid red or black and tan."

"Oh, and you fear an influx of splotchy dachshunds is going to cascade over the horizon?" I could envision such an event in my mind's eye, and it made me smile.

"I'm not sure. Unusual colors have, of course, always appeared, but responsible breeders have always attempted to conform to the breed standard. Why, a dachshund with patches of white on it would be dead in the hole!"

Dead in the hole? "Um... I'm not sure I understand what that means, dead in the hole."

"Dachshunds were originally bred to go after badgers, Daisy. You know that."

"Yes. Yes, indeed." Mrs. Bissel had told me that before she gave me Spike, and Mrs. Pansy Hanratty had told me again when I took Spike to her obedience classes.

"Well, how do you suppose any self-respecting badger would react if it saw something white digging into its burrow?"

"Um... not well?"

"Of course not well! Badgers are mean and nasty. They'd rip a dog with a white coat to shreds. Then you'd see red, all right. Blood red."

Ew. "My goodness. Do you really think the AKC will incorporate multi-colored dachshunds into its... whatever you called it?"

"Breed standard," said Mrs. Bissel firmly. "And if they ever try to do so, they'll have *me* to deal with!"

"Oh, my. Uh, well, I'll be happy to conduct a séance for you, Mrs. Bissel. Let me check my calendar."

I've already told you about my nonexistent calendar, haven't I?

After holding the receiver to my aproned bosom for a suitable length of time, I lifted it again to my ear. "How about Saturday, August first?" I asked, thinking I really needed to get my own wedding arrangements under control soon, or it might happen without me.

"Saturday, August first, would be wonderful, Daisy. Thank you so much. Oh, dear. When is your own wedding planned? Isn't it in September?"

"Yes. We're aiming for Saturday, September twelfth." The date slipped from my tongue as if Sam and I had been planning on that date for months.

"And do you have a venue chosen yet? You know I'd love to have you walk down the stairs at my house. Wouldn't that be lovely? In fact, the house was built for a fashion designer named Kate Duncan! She had her models walk down those very stairs."

"My goodness. I don't think you ever told me that."

"Well, it's the truth, and she did."

"Very interesting. Thank you very much for the offer, Mrs. Bissel. Yes, I agree that would be lovely, but I do believe we'll hold the ceremony in our church."

By golly, two decisions out of the way in the space of one telephone conversation. Now all I needed to do was get in touch with Pastor Smith and see if the date I'd blabbed was available. If not, I would be perfectly happy to wed Sam in either his or our back yard, both of which were beautiful. His (soon to be ours) was more park-like than ours, but not by much.

Of course, if Pastor Smith wasn't available on September twelfth, who'd we get to marry us?

Johnny Buckingham!

Ha. Only needed half a second to figure that one out.

I tell you, sometimes decisions come easily. Other times...

"However, I'll be happy to hold a séance so you may speak to Mrs. Baskerville on August first."

"That's wonderful! Well, thank you, Daisy. I truly appreciate this."

"Thank you. Um... Since you brought up the subject of Mr. Darlington's questionable reputation—"

"Ha!" exploded from the telephone receiver, shocking me. Generally it was Mrs. Pinkerton who tried to burst my eardrums. "There's no question *at all* about that awful young man's character. He had none. Why, do you know he actually affianced himself to Miss Gloria Shipman when he was already engaged to Miss Sarah Holcomb?"

"What? But I thought he was engaged to Miss Madge Hawley while he was engaged to Miss Alma Jervis? I mean, I thought two was bad, but *four*?"

"According to Patsy"—Patsy was Mrs. Bissel's daughter-in-law— "there may be even more. The Darlington cad and several of his coterie of wastrel friends decided it would be amusing to see how many young women Cecil could trick into becoming engaged to him. And then, you know, he would try to take things even farther."

"Um... farther?"

"My goodness, Daisy, you're still a young woman. I can't believe you don't know how loose the morals of some young people are in this decadent day and age. I understand from Patsy that he actually impregnated one young woman. Patsy either didn't know or wouldn't divulge the name of the girl. The poor thing had to go away and have the baby at a relative's home in some other city, because Cecil denied culpability. I think the child eventually went to live with an aunt and an uncle on a farm somewhere."

"The cad!"

"Cad is one word for it."

And I'd bet Mr. Lou Prophet could come up with lots of others. Good heavens. I wondered if Sam had discovered the length and depth of Mr. Cecil Darlington's duplicity and depravity. He and his friends thought becoming engaged to and defiling young women was a *sport*? To place *wagers* on?

"I had no idea. I'm glad he's dead." Boy, I don't think I'd ever said those words to a client before.

"You're definitely not the only one. But Mrs. Baskerville was a fine lady, and she will know, if anyone does, if the AKC is going to allow piebald coloring to sully the purity of the dachshund breed."

Still reeling from the news she'd related, it took my nimble brain a somersault or two to remember why Mrs. B was talking about Mrs. Baskerville. Ah, yes. "Indeed. I'll be happy to have Rolly ask for you, Mrs. Bissel. Saturday, the first of August."

"Thank you so much, dear."

"You're more than welcome."

Phew! I rushed to my bedroom to find a piece of paper and a pencil, which wasn't difficult to do, since I always left paper and pencils in my bedside drawer. When I had the pencil poised, I started writing down the names of the poor maidens—or perhaps no longer maidens—to whom Mr. Cecil Darlington had affianced himself. The scoundrel. The fiend!

"Okay, Spike. One of them was Sarah Holcomb, and the other one was Gloria... Gloria... Oh, bother."

Spike, annoyed by my poor memory, gave a sharp *yip*, and darned if Gloria's last name didn't pop into my brain.

"Shipman!" I smiled fondly down at my wonderful hound. "Thank you, Spike."

He gave me a happy wag. Then he and I went back to the kitchen, where I finished washing the last of the windows.

As I washed, I thought. Piebald dachshunds. Where in the world was I supposed to find out about piebald dachshunds? Probably the Pasadena Public Library would be a good place to start. Then perhaps I could chat with people in the dog world. Unfortunately, the only two people whom I knew to be dedicated dog-show-going people were Mrs. Bissel herself and Mrs. Pansy Hanratty, and they knew each other. In fact, they'd probably both be at the upcoming séance. Nertz.

This sounded like another case for Harold Kincaid. If he didn't know everything, he at least knew somebody who might know somebody who might know what someone else needed to know. I hope his list of acquaintances carried over into the dog-show world.

Although I was almost certain he wasn't at home, I decided to telephone his San Marino residence anyway. I could give my message to his houseboy, Roy Castillo, who would relay it to Harold. And that's precisely what I did.

"People who know about dog shows?" repeated Roy, as if to be sure he'd understood correctly.

"Yes. I know it's a strange question, but I have to learn a whole lot about dachshunds in nine days' time, and the only person I can think of who might know people who are interested in breeding and showing purebred dogs is Harold."

After a significant pause, Roy said, "Mr. Harold knows a lot of people."

"He certainly does."

"I will give him your message, Mrs. Majesty."

"Thank you very much."

"You're welcome."

Roy had the most wonderful accent. He came from the island of Tortuga, which is near Haiti. I'd never heard of it before Mr. Leo Bannister tried to murder his wife. But that's a whole 'nother story and I won't go into it now. The end result of that imbroglio, however, was the incident during which Mrs. Gaulding had tried to kill my Sam, which was why he had to go to court this morning.

Good Lord, but life can be complicated sometimes, can't it?

I finished washing the windows, then hung up my apron and went to my room with Spike for a little rest before lunch.

I must have fallen into a deep, deep sleep, because Pa startled me awake by knocking on the door to my bedroom some time later. Groggily, I glanced at the clock on my bedside table and saw that it was one o'clock! Spike and I had conked out a little before noon. I zipped out of bed and walked in stockinged feet to the door.

"Hey, Pa," I said, wiping my bleary eyes.

"Hey, Daisy. Sorry to wake you, but I just dished out the last of Vi's dinner salad into two bowls. I figured maybe you and I should each eat one of them."

"Merciful heavens. You're right. I really conked out, didn't I?"

"You certainly did. But the house looks great," said Pa. "So you deserved your nap."

"Thanks. Wish I hadn't slept for so long. I feel a little wobbly."

"Naps are funny things. Sometimes they help, and sometimes they don't."

A philosopher. That was my darling father.

"Let me just slip into my shoes and I'll join you at the table."

"It's not much. Just a bowlful of salad and an orange."

"That's not just a salad. It's a meal in itself," I said.

"Correct as always," said Pa with a grin.

Have I mentioned that we had oranges pretty much all year long because we had both a Valencia and a naval orange tree? Well, we did. I loved them both. The Valencias had seeds in them, but the oranges were sweet as nectar. The navels weren't quite as sweet as the Valencias, but they were yummy and *extremely* easy to peel. Also, they had no seeds.

Vi's leftover salmagundi salad was a trifle wilty, but it was still darned tasty. Munched along with an orange, it made a perfect lunch for two, with a couple of nibbles of chicken and egg for a delighted Spike, who always sat at our feet during meals and was seldom disappointed.

TWENTY-NINE

As plans sometimes do, our plans for dinner with the Wilsons that night went slightly askew.

Mr. Prophet showed up at our door at 5:30, Spike announcing his presence with delight and yips.

"Hey, there. Come in."

"Thanks, Miss Daisy." He limped into the house. I peered around outside, waiting for Sam to appear.

"Sam's gonna be a little late tonight," Mr. Prophet told me, having correctly guessed why I was searching the great out-of-doors for a person who wasn't there.

"Oh. That's not good. He's supposed to be here to interrogate Pudge Wilson after dinner."

"He'll be here. He'll just be a little late."

"Why?"

"Told me the court hearing took longer than he expected it to."

"Well, bother. I have some news for him. And you, too, if you're interested."

"Of course, I'm interested." Mr. Prophet appeared a trifle put out.

"Okay. Well, come into the living room. I'm not sure I want my mother and father to hear this stuff."

"Shee-it, must be bad if you think it'll scare your folks."

A trifle exasperated, I snapped, "It won't scare them. But it's... well, kind of unsavory."

"Like me?"

"Yes," I snarled. "Like you."

"They don't seem to mind me a whole lot."

"I have no idea why that is," I told the old rip.

He only grinned and sat on the sofa. "Okay, Miss Daisy. What's this news that's so shocking you're embarrassed to tell your folks?"

Darned if he hadn't pegged me right down to the ground. So to speak. I heaved a sigh and said, "You're right. I'd be embarrassed to tell Ma and Pa about this. Nothing shocks you."

"Ain't that the truth." It wasn't a question.

So I told him Mrs. Bissel's revelations about the late Mr. Cecil Darlington, Miss Sarah Holcomb and Miss Gloria Shipman. "She said there might even be more girls, one of whom reportedly had his baby out of wedlock because he refused to claim it."

"Cripes. And I thought I got around."

"I'm sure you did."

"Yeah." His grin broadened. "I did. She didn't give you the name of the one who had the baby?"

"No. Unless it was one of the girls already named. She didn't know which one it was."

"And she said this was some kind of game he played with his friends?"

"Mrs. Bissel said they made a wager that Cecil Darlington couldn't get himself engaged to five women at the same time without at least one of the women finding out about it."

"Did he make it to five?"

"I guess so. Unless the four whose names we know are all of them, and one of them got pregnant and had to leave town to have her baby."

"Huh."

Before I could stop myself, I blurted out, "Now you see? *This* is why I think so many men are pigs! You don't mind sowing your seed here, there and everywhere, but then you merrily bounce off without a care in the world. It's the *women* who have to bear the shame. *And* the babies!"

"Yeah. You told me as much before. Mrs. Bissel didn't happen to name any of the other men who were part of this wager, did she?"

I sucked in a houseful of newly dusted and waxed air and let it out in a whoosh. Leave it to Mr. Lou Prophet to take the winds of indignation out of my sails simply by sticking to the topic at hand. I tried not to resent him for it. "No. The only one she told me about was Cecil Darlington himself." Because I was still mad at a world over which I had so little control, I added bitterly, "I no longer think of him as a *victim* of homicide. I think he got what he deserved."

"Yeah. I figured that one out on my own. Sam can ask the Wilson kid's friend if his big brother knew Darlington. He might be one of the gamblers."

"Good Lord, you're right. He might well be one of them. I don't know how this gets anyone closer to who killed him, though."

"You don't even care at this point, do you?"

"Well, yes, I do. If it's one of the gang of cads who made that evil wager with him, I want the man to hang."

"Accordin' to Sam, California don't hang people anymore. They fry 'em."

"I think they should fry them all," I muttered.

The doorbell scritched, and I had to stop venting my spleen. Curses.

"That's probably the Wilsons. If I don't have time to tell Sam Mrs. Bissel's news, will you do it for me?"

" 'Course I will. Probably won't impart the news with such impressive passion, but I'll tell him."

I frowned at the man who, if he didn't look so dissolute, might have passed for an angel peering up at me with that innocent expression on his dried-apple face. Nertz.

Spike, naturally, made his way to the front door before I could, so I said, "Spike. Sit." And Spike sat. Bless the dog. He was the only male in my life over whom I exercised any control at all. "Good boy!"

Wagging his tail hard enough to stir up dust, if I'd left any on the floor, which I hadn't, Spike still sat and woofed at the door. I opened same to reveal the Wilson family, mother, father and son.

"Good evening! It's so good of you to come over for dinner tonight," I said. Then I took pity on my dog and told him, "Okay!" which was the word releasing him from durance vile. Spike took advantage of the word to leap upon Pudge and lick his chin, which he could reach because Pudge obligingly bent over to pet him.

"Thank *you*," said Mrs. Wilson, handing me a bouquet of roses I'm sure she'd picked from her backyard garden. We had a backyard garden full of roses, too. I loved them. "It's always a pleasure to eat your aunt's cooking."

"I'm afraid tonight's meal is going to be a cold repast," I said. "She didn't want to have to turn on the oven and heat the house.

"Sensible woman, your aunt Vi," said Mr. Wilson, rubbing his hands together.

"Why don't you join Mr. Prophet in the living room while I get a vase for these gorgeous roses," I told the Wilsons. "Sam is running a bit late this evening, but he'll be here for dinner." I hoped.

"Thank you."

Pudge, who was in slightly frightened awe of Mr. Prophet, grinned like an imp, and swaggered into the living room. I have a feeling he was trying to act like a cowboy. If he only knew how *real* Old-Westerners behaved, he'd have been shocked, turned brick-red, and probably run home again. Good thing the flickers had cleaned things up for the little ones.

"Need any help, Vi?" I asked, carrying the roses into the kitchen so she could see them.

"No, thanks. Oh, my, aren't those lovely?"

"What are lovely?" asked Ma. She appeared in the kitchen door leading from the hall and said, "Oh, how gorgeous! Are the Wilsons here?"

"They are, and they brought these," I told my mother. "I'm getting a vase for them."

249

"I think I put some extra vases in the service porch cupboard," said Ma. "I see you've already put an extra leaf in the table and set it, so if Vi doesn't need me, I'll get your father and take him with me into the living room to chat with the Wilsons. Are Sam and Lou here yet?"

"Mr. Prophet is. Sam will be late," I said, reporting things as I'd been told them.

"Don't need you, Peggy," said Vi cheerfully. "After Daisy finds a good place to put those lovely roses, she and I can get the meal on the table."

"Sounds good to me," I told both the women in my life, wondering as I did so why I was the only one in my family who didn't feel comfortable calling Mr. Prophet Lou. Just one more mystery of life, I reckon.

Sam arrived at the house, nearly panting, at the stroke of six o'clock, when Vi and I were setting out viands. We set the lovely cold ham at Vi's place. She'd slice it and serve everyone, and then we'd all pass the salads and rolls. Boy, those salads were amazing, too! Potato, green pea, carrot and raisin, and I can't even remember what else, but there were at least two more.

The only reason I don't recall all the foodstuffs Vi served us that evening was my state of agitation caused by Sam being late. Curse it! He was supposed to have come early so we could discuss how to handle the Pudge interrogation. I informed him of my aggrieved state as he was helping me set out the salad bowls.

"There's nothing much to handle," he whispered to me after I'd whispered my accusation to him.

"What do you *mean* there's nothing to handle?" I hissed back at him.

"I'll talk to the kid while you're at choir practice. I'm sending Lou with you. I want you to be safe if those three witches show up again, and they probably will."

"You think they might really want to hurt me?"

"Lou does, and he has more experience with wicked women than I do."

"Well, I'm glad to hear *that*," I whispered snippily.

"Me, too. Good ones have been hard enough on me."

"Nertz to you, Sam Rotondo!"

"I'll walk up to the church when I've finished talking to Pudge and tell you everything. Nobody will leave you out of anything."

"Darn and blast! I wanted to talk to Pudge, too!"

"Calm down, Daisy. Everything will be all right."

"I haven't yet told you what Mrs. Bissel revealed to me today about the Darlington creature."

"If it's about a gang of his pals taking bets to see how many women he could defile without the other women finding out, I already know."

Well, *that* pretty much called an abrupt halt to my raging frustration. "How'd you find out?"

"Mrs. Bissel called me at the police department. She said after she spoke to you, she thought I might like to know about Darlington."

"Oh. That was good of her. Mrs. Bissel has a good head on her shoulders, unlike some wealthy women I know," I said.

Chuckling, Sam said, "Yes, she does. She also told me all about piebald dachshunds."

"Oh, dear. She's dead-set against them."

"She sure is."

"Do you have the names of others besides Madge and Alma?"

"Yeah. Three more."

"That's one more than Mrs. B told *me* about. The ones she told me about were Gloria Shipman and Sarah Holcomb."

"Yes. She remembered a couple of other names. There were a Franklin and a Trunick in the mix."

"Good Lord, that makes six!"

"I have a feeling there are more. I'm going to talk to both of the Jervis boys tomorrow. Maybe I can shake some information out of them."

"I'm glad Cecil Darlington is dead. Too bad he's not still alive for all those women to stick pins in."

"Nothing vindictive about you, is there?" whispered Sam.

"Vindictive, am I? Well, maybe I am, but he deserved worse than he got."

"I promise never to play around on you, Daisy."

"You'd better not."

"Trust me. I wouldn't dare."

"Good thing, too."

We both burst out laughing. Vi appeared in the kitchen door and stared at us as if we'd both lost our minds. Maybe we had. There really wasn't anything funny about Cecil Darlington's life *or* his death.

"Will one of you hyenas please get this bowl of mustard and take it to the table?"

"I'll get it, Vi," I said, still giggling. Don't ask me why I laughed. I hadn't noticed anything amusing around me for days.

Naturally, nobody else knew about my personal edginess. Well, except for Sam and Mr. Prophet.

Do I need to say anything about dinner being delicious? No, I didn't think so. The ham was absolutely wonderful with the mustard sauce Vi had created to go with it. I'm not sure why, since I couldn't create mustard if I'd been given mustard seeds and pounded them myself, but I asked her what was in it. She said a little coarse-grained mustard (whatever that was), a little mayonnaise (of her own making) and a dash of grated horseradish. We got into a conversation about horseradish at the table, but I don't think we came to any conclusions about it as a foodstuff. I was surprised when Vi said the horseradish she'd grated to go in her masterpiece came out of our own kitchen garden.

"I didn't know we grew horseradish in the garden!" I cried, amazed.

"That's because you only like tending the flowers," said Vi, grinning.

And here I'd always thought I had something of a greenish thumb. I swear, I was even more useless than I'd heretofore believed, and I'd believed myself to be useless for eons.

"It's good," said Pudge, whose table manners that evening were impeccable. This amazed me a little, too, since every time I turned his way, he seemed to have his worshipful gaze on me. The kid had it bad. I hoped Sam would turn Pudge's devotion to good purpose, although I remained irked that I couldn't be there to watch.

Oh, very well, I'd have butted in, too. Maybe Sam had been late on purpose.

At any rate, we'd finished the ham and as much of the various salads as anyone could stuff into his or her body when Vi asked me to clear the dishes because she was going to prepare our desserts.

"Oh, my goodness, I'd forgotten all about dessert!" I cried, fairly leaping from the table.

"That's not like you, Daisy," said Vi with another grin.

"No, it's not," I agreed, hurriedly piling dishes on my arms like a waiter at the Castleton's fabulous restaurant.

"I'll help," said Ma, also rising.

"Don't disturb your digestion, Peggy," said Sam, who rose from his chair, too. He was bigger than anyone else, so even Ma obeyed him.

"Oh, good. I can use you, Sam," said Vi happily.

And she did. She scooped ice cream into eight fluted bowls— maybe I could get some of those at Nelson's Five and Dime. I didn't want to pay Bullock's prices for them, even if they were beautiful. Tonight she arranged them all on a pretty tray she must have borrowed from the Pinkertons, because I didn't recall seeing it before.

"Sam, will you please take the tray to the stove?" She rendered the phrase as a question, but it was a command, and Sam obeyed nicely.

At the stove, she picked up the pot she'd left on the warming tray, using a potholder I'd made donkeys' years ago. Then, using a special ladle with a dent in its side, she drizzled hot-fudge sauce over the ice cream in all the bowls. Sam followed her, still holding the tray, from the stove to the counter, where she spooned out lots of chopped, toasted almonds. Then Sam followed her to the Frigidaire, from which she lifted out a bowl into which she'd already placed the cream she'd whipped earlier and proceeded to top each chocolate-

253

fudge-and-nut-covered ice cream blob with a big dollop of whipped cream.

The entire process reminded me of pictures I'd seen of automobile assembly lines. As soon as the last blob of whipped cream was plopped on the last fluted glass, Vi stood back with understandable pride. Fists planted firmly on her hips she said, "There. Now if you'll please take the tray to the table, Daisy and I will set desserts at everyone's places."

So he did. And we did. And everyone at the dinner table, even those of us who'd tasted hot fudge sundaes only the day before, were delighted, astonished and basically knocked all of a heap. I read that expression in a British crime novel once, and loved it.

Nobody but me knew my private thoughts, but there was no doubt about anyone's reaction to Vi's fabulous dessert. Wish Mr. Prophet and I hadn't had to leave the table before Vi dished out seconds, but I had to get to choir practice.

Darn Cecil Darlington's evil ways! He even made me miss my seconds! Well, Mr. Prophet missed his, too, but he'd surely committed plenty of evil deeds to make this omission fair.

THIRTY

A nd, sure enough, the three witches—that is to say, the two Misses Hawleys and Miss Alma Jervis—awaited Mr. Prophet and me when we got to the church.

Because I entered the church using the door to the choir room, I was first to see them, although "first" in this case only means between Mr. Prophet and me. The rest of the members of the choir who were there already had seen them, too, and appeared puzzled by their presence. Couldn't blame them.

Of course, as soon the threesome saw me, they smiled. I smiled back.

Then Mr. Prophet entered the church using the door that led into the sanctuary rather than the choir room, and their smiles disappeared.

"Well, how-do, ladies?" he said in a cordial voice. "Figgered you'd be here tonight."

"Why'd you figure that?" asked a sullen Alma Jervis. I suppose being engaged to a fellow who already had four or five other fiancées might make anyone sullen, but she took sullenness to an extreme degree in my not awfully humble opinion. Besides that, neither Mr. Prophet nor I deserved her attitude.

"Why, because you enjoy aggravating Miss Daisy, of course," he said agreeably. Then he moved the pistol he generally tucked under his belt at his back to his side, drawing his jacket aside so the women could see it. Before seating himself, he replaced it behind his back, but the three witches knew it was there.

The women scooted farther over on their pew. Mr. Prophet grinned at them as they did it, and drew a knife from his boot scabbard in a way only they could see. He clearly didn't intend to put up with any nonsense from those three. Madge Hawley, after peering unhappily at Mr. Prophet, moved across the aisle to the other side of the church. Her two acolytes joined her. So did Mr. Prophet.

"Mrs. Majesty, are you with us tonight?" asked Mr. Floy Hostetter, our choir director.

I jumped, not realizing my attention had been focused on the play being enacted in the first row of pews in the church. Turning quickly, I saw the entire choir staring at me. Whoops.

"Sorry, Mr. Hostetter. Just wondered what those three women were doing in our church." I spoke loudly enough for the three women to hear me.

"Anyone may visit as we sing to the glory of God. May our music be a blessing to them," said Mr. Hostetter pompously. Pomposity was normal for him, so I didn't cringe or anything. "But let us begin our practice. We'll sing a few scales first. Mrs. Fleming?" He nodded to our wonderful pianist/organist, Mrs. Fleming, and she gave us a starting note.

So I sang scales like a good alto should. I decided not to pay any attention to the three interlopers. Maybe Mr. Hostetter was correct, and they'd be blessed by our singing. I kind of doubted they would be, since they seemed to have their attention fixed on another motive entirely. Wish I knew what it was.

Our anthem for the coming Sunday was "See How Great a Flame Aspires." I like it, and it was written by Charles Wesley, so it was perfect for us Methodist-Episcopals.

But back to our scales-singing.

"Very good. Now, during our anthem, I'd like it if you, Mrs. Majesty, and you, Mrs. Zollinger, would please sing a duet on the second verse. The soprano and altos will sing the third verse." He paused and squinted at the basses and baritones. "I don't think we'll have any other special singing. We'll all sing the first and fourth verses together."

Lucy looked at me, and I looked at Lucy. We both shrugged together, which was pretty much the way we sang. Together. We did it really well, too, by gum. Although I felt like smirking at our audience, I didn't, and was proud of myself. So there, you trio of evil cows!

Very well, so my inner thoughts weren't geared toward blessing the threesome.

"Excellent," said Mr. Hostetter who, if he'd had feathers, would be preening them. "Now let's go through the hymn once more. Let's make sure we convey our message through proper dynamics. Everyone, medium-loud on the first verse. Mrs. Majesty and Mrs. Zollinger, you're both fine. And *forte* on the last verse, everyone."

"That means loudly, right?" asked Mr. Finster, one of our basses.

"Yes, *forte* means to sing loudly," said Mr. Hostetter. "*Mezzoforte* means medium-loudly."

"Thank you," said Mr. Finster.

I'm sure most of the rest of the choir members were glad Mr. Finster had asked the question. Except for those of us who played the piano or read music, probably everyone else wondered what those terms meant, too, but had been afraid to ask. Mr. Hostetter didn't use musical language often, and I suddenly realized he was showing off for his audience. I glanced at said audience. Except for Mr. Prophet, who sat with his arms crossed over his chest and smiled gently—I considered it a miracle he could still do anything at all gently—the rest of the listeners appeared merely grumpy. And nervous, if I were to judge—and I guess I just did.

Ha.

So we sang "See How Great a Flame Aspires" through once more, paying special attention to the dynamics. At the end of the hymn, three people in the sanctuary applauded. Surprised, I glanced down and saw that Sam had joined the party, along with

Pudge Wilson. Sam, Pudge and Mr. Prophet were the clappers. I grinned and gave all of them a finger wave, and Pudge beamed at me. Guess he was glad I wasn't angry with him.

Mr. Hostetter then took the choir through our introit. "Remember, the first two verses only," said he.

So we sang the first two verses of "Spirit Divine, Attend our Prayers," and did so quite nicely. I peered into the sanctuary again and saw Sam and Mr. Prophet talking softly to the three witches. Although it didn't look to me as though they wanted to, they got up and followed Sam to the side door of the church. Mr. Prophet brought up the rear. Pudge continued sitting on the first pew, looking a trifle uncomfortable now that his entourage of strong men had left him. Yet he sat, silent and still, as he'd probably been ordered to do.

Dang! I wanted to be with Sam, Mr. Prophet and the trio of menaces! *Too bad, Daisy Gumm Majesty. Your job is to sing in the choir.* So I did. If Sam didn't tell me what went on after they led the menaces away, I aimed to kill him.

My, what a truly loving and Christian thought, huh? Oh, well.

Mr. Hostetter had us sing the first verse of "More Love to thee, O Christ" as our benediction. Then he made us go through our anthem for the following Sunday, which would be the second Sunday in August, by golly! Holy Cow, that meant my own nuptials were a little more than a month away. I nearly fainted when the thought hit me but I didn't, praise the Lord.

See? I'm not always thinking sinful thoughts.

"Our anthem for August second will be "I Heard the Voice of Jesus Say." There are three verses, and I think it would be good to have a duet or a quartet for the second verse. Mrs. Zollinger and Mrs. Majesty, are you willing to sing the soprano and alto parts?"

"Yes," Lucy and I said in a perfectly tuneful duet.

"Very good. Mr. Finster and Mr. Warden, can you take the tenor and bass parts, or do I need to get another tenor?"

"I believe I can sing the tenor part," said Mr. Warden gallantly. He generally sang bass, but I guess he had an extensive vocal range.

"Let's try it." Mr. Hostetter glanced at Mrs. Fleming. "Mrs. Fleming?"

"Would you like me to accompany the anthem on the organ, Mr. Hostetter?"

"Are you comfortable playing the organ for this hymn?" asked Mr. Hostetter of our *extremely* competent pianist.

"Yes, I am," said she serenely.

I wanted to be more like Mrs. Fleming, who seemed serene under almost all circumstances. Heck, even when an old lady fell over dead during the communion service a couple of years back, Mrs. Fleming didn't flinch. Well, maybe she flinched, but she didn't scream or titter or anything of the sort, which was more than one could say of many congregants.

So we practiced "I Heard the Voice of Jesus Say," and we all did a good job. Mr. Warden messed up once, because he was used to following the bass line, but he quickly corrected himself. That was a good thing because our tenor section was rather thin at the moment, two of them having taken off on holidays.

After we'd sung as much as Mr. Hostetter deemed appropriate, he said our closing prayer, and the choir straggled from the chancel. Because I didn't want Pudge to feel abandoned, I walked down the chancel steps to sit in the front pew with him for a bit.

He jumped to attention as soon as he deduced my intention, and stood straight and as tall as he could. As he was maybe twelve, and of about average height for his age, that wasn't too tall.

"Miss Daisy, I'm so sorry!" he began. "I didn't know Mr. Jervis was only asking about you because he wanted his cousins to bother you. Please forgive me. I promise never to tattle to anyone about you again."

The poor gallant kid had tears in his eyes. I knew how hard it was to apologize when you were twelve—or, heck, almost twenty-five—so I smiled sweetly at him, and gestured that he should sit again. So he did, and I sat next to him.

"So it was your Boy Scout leader who asked questions about me?" I asked gently.

Pudge nodded hard. "Yes. I didn't know why. He said his cousins were worried about you, and that's why they wanted to go to the places you went.

Interesting. "Why were they worried about me?"

"He said somebody got killed at a wedding, and the murderer might be after you next."

"Why would anyone want to murder me? Did he say?"

"He said it was a conspiracy." Pudge's voice dropped to a thrilling whisper on the last word.

"A conspiracy?"

"Yes."

"Who was conspiring to do what?" I asked, fascinated. When I was a twelve-year-old, I was already earning money by reading palms and plying the Ouija board for people, so I guess I didn't have much time to think about conspiracies.

"Mr. Jervis didn't know, but he said he was worried about you."

"He was, was he?"

Pudge lowered his head, abashed. "That's what he said, but Mr. Prophet and Detective Rotondo said he was lying. I didn't think a Boy Scout leader *could* lie. It's against the rules."

What a sweet, innocent child. You'd never know that, just over two months prior, he'd been instrumental in capturing a crook. Guess he didn't think Boy Scouts or their pack leaders were capable of crookery. Growing up was just one shattered illusion after another, I reckon.

"I'm really sorry, Miss Daisy." He looked up at me, hope writ large on his skinny, freckled features. "You're not mad at me? I wouldn't blame you for being mad at me, because Detective Rotondo said those ladies were scaring you, but I didn't mean—"

Putting an arm around his bony shoulder, I squeezed gently. "It's all right, Pudge. Nobody's mad at you. I'm certainly not, and I'm sure neither Detective Rotondo nor Mr. Prophet are, either. I'm sorry you were tricked. I'm mad at the people who tricked you, but not at you."

"Th-thanks, Miss Daisy." Pudge sniffled. He only did it once, because he was a *Boy Scout*, and too tough for tears.

"Thank you for helping Detective Rotondo and Mr. Prophet

figure out where those three women were getting their information about my movements."

"I wouldn't have told anyone if I'd known you didn't want me to."

"I'm sure that's true, Pudge. But let's not worry about it now." I glanced up and peered around the sanctuary, which looked entirely empty of people. Mr. Hostetter and Mrs. Fleming still occupied the chancel. They appeared to be studying some music. Normal activity for both of them, but I wasn't sure what to do now.

Then the side door to the church opened, and Sam said, "Daisy and Pudge? Can you come out here for a second or two?"

"You bet!" Pudge leapt to his feet and took a giant step toward Sam before he recalled me, sitting in the pew. "I'm sorry, Miss Daisy. May I please be excused?"

"Yes, you may, Pudge." To Sam, I said, "I'll be right there. Just have to put my hymnal and book away."

So Pudge recommenced scampering to the side door, and I walked up the chancel steps, turned left, walked down the steps to the choir room, and put my choir trappings in their assigned cubbyhole. Lucy and Albert Zollinger hadn't left the choir room yet. They seemed to be waiting for me. I smiled at the couple.

"Everything all right, Daisy?" asked Lucy, sounding worried.

"Yes. Fine, thanks."

"What were those three women doing in the church?"

"Keeping track of me, I guess," I told Lucy.

"Why?"

"I don't know, but I'm hoping Sam will be able to answer your question. He's waiting for me outside."

"Oh," said Lucy, sounding dissatisfied not to have had her curiosity satisfied.

Didn't blame her. I wasn't keen on mysteries myself, except in fiction. "I'll let you know Sunday if I can," I said, hoping to reassure her.

"Thanks, Daisy."

"Good evening, Mrs. Majesty," said Mr. Zollinger, who was a rather formal gent. He lifted his hat at me.

"Good evening. Have a good rest of the night, you two."

"We will. Thanks, Daisy. We're going to host an open house as soon as we're all moved in to our new house."

"Wonderful!" I probably sounded a little too cheerful, but was happy for Lucy and her hubby. He was, in my opinion, a little old for her, but young men were thin on the ground since the war and the flu pandemic and she seemed contented, so I was happy for her.

The door to the outside opened, and Mr. Prophet stood there, holding it and scowling at me. "You comin' out or you want us to go in there?"

"Be right there," I said, hoping Mr. Zollinger didn't have a weak heart, because he'd given a huge start of alarm. "Sorry about Mr. Prophet, Lucy and Mr. Zollinger. Guess Sam's getting impatient."

"It's all right," said Mr. Zollinger, who still appeared slightly ruffled.

But Lucy took him by the arm, and they sailed out through the door Mr. Prophet still held open and walked arm in arm to the curb where their automobile was parked.

"For pity's sake, you can't let a girl put away her choir books and talk to a friend or two before hollering at her?" I asked Mr. Prophet as I stomped past him to the Marengo side lawn of the church.

"Cripes. You took your sweet time," said he. "Sam's been waiting with those three witches for an hour."

"He has not!"

"Seems like it."

"Pooh."

THIRTY-ONE

Poor Sam did look a teensy bit disgruntled when Mr. Prophet and I neared him.

Hmmm. There's another interesting word. You never hear about people being gruntled, do you? Aw, well. The English language is a fascinating tool.

At any rate, Sam stood behind one of the pretty stone benches the trustees of our church had commissioned to be made late in the last century. Huddled on the bench were the three young women who had dogged—pre-dogged?—my footsteps for a week or more. I frowned as I approached the group. Pudge, standing off to one side, looked merely perplexed.

"Hey, Sam, have they told you why they're stalking me?"

"Yes," said Sam. "According to them, you killed Mr. Cecil Darlington."

"*What?*" Pudge and I didn't sound bad as a duet, by golly.

"What in the world—?" Me

"Miss Daisy would *never*—" Pudge

"She *did*." The Hawley sisters and Miss Jervis. They didn't sound nearly as musical as Pudge and I had.

"I did not!" Me.

"She did not!" Pudge.

"Cripes." Sam.

Ka-*boom*! Mr. Prophet, who pulled the trigger on his pistol, sending a bullet into the green church lawn and effectively shutting us all up.

I frowned at him. "There was no need for that."

"The hell there wasn't. I'm so sick of jabberin' wimmin, I couldn't stand it another second."

"Tell her," said Sam, speaking to the trio of witches.

"You were the only one who could have killed Cecil," said Miss Madge Hawley.

"Yes, you are!" said her sister.

"They're right," said Miss Jervis.

"Hellkatoot," said Mr. Prophet.

"You see? They think you're the only one who could have done in Mr. Darlington," Sam told me in a conversational tone.

"How'd you come to that conclusion?" I asked the trio, honestly curious.

"You were the only one with him."

"I was outdoors waving Regina and Robert off, along with Sam and about twenty other people when Mr. Darlington was killed," I said. "I never saw Mr. Darlington in my entire life until I discovered his body, and I wish someone else had done that."

"I'll just bet," said a scornful Alma Jervis. Scornful seemed to be her normal state.

"You'd lose," I told her.

"Huh," said she.

"According to the doctor," I said then, trying like anything to hold on to my patience, "it took more than one person to kill your precious Mr. Darlington. At least one person had to hold him still— probably two people—while another person stuffed his mouth full of engagement ring, tennis ball and flowers."

"And filmy fabric," said Mr. Prophet.

"Oh, yes. I'd forgotten the filmy fabric." Then I recalled the bruises on Miss Jervis's arm and her lack of a ring and the seemingly rough way it had been removed from her finger. "You claimed you were engaged to the bounder, too. Where's your engagement ring, Miss Jervis?"

"*My* ring?"

"And where's yours, Miss Hawley?" I asked Madge.

"I… have it at home," Madge said, having to think quickly, something she wasn't accustomed to doing.

"And Miss Jervis?" I asked of Miss Alma Jervis, this time more sharply.

"I never had a ring," said she. "*I* wasn't engaged to Cecil."

I slanted a questioning glance at Sam.

"That's not what your brother and your cousin told me," said Sam.

"Well, they were wrong," said Miss Jervis.

"I call bullshit," said Mr. Prophet, shocking the three women and Pudge into gasps of mortified civility. He reached out and grabbed Miss Jervis's left hand. "What happened to the ring that used to be on that finger? And how'd you get them bruises?"

Under the street lamps—Pasadena had been electrified since the late nineteenth century—Mr. Prophet displayed Alma Jervis's hand and arm, both of which still bore traces of bruising.

Trying and failing to wrench her arm out of Mr. Prophet's grip, Miss Jervis pursed her lips together and didn't speak.

"Well?" asked Sam. "According to your cousin and three of his other buddies you, Miss Hawley, Miss Trunick, Miss Franklin, Miss Shipman and Miss Holcomb had all received engagement rings from Mr. Cecil Darlington. You were all the subjects of a wager. Also according to your cousin and his pals, one of the women to whom he gave an engagement ring became pregnant by him. He denied responsibility for her condition, and she had to leave the city to have her child, who is now being reared on a farm in central California. Your Mr. Darlington was true scum of the earth, but he lost in the long run and ended up dead on the floor in the Brownings' home with a bridal bouquet stuffed into his mouth. Along with the other items mentioned."

"*What?*" Madge Hawley screeched. She tried to stand, but Sam's big paw held her pinned to the bench. "That can't be true!"

Silence reigned for what seemed like a century or three, but was probably ten seconds at most. Then the ever-sullen Miss Alma Jervis suddenly burst into tears and crumpled on the bench. Sam grabbed her so she couldn't fall off, in case she'd planned to.

"It *is* true!" she sobbed when she found breath with which to speak. Or squeak.

"Wh-what?" the Hawley sisters whispered in unison.

Suddenly recalling the repugnant nature of the conversation, I glanced at Pudge. I'm not sure how much he understood, but he stood there staring at us all. Fudge. I couldn't very well send him away to walk home alone.

"It is true," Miss Jervis repeated in a whisper. "Cecil was a cad. I heard Jeff and Ferrell laughing about him, so I listened. They were saying how funny it was that so many girls were fools for Cecil. They thought it was funny. *Funny*!"

"Jeff is Jeffrey Jervis, Miss Jervis?" Sam asked.

She nodded and said miserably, "Yes." Then her face took on a stormy cast. "So I barged in on their conversation and belted Jeffrey. They were still *laughing*! They're *awful*! I *hate* them! In fact, I hate all men. They're such... such... such swine."

Well, I guess that explained her attitude, huh?

"Did one or both of those fellows kill Mr. Darlington, Miss Jervis?"

"What?" Miss Jervis lifted her tear-ravaged face and squinted at Sam. "No! They didn't kill him!"

"Then who did? Did you kill him?"

"No! I hated him, but I didn't kill him. When I heard Jeff and Ferrell talking about him like that I... I guess I went nuts."

"What do you mean?" asked Sam.

With a shrug, Miss Jervis said, "I was so upset, I barged in on them and tried to beat Jeff to death, which I couldn't do because both Jeff and Ferrell are larger than I am. That," she said, back to being sullen, "is how I got these bruises. Ferrell grabbed me, and Jeff tried to fend me off."

"Huh," said Mr. Prophet, who stood with his arms crossed, propped by his leg and his peg and looking as if he'd as soon grab his gun again and shoot all three women as listen to any more blather from Miss Alma Jervis.

"So how'd you get the notion that Mrs. Majesty killed the Darlington fellow?" asked Sam.

Miss Jervis shrugged again. "I don't know. Mrs. Pinkerton held that stupid séance for Mrs. Darlington, and somebody who attended said they thought *she* must have done it because she was the one who found him."

"By she, you mean Mrs. Majesty?"

"Yes."

"Who came to that conclusion? Which person at the séance decided she'd killed him?"

Another shrug. "I don't know. I wasn't there. What was worse was that they tricked my little brother, Reggie, into spying for them."

"Yes, that was pretty low. I don't think your cousin is going to be a Boy Scout leader for much longer," said Sam. "But now we need to figure out who killed Mr. Darlington, even if he wasn't much of a loss to the world."

Madge Hawley burst into tears. DeeDee, who seemed to imitate everything Madge did, took a quick look at her and began crying, too.

"Listen, all three of you. Stop crying," said Sam in his "If you don't do as I say, I'll take you up into the San Gabriel foothills and feed you to a bear" voice.

Oddly enough, they all stopped crying. Not that Alma Jervis had been weeping, but she sure sat up straight on her bench.

"Who killed that man? You must know, or at least suspect, who did him in. Tell me. Now."

"But I *don't* know!" I'm not sure which of the threesome said that, but one of them did. And the weeping and wailing resumed. Bother.

Then Mr. Prophet brought the noise level down again, only this time he did it without pulling his beloved Colt revolver. Rather, kicked the stone bench with his peg leg so hard, the bench wobbled.

Ow. That must have hurt him. I didn't ask, as the timing didn't seem appropriate. The three witches shut up. What's more, they sat up, shocked into good posture.

"Good. Keep yer mouths shut, and let's back up here," he said. "Who's Ferrell, and how'd he get into this story?"

Ferrell? *Ferrell?* What was the man talking about?

Sam must have been at least a little puzzled, because he tilted his head and looked at Mr. Prophet.

Mr. Prophet said, pointing at Miss Jarvis as he did so, "You said you heard Jeff and Ferrell laughin' about the Darlington asshole foolin' so many girls. Who the hell's Ferrell?"

Oh, crumb. I'd forgotten all about Ferrell Hawley, Madge and DeeDee's relative.

Madge swallowed hard, wiped her eyes, and said, "F-Ferrell is our cousin."

"So your cousin and *her*"—he pointed at Miss Jervis—"cousin gassed it up about takin' bets on how many girls the dead yahoo could get himself engaged to?" He scowled at Miss Jervis as he spoke.

She said, "Y-yes."

"When?" said Mr. Prophet.

"When?" she repeated.

"Ain't a hard question. When'd you hear them chinnin'? You said you got mad and slugged your cousin. When?" He pointed at the Hawley sisters, who went cross-eyed as they stared at his pointing finger, which was yellowed with tobacco stains and gnarled with arthritis.

"I-I don't remember," stammered Alma.

"Yes, you do." This time it was Sam who spoke. "When did you overhear their conversation?"

"I…"

"Just tell them, Alma," said Madge, who seemed frightened of Mr. Prophet, if not of Sam.

"I… don't remember."

Mr. Prophet withdrew the Colt from the waistband of his trousers, and she hurried to say, "About a week before the wedding!"

"So, approximately a week before his murder, you knew about

Mr. Darlington's attempt to make money by engaging himself to five or six different women without the women knowing about it?" said Sam.

Alma gulped. Then she whispered, "Yes. About that."

Sam raked all three witches with a scathing glare. "So that means you two knew about Darlington before the wedding, too, right?"

After sharing a frantic glance, Madge and DeeDee muttered, "Yes," so softly I could barely hear them.

"Speak up!" bellowed Mr. Prophet.

All three girls jumped as if they'd been stung by several wasps and said, more loudly, "Yes!" Alma joined in the trio, undoubtedly because she was terrified by this time.

As I was still concerned about Pudge, I shot him a glance, but he'd evidently been turned to stone, because he just stood there, gawking at the scene, and didn't move. I'd get Sam to have a calming chat with him after we got home again.

Scratch that. *I'd* have a calming chat with him. I'd also ask him if he could earn a merit badge if he helped the police solve a crime. I think I'd asked him that the last time he helped Sam, but I don't recall his answer.

"So which of you helped Ferrell Hawley kill Darlington?" said Sam, again using his deadly voice.

"Ferrell didn't do it!" Madge said. "He *didn't!*"

"Then who did?"

"How should I—"

I don't know about anyone else there, but I nearly had a heart attack when Mr. Prophet grabbed his Colt and shot another bullet into the church's Marengo-side lawn. Poor lawn.

Suddenly DeeDee, evidently the leakiest of the three idiotic vessels, fell apart and shrieked, "We *all* did it!"

"Eh?" said Mr. Prophet, still holding his Colt, but not pointing it at anyone.

"Shut up, DeeDee," said Madge, elbowing her sister in the side. Hard, unless I miss my guess, since DeeDee nearly slid off the end of the bench. Sam grabbed her so she couldn't.

"It's *true!*" wailed DeeDee. "I'm sorry, Madge. I can't stand it any longer! I can't sleep, I can't eat, I can't even walk on the street without fearing somebody will shoot me or run me down or kill me! We all did it. Madge and Alma and Gloria and Phoebe and Betty and Sarah. Betty is the one who had his baby. She had to go to San Francisco to have her baby, and then had to give it up to an aunt and uncle in Fresno. I felt *so sorry* for her! And for Madge and Alma. It wasn't fair, what that horrid man did to them. And the other men thought it was funny! I hate men as much as Alma does!"

Mr. Prophet slitted his eyes and said, "Huh? How'd they do that?"

Sam, more accustomed to interrogating suspects than Mr. Prophet, asked a pertinent question. "How did the other women get into the house to do the deed? No one else saw them. Were they guests at the Brownings' wedding?"

Snuffling, DeeDee said in a feeble, faded voice, "They waited behind the garage. During the reception after the wedding, Fer— um... I went outside and brought them up the back staircase."

"You were going to say Ferrell, weren't you?" I asked, butting in. I know, I know. But can you blame me?

Oh, go ahead and blame me. Sam did, for sure. "I'll handle this, Daisy," he said, glowering at me.

"No. No. It wasn't Ferrell's fault."

"Cripes," said Mr. Prophet. Actually, he didn't. He took the Lord's name in vain, but I won't do it here.

Sam turned to me. I stiffened. Shoot, I'd only butted in once!

"Daisy, will you please take Pudge home? These ladies, Mr. Prophet and I are going to go round up a bunch of women. *And* Ferrell Hawley."

"No, not Ferrell!" shrieked Madge.

"Yes, get Ferrell, too," said Alma Jervis, snarling.

"Go on, Daisy," said Sam. "Lou, help me with these three."

Dagnabbit! I hated when Sam and Mr. Prophet did things behind my back! Then again, I guess it was Sam's job. And he'd kind of adopted Mr. Prophet as his sidekick.

I heaved a huge sigh and said, "Let's go home, Pudge. When we get home, we can talk about what happened here, and I can maybe help you feel better."

"Can't I go along with them?" said Pudge, gesturing with despair at Sam and Mr. Prophet. "I wanna see what happens next!"

Crumb. Maybe Alma Jervis was right and all men really *were* pigs. But no. Pudge wasn't a pig. Yet. I suppose there was still time.

What a melancholy thought.

THIRTY-TWO

Thus it was that another murder investigation in the fair city of Pasadena, California, came to a conclusion. It wasn't a particularly satisfying one for me, but that's only because six young women ruined their lives because several young men decided to sport with their feelings. Mr. Cecil Darlington even sported with their bodies, the miserable so-and-so. Mr. Prophet called him a sumbitch, but I don't use language like that.

It was, by the way, Alma Jervis's ring that had ended up in Mr. Darlington's stomach because she wrenched it from her finger and, as several people held on to him, shoved it down his throat. I'm not entirely sure where the filmy fabric came from, but Ferrell Hawley had brought the tennis ball with him, and jammed it into Darlington's mouth. This action seemed uncalled-for by me, although what the men had done was uncalled-for, too. However, Ferrell Hawley had been part of the conspiracy, so he had no moral authority to stuff a tennis ball down Darlington's throat.

If that makes any sense.

After I had a good long talk with Pudge and explained to him, in (I hope) language that didn't sully his freckled young ears, what had happened and why when we were at the church, I walked him home to his parents' house next door. Naturally, Mrs. Wilson wanted to know what was what, so I told her an abbreviated edition of as much as I knew, which wasn't a whole lot at the time, actually.

"Pudge Wilson," said she, "Gossiping about a friend is a despicable thing to do!"

Hanging his head, Pudge said, "I didn't think it was gossiping. I just… He just… Aw, gee, was I really gossiping?"

"Yes," said Mrs. Wilson.

"I'm afraid so, even though you didn't mean any harm to me," I said, believing firmness might be called for.

"I'm sorry," said Pudge. Then he sniffled a big sniffle.

"Well, you know better now, don't you?" said Mrs. Wilson.

"Yes," said Pudge.

"Thank you for helping Detective Rotondo and Mr. Prophet tonight, Pudge. You've been useful to the police again. I think that counts more on the good side than gossiping does on the bad side."

"Really?" He lifted his head and looked at me. Worshipfully, I regret to say.

"I think so," I said.

"I'm not so sure," said Mrs. Wilson. "But it's past your bedtime, Pudge. So say goodnight to Mrs. Majesty and be off with you."

"Okay," said a sorrowful Pudge. "C'n I take Samson with me?"

With a sigh, Mrs. Wilson said, "Of course, you may."

So Pudge trudged off to bed, Samson the cat following him and switching his tail, probably to show me *he* was king in this house, no matter how many dachshunds might chase him when he was outside.

After Mrs. Wilson and I heard the door to Pudge's bedroom close, she leaned over and whispered to me, "I'm sorry Pudge was duped by those fellows. Heavenly days, though, what a ghastly man that Darlington person was. As much as those girls were wrong, both to have allowed themselves to be fooled and then to have killed him, I really don't blame them. I, for one, am glad he's dead."

So there you go. The worst part of the saga was that I didn't blame the poor girls either. I guess that just goes to show that we all have weaknesses of character. I seem to have more than most people. Not only am I useless as an accomplished woman, but I was glad a young man had lost his life in a relatively gruesome manner.

On the other hand, he was even more useless than I, and infinitely more disgusting and depraved.

It was long past ten p.m. when I left the Wilsons' home. I knew my parents and Vi had already gone to bed, and I wasn't expecting to find Sam and Mr. Prophet either at my parents' house or Sam's. My expectations were met. The two men would have had to spend a good long time rounding up suspects and taking them into custody. Then there would be endless hours at the police station, what with so many people with whom to deal.

So I went inside our house, petted my darling hound, brushed my teeth, and went to bed. With my darling hound. Overall, it had been a pretty dismal evening, but at least Flossie and her bevy of Salvation Army ladies would probably provide a delicious pre-bridal luncheon for me on the morrow. And Mr. Prophet. Mustn't forget Mr. Prophet, or little Billy might never forgive me.

At about seven Friday morning, Spike and I arose. The whole family and Mr. Prophet had gathered in the kitchen, where Vi was dishing out pancakes and bacon with ease and vigor. I'll never know how she accomplished such amazing things, but we all know that by this time.

"Morning, all," I said. Knowing the place would be abustle, I'd already dressed in an old blue day dress, although I wore my slippers with it. I wanted to be comfortable for as long as possible.

Various mutters and greetings responded to my salutation. Pa, Mr. Prophet and Ma sat at the table.

"Daisy, will you please carry this plate to your mother? She needs to get to work." Vi squinted at the clock on the kitchen wall. "And so do I. Can you drive us, dear?"

"Happy to," I said. I took the plate she held out for me, which held two slices of perfectly cooked bacon and a stack of three ideal pancakes. My aunt, the miracle worker.

"Thanks, Vi," said Ma. "Thanks, sweetheart."

"I'm only the waitress," I said, wishing I could cook.

"That's somethin' you kin do if you stop talking to dead folks," Mr. Prophet said before taking a big gulp of the coffee in his mug.

"You won't need to work as a waitress," said Sam, who looked droopy eyed and tired.

"Long night?" I asked him.

"Yes. Much too long," said he.

"You'll have to tell me all about it when you can."

"Will do," he said.

I waited, but he added no caveats. Well, glory be! Maybe he really *would* tell me all about it!

"Here's your plate, Daisy," Vi said from the stove.

"Thanks, Vi." I hurried to my magical aunt and got my own plate, decorated along the same lines as my mother's, and took it to the table, where I sat in the spare seat. Glancing up, I asked, "Have you already eaten, Vi?"

"Oh, mercy, yes! I ate first. You don't think I'd wait until you'd finished up and hoped for leftovers, do you?"

"You're a smart woman, Vi," said my father, sitting back in his chair with a happy smile on his face, replete, if I were to judge.

"Definitely," said Sam, popping what looked like his last bite of pancake dripping with real maple syrup from our kin in Massachusetts into his mouth.

"You want any more, Sam, before I turn off the burner and get ready for work?"

"No, thank you. You've fed me amply. Delicious breakfast, Vi," said Sam.

"You always say that," said Vi with a laugh.

"Because it's true," said Sam. He, too, sat back in his chair and appeared as replete, if more fatigued, than my father.

"What time did you guys finally get home?" I asked as I cut into my stack of pancakes. I always put butter between the layers, if anyone cares, then poured syrup on top of the whole pile. I tried to keep my bacon out of the syrup.

"About three this morning," said Sam.

"Good heavens, you must be absolutely dog-tired!" I said, peering at my beloved with my dripping fork poised over my plate.

"You betcha," said Mr. Prophet. He appeared bushed, too. "What time's this shindig I gotta attend at the Buckingham place?"

"Flossie said the ladies will feed us at one p.m.," I said. "So maybe you can take a nap before then."

"Sounds like a good plan." He squinted at me across the table. "I *really* gotta go to this thing? It's gonna be all wimmin, ain't it? All *good* wimmin?"

"Little Billy is counting on you," I said primly.

"Shi-oot," said the old reprobate. "All right. I'll go, but I gotta catch some winks before then."

After peering at the clock and swallowing my bite of pancake, I said, "It's not even eight o'clock. You go across the street and sleep, and I'll fetch you at about twelve-thirty. That should give you time for a good nap."

"Yeah, I guess," he said.

"I don't have to go to the department today," said Sam. "The uniforms will take statements from everybody."

"Oh, good!" I said, happy. "Then you can tell me everything that happened after Pudge and I went home last night!" Seeing the sour expression on his face, I added, "Then you can go home and take a nap, too."

"Daisy," said my mother, having finished her own breakfast and rising from the table to take her dishes to the sink. "Don't pester Sam."

"I'm not pestering him!" I said, peeved. "Those three witches followed my every footstep for a week or more, and they scared me! I deserve to know what happened."

My mother opened her mouth, I'm sure to argue with me, but Sam held up a big hand. Well, both of his hands were big, but he only held up one of them. "It's all right, Peggy. She's right. She does deserve to know, so I'll tell her."

"C'n I go home first?" asked Mr. Prophet, sounding for all the world like an elderly Pudge Wilson.

"Of course, you may," I told him, attempting to sound gracious. "You already *know* what happened."

"Yeah," he said. "Those girls are all crazy as peach-orchard sows."

Whatever a peach-orchard sow was. I'd ask later.

What eventually happened was this: I took Ma and Vi to work, then went home. Pa told me both Sam and Mr. Prophet had gone to Sam's house across the street to nap, drat them. However, I attempted to possess my soul in patience, as St. Luke recommended. I'm not very good at patience, but taking Spike for a walk with Pa helped.

By the time we got home, and after I'd bathed and washed my hair and slathered my entire body with cream Harold said *all* the movie stars used, Sam still wasn't at our house. Curses. Therefore, Spike and I retired to my sewing room, where I basted together Ma's mother-of-the-bride dress. Just as I'd ironed the dress and hung it up so Ma could try it on that evening, a knock came at the sewing-room door, and Sam poked his head in.

"You're here!" I cried joyfully.

So did Spike. Well, he didn't say the words, but he was joyful.

Sam took me to the living room, where Mr. Prophet, looking clean and pressed, also sat, along with Pa. Sam and I sat on the sofa next to each other, with Spike on my lap. Mr. Prophet and Pa sat in chairs they'd pulled up close to the sofa, and Sam began his tale.

"I radioed for a couple of prowl cars to pick up Ferrell Hawley, Jeffrey Jervis, and the rest of the female pack of avenging angels."

"Avenging angels," I murmured. "That's one word for them."

"It's two words," muttered Mr. Prophet.

Rather loudly, Sam said, "We got them all and took them to the station."

"All six of the women Darlington engaged himself to?" I asked for clarification.

"Yeah. All of them. And Ferrell Hawley and the Jervis fellow."

"Ferrell Hawley is the Hawley twins' cousin, right?"

"Yeah."

He stopped speaking and scrubbed his face with his hands, looking glum.

"What's the matter, Sam?" I asked, concern suddenly flooding me.

"I made a mistake," he said.

Big help. "What mistake?"

"I didn't search the Hawley twins or the Jervis woman."

"Did they need to be searched?" I asked, puzzled.

"Yes. I did have them empty their handbags and take out their hairpins and so forth, but I didn't have them disrobe because there wasn't a police matron on duty by the time we got them all to the station."

"That makes sense to me," I told him.

"Made sense to me, too, but I was wrong."

"What happened?" My concern turned to dread.

"Have you seen photos of women carrying bottles in their garter belts? I think the *Saturday Evening Post* ran an article about bootlegging not long back with a picture of a woman looking sly and lifting her skirt to expose the bottle she'd tucked under her garter."

"I remember that, yes," I said.

"Well, Alma Jervis didn't have a bottle. She had a gun."

"Oh, no," I whispered, lifting my hand to my mouth in dismay.

"Could have been worse. She wounded Madge and Ferrell Hawley, but then she shot herself in the head before Doan could tackle her. She might not make it."

"Good Lord. Oh, Sam, I'm so sorry."

"Yeah. Me, too."

"That gal was crazier than a loco shoat," said Mr. Prophet, not sounding the least bit distressed. "She'll be better off if she doesn't make it. If she does, she'll be tried for murder and attempted murder. The others only have one murder on their consciences. If they have consciences."

Sam, Pa and I stared at the man, transfixed by his logic. At least I was. Not sure what Sam and Pa were thinking.

"She did seem like the worst of the lot," I muttered after a few seconds.

"I still should have had them searched," said Sam, as if he actually *wanted* to feel guilty about Alma Jervis's insane antics.

"Who was going to search her? I thought you needed a woman officer to search a female prisoner."

"Yeah. Male officers aren't allowed to search female suspects or prisoners."

"Damn shame, that," said Mr. Prophet.

My father actually chuckled. Then he said, "From everything Daisy, Lou and you, Sam, have told me about those three girls, I don't think you need to feel guilty about anything at all. You did your job. If the… Jervis, was it?"

"Yes," I said.

"If the Jervis girl was unwise or insane enough to carry a gun around with her, and actually shot her friends and herself, I think Lou's right. If she recovers, she probably should be sent to an insane asylum or something."

We all sat and thought hard about Pa's words for a while.

At last, Mr. Prophet broke the silence. "You're right, Joe. I saw those women and talked to 'em, and the Jervis gal was crazy as an owl in a lightnin' storm."

"I've never seen an owl in a lightning storm," I said. "Or a… What else did you call her? A peach-orchard what?"

"Crazier'n a peach-orchard sow," said Mr. Prophet. "Fruit falls from the trees and ferments. The pigs eat the peaches and get schnockered. Nothing quite as dangerous as a peach-orchard sow. Them things is big, and if you get 'em drunk, they're liable to stomp on you and eat you."

My mind flew back a year or so when the then Regina Petrie confessed her cousin Percival used to kill young women and feed their bodies to the pigs on his parents' farm, and I shuddered. "Do you really think she's that bad?"

"Yes. I do," Mr. Prophet said decisively.

"Good Lord."

"Doesn't sound like the good Lord lived in the hearts of those females," said my adorable father. "Sounds like they sold their hearts and souls to some other entity entirely."

"I think you're right, Pa." I turned to Sam, who still looked glum. "I don't think what Alma Jervis did or didn't do is your fault,

Sam. Offhand, I can't think of anything you might have done to stop her. I mean, that police station isn't big enough to isolate anyone, is it?"

"Not really," he admitted.

"And you didn't realize she was nuts enough to try to shoot everybody, for Pete's sake! You can't be held responsible for her actions. Nor can Doan. Was he the one with them when it happened?"

"Yeah. I was checking in the rest of the gang."

"A gang of wickedly deceived young women." I shook my head. "I think most of them should get off with a light sentence. Maybe have them work with orphaned children or something to give them an idea about how most of the world lives. They might not know it yet, but they're all privileged young women. They should have to work a stint at the Salvation Army or something."

"What about Jeffrey Jervis and the Hawley twins?" asked Sam. "And Ferrell Hawley and Alma Jervis?"

After thinking about the people Sam mentioned for a second or three, I said, "Madge is the leader of the twins. DeeDee is all balled up. I don't think she does anything at all unless Madge tells her to. I think Mr. Prophet is right about Alma. I think she's crackers and should probably be sent to the loony bin. I don't know Ferrell Hawley at all, so I can't say."

"According to all reports, he's the one who held Darlington while the girls stuffed his mouth with the ring, the tennis balls and the wedding bouquet," said Sam.

"And the filmy fabric," added Mr. Prophet.

"What do you find so fascinating about the filmy fabric?" I asked him. "You always remind us about the filmy fabric, because we're always forgetting it."

He shrugged. "Just struck my fancy, was all. Where'd the filmy fabric come from, anyhow? Was it lyin' around on the floor? Part of some lady's gown? Off some fancy lady's hat? Just curious."

I looked at Sam.

Sam looked at me.

We both looked at Mr. Prophet.

Then Sam said, "Darned if I know. Daisy?"

I shook my head. "Not a clue."

So we never did learn where the filmy fabric had originated. In fact, it remains a mystery to this day. I hate mysteries.

That being the case, I asked Sam, "Why did the three weird sisters decide tormenting me was a good idea? Did they tell you? Or did you even ask?"

"I asked," said Sam. "They figured if they followed you around and pretended they thought you did the deed, nobody would suspect them."

I'm not sure how long I stared at Sam, incredulous, but it was a long time. Finally I said, "That's it? That's the reason they badgered me?"

"According to Madge Hawley, yes," said Sam.

Good Lord.

The ladies of the Salvation Army welcomed both Mr. Prophet and me (Sam politely declined to attend, even though Mr. Prophet all but begged him to go with us) with open arms. Flossie, looking bigger than the last time I saw her, even though that was only a week or so earlier, gave me a big hug.

As soon as little Billy spotted his hero, his face lit up like a Christmas candle and he ran to us all but yodeling, "Mistew Pwophet! Mistew Pwophet!"

Mr. Prophet stopped whining and swung little Billy up into his old gnarled hands. "How-do there, Mister Billy!"

Flossie and I watched the old man and the little boy, and darned if we both didn't begin dripping tears of silly sentiment. Fortunately, we didn't cry for long, probably because I remembered the thick envelope Mrs. Pinkerton had insisted I take to the Salvation Army. I hauled Flossie into the hallway where we could be alone and handed the envelope to her.

When she opened it, Flossie was too shocked to cry. "Daisy! There's a thousand dollars in here!"

"Really?" That was a lot of money. I guess Mrs. P truly *did* appreciate the Salvation Army.

Flossie frowned at me. "What do you mean, 'Really'? You can't afford to give us this much money, Daisy Majesty! Here." She thrust the envelope at me.

Holding my hands up as if she were pointing a gun instead of a paper envelope, I said, "It wasn't me!"

Tilting her head and appearing skeptical, Flossie said, "Oh, really?" She sounded skeptical too.

"Honest!" I cried. "It's from Mrs. Pinkerton! She wanted to be anonymous, but phooey on that."

Flossie's mouth dropped open. Couldn't say as I blamed her.

Luncheon was delicious, the ladies were warm and wonderful, and Flossie gave me a sampler she'd embroidered herself and Johnny had framed. It was beautiful.

"I want you to hang this where you can see it every day, Daisy," said Flossie. "Just to remind yourself how good you are."

"Even though I can't cook or anything?" I asked, sniffling a little and feeling silly.

"Cooking is overrated," she announced. "You know, we here at the Salvation Army take First Corinthians, chapter twelve to heart. The verse goes, 'If the whole body were an eye, where were the hearing? If the whole body were hearing, where were the smelling?' In other words, we're supposed to use the skills God gave us, and He doesn't give all of us the same skills. For instance, I could no more conduct a séance than I could fly to the moon."

"Conducting séances isn't much of a skill," I muttered, still feeling a little weepy.

"Fiddlesticks. You've earned a living for yourself, your family and your late husband using the skills you have, and you've done it well. So, do as I say. Take this and hang it in a spot where you'll see it *every day*." She laughed and thrust the sampler at me.

"Yes, ma'am." I laughed, too. Then I read the sampler, and I cried again.

Flossie had embroidered a quotation from Henry Van Dyke, who wrote one of my favorite stories of all time, *The Story of the Other Wise Man.* I'd given it to Flossie for Christmas in 1924.

The sampler read: "Use what talents you possess; the woods would be very silent if no birds sang there except those that sang best."

Full of good food and happy at last, I drove Mr. Prophet and myself home later that afternoon. The back seat of the Chevrolet was packed with cakes and cookies and all sorts of wonderful leftovers from the pre-bridal luncheon at the Salvation Army. I loved my friends.

The weeks leading up to September 12, 1925, were totally free of melodrama, for which I could only be glad.

I attended the luncheon Mrs. Pinkerton planned for me with a little trepidation, but oddly enough, I had a good time. Mrs. P and good times were such an anomaly, I talked about it so much, Harold finally told me to shut up about it. So I did.

Mrs. Bissel was disappointed to learn from the late Mrs. Baskerville that piebald dachshunds might eventually be recognized as a legitimate color by the AKC. Mrs. Baskerville told her not to worry, however. She said—because a dog-loving friend of Harold's had passed on the information—that this process would take so many years, Mrs. Bissel probably wouldn't be around to decry the decision. Mrs. Bissel wasn't too badly distressed.

Miss Alma Jervis survived her suicide attempt, although the shot to her head would impair her hearing and eyesight for the rest of her life. That's according to Dr. Benjamin. I have no idea if the woman lived to go to trial. The two Hawley relations Miss Jarvis shot also recovered from their wounds in time to stand trial for the murder of Mr. Cecil Darlington.

The other young women who had been involved in Mr. Darlington's death received suspended sentences, because the jury decided they'd suffered enough, especially poor Miss Betty Trunick, who had borne Mr. Darlington's unacknowledged baby, and who'd had to go to a sanatorium to regain her mental and physical health. Those sentences were okay by me.

DeeDee, being Madge's acolyte, also received a suspended sentence. Madge had to serve a year at the women's ward at San Quentin Penitentiary, where Mr. Eustace Kincaid was also imprisoned. Only Mr. Kincaid wasn't in the women's ward. San Quentin is located a little north of San Francisco, so I imagine the prisoners get a nice view if they're ever allowed to look out at the Pacific Ocean.

Because Jeffrey Jervis hadn't participated in the murder of Cecil Darlington, he escaped a prison sentence. However, I do believe the de Molay organization decided it didn't want to be associated with him any longer. I guess someone tattled on him instead of me for a change.

Mr. Ferrell Hawley, who survived his gunshot, never made it to his own trial because he hanged himself in his jail cell in the basement of Pasadena City Hall. Sam was furious because, he said, Mr. Hawley should have been watched more closely by the jail guards.

Oh, well. Saved the taxpayers some money. That's according to my father. Sam eventually agreed.

THIRTY-THREE

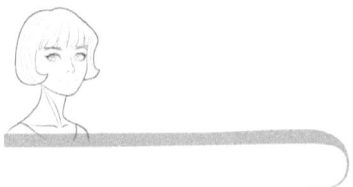

I became Mrs. Sam Rotondo on Saturday, September 12, 1925, in the Methodist-Episcopal Church on the corner of Marengo Avenue and Colorado Street in Pasadena, California. Although it was a second marriage for both of us, you'd never have known it from the floral extravaganza prepared by Harold Kincaid or the packed-ness (I'm sure that's not a word) of the church itself. I swear to heaven, everyone I'd ever known in my entire life came to our wedding! Including the Jackson family and Hattie and Cyrus Potts. They sat in the middle of the church pews as if they belonged there. Which they did, darn it!

By the way, Harold had been absolutely correct about people giving me presents of china, glassware, cookware and silverware. The home in which Sam and I would live when we got back from our wedding trip was filled almost to its rafters with boxes of dinner-ware, tea sets, coffee sets, chocolate sets, silverware, glassware, and I don't know what else.

"I don't even know who sent us all this stuff," I moaned to Harold as he attended to my wedding attire before driving me to the church, where everyone was gathering.

"Don't worry about it. I'll come back here after you two tie the knot and write down who gave you what. Please be sure to tell Lou Prophet not to shoot me when I come in to do that."

"Harold, you're the best friend I've ever had," I told him, getting teary-eyed for a second.

"Dry the waterworks, dammit, Daisy!" Harold ordered. "Never mind. I'll tell Lou myself. Here." He shoved a box of mono-grammed stationery into my hands.

"What's this for?" I asked numbly.

"Note cards. I'll send you the list of gifts and givers, and you'll get to spend your entire honeymoon writing thank-you notes."

"Oh," I said, even more numbly.

"Don't worry. It won't take you your *entire* honeymoon."

"Oh."

My mother looked beautiful in her light rose-colored gown, and Vi looked beautiful in her own darker rose-colored gown. My sister Daphne made a spectacular matron of honor in her emerald-green gown. My nieces, Daphne and Daniel's daughters, Peggy and Polly, were adorable bridesmaids.

My brother Walter, along with my brother-in-law Daniel, guided people to their seats when they came to the church. Pudge Wilson, who seemed a trifle down in the dumps that I hadn't waited for him to grow up so that he could marry me, manned the guest book in the church's lobby.

We didn't have a bride's side and a groom's side, since all the attendees knew both Sam and me, except for Sam's sister and her husband, but it didn't matter. People sat wherever they wanted to sit, and they made for a colorful crowd.

Flossie was as big as a house, as she'd predicted she'd be. She sat near the Jackson and Potts families in the pews, as did Mr. Lou Prophet, who had declined the pleasure of being Sam's best man. That honor went to Johnny, which I thought was nice.

Although she didn't much want to, Sam's sister Renata Pagano also attended our nuptials. She resented me for not being Italian or Roman Catholic. And for being the target of her idiot son's thwarted attempts at murder. Her husband, Francis Pagano, Sr., attended too, but he seemed happy for both Sam and me. He even

At the ceremony, performed by our pastor, Reverend Merle Negley Smith, Sam gave me a gold ring his father had made to go with the engagement ring he'd also made. The older Mr. Rotondo had crafted rose leaves in gold that fitted perfectly around the emerald sitting in a bed of rose leaves in the engagement ring. Sam's father, for the record, didn't approve of me, either, but he'd crafted the beautiful rings anyway.

All I gave Sam was a plain gold band. I did it on purpose, however, because Sam said that's what he wanted, and if I tried to make him wear anything fancy, he'd rebel. Not sure how he planned to do that, but I believed him. My Sam, unlike me, didn't fib.

I doubt the Hotel Castleton's staff had ever catered a wedding reception at a Methodist fellowship hall before, but they did that day. It was spectacular.

One of the best parts of the ceremony was that my father, whose health had been precarious during recent months, walked me down the aisle. I love my family *so* much.

The *absolute* best part of the ceremony was that Spike, the dachshund I'd acquired for my beloved first husband Billy Majesty, had been smuggled into the church. I never did know by whom, but I suspect a collaboration between Harold and Mr. Prophet. He sat next to Pastor Smith, who stared down at him in confusion until Harold told him I wanted Spike there, which was the truth. I heard a few gasps, but more chuckles than huffs. Mrs. Bissel and Mrs. Hanratty were both overjoyed. I know they were, because they told me so at the reception.

So my beloved dachshund wagged his tail as I became Mrs. Samuele Gabriele Rotondo at long, long last. I don't know about anyone else, but I hadn't honestly believed I'd live to participate in the day's festivities.

After Pastor Smith had pronounced us man and wife, Sam took my arm to walk me down the chancel steps and into the center aisle. Everyone in the congregation smiled, stood, and applauded for us. It was then I realized that "family" included not merely those with whom one grew up. It included everybody one loved.

And then, as if someone had spoken into my ear, I heard a voice in a thick Scottish accent say, "Ay, lass, ye've got yerself a good one at last."

I might possibly have gasped in astonishment, but I don't think anybody noticed. But had Rolly truly blessed my union with Sam? I'd never tell anyone, ever, but I do hope so.

Harold drove Sam and me to the Santa Fe Train Station later that afternoon. His fabulous Hispano-Suiza was followed by a host of other automobiles, old and new, all honking and waving for us. From the Santa Fe Station, we began our long, long train trip across the massive geography of the United States of America. We aimed to travel from the west coast to the east coast.

Sam made me swear that if I stumbled over a body along the way, I'd keep the information to myself.

"Kick it outside the train, if you find it near a door."

I don't think he meant his words, but I'm not sure.

The End

Aunt Vi's Raisin Pie

Ingredients:

2 cups raisins
1 ½ cups boiling water
1 cup sugar
4 Tablespoons cornstarch
Juice of two lemons
1 Tablespoon grated lemon rind
1 Tablespoon grated orange rind
1 cup chopped walnuts

Directions:

Cook raisins in boiling water for five minutes
Mix sugar and cornstarch together and dump into the raisin mixture
Cook until thick
Remove from fire and add other ingredients
Pour the hot filling into an unbaked pie shell, put on a top crust and cut slits in it (or you can make a lattice crust). Bake in a hot oven (450 degrees) for 20-25 minutes, until crust is golden brown. No need to bake any longer since the filling is already cooked.
Serve with vanilla ice cream or custard sauce.

DOMESTICATED SPIRITS

A DAISY GUMM MAJESTY MYSTERY, BOOK 17

Sam came to the window, stood next to me and put an arm around my waist as he, too, peered out the window. "It does look like a cat. At least I think it does."

"Huh. Wonder where it came from," I mused.

"And how it got that way," said Sam.

"Looks like it's been in a fight or three."

"Or four."

"I hope the cat vanishes before Pa brings Spike over. Spike is notorious for chasing cats. If that cat is still ailing from whatever happened to it, Spike might kill it. If it's healed and those injuries made it mean, the cat might kill Spike."

A knock came at the front door.

"Speaking of Joe and Spike," said Sam. "I'd better intercept them before Spike sees that cat."

"Good thinking. I'll help."

So Sam and I walked from the kitchen to the small entryway of our lovely bungalow on South Marengo Avenue in the beautiful city of Pasadena, California, and greeted my father and Spike. I'd left the front door unlocked for them, so their knock had been only to let us know they'd arrived.

"Morning, you two," said my father, giving me a hug and then shaking Sam's proffered hand.

"Hi, Pa," I said. I spoke from the floor, because I'd knelt to give Spike the greeting he deserved. Well, my father deserved a hearty welcome, too, but I'd already hugged him, and Spike preferred his humans to pet him. "Glad you brought the leash with you."

"I don't like to walk him across the street without it, just in case he spies Samson and darts out in front of a car to chase him," Pa said.

"Oh, shoot, I forgot about the cat," I said, grabbing for Spike's collar. Pa had unhooked his leash.

"What cat?" asked Pa, gazing out over our back yard. Sam and I had big plans for that yard.

I peered, too. "Huh. Guess it went away. The ugliest cat I've ever seen in my life was out there a few minutes ago. Not sure where it came from or where it went, but I'm glad it's gone, because I didn't want Spike to chase it."

"What color was it?" asked Pa. "Was it Samson?"

"No, it wasn't Samson. Samson's a handsome, sleek, well-cared-for cat. This cat was... Well, it was ugly. Looked as if it had run into a big dog or a car. Maybe a freight train or combine. It was orange like Samson, but it was... Damaged, I guess is the best description I can think of."

Spike had descended the porch steps and was sniffing his way around the yard, watering plants here and there and in general having a grand old time. This was a relatively new yard for him. He hadn't explored all of its intricacies yet.

"Oh, shoot, is that the cat?" asked Pa, pointing to where the naked arbor stood, planted between two neatly pruned sides of the buckthorn hedge separating Sam's and my house from that of Mr. Prophet. Well, Sam and I owned that one, too, but Mr. Prophet lived in it.

The cat had come back—that's almost the title of an old, old song, not that it matters. It sat in the center of the arbor, gazing at Spike and us as if inspecting interlopers into its domain. Stupid cat.

"Crumb. Catch Spike, will you? By his collar?" I felt panic rise in my bosom. "I really don't want a bloodbath on this glorious day."

"Good idea," said Pa, holding out the leash.

But Spike hadn't moved. He stood as still as a black-and-tan statue, staring at the ugliest cat in the universe, his nose quivering as if he smelled something interesting but wasn't sure he wanted to investigate it.

Quickly Pa clipped the leash to Spike's collar. My panic subsided.

Although I expected the cat to sprint—or maybe stagger—off as Spike and I approached, it didn't. It just sat there, looking at us. Kind of like a miniature tiger, actually. A miniature tiger that had been run over by a lawn mower maybe.

Then something happened I wouldn't have believed, except Sam and Pa saw it too and were as flabbergasted as I.

Spike leaned his long nose forward as if to sniff at the mangled cat. The cat lifted a paw—I squinted to look for claws but saw none—and extended it. Spike's nose and the cat's paw met in the middle, and darned if the silly animals didn't seem to be introducing themselves to each other.

I don't know how many seconds ticked by as Spike and the cat made friends. Seemed like hours, perhaps because I was squatting in an uncomfortable position. But I feared to rise lest I startle the cat into hissing and scratching or the dog into barking and biting.

Because I didn't know what else to do, I said, "Hello, cat. Where did you come from and what happened to you?"

"Aw, hellkatoot," came the voice of Mr. Lou Prophet from behind the cat. "So that's where you got yourself off to." And darned if I didn't hear him stumping his way down the orange-tree lined path from his cottage to the arbor.

"Is this your cat?" I asked him as he came into view and stopped short. Appalled, unless I missed my guess to judge by the look on his face.

"*My* cat?" he asked in an odd voice. "What the hell would I be doing with a damned cat?"

From this speech, I knew he was rattled. His language was colorful, but he tried to contain the swear words when he was around regular human beings, which included my family and me.

If Mr. Prophet had possessed two legs, he'd be digging the toe of one of his boots in the soft earth of the garden path. I'd never seen the old scoundrel appear so abashed.

"Well, hell, I guess so. The critter crawled up onto my porch while you were in New York. Don't know if he was hit by a car or got into a fight with a mastiff or what, but he was a wreck. So I just kinda nursed him. He was just a kitten when I found him. I guess he's a... what are they callin' 'em in the newspapers? A teenager? I guess he's a teenager now."

"Oh, that's so nice of you!" I cried, making Mr. Prophet wince. "You bandaged his shredded flesh and rips and stuff?"

"Took him to the veterinarian," admitted Mr. Prophet, who had owned a horse he'd named Mean and Ugly during his bounty-hunting days.

"What did you name your cat?"

"Ain't *my* cat," said he gruffly. "He just comes around, is all."

"Very well, so he's not your cat," I said to appease the old sinner. "What do you call him? You called your horse Mean and Ugly. Do you call this animal something equally awful?"

"Mean and Ugly wasn't an awful name. Fit the animal to a T." He stopped speaking, but when I opened my mouth to repeat my question, he said, "I call the cat Yuyu."

"Yuyu?" I peered at the old man, still trying to shake my left foot into life. "What does that mean?"

"Mean? Don't expect Yuyu means anything by itself."

Becoming annoyed by his prevaricating, I demanded, "Well, what does it mean if it isn't by itself?"

"Yuyu's short for Yuyutsu."

I stared at the orange and white striped cat who was now what I could only call cavorting with my ferocious hunting hound, Spike the dachshund. I'd *never* anticipated Spike would like, much less play with, a *cat*, of all creatures. "Was there somebody named Yuyutsu you knew in the bad old days?"

"They wasn't bad old days. They were *my* days, and they were grand. And yeah. Indian fellow. Yuyutsu. Mescalero Apache. Fought like hell and loved it. That's what the name means."

"Yuyutsu means he fights like... heck?" Was I embarrassingly prissy, or what?

"Means he *liked* to fight like hell, yeah. Figured that cat was a fighter, and he might as well have a fighter's name."

Gazing again at the adolescent cat, now positively *playing* with Spike, from whom Sam had unclipped the leash, I said, "He sure looks like he's been in a fight or two. Or three or four."

"Exactly. All the Injuns got beat up, not just the Mescalero. They all did." Mr. Prophet shook his head. "We white folks beat the hell out of all the Injun tribes. The Mescalero Apaches got dumped onto a reservation in the Sacramento Mountains, and they live there now. At least it's pretty there. Most Injuns didn't get so lucky."

"The Sacramento Mountains? In California?" I asked, puzzled, never having thought of Apaches as having anything to do with California. Truth to tell, I couldn't precisely tell you what, if any, Indian tribes used to live in California. Or still did, for all I knew.

"No, not in California," said Mr. Prophet disdainfully. "They're in New Mexico. The Sacramento Mountains in New Mexico."

"I didn't know New Mexico had any mountains at all," I admitted.

"Don't surprise me none." Still disdainful.

I got the impression Mr. Lou Prophet, former Confederate soldier, bounty-hunter, womanizer, gunslinger, and all-around rough customer, was embarrassed to have been caught being kind to a bedraggled cat. The notion made me smile, actually.

Suddenly Pa said, "What the heck does that cat have in its mouth?"

"Looks like a stick," said Sam, squinting at Yuyu, who sat in the center of the arbor's archway and nudged something with his paws. Spike had gone elsewhere for the nonce. "Never saw a cat playing with a stick before. Thought it was dogs who liked to play with sticks."

I was about to shrug and get back to mounding earth, when Mr. Prophet said, "I don't think that's a stick."

Looking up again, I saw he'd risen from his chair and was thumping over to the cat, which looked up at him and grinned. I swear to you, the cat grinned.

"What *is* that?" asked Sam, removing one of his gardening gloves, standing and moseying over to Mr. Prophet and Yuyu. He squatted before the cat. Then he said, "I don't believe it," and lifted his bare hand to cradle his head.

What the heck? Sticking my trowel into the ground, I rose too, and went over to see what was up with the cat and the men in my life.

"Oh, my word," I muttered as I peered down at the cat.

Then Spike bounded up to us. In his jaws he carried the jawbone of a defunct person. It looked like the jawbone of a person who had been defunct for quite some time and buried. In *our* yard.

"Spike! Drop it!" I bellowed.

Spike, startled, nevertheless heeded his obedience training and dropped the jawbone. I walked over to him, knelt, stroked his back, said, "Good boy," and picked up the bone in a garden-gloved hand.

"Good Lord," said Sam. Then he repeated, "I don't believe it."

"Holy Moses," said Pa. "Those are *bones*."

Available in Paperback and eBook from Your Favorite Bookstore or Online Retailer

ABOUT THE AUTHOR

Award-winning author Alice Duncan lives with a herd of wild dachshunds (enriched from time to time with fosterees from New Mexico Dachshund Rescue) in Roswell, New Mexico. She's not a UFO enthusiast; she's in Roswell because her mother's family settled there fifty years before the aliens crashed (and living in Roswell, NM, is cheaper than living in Pasadena, CA, unfortunately). Alice would love to hear from you at alice@aliceduncan.net

www.aliceduncan.net

 facebook.com/alice.duncan.925

www.ingramcontent.com/pod-product-compliance
Lightning Source LLC
Chambersburg PA
CBHW020542020726
47494CB00006B/1886